ALSO BY TODD HASAK-LOWY

The Task of This Translator

Captives

TODD HASAK-LOWY

Spiegel & Grau

NEW YORK

2008

PUBLISHED BY SPIEGEL & GRAU

Published in the United States by Spiegel & Grau, an imprint of The Doubleday Publishing Group, a division of Random House, Inc., New York.
www.spiegelandgrau.com

SPIEGEL & GRAU is a trademark of Random House, Inc.

Library of Congress Cataloging-in-Publication Data
Hasak-Lowy, Todd, 1969–
    Captives: a novel / Todd Hasak-Lowy. — 1st ed.
        p.   cm.
    1. Screenwriters—Fiction. 2. Motion picture industry—Fiction.
3. Hollywood (Los Angeles, Calif.)—Fiction. I. Title.
PS3608.A7895C37   2008
813'.6—dc22

                                        2008013021

ISBN 978-0-385-52773-6

PRINTED IN THE UNITED STATES OF AMERICA

10 9 8 7 6 5 4 3 2 1

First Edition

For my parents

CAPTIVES

LOS ANGELES

It's impossible to explain what anger the screenwriter felt, what humiliation, due to reality of course.

—ORLY CASTEL-BLOOM,
"The Screenwriter and Reality"

And in July of that year, on an otherwise uneventful morning, Daniel suddenly found himself confronting an unmistakable reluctance to continue writing stories. For seventeen years Daniel had dedicated a good portion of his waking life to doing just this, to crafting stories, which in his case took the form of screenplays. He had completed fourteen full scripts, had sold eight of these, three of which were in fact turned into movies. One of these, his eleventh screenplay, entitled *Captives,* grossed over one hundred and sixty million dollars in the United States alone, though the director chose to rename it *Helsinki Honeymoon,* a clause in the twenty-eight page contract giving the headstrong Frenchman permission to do so. Regardless, Daniel had earned for himself and his family nearly five million dollars through the sale of these screenplays, enough to purchase a beautiful, spacious home in the expensive Southern California real estate market, enough to send his son to a competitive, pricey private school, enough to provide his wife the freedom not to work for nine of these past seventeen years. Though not one of Hollywood's leading screenwriters, Daniel's name had become well known and respected, such that a major studio would occasionally approach Daniel with hopes that he might be willing to fix someone else's screenplay, as the studio had decided, either before or during production, that the screenplay required the attention of a professional. Often Daniel would decline these offers, his own projects obviously more important than someone else's, but when the timing was right Daniel would agree and be paid handsomely for his services.

Though Daniel has remained, until this July morning, determined to continue writing his own screenplays, the possibility of script doctoring full-time, on the off chance that he one day finds himself uninterested in or incapable of writing movies on his own, appeals to him as an insurance policy of sorts, because, to be sure, there are times when the pressure, much of it manufactured in his own head, along with the intimidating lunacy of the movie industry, the egos, the indecision, the absurd budgets, the reluctance to take risks, the prevailing culture of remorseless dishonesty, leads him to conclude, nearly, that the work involved in realizing his own screenplays is no longer worth the effort. Not in the monetary sense, in this regard it is undeniably worth it, but rather in terms of the emotional and almost spiritual investment necessary to conceive of a basic story, envision the main characters who would be the agents of its action, select a proper setting in which they would perform these actions, patiently massaging these interrelated but inchoate concepts into being, waiting out the days when he could not concentrate, finding a balance between the steady, clever, and original, but not too original (this being mainstream Hollywood, after all) development of plot, character, and setting, all in order to complete a first draft, at which point it would be necessary to show the script to his agent and then wait a week or even a month for his comments, feedback that often strongly suggested, if not necessarily required, that he perform major, however elective, surgery on his screenplay, a process that was invariably more painful and less enjoyable than the invigorating, though still anxious early days of sketching out the basic contours of his new story, a process that would often be repeated once, twice, even three or four times, at which point the diminishing returns on his sustained effort and anguished focus would nearly get the best of him, bringing him to the brink of despair, which he would only be able to avoid by drinking in the evenings, watching hour upon hour of vapid late-night television and eating vast quantities of imported semisweet chocolate, causing him to gain weight and lose sleep and become, more or less, an insufferable asshole, a man his wife and son, who loved him to be sure, learned to identify and then avoid almost entirely, until one night, it always seemed to happen late, late at night, Daniel would have his breakthrough, and though work would remain, it would all be downhill from there, until two to four months later a well-earned bottle of wonderfully overpriced champagne would be popped open in nearly anticlimactic celebration, while Daniel's checking account would wait with silent and cooperative patience to be inflated to the tune of six figures or more.

The negative features of this process were only heightened by Daniel's knowledge of what awaited his screenplay once it was acquired by a studio, as a clear majority of studio executives, directors, and leading men thought nothing of altering his screenplays beyond recognition to suit their infantile needs and desires, needs and desires that invariably led to a final cinematic product of undeniably lower quality than what would certainly have been produced had this executive, director, or leading man done his best to faithfully translate the words in Daniel's script into the visual and aural language of film. After the success of *Captives,* that is, after the success of *Helsinki Honeymoon,* Daniel sought to leverage his newly well-earned clout within the industry into more control over the various complicated and high-stakes processes that took place between the initial sale of a script and that unlikely final and fateful moment the very first moviegoer voluntarily approaches the box office to buy a ticket. Daniel joined forces with an up-and-coming director who had recently completed his first feature, and the two set out to take Daniel's next screenplay, *Locked Up and Loaded,* which the up-and-coming director read with great enthusiasm, and sell it for a truly enormous sum of money to the studio that had produced the up-and-coming director's successful first film, with this director signed on as director and with the two of them signed on as producers, all with an eye on not just turning Daniel's outstanding screenplay into precisely the great movie this screenplay could be, but, in the process, on turning the two of them, Daniel and the director, into major players in Hollywood, into an unstoppable two-headed creative force that would leave its mark on American popular cinema.

Despite the dense character of this opening, a full account of what stood between Daniel, the director, and the realization of their ambitions would simply be too involved to detail at this time. Suffice to say that the pathological lunacy of the movie industry, in particular the egos and the remorseless dishonesty, seemed, in Daniel's eyes, to grow only more unpredictable and treacherous as the daunting peak of this foolhardy madness finally came into full view. None of this was helped by the fact that the up-and-coming director turned out to be a very different man than the man Daniel had initially thought him to be. Most of all, Daniel learned that the successful navigation of the decidedly rockier terrain of actual production required all manner of endurance and fortitude that easily outmeasured the endurance and fortitude that one had to bring to bear on the creation of an industry-worthy screenplay, this more substantial endurance and fortitude involving not just sustained focus and creativity, but the ability to outlast and simply intimidate rivals and adversaries. What Daniel learned was that while the far-from-modest demands involved in successfully writing and selling a screenplay were, indeed, far from modest, when considered against Daniel's character, in particular his strengths and weaknesses, it turned out that the fulfillment of such sizable screenwriting demands was not such a surprise after all. By contrast, Daniel and his character, his strengths and weaknesses, turned out to be ill suited to the realization of the more considerable demands at the heart of taking a promising screenplay, or even, or especially, a truly great screenplay, and turning it into a movie that might find its way to thousands of cineplexes here and abroad.

What Daniel learned was that he was not equipped to overcome the various interpersonal obstacles that invariably present themselves on the path to postproduction, the lying, the confrontations, the final, decisive act of resigning oneself to the fact that a mortal, lifelong enemy, an enemy with considerable power and clout in the industry, has been made in order to properly realize, say, the relationship between leading man and leading lady. To be sure, Daniel had come to dread the various difficulties that predictably emerged during the extended solitude of writing a screenplay, but the amount of drinking and late-night television and bittersweet chocolate Daniel found himself having to consume to surmount these production-related interpersonal hurdles transformed him into a purely insufferable and truly self-loathing asshole, such that his wife, a woman who certainly has her own shortcomings, told him one evening, with an impressive lack of ceremony or even warning, that marriage contract or no marriage contract, she was most certainly not willing to share her life and raise a son with the contemptible prick that Daniel had become while wrestling with the world-famous action hero over whether or not his character would get the girl in the end. Though their personal finances had never been better, this movie having more than funded his and his family's much-needed getaway to the South of France that spring, Daniel unequivocally regretted, or at the least most certainly enjoyed no aspect of the experience that was transforming the screenplay *Locked Up and Loaded* into an actual movie, a movie the viewing public, or the disappointingly small portion of the movie-going public that actually bothered to see it, knows by its unimaginatively, though highly contested, shortened name, *Loaded.*

Remarkably, however, none of this played a direct role in Daniel's sudden disinclination to continue writing screenplays. Though, as stated above, crafting a screenplay, even for the highly experienced Daniel, wasn't easy, he was still more than capable, in fact, his ideas seemed, in terms of originality and crowd-pulling potential, to be evolving in promising directions. And it is his latest premise, an initially intriguing premise, that turns out to be the cause of his problems. Daniel's specialty as a screenwriter is located within the larger genres of action and suspense. All of his scripts contain and in fact revolve around violence, in particular the specter of violent acts committed by characters who, though demonstrating the potential to perform such acts, are not lifelong criminals or even remotely violent people. In this regard there is an unmistakable psychological component to Daniel's stories. While the rest of the industry steadily migrates toward higher body counts and louder explosions, Daniel tells stories in which hesitant and often solitary individuals are drawn reluctantly toward this violence, eventually surrendering to its seemingly irresistible pull in surprising and often disturbing ways. In the world of Daniel's thrillers, violence, even the mere threat of violence, possesses a overpowering contagious force, such that previously nonviolent people can, and often do, commit acts of horrible violence, having been irreversibly altered by the mere exposure to the possibility of becoming targets of violence themselves. Revenge, in other words, is always at the center of Daniel's scripts, as is the transformation of a placid setting, a suburban home, a modest church, a country store, into a site of bloodletting. What pleases Daniel most about his scripts, and what he has found himself working to isolate and cultivate in the development of his screenplays, is the morally ambiguous nature of the violence in his stories. The vengeful acts his previously nonviolent characters commit are often out of all proportion to the threat they encountered or even the physical harm they themselves suffered. For instance, in *Captives*, or *Helsinki Honeymoon*, a man takes a woman hostage, but over the course of three sleepless nights comes to regret his decision and perhaps falls in love with his captive, while she becomes consumed by her desire to subject her captor to the sort of anguish she endures even though she may have feelings for him as well. The captor's decision to set her free, to undo what he had done, allows her the opportunity to do just this, only she cannot, once given the upper hand, restrain herself, leading to various unpleasant acts, all of which are colored with a disturbing and not-so-subtle sexual overtone. This is Daniel's imaginative terrain.

His latest project, still in its earliest stages, would open as follows: It is a sunny, early morning in an extremely affluent and sparklingly new suburban community. Much of this opening sequence is set primarily in a single residence, though there are steady cuts to the rest of the neighborhood, where, for instance, newspapers are delivered, women jog, automatic sprinkler systems are activated, a security vehicle makes its rounds, immigrants attend to lawns and landscaping, and uniformed personnel in the guardhouse at the entrance to this gated community carefully filter early morning visitors and briefly acknowledge residents heading out to work. The unmistakably tranquil character of the neighborhood, the order, the quiet, the calm, the safety, would seem to suggest an ironic reading of the guardhouse and the security vehicle, though Daniel hopes that the director would present them as neutrally as possible. Inside the main residence, a family continues to sleep except for one man, a father-husband, who rises quietly from bed, puts on a perfectly white terrycloth robe, slips on a pair of nearly new leather slippers, and wanders through his expansive home, where he passes through its all-American upscale décor, complete with professional family portraits and giant televisions and an impossibly clean custom kitchen. This man, in his late forties, is tall, fit, handsome, and clean-cut, though a shave is perhaps in order. As he wanders through his house it remains unclear precisely what sort of state this man is in. He appears restless more than anything else, opening his top-of-the-line refrigerator but not removing anything to eat or drink, peeking his head briefly into a fully equipped exercise room but not exercising, even looking in at his expensive automobiles in his garage but obviously not going anywhere. He stops longest in his tastefully furnished home office. Without sitting down, he checks something on the computer and then leaves, the camera pausing briefly on an answering machine, where a high number, eleven or sixteen, blinks in red. Finally, still in his robe, the man disarms an alarm system, opens his front door, and walks partway down his perfectly green lawn to retrieve the morning paper. He removes it slowly from a plastic sleeve and scans the front page, where, after a moment, his expression shifts slightly, his eyes closing and opening again. The camera pans a hundred and eighty degrees, stopping behind his shoulder and thus allowing the newspaper to come into focus. There on the front page, just below the fold, is a picture of this same man, in a dark blue suit, leaving a courthouse, where, the headline explains, as the former CEO of a scandalously failed multinational corporation, he has been arraigned. Just then a slight noise is heard. The man falls and tumbles over, blood running out of a fresh hole in his forehead and pooling into the newspaper that contains his picture. At this point the camera cuts to the assassin, who is most likely in a van, though Daniel was still considering a tree, a rooftop, or even a neighboring house. The man quickly but calmly lowers his high-powered rifle, dismantles it, and carefully stores it in a padded briefcase, which he then closes. Moments later this second man drives out through the front gate, quickly blending, over the course of a few jump cuts, into the ever-thickening morning traffic.

Here are the other features of the story Daniel had already envisioned: The main investigator into this murder, probably a federal agent, would, it turns out, have a presently deteriorating father who himself suffered greatly from the collapse of a giant corporation and/or the misconduct and deception of its executives. Daniel knew this would have to be handled gingerly, so as not to make the investigator's potential ambivalence too obvious, but clearly the agent, in addition to subscribing to the widely held opinion that the murdered executive was a despicable person, would himself have had to experience up close the way such corporate deceit ruins the lives of actual people. Meanwhile, in another minutely choreographed scene, a second well-groomed, if slightly fleshier and clearly unctuous, affluent man is similarly assassinated, by the same still-anonymous sniper.

This second victim is not from this same failed corporation or even from a different corporation. Rather, and this would be made perfectly clear from the second victim's single scene, he was located somewhere between the worlds of business and government, a consultant, perhaps, or even a lobbyist. Perhaps the viewer would be introduced to him at the tail end of an extravagant business lunch, in which this man addresses a different man as "Senator" or "Congressman" as he says his farewell, giving him the kind of handshake that informs the viewer that a questionable, you-scratch-my-back-I'll-scratch-yours deal has just been struck, before casually walking to his expensive sedan on the roof of an urban parking structure, where he will be shot from a nearby rooftop. In short, what the viewer will learn in the opening act of the story is that someone is assassinating a series of unsympathetic and powerful individuals and that the federal agent given the responsibility of capturing the elusive, efficient assassin, though himself clearly a dedicated professional, may be susceptible to harboring sympathies for this vigilante.

This still largely embryonic screenplay began for Daniel with the idea of an assassin whose preferred method is the high-powered sniper rifle. Though the figure of the sniper had, in various ways, been treated in other, earlier films, Daniel in particular being fond of the sharpshooter from *Saving Private Ryan*, he still believed strongly that there remained much unexplored territory. Daniel's minimalist tendencies, his preference for scattering a handful of precision-crafted, highly contained acts of violence over his ninety-minute stories, made the sniper an obvious choice for him. The inherent sterility of the sniper's violence, the distance, the brevity, the suddenness, also provided a new and fascinating challenge when it came to investing these acts with emotional weight. Daniel wasn't really sure how he'd manage this, but was hopeful, and did have a general sense of gradually devoting more and more attention to the assassin as the story progressed, showing how his apparently seamless and essentially affectless acts were, in fact, riddled with misgivings and thus slowly tearing him apart. There was even the possibility of the sniper and the agent chiasmatically intersecting and thus passing by each other in regards to their respective stances on the justice of the sniper's program to surgically remove a handful of horrible, powerful individuals from among the living. In other words, maybe the federal agent would decide to actually assist the sniper, while the sniper, aware of the agent hot on his heels, would wait expectantly to be caught, having come to see the error of his ways.

The sniper's targets came second, and it was conjuring up this collection of somewhat fictional and possibly deserving victims that ultimately spelled trouble for Daniel. His stories had never been political before. Indeed, the sort of violence Daniel imagined and represented was not only limited, it was necessarily contrived, nearly to the point of allegory. If real-world politics entered into his screenplays it was solely to round out a character's background, provide an initial motivation, or adequately ground the setting to placate some narrow-minded studio executive. Sometimes it helped set things in motion if, for instance, someone could be shown to have spent time in the military, but Daniel was never interested in making a statement about the military's recruitment strategies (*Unlisted*) or bodyguards (*Body or Soul*) or rural America (*Get Away*). But in this case Daniel found himself disinclined, for reasons initially unclear to him, to have his sniper target random, everyday individuals, in part, he realized, since regular people can be killed up close. A sniper hits targets from a distance precisely because these targets cannot be reached in any other way. During wartime such distances are a function of impregnable battle lines and contested topography, but Daniel's distaste for the cluttered chaos of war made this an unattractive choice of settings. To tap into Daniel's screenwriting strengths, this sniper would have to target people who felt perfectly safe, but people who necessarily, for some reason, would have to be killed from a distance. And who were these people, these people who lived in perfect safety, but were in fact suitable targets for a serial sniper? The powerful, the apparently untouchable and powerful: corporate executives, politicians, etc.

Now prior to the development of this screenplay, Daniel's personal desires and concerns never much entered into his stories. Daniel is not one of those screenwriters who, above all and deep down, longs to tell his story. He has never once felt the urge to write a screenplay about a guy like him growing up in a place like the place where he was raised, a guy falling in love or feeling alienated or watching his family fall apart. Indeed, Daniel first fell in love with movies, like so many before him, thanks to the escape they promised. As has been demonstrated, while Daniel is without doubt emotionally invested in these various projects, this investment manifests itself not in the content of the screenplays but rather in their stubborn, sustained composition. Related to this, it should be mentioned that for most of the seventeen years Daniel has written screenplays he has never been much more than mildly interested in politics or the state of things. Growing up, Daniel detected a vague displeasure and even occasional hostility being directed toward those responsible for whatever it was that went on in the 1980s. His distinct pleasure, in the early nineties, to find himself suddenly living under a government he didn't instinctively identify against surprised him, but this pleasure, too, soon faded, and once more Daniel retreated from these matters into the pretend, self-contained, punctuated-with-violence world of his screenplays. Perhaps this violence was, then, in some sense, a response to his long-running disappointment with the state of things. Perhaps there was some sublimation involved. Daniel would not necessarily have denied this, but neither would he be much moved by its possibility.

Over the last half-dozen years or so, however, Daniel has been sensing a slight but steady shift within himself when it comes to thinking about the state of things. His previously longstanding, reliable, but somewhat limited cynicism and distaste for this state of things had once allowed him, encouraged him even, to turn his back on the possibility of working to improve it. Things weren't great, perhaps they were quite dire in certain areas and from certain perspectives, but they appeared stable enough and bearable enough, at least, or especially, for him, not to mind it all that much. He occasionally encountered words like *responsibility* and *duty* and *urgency* and *unsustainable* in discussions, private discussions even, about this state of things, but these words slid off his back, or he turned his back to them, something facilitated by the overall political apathy of Hollywood, where the only activists were movie stars, whose activism was so clearly a form of vanity that it served to distance Daniel and his ilk yet further from the very possibility of political engagement directed at improving the state of things.

But this new decade, which happened, dramatically enough, to be a new century and, if that weren't enough, a new millennium as well, seemed to augur something else entirely. Each passing day Daniel found himself more and more preoccupied with thoughts about the state of things, a state that was bad and getting worse. Small talk at casual get-togethers gravitated more and more toward a predictable meditation on this state of things, leading quickly and inevitably toward an abject, forlorn consensus that things were bad and getting worse. And while in the past a conclusion of this general, if not as severe, sort was often reached largely, it appeared, in order to generate a bond between those participating in this pessimistic consensus, now this consensus was at best cold comfort, because, and everyone knew that everyone agreed on this before the predictable conversation even began, things were really very, very bad and getting much, much worse. To the point that Daniel had recently become haunted by a certain intractable rage at those responsible for this state of affairs and a similarly persistent frustration with himself for doing nothing at all, beyond voting in the electorally irrelevant state of California for president once every four years, to change things. All of this may have been exacerbated by the growth and maturation of his son, Zack, who from time to time asks for explanations about this or that news item, and who, moreover, represents, not at all metaphorically for Daniel, the person who is to inherit the world that Daniel's generation is making for him. While Daniel hardly enjoyed having inherited a broken world himself, he appeared to have managed well enough, but the notion of failing to assume any real responsibility to fix the world that his son will inherit, a world that is perhaps, likely even, to be qualitatively worse than the world he inherited, such that there is a decent chance that Zack is going to inherit a world so broken that he is almost certain to suffer or at the least witness up close some really, really unpleasant things, was not something he could ignore, nor could he ignore the troubling implications of experiencing and understanding this new sense of responsibility by suddenly and sincerely subscribing to the cliché "the world our children will inherit," a cliché he had previously dismissed for years as the stuff of laughable sanctimony.

And so that July, one clear July morning in fact, as he sits trying to write this screenplay in the quiet, peaceful guesthouse behind his family's luxurious home, Daniel suddenly makes some unhappy realizations. First, Daniel realizes that the assassin's actions represent a form of wish fulfillment. While in the past there may have been elements of wish fulfillment in his screenplays, while perhaps Daniel indeed wanted to know and thus imagined in detail what, for instance, was involved in taking revenge on one's captor, this was always carried out on a solely abstract level, one limited to isolated individuals encountering and responding to existential and thus universal dilemmas. The real world simply didn't enter into it. But with the assassin things had changed. The assassin's targets were chosen as targets precisely because of who they are and what they represent in the real world of today. Moreover, Daniel realizes that even more than staging these murders with exquisite precision, Daniel wants to fantasize, at length and in great detail, about the systematic murder of a short list of individuals he feels are responsible, or at least emblematic of the forces responsible, for the current state of things. This screenplay, it turns out, is another revenge story, only the vengeance is fueled not by a particular, isolated act confined to the imagined world of Daniel's story. Rather, Daniel's assassin is taking revenge on actual people, or fictional characters who are clear stand-ins for actual people, for what they have done to create this state of things, and in so doing have created the world that Zack is to inherit. Daniel, he realizes as he stares out onto the family pool and nervously chews an innocent pen to the point of no return, unequivocally wants a number of real people dead, and this, he realizes, is perhaps the most efficient and promising way of going about expunging them, at least in his imagination, from the human record. Finally, the great potential of this screenplay stems not merely from its various narrowly understood cinematic qualities, its suspense, its development of character through action, its use of powerful visual images, in particular the inherently pleasing aesthetics of seeing a soon-to-be dead man positioned just so in a sniper's crosshairs, to enthrall its audience, but more so from the way this movie will, Daniel imagines, tap into a collective rage, a collective desire and even need for, in lieu of actual violent revolution, the staged murders of a representative swath of leaders responsible not only for the dismal state of things, but for a state of things that includes, necessarily, the widely held conviction that the collective for whose welfare these leaders work has been rendered utterly powerless and politically irrelevant, so much so that they might well be allowed to gather in large numbers in darkened movie houses to view a fictional story in which leaders who strongly resemble their own leaders are taken out by a lone sniper as punishment for systematically and intentionally disregarding the needs of this very collective.

After this large and distressing conclusion comes into perfect focus, Daniel turns his head quickly away from the pool and removes the withered pen from his mouth, hoping that this abrupt motion might permanently dislodge from his mind this conclusion and the long trail of thoughts that led to it. Without moving, frozen in fact, paralyzed even, Daniel runs as fast as he can from this realization, whose full consequences he still hasn't sorted out, but whose general implications he already recognizes. Simply put, Daniel should not write a screenplay that gives voice to such a bleak view of the world. Either Daniel will have to convince himself, really and truly, that he doesn't think things have gotten to the point that various powerful individuals need to be erased, or Daniel will have to do something about the world, not kill people of course, but rather get off his financially secure and undeniably privileged and flat-out-lucky ass and devote long, long hours to fixing the world. Right away Daniel senses that neither of these possibilities is tenable or appealing. He looks around, unsure how to proceed. After a full minute he stands up and leaves the guesthouse.

Still not entirely willing to admit he now occupies the unenviable position produced by this dilemma, Daniel spends the rest of the day compulsively performing the various activities he performs when stuck in his effort to make progress on a script that does not involve the need to come to terms with his murderous rage or recognize that he is accountable, ultimately, for the state of things. Daniel slowly walks Alfred, the aging, arthritic, loyal family dog, who silently refuses to respond to his master's pleas for help, runs three miles in place on a treadmill, eats a delicious, overpriced lunch by himself in public, goes to a hideously bad matinee, where he sits in the dark by himself in public, and, finally, drives to the ocean and stares out at the beautiful thing hoping for some ministration, or, at the least, some pity. Daniel's wife, Caroline, calls his cell phone twice, but he does not answer. Over the last two years, watching her husband and his swollen ego suffer, Caroline's distaste for the movie industry has fully metastasized into an unruly, intransigent, and volatile rancor that is so not fun to be around that Daniel has more or less stopped sharing with her any of his screenwriting and deal-making experiences, save the most innocuous and predictably welcome. This is, of course, a problem and not really the kind of thing that can continue unaddressed for much longer, since Daniel's identity and sense of self revolve in large measure around his screenwriting and deal-making experiences, but since Daniel had been an insufferable asshole, closed up, selfish, restless, irritable, and finally cruel, for over four straight months during the previous spring and summer, he figures she can be accommodated for now. In another couple months, when Caroline finishes her latest interior-design project, they might perhaps decide on a policy going forward. He stares at his phone after ignoring her second call, briefly wrestling with the guilt and resentment. Then he calls Holden, his agent.

—Bloom, what's up?

—I'm at the beach.

—Ouch. Four o'clock on a Tuesday. Not a good sign. What's up? Do you need talking down?

—Yes. But in person.

—Today's no good. How's breakfast tomorrow?

—Fine.

—Nine sharp, at the corner of Highland and Third. There's a new place.

—Sounds good.

—Go home. Watch the first half of *The Graduate,* up until Hoffman starts dating the daughter. Then watch the opening of *A Thousand Clowns,* until the social workers show up. If things get really bad, try the opening of *Harold and Maude,* or the middle of *E.T.*

—I can't watch the end of anything?

—Absolutely not. And do not, under any circumstances, so much as touch *The Deer Hunter.*

2

The following morning at nine fifteen, Daniel watches from an outdoor table as Holden arrives on an old red Vespa, a shiny black helmet in the shape of a perfect half circle fastened to his small, aerodynamic head. Holden's face is preposterously thin. An enormous bent nose seems to take up a good 20 percent of his overall head volume, apparently stealing bone from what should be a normal chin and forehead. He's stuck with a pronounced overbite as well. But his green eyes are beautiful, and in general Holden doesn't appear to give a shit that he looks like a cartoon.

—Top of the morning, Bloom. How are we today?

—Not sure. Let's eat.

Holden's name is not, or at least hasn't always been, Holden. Daniel's fairly sure his original name is Scott, but this may merely have been the name he was using when they first met eleven years earlier. Holden changes his name every three to six months, typically, but not always drawing his names from film and literature. He has been, since Daniel met him, in no particular order, Vito, Darl, Kane, Marlowe, Zelig, Leopold, Huck, Tristam, and Dolemite, among others. He never changes his last name, Stein, but he refuses to answer to it or to any monikers derived from it. Nor is one allowed to alter his present name in any way, either. He is an excellent agent.

—So what's the story?

—I have this idea, and it's really good, but there's some problems.

Daniel tells his story while they order, drink their morning beverages, and wait for their food. Holden is the first to hear any of this, and Daniel hopes it might sound less ominous as it comes out of his mouth and into the world, but it doesn't. His monologue is long, Holden listens patiently, until Daniel finally digs into his eggs, newly and reluctantly resigned to one of two fates.

—That's genuinely fucked up, Mr. Bloom.

—Fucked up in a good way or a bad way?

—No, in a bad way. I mean, it's really fucked up.

—Do you think, as a story, it's a good idea?

—Do you mean is it compelling? Would it make a good movie?

—Yeah.

—It could be. I doubt it would be easy to get the federal agent right, especially his relationship with his father. But people like it when any kind of event, especially murder, repeats itself. It would be like the inverse of the recruiting segments from *Seven Samurai*, sort of.

—Those would be fun to write. But what about, you know, the main problem?

—It's a problem. No studio would get behind it. Not if it was set here. Have you thought about setting it somewhere else?

—Like where?

—I don't know. England? France? Some imagined country in the near future?

—I hate that kind of shit. Too thinly veiled. There's no way to get the audience to buy into it unless they recognize it.

—So it's a problem. You can go ahead and write it. By the time you're done, who knows, but it's pretty fucking unlikely.

—What about my other problem?

—What other problem?

—That I think I want this to actually happen. That I want someone, I think, to go around taking out elected officials and corporate executives.

—You really want that to happen?

—I think so, yes.

—Deep down, deep inside, you think the world would be better if someone assassinated Ohio's secretary of state? The CEO of Exxon?

—I'm not sure if it would ultimately make the world a better place, but yes, I think I'm willing to take the chance that it would.

—You're serious? Summary executions carried out by a judge and jury of one?

—Yup.

—That's fucked up.

—You said that already.

—But it is, it's fucked up.

—What do you think? Don't you want some of these people gone?

—Of course. If the president was flattened by that long helicopter of his, I'd be dancing in the street. But I want to bonk our waitress, too. I want to bonk all the waitresses in this town. Doesn't mean it should happen.

—What if it's just if you bonk our waitress?

—What could be just about bonking a waitress?

—I mean, what if it's just if the president's helicopter flattens him? As opposed to only something we want? Then what?

—Does the celebration in the street deteriorate into something so carnivalesque that our waitress agrees to bonk me?

—Stop it, I'm serious. I mean what if their deaths, their intentional deaths, were the right thing? Some needs-of-the-many-outweigh-the-needs-of-the-few situation?

Holden doesn't respond. Cuts into his steak and eggs, then holds up his fork complete with square of impaled steak and points it all at Daniel.

—Tell me something, have you ever even shot a gun?

—No.

—You're kidding. You've written all these violent movies and you've never even shot a gun?

—So?

—So, I think that makes you a pussy somehow.

—How does it make me a pussy?

—It's like you think you're a tough guy, getting all these imaginary people to shoot and stab and maul one another, when you've never even fired a single shot.

—What the hell does one have to do with the other? What if my screenplays are a critique of violence?

—A critique of violence? Really. Do you seriously mean to tell me that your movies are a critique of violence?

—Well, I don't think they're a celebration of violence.

—No, they're not. They're a violence-can-be-really-interesting-and-more-than-a-little-entertaining study of violence. *Shoah* was a critique of violence, *The Elephant Man* was a critique of violence.

—How was *The Elephant Man* a critique of violence?

—Trust me, it was a critique.

—So why does it matter if I've never shot a gun? Anyhow, I have held a gun.

—When?

—When I was sixteen, on a trip to Israel. We had this guard on our bus, Rafi. I held his Uzi.

—What was that like?

—It was heavy and cold.

—Was it loaded?

—I don't remember. Probably not. So what's your point?

—You need to shoot a gun. You need to go somewhere where you can shoot a gun. And then you need to shoot one, and then you need to think about killing someone by shooting it. You should do this a few times. You should really go hunting. That would be the best thing for you. You should try to kill an animal by shooting it. Then we'll see if you still want someone shooting people.

—I don't think there's much hunting in Southern California.

—You'd be surprised.

—I'm not going hunting.

—So go to a shooting range or a firing range or whatever the hell those fascists call them. Go there and shoot and pretend, in that dark head of yours, that you're killing someone. That will cure you of your fantasy.

—Holden, think how many people we're killing. Executions here, bombings there, all that kind of shit.

—But you think that's bad.

—It is.

—So why do you want to kill more people? Even bad people?

—I don't know. Desperation. A feeling of helplessness.

—No one will fund it.

—Will you go with me?

—Where?

—To the shooting place, the range.

—I think you should go alone.

—See? You're a pussy.

—I am not a pussy.

—You drive a moped. You are an enormous pussy.

—I drive an Italian scooter, which not only makes me not a pussy, it makes me sexy. Anyhow, I do it for the environment.

Their waitress approaches. Daniel asks her, is a man in his forties driving a moped—

—A scooter, Holden interjects, this scooter, pointing to the Vespa.

—Is a man driving this scooter made more sexy by driving it?

—Whose scooter is it?

—Not important. More or less sexy?

—More. A little bit more.

She clears their plates and walks away.

—You're still a pussy.

Holden picks up the bill and puts down a twenty, gets up, walks over to his Vespa, puts on his helmet, and starts the engine.

—Shoot something, then we'll talk.

—Will do, maybe.

—Oh, and starting Monday my name will be Max. Please make a note of it.

3

Now at around this same time, the entire Bloom family, Daniel, Caroline, and Zack, are making their first preparations for Zack's bar mitzvah, such that only two days after his somewhat, but-not-really-all-that-helpful breakfast with Holden/Max, the whole clan gets in the car and drives a few miles east to Temple Beth Israel to meet with Rabbi Kaufman. Not since the previous September has Daniel entered this house of worship, though he has pulled into the parking lot a couple times a month to pick up Zack from his Hebrew lessons. Despite the infrequency of his visits, the Blooms are paying members of Beth Israel, a Reform outfit, though this is exclusively, and one might say cynically, in order to have the right to hold Zack's bar mitzvah in its semihallowed sanctuary.

On an assimilation scale of one to one hundred, one being residence in the ultraorthodox neighborhood of Mea Shearim in Jerusalem, one hundred being only the vaguest sense that a maternal grandmother may have been Jewish, the Blooms are, as an aggregate, about a seventy-eight. The home in which Daniel was raised was, at the time of his birth, just the occasional very guilty BLT over fifty, but the Cleveland suburb to which they moved just prior to Daniel beginning kindergarten turned out to be much, much less Jewish than they expected, and so by the time Daniel headed off to college both he and his family had slipped or migrated into the low seventies, something that caused Daniel's mother a good deal of grief. Caroline, for her part, came from a home outside of Boston that held steadily in the midsixties, her family having been in the United States one generation longer than Daniel's, and having settled in a permissive but decidedly Jewish neighborhood before Caroline was born. But the relocation to California and the establishment of their own nuclear families severed them from the relatively stabilizing forces of their own families, communities, and hometowns, such that they were now free and in a sense even forced to decide just how assimilated and/or Jewish they wanted to be. Of course, it was possible for them to avoid actively deciding or addressing or even recognizing that this was something they could or should or must decide or address, in which case their passivity would give them a nice little nudge toward the higher end of the assimilation scale, since assimilation, at this time and in this place, isn't exactly something a Jew need write down on his or her to-do list. Only a few mostly local factors have prevented them from rising up and into the often point-of-no-return mideighties: the prevalence of a certain latent Jewish cultural sensibility in the entertainment industry, this being a fairly watered-down version of borscht belt, Yiddishkeit, vaudeville humor, crossbred with but later intermarried away from the dominant Jewish presence in the origins of the American movie industry; the similarly high frequency of nevertheless highly assimilated Jews at Zack's various private schools; the minor, nagging identity crisis Caroline suffers each December confronting and trying to explain to Zack the bewildering salience of the unfortunate annual simultaneity of Hanukah and Christmas; and, finally, Daniel's mother's various efforts, typically designed for and directed toward her daughter-in-law, to reroute her son's family back down the assimilation scale. Rabbi Kaufman figures as much even before the Blooms enter his office this afternoon. His congregants, for the most part, aren't buying what he's selling, though, oddly enough, they pay him generously for trying. The commercial metaphors are, obviously, entirely not in the spirit of the operation, a sign of just how dire things have become from a rabbinical perspective, but Rabbi Kaufman can't help but see it in these terms. He warmly welcomes the Blooms into his spacious office, trying to shake hands more like a doctor than a salesman, offering Zack a slang version of the greeting he uses with Zack's parents. Rabbi Kaufman knows, or at least thinks, that his congregants, especially his rarely seen congregants, approach him with the guilt a disobedient subject has for a disappointed authority, but nevertheless the rabbi relates, or attempts to relate, not to their shame, but rather, straining to reach it, that small part of them that still believes there remains some Jewish something, a ritual, an activity, an incantation, that might in fact give their life more meaning. Rabbi Kaufman is not particularly optimistic at this point that he can reach this, especially with a family like the family he anticipates the Blooms to be, but any other strategy only discourages him even more, accelerating yet further his decision to search for work as something other than a pulpit rabbi.

—Well, welcome everyone, I'm glad to see you here today. Today is a special day, because today, Zack, you're starting on the final leg of your path toward your bar mitzvah, toward becoming a man according to Jewish law and custom.

And he smiles, trying to smile in response to the still-pleasing, abstract notion of Jewish boys becoming Jewish men, as opposed to the more specific and sobering idea of an unenthusiastic and undereducated Jewish boy like Zack becoming a similarly unenthusiastic and undereducated Jewish man.

—Now, of course, Zack, you have been coming to Beth Israel weekly for a couple of years to learn Hebrew. Why do you think that is?

The rabbi smiles.

—So I can read from the Torah?

—Right! So you can read from the Torah. So really you've been heading toward your bar mitzvah for a couple of years now. And Ms.

Lamdan tells me you're a fine student, too. But today, today is the day that you break off from your peers and start out on your very own path.

Rabbi Kaufman is giving most of his eye contact to Zack, turning to Daniel and Caroline just enough to let them know that he knows they're in the room. He doesn't like the added challenge of trying to bond with Zack as a sort of performance for Zack's parents, all the while trying secondarily to bond with Zack's parents, but this, too, is out of his control.

—So what we're going to do today is talk a little bit about what your responsibilities will be on the day of your bar mitzvah, on the day you lead our congregation in prayer. Then we'll talk a little about what exactly we're all going to do to get you ready to do that. How's that sound?

Cooperative nodding and mumbling from the Blooms.

—Now the most exciting part of all of this, the highlight, really, is the moment you actually read from the Torah. This is called an *aliyah*. *Aliyah* means going up or ascending, it's the same word we use when we talk about moving to the Land of Israel. You will go up to the Torah and read, something that's been done by millions of young Jews for centuries. I'll tell you what, it's a pretty cool feeling. Now the week you're going to read from the Torah . . .

At about this time Daniel stops paying attention entirely, which would surprise none of the other three in attendance, not that any of them are really paying attention to him in the first place. Daniel compensates for the guilt he feels at being unable or unwilling to listen to a perfectly fine rabbi introduce them to Zack's bar mitzvah portion by deciding to think about his own relationship to Judaism and this temple, as opposed to worrying anymore for now about the obviously pressing question of what it means that he wants to write a screenplay about a man who systematically commits a series of premeditated murders in order to rid the world of some very evil men, and women, there will have to be at least one woman, who also happen to be very powerful and not evil at all in the eyes of many other people. Daniel realizes right away that he doesn't really give a shit about Beth Israel, and that most of his thoughts about his son's imminent bar mitzvah relate to the various logistic and financial complications it will invariably present to him and Caroline. Beyond that he wonders a little what Zack thinks about all of this, while a very small part of him is beginning to brace himself for Caroline's reaction to this meeting, which actually matters to her a little, enough that she might want to have a long conversation about the possibilities of somehow getting up for it all a bit more. Daniel isn't opposed to Jewish practice enough to oppose Caroline or even Zack's potential desire to dial up their Jewishness, but he himself is entirely not interested. And hasn't been for some time, which overall and in general doesn't bother him.

But what happens, as an animated Rabbi Kaufman talks about the trials of some biblical somebody, is that the big, persistent, and stubbornly looming problem that Daniel is persistently trying not to think about but stubbornly thinking about anyway, the one having to do with the debilitating screenplay project, finds a backdoor into Daniel's present thoughts about Judaism. What the screenplay project, as a crisis, now engaged once more, gets Daniel to realize is that maybe, just maybe, this is a crisis that asks for some religious or spiritual response. Maybe, just maybe, that is one way to think about the measure of the entirely unfamiliar disquiet it gives rise to in Daniel. As a problem it's categorically different than his previous problems, so the solution must be located elsewhere, far, far away from his agnostic, secular, rational, intellectual, liberal, lefty, cynical, ironic, sarcastic, unbelieving self. Not just in the other direction, but in another realm entirely, way down along some alien axis of thought and conviction and faith, yes, even faith, that he doesn't believe even exists inside him, but that he may need to relocate or simply construct from the scraps of all the people he refused or failed to become, scraps that just might be piled up in various long-neglected corners of his person.

This thought strikes Daniel straight across the jaw, with just about as much force, but coming from the other side, as the initially horrifying realization he had back in the guesthouse a few days earlier, because opening himself up to religion, making himself vulnerable to its views on things, scares the hell out of him, because he isn't simply very assimilated, he is intentionally secular in his worldview, most certainly not believing in things he can't see, and most certainly not at all tempted to try and see the things he can't see according to the various Jewish ways of trying to see these things, whatever they are. As he looks back up at Rabbi Kaufman, who is saying *tabernacle* and apparently illustrating its dimensions with his hands, Daniel tries hard not to think about how some sort of religious practice might help him through this. He takes his wife's hand, and she almost smiles in response.

—So what now? The rabbi smiles, brushing his thumb up against his amazingly well-groomed beard. Well, in less than a week we have a new rabbi joining our congregation, a young man named Rabbi Ethan Brenner. Rabbi Brenner, who is dynamic and bright and not your average rabbi, let me tell you, Rabbi Brenner will be in charge of this year's b'nai mitzvah class, meaning, Zack, you and your peers will meet with him once a week to talk about what it means to become a bar or bat mitzvah. But before he meets with all of you, he wants to meet with everyone's parents. So, Daniel and Caroline, seven thirty Monday evening.

Back in the car, Daniel checks his voice mail. Max, reminding him he is now Max and asking him if he's shot a gun yet. Caroline and Zack quickly scatter after they get home, leaving Daniel a big house soon filling up with thoughts about dangerous scripts, firearms, and rituals. He takes down the yellow pages with the hope of getting Max off his back. Shooting galleries, gun shops, firing ranges, Daniel doesn't even know where to find whatever it is he's looking for, but eventually he finds the right page. The Greater Los Angeles area has eighteen listings, six of which thought it worthwhile to place ads in this volume. Four of the six ads contain pictures of guns, and Daniel decides to penalize them for this. He dials the remaining number in his area code, not bothering to figure out first what he'd say.

—Dave's Firearms and Shooting Range. This is Pete.

—Hi.

—How can I help ya?

—Yeah, I'm thinking about getting a gun.

—Guns we've got. What you looking for?

The man, Daniel decides, has a moustache and wears a denim vest with patches detailing his service in Vietnam and his affection for motorcycles. He's chewing something.

—Well, I'm not really sure. That's the thing—

—What's it going to be for? Hunting, home security?

—No, not hunting. Something for the home.

—No problem. We can definitely set you up with something.

He doesn't have a rural or southern accent, but he sounds different all the same. His words are somehow clipped and drawn out at the same time. It's the kind of voice that would be potently emphatic when pissed.

—Because a couple days ago someone somehow got into our house, I don't know how. He didn't get much, just some electronic equipment, but, you know, it got me pretty rattled.

—I don't doubt it. Sons of bitches.

—You know, I've never thought about it before, but I realized, what the hell am I going to do if someone like that enters our home at night?

—You got a wife? Kids?

—Yeah. A son. And a daughter.

—And you need to protect them. Because the boys in blue aren't all that much help when you got some desperate crackhead burglar tearing apart your living room.

—Right.

—Partner, I hear you. Well, we're open until six all week, why don't you come by and we'll see if we can't get you situated. Bill! Go around back. Delivery. Sorry. So yeah, come on by, we'll get you a little peace of mind. This would be your first firearm?

—Yes.

—So you ought to know that you won't be able to leave with anything the day you come out.

—No?

—The great State of California imposes a ten-day waiting period before your firearm can be released to you.

—Really?

—I kid you not. Not to mention that you must also get yourself an HSC.

—HSC?

—Handgun Safety Certificate. Basically, you've got to pass this written test on handgun safety. And also, you must perform a safe-handling demonstration with the handgun you're gonna buy. We've got a few DOJ, sorry, Department of Justice–certified instructors, including myself, so we can take care of that here, but you might want to find yourself a copy of the Handgun Safety Certificate study guide. It's online.

Daniel had started taking notes, but gave up after writing "DOJ." He considers asking for all this to be repeated until he remembers the main goal here.

—But if I come out there, can I still try out some firearms?

—You want to fire off some rounds?

—Yes. If that's possible.

—You ever shot a gun before?

—No.

—Never?

—Some BB guns back in junior high.

—BB guns. That's funny. BB guns don't count.

—I didn't figure they—

—A virgin. Alright, no problem, we can set you up.

—Great, great.

—We're open until six this evening. Come around five thirty, I'll give you a lesson, show you some options. Make sure you've got a valid California driver's license and something like a recent utility bill. You coming out today?

—Sure, I guess.

—What? Bill, excuse me, Bill, what do you need? Ah, crap. Hey, it looks like they need some help out back. So I'll see you, what's your name?

—Daniel.

—Alright, Daniel, I'll see you this afternoon.

Allowing for traffic, Daniel figures he has about three hours before he needs to head out. First thing, he has to come up with an excuse for leaving at that hour, which will mean missing dinner, something highly abnormal at the Blooms', especially on such late notice. But Daniel knows he can enlist Max in the cause, since Max has forced Daniel to enlist in the first place. He calls Max.

—Hey, how's my lone gunman?

—I'm heading out to a place this afternoon. Caroline will think me and you are meeting with a producer about a new pitch. So don't call here then.

—Why would I call you?

—Just don't.

—You're really going out there today?

—You heard me. A guy named Pete is going to let me *squeeze off a few.*

—Nice. Hey, do me a favor, pretend to kill actual people.

Daniel is unsure how to dress for the occasion. Recently, including at this very moment, he's been wearing worn jeans with short-sleeved button-down shirts that he leaves untucked. He'll put on newer jeans and tuck in his shirt, plus he'll switch shoes, from his black leather slip-ons to some running shoes. And a shave. There's nothing he can do about his glasses, a designer rimless model that cost him an arm and a leg, that will peg him for Pete right away. He'll compensate by wearing a baseball hat with an American flag on it, something he put on awhile back while doing an imitation of the president when he went out on a producer's boat the previous September. The sun was brutal and he forgot his sunglasses. Everyone joked about the American flag, and at the end of the day the producer refused, theatrically, to take it back. It has been in the back of a closet ever since.

———

Daniel's suspicion was right, and the traffic heading east at this hour is staggering. It's been a few years since he's driven this far in this direction, and the continued sprawl, while hardly surprising, astounds him all the same. To avoid thinking about the task that lies ahead, as well as his mild stomachache, Daniel turns his attention back to the screenplay. While the assassin would start with the corporate scum, he'd slowly move toward the politicians, something already suggested by his second target, the lobbyist. But eventually, there's no way to avoid it, he'd have to take out elected officials, or high-ranking appointees. This is where Daniel would really get into trouble, but like so many other projects this story has a logic of its own, and either you draw it out faithfully, getting it down on paper and somehow transposing all the images into plain English, controversial and morally questionable stuff and all, if only as a necessary initial exercise, or you forget the whole thing and just settle for variations on your earlier themes. So when it comes to elected officials, Daniel sees he has two options, either you have the assassin target real low-level functionaries, state representatives, and circuit judges, the kind of people who are surrounded by little or no security, or you confront the problem of security. Daniel has absolutely no interest in bringing security details and bodyguards and counterterrorism experts into his story, they're already getting too much attention, the anointed heroes of the currently dominant and totally, or just about almost totally full-of-shit, or at least vigorously overblown, nation-as-vulnerable story line. It was precisely the people who were exploiting this collective fear that Daniel's assassin would punish, it was a matter of punishment, but how to get to them?

About twenty miles from his house, Daniel exits the interstate and starts heading north on a pleasantly underdeveloped state highway he'll take for another eight miles. A few minutes later he spots a small stand selling fruit and nuts. Despite feeling queasy, he can't resist the urge to pull over. He hasn't eaten since lunch, and dinner remains a couple of hours off. Not to mention that these stands are the kind of under-the-radar, one-man businesses he can't help but support, it seems like a matter of duty to him by this point. Hearing the gravel crunch under his tires, Daniel takes some pride in the way this adventure has brought him out here to the edge of things. The dry air tastes uncontaminated, the chaotic brush nearby has been left unsupervised, the kind of detail location scouts kill for. Ignoring the fruit, Daniel, in his suddenly pleasing costume, inspects the nuts, a half-dozen kinds, almonds, cashews, hazelnuts, types he can't name, all packaged in small plastic bags with twist ties. The short immigrant running the place points him toward a stack on the side, special, he says. In a Dixie cup there are free samples, and Daniel tries some, he can't quite locate the spices, a little sweet, a little salty, but something else, too, something delicious and irresistible. Daniel grabs a bag of almonds and holds it up, the man responds by patting a large cooler, drink, he says. Daniel walks to it and looks inside to see mostly melted ice and a handful of lonely bottles floating, a couple Cokes, an iced tea, and a few plastic bottles shaped like columns. He reaches his hand in the freezing water and pulls one out, apple juice, made, according to the label, just up the road.

Back in the car, Daniel races through the tasty almonds and the tangy apple juice. The jolt of energy gives him renewed focus, bringing him quickly to a wonderful but truly questionable idea, the assassin will locate and target individuals from the first concentric circle of relatives lying just outside the immediate, protected circle of the people at the highest level of government. The president's children are off-limits, of course, but what about his cousins? The secretary of defense's wife can't be touched, but what about a brother-in-law? This idea, targeting not just innocent, but possibly virtuous people solely by virtue of their relationship to some vile, but invulnerable, politician, is at once absolute genius and absolute madness. If the project was probably unfundable before, there's no question what this little wrinkle would do to it. Would probably get him his own file at the

FBI, if not a visit by them to his house. Daniel grabs his cell phone but then resists the urge to call Max. Stuffing some more almonds in his mouth, he explores the idea, it's a form of collective punishment, targeting people solely by virtue of birth or marriage, but in a roundabout way there's a certain poetic justice, or at least poetry, to it, since our main complaint about these leaders is their unprecedented selfishness, their disregard for others, especially for people who can't take care of themselves. It was all too much to be sure, but the beauty of making them responsible for these nearly meaningless deaths, wait until Max hears.

Wiping his fingers clean on the side of his seat, Daniel checks the directions again, he should be there by now. The cold juice fizzes down in his stomach, he'll need to piss when he gets there, he might need to take a crap. Or maybe it's just excitement or nerves or something in between, he's about to shoot a gun. Two signs come into view up ahead, a simple, massive white sign, the four oversized red letters, GUNS, just about filling up the background, and below it, much smaller but almost as wide, black letters on yellow, DAVE'S FIREARMS AND SHOOTING RANGE, the D flattened and elongated into the shape of a bullet, the entire name shot out of the barrel of a revolver. The paved parking lot is mostly empty, no pickup trucks with gun racks, just a Buick and a Japanese minivan. Still, his Audi looks out of place. Thank god he doesn't believe in bumper stickers anymore.

Unfastening the seatbelt and standing up out of the car reveals new pressures down below, definitely must visit a bathroom. Inside, a man in shorts with his back to Daniel stands near the intersection of two large glass display cases brought together in the shape of an L. On the other side of this L, talking to the man in the shorts, stands a squat man in a generic green polo shirt. His thick hands, hands much too big for the rest of him, lay flat on the glass countertop. Below his hands, on two separate levels and radiating out to fill both display cases, are guns, lots and lots of guns. At least two hundred, mostly handguns. Behind the man, up against the wall, are another fifty rifles and shotguns. Daniel has never been in the presence of this much weaponry, and the danger and fear and anger radiating from this collection tugs and pulls at the pressure in his abdomen. He should turn around, go home, forget the whole thing. All this potential death, proudly displayed for sale, it's just too much. Daniel's far from interested in having a debate about the Second Amendment, or even an extended conversation about why and under what circumstances an otherwise perfectly agreeable person might reasonably want or even need a gun, but there's just no getting around the fact that the underlying values here are not his own. Alright, Mike, the man raises one of his enormous hands and offers it to the man in shorts, you take care. Mike turns and passes Daniel, who remains standing near the entrance.

—You must be Daniel.

—Pete?

—None other.

—Pete, do you happen—

—Look, Daniel, turns out, I—

—Yes?

—Hmm. You drove some to get here, didn't you?

—Fifty minutes or so. Do you—

—Damn. Alright, I don't want to make you drive out here again, but we're gonna have to hurry, son's got a game I all but forgot about.

—Do you have a bathroom?

—Sure. Let's get a move on.

Pete walks to the end of the longer counter, raises a board to let Daniel through and into the back, points to a door at the end of a short hallway, and says, handguns, right? As Daniel races to the door, he hears Pete say to himself, Damn, we're gonna have to hurry. Daniel sits on the toilet, not quite knowing what will come from where. As he pisses, a single loud fart, apparently tangled up in all that abdominal pressure, breaks free. Perhaps more work remains here, but he doesn't want to keep Pete waiting. The moment he opens the door, Pete yells, Up here, come back to the front.

On the counter, three guns of various sizes lay on a gray square of rubber padding.

—Alright, let's get started, shall we?

Pete looks to be in his midforties. Dark hair, cut short, though a small ponytail, almost in the shape of a rabbit's tail, is gathered in back. He wears plain, silver-frame glasses, the lenses of which have about three times the surface area of Daniel's more stylish pair.

—Now, there is no such thing as a perfect first firearm. Everybody's different. Different needs, different budgets, different bodies with different strengths. But one of these three is pretty likely to suit your needs. You look like a guy willing to pay a little extra to get a new piece. Yes?

—Sure.

—We stand by all the used models we sell, but trust me, overall you're much better off being the very first man to take your gun home.

—Right.

—So what do we got here? From my left to right, the Browning M One-Nine-Three-Five, not a clone, the Beretta M92 FS, and my personal favorite, the Colt M One-Nine-One-One A-One, Combat Commander. Now these are all nine millimeter autoloaders, meaning they're not revolvers, meaning that the weapon takes the recoil from a fired cartridge and uses it to eject the empty cartridge, load the next one, and cock the hammer. You can thank Mr. John Browning for that little bit of ingenuity. Some guys will tell you if you just want something for the home and don't plan on practicing all that often, then settle on a four-inch .38 Special, a revolver. Fair enough, but I say why settle, right?

Daniel, even though he has absolutely no intention of buying these or any other guns, tries hard to follow Pete, but between the terminology, bits of which he seems to recall having plugged into various scripts but none of which really means much to him, and the sight of all these guns, which seem alive to him, he can't manage to focus on any one thing. Pete's fingers, if not professionally manicured, are meticulously cared for, and overall there's something disarmingly neat about him, even his shirt, at the end of the day, shows not a single wrinkle or crease.

—Why don't we head back to the range? We don't got much time, but you'll get a taste, and we can take it from there next time. Now you're not just gonna fire off one of these here, because I want to give you a taste of some other calibers.

After watching Pete lock the front door and activate an alarm, Daniel follows him into the back again, this time heading down a different, longer hallway. Pete removes a large key chain from his pocket, finds an unusually intricate key, and opens the door.

—This here is our shooting range. Six lanes, fifty yards deep. On the weekends, man, you should see it, this place is packed. But at, at six P.M., crap, it's already six P.M., at six P.M. on a Thursday looks like it's just me and you. Not a bad way to go about it your first time.

Pete walks Daniel to the second lane and tells him to wait. Everything in the entire room is brown. Shades of brown. The ceiling, dark brown, the partitions between each lane, light brown, the floor, an even lighter brown. For a place that's seen so much gunfire, it, too, seems awfully clean, sterile even. Daniel inhales, hoping to smell some spent gunpowder, but even this is faint. Remembering for a moment the ridiculous reason he's here, something to do with learning what it really means to shoot a gun with the aim to kill, Daniel attempts to visualize himself shooting, if not Pete, then someone real, some crook who, beyond foolish, attacks them a minute after Pete returns with a few loaded weapons. Sure, this experience will wind up in one of his scripts at some point, maybe even the one he is trying to snuff out by coming here, but truth be told he'd really like some more time in the bathroom.

—Alright.

Pete approaches with three new guns hanging from a metal rod strung through the trigger guard of each. He places one end of it on the waist-high shelf at the head of their lane and slowly tilts it, until the first gun, Pete holds the other two back, slides down. He repeats this until all three are at rest in a neat line, a few inches apart from one another.

—What are we looking at? This little pip-squeak is a single-action .22-caliber magnum revolver. You won't want it, but you'll be glad to know what it's like to shoot it. We'll start with that. This here is a bit of what I like to call combat Tupperware, the Glock model 17, made out of some newfangled polymer the Austrians came up with. I still like metal myself, but it's hard to argue with the results in this case. Last, the Ruger P89. Butt ugly, but a damn fine double-action autoloader nevertheless. Now normally we'd spend about twenty minutes going over a shitload of safety issues, and if the DOJ knew what I was about to let you do, they'd rescind my license and my right nut along with it, but seeing how my wife would be threatening me with one of these here if she knew how late I'm gonna be regardless, well, what the DOJ don't know won't bother them, right?

Daniel tries smiling, but has no idea what he might look like. He reaches up and adjusts the American flag on top of his head. His stomach is trying to talk him out of it.

—Now how's this gonna work? Shit, I forgot to pull up the targets. 'Scuse me.

He leans past Daniel and depresses a silver button on the partition. Daniel hears a whirring as a large rectangular target approaches from the far wall, the bottom flapping slightly. The outline of the upper half of a human form, complete with concentric rings, comes to a stop about fifteen yards away.

—We got ones with Saddam and Osama. They're even selling some with Hillary Clinton, I hear, but, hell, even I have my limits. Now. The safety is on all three guns. After you put on these little earmuffs to protect your hearing, you'll come up to the shelf, pick up the .22, this one, turn off the safety, which is this little switch right next to the sight. I'll be standing over your left shoulder, a few feet back. Once you turn off that safety, do not, I repeat do not turn toward me with that gun in your hand. If you do, I will protect myself, and you will absolutely regret that you turned toward me with a loaded gun in your hand. I will not ask you as you turn around why you are turning around, and I will not remind you not to turn toward me with a loaded gun in your hand that's had the safety turned off. I will simply prevent you from doing so, and in a manner that will make you really wish you'd followed this little bit of instructions. Are we clear?

—Yes.

—Good. Alright. Once the safety is off, take the gun in both hands, none of that Hollywood nonchalant one-handed bunk, take it with a firm grip, left over right, assuming you're right handed, then get a good, firm stance, like this, bend your knees a bit, try feeling the floor through the balls of your feet, raise it, cock the hammer, that's this thing, look down the barrel using the sight, and try holding the gun still. Then squeeze the trigger. When you squeeze it, try moving just your forefinger without adjusting or tensing the rest of your grip. That's key to hitting what you want to hit, but it's a bitch at first. Questions?

Daniel wants to request a bathroom visit, but there's just no way. It's hard to say just how much of this little lesson he's absorbed, so he's trying to concentrate on just a couple things: Don't turn around with a gun, shoot it instead.

—I think I got it.

Pete hands Daniel a pair of earmuffs and steps back. Daniel approaches the counter, gets the earmuffs in place, and takes the .22. It's quite small, but it appears to be a gun, one that, unless Pete is keeping something from him, contains actual bullets. He lifts it up from the counter and feels that it's a good bit heavier than anything else its size Daniel has ever held. He switches the safety off and realizes that while he probably can't shoot Pete, he could, he supposes, literally shoot himself in the foot, so he tries very hard not to point the gun toward the floor. Wrapping his oddly dry hands around the weapon, he can't seem to find a good grip, the gun is incredibly hard. He fusses with it for a moment, but after remembering the bathroom and Pete's wife he decides just to try and squeeze it as tight as he can. Looks down the sight and toward the human form on the target. He will now kill the target. Squeezes the trigger. Nothing. He needs to squeeze harder. Squeezes again.

Because of the earmuffs, the sound, the actual noise traveling through the air, is, if not negligible, secondary to the force of the gun recoiling back into his hands. Despite his grip, which was, admittedly, already fading by the time he squeezed hard enough, typing and eating chocolate apparently won't get you hands and forearms like Pete's, the gun nearly breaks free to fly over his shoulder. His elbows and shoulders, especially on the right side, ache horribly, as if he's been in a minor car accident in which he failed to let go of the steering wheel. Though he'd been bracing himself, the flattening path of the startling sensation through his entire body, including down through his shaken legs, makes him wants to curl up into a ball and be hugged by Caroline, or better yet, his mother. And it is only after taking this initial inventory of his devastated appendages that Daniel senses a strange change in the pressure near his bottom, where, it seems, there is less pressure in some places and more elsewhere, but overall, clearly and ominously, he's lighter. Without even lowering the gun, Daniel grows quite certain of the fact that his rectum, in all the excitement, had a momentary lapse, allowing his bowels to lurch forward without the rest of Daniel's knowledge, let alone consent. Trying not to move any more than necessary, so that the feces now somehow clinging to the borderland at the intersection of ass and inner thigh don't break free, Daniel slowly lowers the gun to the wooden shelf, brings his hands to his sides, then lifts his sore left hand to remove his earmuffs, after which he turns to Pete and says, trying very hard to sound casual, You know, I think that's enough for today, I think I get the basic idea and you ought to get to your son's game. But do you think first, before you go, could I use the bathroom again? Pete obliges, a bit confused by the brevity of it all. Discouraged, he doesn't even bother trying to lay the groundwork for a future sale. Nor does he think it worthwhile to tell Daniel that even at fifteen yards he still missed the target completely.

5

Four long days later, Daniel walks back into Beth Israel with Caroline for the second time in a week. These four days have not been easy. The screenplay idea refuses to leave him alone. He spends half of each day trying to get away from it, the other half working on it. One morning he took his car in for some work, then got himself and the rheumatic dog groomed, lovingly slapping the always agreeable Alfred on the shoulder afterward, hoping the animal might somehow come to his rescue.

In the afternoon he wrote a scene between the federal agent and his father, set in his father's new, barely furnished, poorly lit apartment. The agent helps his father work on his résumé, the camera settling for a moment on the word *Employment,* which contains some text and the dates *1978–2005,* looks in the mostly empty refrigerator, fixes him a sandwich, passes by framed pictures of his obviously dead mother, inspects the nearly empty pill bottles in the plain bathroom. The scene will be long but contain little in the way of dialogue, as the two men, left womanless, the agent is either long divorced or forever single, probably divorced, don't have what it takes to maintain a conversation in order to conceal discomfort and unhappiness. Throughout much of the scene his father will be diligently polishing a couple of pairs of worn-out shoes. Just as the agent is getting ready to leave, putting on his jacket, his father will say, not looking up from his shoes, I'm sure you heard, someone killed Wenders. Yep, his son responds, not interested in talking about it. Bastard had it coming, I tell you, they all got it coming. The agent doesn't respond, just places his hand on his father's shoulder and tells him to eat his lunch.

It isn't Daniel's best work, but he's pleased by the idea of introducing the agent, this will be the agent's first scene, through his relationship to his father and not through his work, as it makes him out to be both nurturing and helpless, two traits that hardly lend themselves to an audience's typical notion of a federal homicide detective. Daniel even has an idea of ending the scene with the camera coming to rest on the men's feet, when the viewer will see the poor state of the agent's own shoes. Something that will suggest that he isn't much better off than his father, and that, of course, there will be no inheritance coming his way. Perhaps it simply reflects the way the entire project makes Daniel feel, but he senses that this scene, that all the scenes with the agent, must contain an element of doom and failure, that even as the agent draws closer to capturing the assassin he will take no satisfaction in his progress, he won't even believe he's getting closer. The agent's world will be encased in impotence, something that will be evident in everything from the pitiful state of his car to his inability to connect with coworkers to, above all, a persistent, however elusive, tone suggesting that what he is doing just doesn't really matter. Daniel has only the slightest sense how this would be communicated, he imagines unconventional editing could frustrate the audience's sense of pacing, that key scenes could be shot without close-ups or money shots of any sort, all this to prepare everyone for the coming anticlimax.

As Daniel sits down next to his wife in a nicely upholstered, but already uncomfortable rigid burgundy chair in one of the temple's mid-sized social halls, he reviews this and the other largely unsatisfying events of the past four days, including his unsuccessful and slightly humiliating call to the studio he'd done some script doctoring for a year earlier, a call that accomplished nothing outside of planting a seed in the always-fertile imagination of the loudmouth executive he spoke with that Daniel Bloom was, simply put, washed up.

—Shalom. Good evening everyone. Thanks for coming out. In case you haven't met me yet, and you probably haven't, my name is Rabbi Ethan Brenner. I thought we'd jump right in here. So my first question: Why aren't you looking forward to having your child bar or bat mitzvahed? ·

Perceptible chair rustling, whispering, and a single awkward guffaw. Daniel smiles at Caroline, who stares at the rabbi, nearly grinning herself.

—Why are you dreading this? Why do you wish that after another long, long day of difficult work, you just didn't have to deal with this? Why do bar mitzvahs, let's not beat around the bush, burning or otherwise, suck?

This time no one laughs, the room has grown very quiet. Daniel sees a few couples crossing their arms in displeasure. He turns back to the front of the room to see the rabbi remove his wallet.

—Here is ten dollars. I will give this ten dollars to the first person who will share with the rest of these proud parents here one reason why it might not be so easy to smile for the high-priced photographer you may or may not have already arranged for the big day. I know it won't do much to offset the cost, but it's a start.

Finally, a hand goes up near the back.

—Yes. A soon-to-be-wealthier volunteer.

—My daughter won't practice her portion.

—Your daughter won't practice her portion. What's her portion about?

The man turns to his wife. She leans forward and whispers something.

—It's from Genesis.

—Genesis. Well, you could do worse than Genesis. Anybody got stuck with Leviticus? The biblical cure for insomnia. Which story from Genesis?

—I'm not sure.

—Abraham, Isaac, Jacob, Joseph? Any of those ring a bell?

—Jacob, maybe. I'm not sure.

—Never mind. She won't practice. Why not?

—I don't know. She has homework. TV. Friends. Clarinet. Soccer.

—Another underachiever.

—She just doesn't want to.

—Have you offered to help her?

—I don't know Hebrew.

—I see. Good. Good. Thanks for sharing. Here's your ten bucks. Could get you a Hebrew lesson, if you're interested. Who else? Yes. In the back.

—We're putting our party together, and it's really starting to add up.

—Ah, the party.

—First the place, then the DJ, then the photographer, then the videographer, then my son wants us to have one of those guys who takes pictures of everyone dressed up like they're cowboys, and you need the T-shirts, and on and on.

—More bar than mitzvah. Anyone else share this concern? It's common. Who else? Yes, Jocelyn.

—My son says it's stupid.

—Ouch.

—Stupid.

—What do you tell him? How do you convince him it's not stupid?

—I told him that we've been doing it for generations. That it's tradition.

—Alright, but in my family we've been overeating whenever possible for hundreds of years. It's not much of a reason to keep pigging out. Tradition is just habit in dress clothes. Anybody else dealing with this one? Yes, not unusual. Who thinks this themselves, at least a little. C'mon. Somebody. That was my last ten dollars, so you'll have to be brave for free this time. No one? You're all firm believers in the value of forcing thirteen-year-olds to read from the Torah, a book most of us don't know much about, all so our annoying uncle from Minneapolis can come to town for a few days. No one? Alright, so I'll say it: I think most bar and bat mitzvahs are, when you get right down to it, a pretty big waste of time and money. That's what I think. I think usually in the end everyone manages to enjoy themselves, so long as you don't compromise your home equity too much, and so long as the marriage survives, because, let's face it, sometimes it doesn't. But I think that the joy we take from these events doesn't come much from the rituals, they come in spite of them. And I think that's pretty pathetic. And this isn't about me, but I'll tell you how it looks from my perspective. You know near the end of the service, when the rabbi calls up the bar mitzvah boy and his parents, after he's read a hundred words that he doesn't really understand and given his little clichéd speech and the president of the sisterhood presents him with a Kiddush cup and the Torah is back snug in the ark but the doors are still open? Then the rabbi blesses the bar mitzvah. You get to put your hand on his head and say a prayer and wish everyone well. You know what most rabbis think then? Just between you and me? When's lunch? Did my wife pick up my dry cleaning? If the weather holds up, I wonder if I'll be able to get in nine holes this afternoon. We try, we really do. But after a while, we're only human. I'll level with all of you: I took this job, I came here, moving from New York, because I think I can make a difference and I believe in this book and these rituals and this crazy religion, but if you don't all step up, I'm just a hired hand. I don't have magic holy dust that I can sprinkle on your children. If you want this to matter to your children, you've got to figure out a way for it to matter to you. If you're ignorant about the text and the tradition, you shouldn't expect your children to want to do something about their own ignorance. If you spend all your time worrying about the party, that's what your kids are going to care about. Making any of this matter the way it should matter is a lot of work. If you want to spend fifteen thousand dollars so that your daughter can have a glorified thirteenth birthday that includes people making speeches with the word *simcha* in it, by all means, that's your business, I won't stand in your way. If you want to worry more about the florists than the prophets, that's your decision. But I'll be honest with you, I'm not going to smile about it and pretend that that's alright with me. I could have gone to med school and moved to Africa to fight AIDS. I could have started a nonprofit dedicated to spreading literacy in low-income neighborhoods. But I decided to be a rabbi, and I refuse to waste my time. So we've got some work to do. Here's your homework: For next week, write down, each one of you, your fondest Jewish memory. I'll leave it up to you to decide what that means. But write it down. If you don't bring it, I won't let you in. And read Genesis 22. It's short. If you don't have a Hebrew Bible, aka the Old Testament, buy one. We have them in the gift shop, and you can find one in any decent bookstore. Oh, and I'm looking forward to this. When you stop wasting your time it can be great fun. Here's my e-mail address. I check it obsessively, so if you want to tell me I shouldn't have been hired, I'll keep it confidential.

Before leaving, Daniel approaches the rabbi and asks, Do you have some time to meet this week?

6

—**Since when** do you have your own ball?

—A couple months.

—Why?

—Why what?

—Why do you have your own ball? You don't even bowl that much.

—I got sick of not being able to find one that fit my hand. I got these thin fingers, and I'd get stuck with the kiddie balls. You ever try getting a strike with a nine-pound ball?

—How much does that weigh?

—Thirteen. I'm not that strong.

—You bought a thirteen-pound ball.

—Which I will presently use to kick your ass. Like so.

—Money, meet Mouth.

—So you went out there and shot a gun.

—I did.

—And?

—Explain again why you thought that would help me.

—What happened?

—Oh, you know. Nothing too out of the ordinary. Just soiled my pants, that's all. I pulled the trigger, crapped my pants, and that pretty much marked the end of my relationship with firearms.

—You shit your pants?

—First time since second grade.

—You shit your pants in second grade? Take a turn while I wrap my head around that one.

—Now the big problem was what to do with my underwear. I asked to use the bathroom, got naked, with great care, from the waist down, cleaned up as best as I could. But I couldn't figure out what to do with my underwear, which was now soaking wet, but still only about 95 percent clean, which, when you're talking about your own shit, is a lot less clean than you'd like it to be. The obvious choice would be to just throw them out and ride home commando style, only the garbage can in the bathroom is completely empty and lidless to boot. So if I leave them there, I'm just announcing to Pete, the guy working there, who maybe even has my home phone number on his caller ID, that I chose to leave a soiled pair of underwear in his bathroom. Another possibility is to just wear them out. But they're really wet and would soak right through my pants, potentially creating a different but similarly embarrassing situation with Pete—

—Do you mind if I go? By go I mean go bowling, not go to the bathroom in my pants.

—Be my guest. It will give me time to craft my ending.

—You've been practicing, haven't you?

—Full disclosure?

—I'm telling you about cleaning my own crap off my underwear.

—Right. Yes, I have. Couple nights a week.

—What's the appeal?

—Beats renting movies.

—It's a pretty silly pastime.

—Exactly. Bowling is silly. So you've got that taken care of. When I'm bowling I'm not haunted by the question, Is this stupid? Is this ridiculous? Am I wasting my time? Because I know that on a basic level, it is, and I am. So I recognize it, accept it, and bowl. Whereas if I was golfing or mountain biking, I wouldn't be able to decide if it was stupid overall or not. I would think, Wow, this is really cool, and then I'd think, But is it? Maybe it's lame. Maybe I'm a total loser. Bowling is lame and I'm a total loser, but it isn't only lame, and I'm not only a loser. That's when the fun begins. Your turn.

—You're not interested in the denouement of my doo-doo?

—Channel it. I doubt we'll forget.

—You should get your own ball. That one's all wrong for you.

—My birthday's coming up. Feel free.

—Noted. Okay, so you're naked from the waist down in a gun shop with a pair of your still 5 percent-soiled underwear in your hands. How'd you smuggle them out without getting caught?

—Would you like to guess?

—I would not.

—I put on my pants, no underwear, folded up the underwear, nastiness on the inside, and, I really think this will make you proud, removed my hat, placed the crap-stained underwear on my head, put my hat back on, and walked right out the front door.

—Well played, Bloom, well played. How far did you drive like that?

—About a mile. Then I tossed them out through the passenger window, didn't even slow down.

—Just like that? No garbage can?

—Nope.

—You littered your own crap.

—Guilty as charged.

—They can test for DNA on something like that. You could be identified.

—Now that's an idea for a movie.

—Pardon me.

—I'm still stuck on this idea for the sniper movie.

—Have you been working on it?

—Mostly just thinking a lot about it.

—What else have you come up with?

—He kills distant relatives of the president. Second and third cousins. Plus in-laws of various cabinet members.

—Take your turn, I need more time to shake my head in disbelief, you sick bastard.

—He's actually going to kill these people? How will the audience even know they're related? You can't have them with the president or the secretary of transportation, because then there'd be security.

—Someone could be in a bar, making a wager with some other guy, playing two truths and a lie or something like that. Drawing out the family tree on a cocktail napkin, then he walks out into the night, turns around a corner, boom.

—Does this make you feel sick? Thinking about this?

—I—

—Don't answer, think about it. I want a serious response.

—High five for the Spare Doctor.

—Impressive.

—So?

—Serious. I told you. The idea is really fucking me up. But I also think it's the best idea I've had in a long time. There's something real about it. You can't tell me a lot of people won't identify with him.

—You do understand it will never get made.

—Probably.

—Not probably. It will never get made. You probably won't even be able to sell it.

—You're probably right.

—So some advice. As your agent.

—Yes.

—Bowl.

—When's the last time you bowled?

—I don't know. I took Zack over winter break.

—Because with all due respect, you kind of suck.

—And you have a big fucking nose.

—Touché.

—Was that the extent of your advice?

—Leave it. Just leave it.

—But I feel like I'm tapping into something here. Something about me and, I'm pretty sure, something about a lot of other people.

—Keep a journal. Find a therapist. Don't waste your time with this. If you get anywhere with it, you'll find it's going to be professionally and politically very risky for you. The guys who worry about packing them in in Nebraska and Arkansas are not going to want to get near this, and that's assuming that they themselves don't find it repulsive.

—You can't tell me that a lot of people in the industry won't identify with the premise.

—You bowl instead of facing the truth.

—My bowling is the truth.

—True or false: These are dark, dark times.

—False. These are dark, dark, dark times.

—So what do you do?

—I bowl.

—And that makes everything better?

—The goal is not to make everything better.

—Why not?

—You saw *Titanic*, yes?

—I'm going to stand up and bowl. When I come back, you will apologize for that.

—I'm making a point. You saw it, no?

—You've ruined the word *it*.

—When the big fucking boat's nose is pointing up in the air and men with moustaches and wool overcoats are tumbling down the suddenly vertical ship deck, was anyone trying to make everything better? We're past making everything better. The only difference here is that we're sinking very, very slowly. But this is it, this is the end of the empire. My ego isn't big enough to believe in making everything better.

—So what do you do?

—I bowl for those who cannot.

—You feel no obligation to try?

—Most days I'm just glad to be in one of those lifeboats with the lucky ones.

—But we actually have a voice. Do you know how many millions of people saw *Captives*?

—You mean *Helsinki Honeymoon*.

—Do you know how many people saw it?

—Precisely because it wasn't psychotic preachy bullshit. Daniel, you are my third biggest client. My second has just finished a documentary trilogy about the aftermath of car accidents, each one set in a different decade and continent, a trilogy that is somehow all the rage in Europe. And my biggest client has written and directed a series of children's movies, all of which revolve around animals playing professional sports, that together have grossed over one billion, one billion dollars, worldwide. We should have no illusions about our industry's ability to speak truth to power. We speak nonsense to indifference. Please bowl, lest I continue in this vein.

———

—But can we talk about it, anyway?

—About your shitty bowling?

—No, the movie.

—Why?

—Just humor me.

—Humor this.

—Here's the thing. The opening is easy. Show a few assassinations, ratchet them up each time, from evil corporate sleazeball to greedy, unethical lobbyist, to advisor, to corrupt senator, then you spend some time with the federal agent. You show his relationship with his dad, you show that he's not doing too well, maybe he drinks, and you start planting the seed of his ambivalence. That's easy.

—So where do you go from there?

—Right. Here's what you do. The assassin calls the agent's cell phone one day. Hello, he says. You don't know me, but you know what I've been doing. He names all the names of the victims. The great thing is he doesn't sound crazy or villainous. He actually sounds kind, sensitive even. I was wondering if you'd agree to meet with me. The agent, who is weary above all, runs through all the angles with him: How do I know you're really the guy, why would you offer to meet with the person trying to put you behind bars or worse? Only the guy is ready, he starts providing details of the victims and the shootings that he couldn't possibly know otherwise, what they were wearing, how their bodies fell, the precise location of the bullet entries, shit like that. And he says, I won't have anything with me, no gun, no anything, there's no way you'd be able to prove anything. Plus, and here's a key early line, maybe I want to be caught. Right, the agent says, and here's the other half of that line, and maybe I don't want to catch you.

—Will you have them meet at a bowling alley?

—No.

—Well, will you bowl then? This is riveting, but I'm working on a double.

———

—So where do they meet?

—Suburban shopping mall.

—Why there?

—It's sort of the twenty-first-century version of the park bench. They sit in the food court. Teenage girls drink smoothies. Moms are cutting up chicken nuggets and feeding them to their two-year-olds. There's even an impotent security guard having lunch a couple tables from them.

—And what do they talk about? No, don't tell me yet. Give me two throws and I'll have some guesses.

—He asks him to guess who's next.

—Not quite. He asks him for his honest answer: How have these assassinations made you feel? Not, Do you think it's right or some-thing that could possibly be justified. How did it make you feel? And again, the guy isn't trying to win an argument here, he's not certain himself. He truly wants to know, he's looking for approval.

—And what does the agent say?

—He won't answer. He refuses.

—He should answer.

—No, it will be gradual. But he doesn't just say, You're full of shit, you're sick, of course I think what you're doing is wrong.

—Take that confidence and show us how Daniel Bloom can really bowl.

—Almost an improvement. How do you end the scene?

—The agent asks him if he knows who his next target is. But he doesn't. He confesses that he was hoping for the agent to give him some direction. Either yes or no. Either stop or continue. And now he doesn't know. Just then the agent's cell rings. It's his father, we only hear his half of the conversation, but obviously Dad's not doing well. The agent is even just a bit shaken. Look, I've got to go. Your father,

the assassin says. He's not trying to flaunt his knowledge, he's not saying it to get some upper hand. He just knows, and he honestly feels
bad. The agent isn't even surprised. Takes a sip from his soda just to
get his composure. And—

—And hits a turkey going into the tenth frame!

—No shame in a spare.

—No, but now I can't get two hundred. That's all I really want.
I'll stop when I get two hundred. I've gotten over one-ninety twice,
but never two hundred.

—I got a two-oh-two in college.

—You're full of shit.

—Nope. Just an honest bowler decades past his prime.

—How do you end the scene?

—I don't.

—What does that mean?

—Just like this in the middle, I—

—You just have a cut right in the middle?

—I think so. It also tells the audience that the point of the inter-
action isn't all the cops-and-robbers stuff, how do they exit the building, how does the assassin know he's not being tracked, all that stuff.
This is about the two of them. There's going to be more scenes like
this.

—But how do you justify having the agent so uninterested in
doing his job?

—He's going through a crisis, too, that's all I know right now.

—That's so funny, I know someone else going through a crisis.
He's writing a fucked-up movie to work through it. Only I'm not in
a crisis, I'm in a bowling zone. Watch as me and Ingrid do our thing.

—One eighty-seven. Nice. Are you going to change your ball's
name, too?

—No, she's Ingrid. I knew it the moment I saw her.

—Did you intentionally order a female ball?

—Round with holes. They're all female. Sorry.

—Does she sleep in bed with you?

—No, turns out she's a lesbian.

—You're ridiculous.

—C'mon. Finish your pathetic game. Three strikes and you can break a hundred.

—Thanks for agreeing to meet with me.

—No problem. Thanks for wanting to meet with me. Come, let's sit over here.

Rabbi Brenner leads Daniel over to a couch. The rabbi sits down opposite him in an armchair, removes his shoes, and crosses his feet under his legs.

—I wanted to tell you I liked what you did the other night with the parents.

—You liked that.

—I thought it was pretty ballsy.

—The Ballsy Rabbi. I like the sound of that. So, what's up? What brought you to the junior rabbi's office? Jump right in. The Ballsy Rabbi disdains small talk.

—Well, I write screenplays for a living. And there's this new project I'm working on, that I'm thinking a lot about, and it's causing me some problems.

—Problems.

—Well, it's still in the early stages, but here's the basic premise: Someone is killing a bunch of powerful people—high-level executives, politicians, people like that. He's a sniper of some sort, and he's steadily knocking off these people. They're bad people.

—I see you write children's films.

—Not exactly.

—So what's the catch, why is it causing you problems?

—I guess because I really want this guy to kill these people. The plot will eventually involve a federal agent who is trying to catch the sniper. But I realize I don't want him to catch him. I just want to write the scenes where the sniper kills all the bad, powerful guys.

The rabbi raises one of his hands, which had been resting still in his lap, toward his patchy, overgrown beard and starts twisting a dozen whiskers together.

—Why is this a problem?

—Well, for one thing, I'll never be able to sell it—

—You've sold screenplays before?

—Yes, a number of them.

—Anything I might have seen?

—*Helsinki Honeymoon*?

—Sure, I saw that.

—It was originally called *Captives.*

—Not bad, pretty violent. That was you.

—Yep.

—Wow. *Helsinki Honeymoon.* I'm honored.

—Thanks.

—Okay, so, you won't be able to sell this one. Can you write it, just for yourself, and then move on? Financially, can you let yourself do that?

—Probably. But it's not just that. I mean, here's the thing. I want to write this screenplay, because, because I've totally lost my patience with everything. It's not just patience. It's more than that. Everything's just completely, completely, do you mind if I swear?

—By all means, let it out. Would the Ballsy Rabbi be the Ballsy Rabbi otherwise?

—Everything's completely fucked. The government, the corporations, everything.

—Are you hoping I'll challenge you on this point?

—I can't stop thinking about it. It's not like I ever thought things were great, or even good, but I just can't believe the deterioration of the last few years.

The rabbi continues twisting parts of his beard.

—And I don't like that this is what it's doing to me. It's made me obsessive. I read the paper, knowing I'll get pissed, and then I get pissed. I have conversations about it with my friends, knowing I'll wind up despondent, and I do. And now, now it's taken over my work.

The rabbi lowers his hand back to his lap.

—So let me get this straight: The world is broken, and you would like this not to bother you so much?

—I'd like the world not to be broken.

—Of course.

—Who wouldn't?

—Who wouldn't. Can I ask you something?

—Sure.

—Why are you here?

—I wanted to talk to someone about this. My agent wasn't much help.

—What did he say?

—He told me to shoot a gun and pretend I was killing someone.

—Interesting advice. And did you?

—Yes.

—And?

—I crapped my pants.

—I see. What about your wife? Have you spoken to her about this?

—No. We don't talk much about my scripts.

—That can't be good.

—No, probably not. It's a long story.

—So you want someone else to talk to about this. Why me? Why not a regular therapist? You should know I have no legal access to Prozac. I know I'm free, but that doesn't look to be an issue with you.

—You just seemed different. The other night. Rabbis don't usually talk like that.

—Should they?

—Yes. Sometimes, anyway.

—But you still haven't really answered my question. So I'm different. So what? I doubt you wanted me only to listen. What else are you hoping for from me?

—I don't really know. I don't like feeling this. I don't like hating the world this much all the time.

—Would you like me to make suggestions of things you can do to fix the world? I could probably come up with a long list of ideas.

Daniel doesn't answer, stares, instead, at some open packing boxes filled with books.

—Daniel, with all due respect, it doesn't appear to me that that is truly what you want from me. Are you hoping I'll encourage you, command you even, to help out at a soup kitchen twice a week? As your junior rabbi, I implore you, buy a hybrid! Protest the war at the Federal Building every Wednesday at five P.M.! You need me to inform you of these possibilities? You need this instruction from me?

—Do you do any of those things?

—Why do you ask?

—I'm curious.

—Bullshit. You're curious. You want me as a role model? You want to be relieved that I don't do any of these things? What is it?

—I want guidance.

—Guidance.

—Yes.

—Well, that was guidance. Go, go and feed the homeless. Recycle. Write letters to your congressman. Make the world a better place for the children of tomorrow.

—You really seem to mean it.

—I'm just starting to get the sense that you're wasting our time here. You're a bright guy. I'm a bright guy. You don't need me for this.

—How do you manage?

—Manage what?

—Living in this world.

—You're assuming I manage.

—You don't?

—I have my better days and my worse days.

—Is that a problem, professionally?

—Elaborate.

—I don't know, the congregants come to you for leadership and guidance and strength. They want someone who manages.

—I'm sure they do. But I'm used to frustrating people's expectations. It's my greatest strength.

—So why are you here?

—Why am I here? I still don't know why you're here.

—If you tell me why you're here, I'll tell you why I'm here.

—You know, once upon a time, back in the good old days when Polish bandits were raping our ancestors, rabbis didn't have to work so hard to get their flocks' attention. Tending the flock was probably never easy, we know that from way back with the prophets, but we weren't always working for you. It was the other way around, if anything. You tried to be worthy of us, you tried to understand us, you provided for us so we could ask the hardest questions. So that's why I'm here, naively. You pay me to study and tell you what I think. I have a few answers, a lot of questions, and a bad habit of being honest.

—That being the ballsy part.

—That and a lack of patience. So when I have someone in my office who won't tell me why he's here, I get unpleasant. Daniel, what the hell do you want from me?

—I want to know if religion can help.

Rabbi Brenner places his hands on the armrests of his chair, lifts his entire body off the seat, recrosses his legs in the opposite direction, and lowers himself back down.

—Thank you. Finally. How long did that take? Don't answer. Religion, meaning what, exactly?

—I'm not sure.

—Help in the form of religion. Sure seems to have made the world a better place overall. What would you like? Some prayer? Would you like me to encourage you to attend the morning *minyan*? I could walk you through *Havdalah*. Would you like that? Or, how about keeping kosher? Daniel, keep kosher. No more lobster bisque for you! Or more reading assignments in Jewish texts. For next Thursday, read Judges and pick your favorite one.

—How did you get this job?

—I can behave if I must.

—But you're, you're a dick.

—Dick Rabbi doesn't sound as good as Ballsy Rabbi.

—But you are. I came here thinking you might be able to help me. I'm desperate. Do you have any idea how hard it was for me to decide to see if this place could offer me anything of substance?

—Substance?

—Rabbi, I came here open to the idea of thinking about being more Jewish.

—More Jewish. What in the world does that mean?

—Listen to you. You're not going to last six months here. I'll just leave, but you talk like this to some of the congregants here, they'll have you tossed out like that. Probably figure out a way to bring a suit against you or even the temple.

—I'm sure you're right. But they'll pay me nicely in the meantime. I've rented a very modest in-law unit, I have limited expenses. I'll do my time, as long as it lasts, I'll try my best, I really will, and when the time comes for us to go our separate ways, I'll have a little budget for the next chapter of my journey.

—Your journey? What does that mean? Some ashram? An organic farming collective?

—Would you prefer I find work at a talent agency and live in the Hollywood Hills? Write movies about snipers and kidnappers?

—Who are you? Where did you come from?

—You couldn't possibly want my life story. But here it is, chapter headings only: child of survivors, only child, Milwaukee, gifted, behavioral problems, boarding school, drugs, different boarding school, Columbia, more drugs, University of Wisconsin–Milwaukee, meditation, a year in India, reconciliation with parents, master's in ancient Near Eastern languages, University of Wisconsin, another year in India, six months in Jerusalem, rabbinical school, India, Jerusalem, New York, here. How's that work for you?

—And still all that anger?

—Stand up. Come here. Seriously. Stand up and come here. You want some advice and guidance from a professional Jew? You ever see a Muslim pray? On your knees. Good. Lower your forehead to the floor. Good. Submit, that's what Islam means. Submission. A moment of humility. Now think whatever else you feel like thinking. Be aware of the new thoughts that come to you in this position. Too many Jews pray without their bodies. It's hopeless. Stand up. Good. So try that. Play around with it. Here, take these. Where are they? Take these two books. Read them, see if they say anything to you. And stop eating animals. For a week. No death in your diet. Eggs and dairy are your call. But no meat, not even any fish. You want my help, that's where we'll start. Next week, same time, same place. Are you happy now? Will you say nice things on your rabbi evaluation form?

8

During the seven days before his next appointment with Rabbi Brenner, Daniel brings his forehead to the floor nineteen times. This act is performed six times in close succession on the morning following their meeting, as Daniel moves from room to room in his home searching for the proper setting. He disqualifies the guesthouse immediately in light of its proximity to his work in general and the screenplay in particular. The conjugal bedroom reminds him too much of Caroline and their slightly strained, possibly troubled marriage. Though it's probably high time for Daniel to address their relationship, whatever it was that the rabbi was pointing him toward by ordering him to assume this position will not be found if thoughts of his marriage occupy him while prostrate. He goes downstairs, but has no luck there, either. The kitchen, living room, den, and dining room, are, respectively, too dirty, too stiff, too cluttered, and too dirty. Plus, Alfred, who, Daniel likes to believe, is otherwise supportive of this act, sniffs at his ass. After the fifth try Daniel says, Fuck it, over a loud exhale, his frustration leading him to conclude that the entire idea is inherently nonsensical. He stands back up and climbs the stairs. He will shower and while showering attempt to figure out a plan for making it through another wide-open day.

At the top of the stairs Daniel looks into his son's room. Messy, but not all that bad. He's taken to keeping out of Zack's room, partially in deference to Zack's supposedly budding autonomy and need for privacy, but more so as a result of Daniel's own inability to enter his son's world. Their bond is solid enough, he likes to think, this in large part thanks to sports, which they play, discuss, and, above all, watch together with great regularity, but Daniel has a pretty good hunch he's missing the bulk of the ever-proliferating complexity that is his son. Caroline, though typically frazzled and easily aggravated and quite possibly emotionally stunted, still possesses adequate instinctive maternal generosity to pay attention in order to make sure that Zack's needs, such as they are, are being met. Even so, Daniel enters the room, sweeps aside a pair of sweatpants and an Indians baseball cap with his foot, crouches to the floor, briefly goes to all fours, and then gently touches what some might call his third eye to the soft, welcoming carpet covering his son's floor. And then, quite instantly, he feels, if not good, then better, yes, somehow better.

Daniel lets himself stay in this position for a number of minutes, perhaps as many as four. At times he focuses on the physical position itself, trying to decide how much weight his forehead should be asked to support, noticing how it allows him to stretch his always tight lower back by moving his butt toward his feet. But mostly Daniel attempts to feel, not so much name, just feel whatever it is that he feels when bent and bowed low. He is not sad, but he notes immediately how suddenly unobstructed the path to his sadness has become. Likewise his tension, his rage, his fear, his absolute sense of helplessness. Motionless and nearly curled up, Daniel sees himself, his emotional topography, laid out naked before him. No feature of its worrisome terrain surprises him, indeed his ability in this moment to face it, to simply survey his vast, raw inner landscape without judgment, without recoiling, without turning and rushing toward the pleasant, the easy, the acceptable, brings with it enormous relief.

It's okay, everything is perfectly okay. For a moment his breathing
swells from the surge of this self-accepting, self-tolerating honesty.
He wonders if he will cry, it seems like something he could and perhaps should decide or allow himself to do. But this passes, leaving
Daniel to enjoy the tranquility that follows his wordless confession,
his willing acquiescence. Then he stands up, taller perhaps, and
heads to the shower.

9

Two days later Daniel is back in Zack's room, touching his forehead to the ground while at the same time trying to think about the possibility that he and his body are not the only things involved here. The day before he tried unsuccessfully to recreate that first wondrous experience, but while he got some unimpeded views of himself and sensed some echoes of that initial calming euphoria, it wasn't the same. Somehow his expectations had turned it, or even him, into just another thing he was after. Either that or he was already too aware of himself taking this supposedly judgment-free survey. Whatever the case, the initial resistance deflected him to the screenplay, his latest ideas for it, his continued reluctance to write it, which was followed by a doomed effort to not think about it, which left him, just moments later, stewing in frustration and self-loathing. He quickly stood up and left his son's room, hoping not to contaminate it entirely. The rest of the day was largely devoted to wondering how he might salvage the act. Apparently he would need to go beyond the first day, though he couldn't figure out what that meant. It wasn't until dinner that he realized, as he swallowed some food he had been chewing, that this meant getting past himself, that it meant, simply, transcending the self. The sudden recognition and use of this phrase in regard to himself alarmed him. He'd heard it, to be sure, and maybe back in college he'd even made the effort to wonder what it meant exactly, but that was as close as he'd ever been to doing it, or trying to do it, or even considering, really, what might be involved in making some sort of sincere effort to prepare oneself for the arduous task of finding out whatever it was that one found or was to look for on the other side of the self.

So what he did, just moments ago as he lowered himself to the forgiving carpet, was think that he was intentionally prostrating himself before something. He tried quite hard not to think of this thing as God or godlike or even god-surrogatelike, at least not godlike in the sense of humanoid or self-contained or in possession of a voice or corporeal or material in any way. The idea was to avoid naming it or giving it shape while at the same time feeling with some certainty that he wasn't alone. Maybe it could be an it, but only as a force, some extremely diffuse and probably ethereal and maybe even sporadic force, but a force that was out there, that was maybe both independent of, and somehow also importantly reliant on people or life, broadly defined, including, then, Daniel, perhaps. Only Max interrupted, banging on Daniel's front door and screaming his name.

After Daniel opens the door, Max idiomatically attributes his client's delay in opening the door to the interruption of his client's masturbation.

—Close, but not quite. To what do I owe the honor of your presence? Why the house call?

—You remember Donny over at—

—Donny Banderberg?

—That's the one.

—Sure. Big-Time Donny.

—Big-Time Donny Banderberg.

—So?

—I ran into him over at this talent agency—

—What were you doing at a talent agency?

—Later. I ran into him, and we're talking, and he's telling me how bored he is with everything they're working on over there. He says, Max, actually he called me Kane, didn't even know about Holden, this industry's doomed. We're making all this crap. None of it's real. Even the documentaries are starting to feel fake. I got all this money, but I've got to make this crap. It's killing me.

—Great word of mouth for the studio.

—So I tell him, You want to hear a killer idea?

—No, you didn't.

—Right there in the lobby.

—What'd you tell him?

—Everything we got so far.

—Stop fucking with me.

—I fuck you not.

—And?

—Big-Time nearly lost his shit.

—But he told you there was no way he could take on a project like that, right?

—He sort of started twitching, scratching the back of his head, making these strange faces. I think he was holding some kind of impromptu negotiation with himself. Big-Time's a big dude, and he kept shifting all that weight, I'll tell you what, I don't envy his arteries, everyone in town is doing yoga and eating organic, and he looks like he's a lifetime member of the Bacon-of-the-Month Club. Anyway, he's getting more and more animated. And then he starts saying things like, Max, I hate those fuckers, every last one of them. For a while he's not even talking about the story, he's just getting worked up, he must have named seven different cabinet members, his big face growing red. It was great.

—So what happened?

—The scene at the mall. That just killed him.

—And?

—He wants the script.

—Does he think there's a script already?

—He thinks there's a draft.

—You're a giant cock, you know that.

—If memory serves me correctly, I believe I was considered a pussy not long ago. Is this an upgrade?

—Max, I don't have a script. I have a premise, a couple scenes, an act and a half at best.

—Well, Big-Time just lit a big-time fire under your ass.

—Not to mention I'm not all that sure I want to see this one through.

—Oh, get over yourself.

—Max, you think this is funny. It's too dark for me. I haven't even been writing it, and it's making me a mess.

—The troubled artist.

—Dickface, do you know what I was doing when you knocked?

—In addition to whacking off?

—I was praying. Or meditating. Or trying to locate some higher power.

Max smiles. It's a friendly smile. Apparently he's trying not to mock Daniel. But there's some pleasure in it, too.

—A higher power. Hey, I think that's great. Go with it. Feel it. Don't let me stop you. But don't let that prevent you from grabbing this. It's a bold idea. You're a bold man, praying at ten forty-five on a Wednesday morning in July, and then admitting it to a guy who looks and acts like me. Hey, which reminds me. You wanted to know why I was at the talent agency. Look at these.

—Why do you have head shots of yourself?

—You like 'em?

—Clearly professional. Though you look, I mean, you look like a bit of a freak.

—Exactly.

—And what's with the bow tie?

—Just part of the look.

—What look? Why did you get head shots? You're an agent.

—Not just an agent.

—And who the hell is Murray Stein?

—That was my dad's name. Now it's my stage name.

—Your stage name? You've never acted in your life. Have you?

—*Guys and Dolls* in high school. But otherwise, no. But I was thinking, look at me. I mean really look at me. I'm a funny-looking guy. I got no illusions about this. I'll never be a leading man, but I've got sidekick written all over me.

—But you can't act.

—No one acts, you moron. I'll be the witty, eccentric sidekick with the big fucking nose. A poor man's Marty Feldman. It'll be fun. I don't need it. But what the hell. I'm in Hollywood, I got connections up the ass. I thought, why not?

—Murray Stein.

—He'd be proud. I tell you, he'd be proud.

—Any auditions yet?

—Friday's my first.

—What's the part?

—Not sure. It's an ensemble piece set at a rehab clinic.

—Comedy?

—Who knows? I'll show up hungover and take it from there.

—Wonderful.

—And afterward, part or no part, I'm coming straight over here to see what you've got, so put that little spiritual journey of yours on hold. Big-Time's got a boatload of money with your little fucked-up name on it.

—Whatever you say, Murray. Whatever you say.

10

Daniel offers to cook most of that week. Household respon-
sibilities at the Blooms', at least in recent years, are largely undefined.
During the time Caroline stayed at home, she covered the domestic
waterfront, groceries, cooking, day care, bills, and whatever laundry
and cleaning needed to be done between weekly, and later semi-
weekly, visits from the south-of-the-border hired help. But since
starting her interior-design business some four years ago, she and
Daniel pretty much just make it up as they go along, each trying, at
least according to the official party line, to pick up the slack whenever
the other one is saddled with a big project or a deadline. In practice,
however, they keep score, unofficially and compulsively, because at
this point both husband and wife, most of the time anyway, feel like
they've got something better to do, something better than cooking
or cleaning, and something better than whatever it is the other claims
he or she has better to do. Regardless, what Daniel has learned, a lesson Caroline may have picked up herself as well, is that it's worthwhile to find something you actually don't mind doing from among
the culinary, financial, and janitorial duties that come with having a
house and child, though, and this is the second half of the lesson,
one should not let on to this, as it would complicate the scorekeep-
ing, since doing something you actually enjoy doing would not then

seem to count. Daniel, for his part, cooks when he can, since he en-
joys the process, though it always seems to take more time than it
should. He thus thinks of himself as the primary cook, and also thus
thinks of this as a truly substantive role, this despite the fact that the
Blooms eat out, on average, four-and-a-half nights a week.

Daniel's primary agenda this week is, of course, not simply to
cook, or even to cook vegetarian meals, but to cook vegetarian meals
without wife or son noticing this as a trend. They don't exactly eat
loads of meat in the house, virtually no pork, red meat on rare occasions, but working around fish and, especially, chicken takes some
careful planning. First night, obviously, pasta, simple enough. Night
number two, a stir fry. He throws some marinated tofu in for good
measure, under the guise of trying, once more, to dress up tofu and
thereby make it palatable. Mixed success. They order pizza on the
third night, Daniel surreptitiously removes the pepperoni from his
slices. On the fourth night, Daniel prepares a curry dish, knowing
this may blow his cover. He has prepared a line of defense, one rely-
ing on his and Caroline's ongoing project of weaning Zack off a diet
revolving around breaded meats prepared in the toaster oven. Still,
things could get tricky.

Luckily, Caroline eats dinner while still aggravated with a client,
and Daniel rides out most of the meal listening to her grumble. While
one might expect her main focus with each client to be the client's
home, in particular the interior of the client's home, Caroline invariably comes to focus on the client him-, or more often, herself.
She develops extremely complicated and rarely neutral opinions
about her clients, opinions that first emerge in direct response to a
given client's tastes and aesthetic sensibilities, but that eventually
break free of such concerns in order to revolve solely around this or
that feature, whether pleasing or repulsive, of the client's personality,
which then comes to dominate Caroline's entire experience with the
client and the interior of his or her home. On this evening, Daniel
earns some points by asking follow-up questions that allow his wife

to elaborate on her initial complaints regarding a client who simply cannot be satisfied. Zack, meanwhile, picks at his cauliflower and lentils, matching his mother complaint for complaint, until Caroline, perhaps recognizing her inability to outgrumble her son on this night, allows the meal to become the centerpiece of the mealtime conversation.

—Some rather funky dinners this week, Daniel. What's the occasion?

—I don't know, just thought I'd try something new.

—It's not bad.

—Is it good?

—It's not bad.

—Dad, can we have something normal tomorrow, this is nasty.

—What's normal?

—I don't know. Not this. Something with chicken. No lentils. They're disgusting.

—We'll see. How about Mexican?

—Mexican's alright.

And with that Daniel dodges a bullet, while also continuing to trick and mislead his carnivorous offspring, who, the following evening, will, unknowingly, eat a textured vegetable-protein burrito.

That night in bed, Daniel tries again to read one of the books the rabbi thrust at him near the end of their meeting. It's not bad. The writer uses words like *revelation* and *redemption* and, of course, *God*, but there's nothing naive about it, and a phrase that shows up early, *faith beyond emptiness*, immediately claims a central place in Daniel's thinking, where it will remain for some time. Still, he's tired, and there's some unfathomable mystical economy that seems to be running through the opening few pages, one dealing in giving and taking and seeking and worshiping that leaves him perplexed and needing the familiar comfort of the nearly highbrow and mercilessly edited political bitching that is delivered to his door on a daily and weekly and monthly basis. But before he can hide the book, his wife, who is leafing through yet another design magazine and with whom he hasn't had sex in many, many weeks, not that either of them is keeping track, asks, What you reading? Rather than say anything, he just shows her the cover. She studies it and after a time says, suspiciously amused, or maybe just suspicious, Where'd you get that? with emphasis on *that*. Unless Daniel is willing and able to manufacture a creative lie, the jig is up. He could, he supposes, claim that it's for a script, an excuse capable of explaining away nearly everything this side of infidelity and crack cocaine. But he's tired.

—I met with that Rabbi Brenner a few days ago.

—You did?

—Yeah.

—Why?

—I don't know. I thought he was pretty out-there with the parents. I wanted to check him out a little more. See if he's always that way.

—Was he?

—Yup.

—What'd you guys talk about?

—You know, I was just trying to get an idea where he was coming from, but he wasn't all that forthcoming. He asked me a lot of questions.

—Like what?

—Like why I was there.

—And what'd you say?

—You know, I told him that with Zack's bar mitzvah coming up, I was starting to wonder myself, again, what the point of all this was. Something like that.

—And what'd he say?

—He asked me what I meant by all this.

—Was he nice?

—Not particularly. But he listened.

—Michelle thought he was a jerk. They're thinking about pulling Cody out.

—Doesn't surprise me.

—Is the book any good?

—Not really. I don't know. I don't think it's for me.

—What's it about?

—So far? God, Presence, Oneness, something like that.

But Caroline's already got her nose back in an article about recessed lighting. Which is just as well. He would really prefer that this doesn't come to be about her, which, if pressed, he might admit is probably wishful thinking. Regardless, she doesn't seem to care. Perhaps she's just relieved that he's in bed and not downstairs watching a B action movie from the seventies that won't end until one A.M. Maybe she'll take her chances with this book announcing the general direction of her husband's looming midlife crisis, it sure looks better than Becky's affair, Gordon's gambling addiction, or Veronica's public nervous breakdown. Or it could be, quite simply, that she really doesn't care, not about the book, and not about what may be her husband's looming midlife crisis, and not, above all, about her husband.

Whatever the case, Daniel calls it a night first. Puts the book down, turns off his lamp, rolls to his side, and briefly kisses Caroline on the lips. They each pass quickly through that awkward moment when it becomes official that tonight, too, will be sex free. He decides to be pretty sure they're just both tired, that it's nothing bigger than that.

Even though her light is off not five minutes later, he remains awake for a time. The screenplay. He doesn't want a montage in the opening act, but he needs to find a way to communicate that the assassin is gradually managing to kill a good number of people. What will happen, Daniel decides, is that in the first scene set at his office, the agent will tell some underling, some clearly junior type in interesting glasses and a bad tie, to put together a list of other potential tar-

gets. Not much later the underling, who's kind of sharp and a bit
nerdy but awkwardly handsome as well, and who will, perhaps,
somewhere in the third act, get a couple of good lines, approaches
the main agent with a small dry-erase board. *Wenders,* the guy killed
in the opening scene, is right in the middle of the board, along with
another half-dozen names radiating out from this. The intriguing
underling, hands at his sides and enthusiastic about either his ability
to come up with this list so fast or the possibility that these other guys
may be targets, too, or even both, starts going over the list with the
main agent, quickly pointing to each name and then quickly returning his hand to his hip and then offering a brief, but not that brief, bio
of each guy, Oh, and this is Dwayne Carmichael, CFO, they called
him the Wunderkind, stuff like that, suggesting that the underling is
the kind of guy who either has been following that corporation's his-
toric scandal all along or is just a quick study, and he can just barely
contain himself and even peppers his presentation with the occasional editorial aside, supposedly a total scumbag, stuff like that, until
the agent, who finds the underling's enthusiasm far from contagious,
gives him a look that right away tells the underling, whom the audience has taken an instant liking to, to cool it. Anyhow, the agent finally takes the board and puts it up against the wall next to his desk
and tells the underling to make sure that division knows about these
other names. After the second assassination, there's another such
scene, much shorter, another dry-erase board, another web of rela-
tions, a very, very brief sentence or two from the underling, who's
wearing another bad tie and saying things like *indicted* and *three
counts of* and *plea bargain,* and, again, seeming to enjoy all this just a
bit too much, and then a quick shot of the agent putting dry-erase
board number two next to the first one. A few scenes later, after the
audience has seen at least one more assassination, and probably after
the scene between the assassin and the agent at the mall, there's another scene set at the agent's office, only this time the underling is
grabbing one of the small dry-erase boards from the agent's desk. He

comes back a bit later, the audience can tell it's the same day because he's wearing the same bad tie, but this time he's holding a much larger dry-erase board, because now the webs are starting to converge, and he explains this briefly to the agent, explains how some guy, perhaps the third or fourth target, was both Wenders's lead counsel at one time and a consultant for victim number two. And, then, of course, much later, after the assassin does the really unthinkable and kills the second cousin of the secretary of state, the underling and his bad tie approach the agent's desk, only this time he's got no dry-erase board, not even a big dry-erase board, and, with awkward deference, he asks the agent to come with him, and they walk through the big office, down a hallway, up a flight of stairs, and down another hallway, until the underling holds a door open for the agent, and he walks inside. Next, there's a cut to a close-up of the agent's face. By this time the audience has got a pretty good idea that the agent, while not doing all that well overall, is seasoned and dispassionate and just way less flappable than the fidgety underling, whom the audience doesn't see yet, but when they do he'll be almost jumping out of his young skin with pride and excitement, but still, the agent's face betrays a moment of shock or stupefaction or simple disbelief. Finally, the camera pulls back to let the audience see what it is the agent has just seen. They're in a large classroom and the underling, it's the same square handwriting, has covered a massive dry-erase board, some six feet high and twenty feet across, with names and titles and lines and arrows. The camera pans the board briefly to show the audience, among other things, the occasional crossed-out name, various strange symbols, and words and phrases like *cousin, stepsister,* and *last seen in Geneva* scattered across the board. The underling, still beaming, interrupts the silent agent to announce that he'd been working on it since the previous night at eight P.M., after which the agent turns to him, still silent, and gives him a look that causes the underling to apologize. Finally, the agent asks out loud, but not so much to the underling, Who are all these people, why them? Sir, the underling says a few moments later, reluctant to interrupt the agent. The agent turns to him. Sir, they're the bad people. The bad people and their relatives. The agent gets another look of stupefaction, this one tempered by a bit of possible outrage, his mouth falls open a bit, and so the underling corrects himself quickly to save his skin, According to our killer, sir, they're the bad people, and their relatives.

11

—I liked the lesson the other day.

—What? When I threw all those people out at the beginning?

—Yeah, that was great.

—You must be strict. If you give an assignment and don't enforce it, there's no point, no one will do it. I'm a firm believer in negative reinforcement.

—My favorite part is when George and his wife, what's her name?

—Jules.

—When George and Jules didn't think you were serious.

—Well, it's good to see there's some of the sadist in you.

—Speaking of which, sort of, I haven't eaten meat, not even fish, since before we met last week.

—You're probably still crapping bacon.

—I haven't eaten bacon in over two years.

—Then a Big Mac.

—Ditto.

—Would you like me to say I am impressed? I am mildly impressed. Has it been difficult?

—Not really. Keeping Caroline and Zack off my trail has been the hardest part.

—They don't know?

—Caroline sort of knows.

—What does she know?

—She saw one of the books.

—You're reading the books.

—I'm trying.

—What does that mean?

—I've read a little bit.

—How much is a little bit?

—I don't know. Five, ten pages.

—Five or ten?

—Four.

—Wow. If it weren't for your busy schedule, you might have even finished the preface. So what does Caroline know?

—That I came to see you and that you gave me some books.

—What did you say when she asked you why you came to see me?

—Because Zack's bar mitzvah got me thinking about the meaning of all this.

—All this. How did she respond?

—She didn't, really. Smiled a little. Seemed fine with it, I think.

—Does she know about the new diet or the prostrating?

—No.

—Are you going to tell her?

—At some point, if I keep it up.

—Do you think you will?

—Maybe.

—What about the screenplay?

—I'm working on it, off and on.

—Why?

—It interests me.

—Is it still bothering you?

—Yeah. But now there's a big-time producer interested in it.

—And you shall choose from the entire nation worthy people, who fear God, men of truth who hate greed. Exodus, chapter 18, verse 21. *Nu?*

—*Nu* what?

—How do you respond?

—To what?

—And you shall choose from the entire nation worthy people, who fear God, men of truth who hate greed.

—Are you calling me greedy?

—Should I?

—I'm a man of truth.

—Explain.

—This screenplay, it's real. It's about all the anger out there. A very specific anger. No one has the guts to write something like this.

—And you hate greed?

—You're going to fight greed? In this town?

—One person at a time. You're more likely to write this now that there's a buyer?

—I'd like to see it get made. Sure, the money would be nice. Am I supposed to write for charity?

—That being an idea so ridiculous you can only raise it rhetorically?

—Hey, we've given to charity.

—I'm sure. Ten percent?

—Of what?

—Of your earnings.

—Do you know how much that would be?

—Much more than you've given?

—Do you give 10 percent?

—Why do you always bring this back to me?

—Shouldn't one lead by example?

—Shouldn't one get off my fucking back?

—A little defensive, are we?

—My work, quite unlike yours, is itself an act of charity. Of self-lessness. I am not, like so many of my peers in the rabbinate, an actor, a prima donna, a megalomaniac. I have no delusions of grandeur. I am, ballsiness aside, quite humble and not that interested in calling attention to myself.

—That's the first thing I've heard you say that strikes me as total bullshit.

—You confuse the drama inherent in my stern treatment of our congregants with a desire to perform in front of an audience. I'd like nothing more than to work with a group of serious, engaged students capable of commanding the spotlight themselves.

—You know you won't find that here. Not even after ten years of hard work.

—What makes you so sure?

—This town is so deeply devoted to appearance, to style, that that's it. That's all there is. There is no substance here, there is no below the surface. Everyone here looks like they're on lunch break from a porno shoot or just getting back from an appointment with their plastic surgeon. Everyone is playing their angle, making a deal, lying every step of the way. It's a sick, sick place.

—So why do you live here?

—If you're a fisherman, you don't live in Kansas.

—If being a fisherman made you sick, would it matter if you were catching a lot of fish?

—This is where our lives are.

—Bravo. That's the stupidest fucking thing I've heard in a long time.

—Thank you.

—Anyhow, there are ways to get people past the surface.

—Such as?

—All sorts of things. Ritual, rigorous textual study, travel, drugs.

—Ah, yes, drugs. The clergy's old standby.

—Depends what clergy you're talking about.

—What clergy are you talking about? Clearly not ours.

—You haven't been to rabbinical school lately.

—Meaning?

—What you heard.

—Fine, so rabbinical students like to smoke weed—

—Among other things.

—You're full of shit.

—Does it frighten you?

—What? Twenty-five-year-old rabbis-in-training doing X?

—No. Full-fledged rabbis dropping acid.

—If it doesn't prevent them from doing their job, that's their business.

—What if it enhances their ability to perform their job?

—How would it enhance their ability to perform their job?

—Have you ever done acid?

—Yes, back in college.

—And you need to ask? Were you paying attention?

—How does everything looking like a face help someone write a moving sermon?

—There's more to it than seeing faces.

—Right. Marc Katz saw colors everywhere.

—Not to mention there's more to being a good rabbi than writing moving sermons. Sermons are, honestly, bullshit. You people love them, especially in this town, because you like a good show. You like seeing someone up on stage. You watered-down Goybrews love your organs and your choirs and your rabbis in those ridiculous robes they make us wear.

—Hey, if all the trappings of this place bug you so much, why are you Reform? We're the only ones with the organs and all that.

—Again, back to me. If this was therapy, you'd be wasting a lot of money trying to analyze your shrink.

—Fine, but it's a fair question. You make about as much sense as a Reform rabbi as Sid Vicious does working Vegas.

—You insult Vegas.

—What's the rub? C'mon.

—That's what I want to know. Am I that fascinating? Is your life that boring? Are your problems, including this troubling screenplay, Oooh, I want someone to shoot the attorney general, is it all just made up—

—Of course the screenplay's made up, what else could it be?

—I mean, you smart-ass moron, is this all pretext so that you can get the dirt on me? Are you just another gossip?

—Not at all. I'm truly curious. I promise I'll leave you alone after this. Why Reform?

—I couldn't get into the conservative seminary, and then I had to leave the reconstructionist rabbinical program.

—You had to leave? What, you got kicked out? Let me guess, a bit too much narcotic-induced spirituality?

—You wouldn't know spirituality if it took a crap on your shoes.

—Lovely.

—You're so far from being ready for true spirituality I don't even know why I suggested a second meeting. You think it's something you buy, or something you find after a week of shutting up for a few minutes a day and laying off the fried shrimp.

—Would it help if I went down to the basement and dug up my old bong?

—Seeing as how you don't have the imagination and discipline required to read the most accessible book ever written about Jewish mysticism, it's probably your best bet. You mock drugs. Even you, Mr. Southern California Lefty Progressive, you bought some of that Just Say No propaganda. Why do you think the Hasids drink so damn much? Because it helps them sing? It's precisely about getting past the everyday, about seeing the connections between all things, about breaking down your rigid habits of perception, about thinking new thoughts.

—Are you suggesting dosing the punch bowl at *kiddush*?

—We could do a lot worse.

—You're out of your mind.

—Most shamans would be considered insane by our standards. But some cultures are wise enough to recognize that not all deviations from the norm are the same. Some people are crazy, others are visionaries. I wouldn't dose the punch bowl, not if children were present.

—But at an adults-only reception you would?

—In the proper setting, at a retreat, say, with a group ready and willing. Absolutely.

—How do you plan to communicate this little programming nugget to your potentially ready and willing congregants?

—They'll come to me.

—Is that so?

—You did.

—Not for acid.

—No, that's not the right drug for you. You don't need to see more, you're perceptive enough. You need to see less, just the things that matter. It's right in front of your face, but you keep missing it.

—What?

—If it was a matter of just saying it, I would have said it by now.

—And is there a drug for that?

—Oh, there's a drug for everything. There are drugs for needs we didn't even know we had before the right drugs came along to show them to us.

—What's the name of the drug that makes you see less? Isn't that called Valium?

—Not at all. Valium just flattens everything. It's all still there, just not enough of it to bother you. There's a time and place for Valium. I'm talking about a drug that cuts away all the other stuff, leaving just what matters, what you fail to see because of all the clutter.

—And what's it called?

—It doesn't have a name yet. Just a number right now. P19. A letter and a number.

—And you've done P19?

—Oh yes.

—And?

—In a few years, assuming the government doesn't get their hands on it at the early stages and wipe it out entirely, P19 will be regarded as the most important psychotropic discovery since LSD.

—What does it do, exactly?

—It's impossible to explain. You'd laugh.

—C'mon.

—Absolute Oneness, that's the best I can do.

—Who's making it?

—Not clear. Rumor has it some chemist living in Prague, but that could just be legend.

—Is it legal?

—You're kidding.

No one talks. Daniel checks the clock, theatrically.

—Would you like to try it?

—P19?

—Yes.

—You have some here?

—That I can neither confirm nor deny.

—Is it dangerous?

—None of the stories I've heard suggest it is. But you'll want to stay away from sharp objects, heavy machinery, including, of course, cars, plus large bodies of water, cliffs, and animals, even house pets.

—House pets? And you recommend this?

—Strongly.

—You're really crazy. You're a rabbi and a drug dealer.

—A drug dealer is paid for the product he pushes. I charge nothing. I am a guide.

—You could definitely go to jail for this.

—I could go to jail. You know what? Go fuck yourself. You're a coward. You think you scare me. But you won't tell anyone, if only because then your wife and son would find out that you've been coming here for spiritual guidance. You're too scared they'd laugh at you, because you refuse to take yourself seriously enough to disregard the fact that this may challenge their own meaningless routine. Not to mention what would happen to your precious, ridiculous career if all the big-time producers in town found out. All those big-time producers whose bloated, diseased tits you suck at for that rich, curdled milk you're addicted to. Get the hell out of my office.

Daniel slowly stands up and heads to the door. Then he turns around and extends his hand.

—What?

Daniel extends his hand a bit further. After a few moments, the rabbi stands up and walks to the other side of his desk. Rummages through a knapsack. Takes out a small plastic film canister. Opens it and shakes something into his palm. Closes and returns the film canister to the bag. Grabs a piece of Kleenex from his desk and places the pill, a bright yellow octahedron, on it.

—Here you go. Some instructions: Make sure you're alone and going to be alone. Somewhere familiar and indoors is best. Have a light meal about an hour beforehand. Find a comfortable place, like a couch, and bring a couple of simple three-dimensional objects close to you that you have positive associations with, like a ball or a flower. No roses, though, because of the thorns. It doesn't last long, maybe two hours, but it comes on very, very fast, so be ready. Oh, and you'll want to do this afterward anyway, but you should start growing a beard.

12

—**Where** we going?

—The mall.

—Why the mall?

—To the food court, to be precise.

—You want to have lunch at a food court?

—I want to hear what else is happening with that screenplay of yours, and I want to do that at a food court because I want another scene to be set at the food court, and maybe having lunch with you at the food court will turn my vision into reality.

—I'll do my best. By the way, Murray, how'd the audition go?

—Don't call me Murray.

—Sorry, Murray Stein, how'd the audition go?

—Do not belittle my father's name. My name is Max.

—For now.

—Max.

—How did it go?

—You know, the usual, Thanks, we'll be in touch. I don't think so great. I was too chipper, too up. I couldn't help it. I'm an aspiring actor!

—Were you hungover?

—Nah. Even though I drank a ton last night. Woke up in my shoes and everything, but I felt fine. Quite well rested actually.

—What was this for again?

—I was auditioning for the part of Dutch, who's back in the rehab center for the fourth time. I say stuff like, There's no point in worrying about it, you'll never get used to it.

—Did you figure out if it was a comedy or not?

—No. And they wouldn't tell me, either.

—You asked?

—Murray did. Murray's an idiot.

—Alright, we got our cinnamon rolls and curly fries and meat on a stick—

—No meat on a stick for me.

—Part of the spiritual journey?

—Apparently.

—You want a smoothie then?

—Sure, afterward.

—Alright, so tell me, you got another scene for the food court?

—I do.

—Oh goodie! C'mon, out with it.

—Alright, so the assassin calls the agent again. This is after the cousin of the secretary of state has been killed. We get another look at another newspaper headline, this one about the assassin, who's being called a terrorist. But it's not one of those media-as-supporting-player movies.

—Good, I hate that crap. Hate it. If I see another fucking news van as someone's idea of set design.

—No worries, we're keeping it small. So we get just enough of the newspaper to know that this is a major story. Anyhow, so he gets another call from him—

—Holy crap, have you tasted these cinnamon rolls? Jesus.

—Yeah, they're pretty strong.

—I mean, how is someone not supposed to eat these? How are we not supposed to be fat as hell with stuff like this around?

—Max, you're skinny as a rail.

—I mean us, the collective. America. Even though I'm skinny, we're not, you know?

—Yep.

—Jesus, we're going to have to get another.

—We, as in?

—The screenplay, talk.

—So he gets another call. Tells him to meet him at the same place. The agent, now not surprised, just says, Drew Kelly. That's the name of the cousin of the secretary of state.

—Drew Kelly?

—We can change it. He just says the name.

—A name other than Drew Kelly.

—He just says the name, waiting for a response from the assassin, but all the assassin says is, I know, I'll try to explain. Again, his voice is not resounding in its confidence. I'll try to explain, because he's not sure he can.

—Nice.

—Cut to the food court.

—This food court?

—Maybe, sure.

—Because that would be so cool!

—Sure, this very food court.

—Wow. I mean what's that like? Do you think they talked about that scene from *The Third Man* up in that glassed-in Ferris wheel car? It's so fucking meta!

—Max, what's up?

—What do you mean? What?

—You're a bit on the manic side today, even for you. Not that I got anything against manic.

—I took some diet pills for the audition.

—What?

—I figured if I'm not going to be hungover and all down, I'll go the other way. Anyway, they never told me what kind of substance Dutch was abusing.

—How many did you take?

—Four.

—Four?

—Or five.

—Are you alright?

—Yeah, yeah, yeah, I'm fine. I just wish this roll was made out of something a little tougher, it's like I'm eating a pillow. A cinnamon roll with the consistency of tree bark. Man, I could use the challenge. You know? Same taste, but make me work for it. I'm fine, I'm fine. Keep going. I'll try to shut up.

—So there's a cut to the food—

—I won't be able to, but I am trying—

—They're walking into the food court. The assassin immediately says, You set up the net today. I can see it, you're checking for something. The agent denies it. You're just paranoid, he says, and you should be. They walk silently for a moment, the agent tells the assassin to choose a table.

—Don't they get anything to eat?

—No, not at first.

—Because, look, I'm really trying to shut up, but think of the dissonance suggested by something as happily delicious, as cheerily oblivious to the dire state of the planet as this very cinnamon roll!

—Fine. The agent stops first and buys a cinnamon roll.

—Nice detail—

—And then they sit down. So why Drew Kelly—

—Not—

—Max, shhh, just chew. He asks, Why Drew Kelly? There isn't much judgment in the way he poses the question. He's simply curious, so curious that it almost explains why he isn't apprehending him, though ultimately that must remain a mystery as well. The assassin says nothing for a long time. A good ten seconds. The audience gets a few seconds close-up of one, then a few seconds of the other. Then a wide shot, giving the audience an uneasy sense that they're getting further from finding out the motivation. Finally, back to the assassin, straight-on shot. He starts speaking, softly. I won't tell you that no one is innocent. I don't believe that. Justin Grace was—

—Instead of Drew Kelly?

—Right.

—Better, not great, but serviceable. Sorry, the assassin was saying.

—Yes. Justin Grace was innocent. But his cousin is not. His cousin, our secretary of state, is responsible for the deaths of thousands, literally thousands of innocents. Thousands guilty of nothing more than being born in the wrong country at the wrong time, of living next door to a home flattened by one of our five-hundred-pound bombs, of enlisting in the Marines with the naive belief that they'd only be called on to fight when absolutely necessary. It wasn't an easy decision. It may not have been the correct decision. Do you know what made me think to do it in the first place? The agent says no. I was watching the news. I try not to at this point, but there are days when I can't help it. I was watching a piece on a soldier, some young man, Kyle or Tyler something, from one of the Carolinas, I can't recall which one, nineteen years old, killed on a patrol. They still have no idea which of the militias killed him. I turn the volume down, I cannot tolerate the way journalists speak these days, but I keep the image on. And then there is a shot of a home, a plain living room in a modest home in the Carolinas, worn couches, an upright piano, old porcelain lamps probably in the family a few generations. Forty people at that tiny living-room wake, every last one of them shattered. The shot lasted no more than two seconds, but it haunted me for days. You could almost make out the entire family tree from that shot, the aunts, the cousins, a grandmother, a brother, a mother, scattered around the room, ashen. Their nephew, their cousin, her grandson, his brother, her son, he says *her son* with great emphasis, gone, their own lives devastated. What was his crime? What was *their* crime? A family of mourners, every last one. And then I realized, let our secretary of state be a mourner, too. Let him watch a young body being lowered into the ground forever, let him think, how tragic, how unfair, how senseless. Let him remember what death really means.

—Is Justin a cousin or a nephew? Because he wouldn't be that young if he were a cousin.

—You're right. Nephew. The assassin continues, Justin was the secretary's favorite nephew. Used to spend summers on the family farm in Nebraska. Justin's parents had a nasty divorce in the early nineties, he spent a lot of time with the secretary and his wife. They had a special bond. So now the secretary can learn what it means to be connected, just like the rest of us, to the killing and the being killed, to the madness that he and his colleagues set in motion. I didn't kill Justin Grace as a surrogate for the secretary, that would be meaningless. I wanted to make the secretary, I wanted to make him *sad*, I wanted the secretary to weep. All the noise, in the newspaper, on TV, all over the Internet, the debates, the editorials, the latest chapter, they all obscure one crucial fact: This is a horribly sad time. Horribly sad. The closest we get to it is rage and fear. I wanted the secretary overcome with grief. On TV he showed that same old steely resolve, we'll catch this murderer, this terrorist, but he has been weakened, has been reminded of death's stubborn finality. It has, the idiom made great sense to me after seeing that Carolina living room, it has, for Mr. Secretary, hit home.

—What does the agent say? How does he respond?

—He looks off into the distance—

—Is there a distance at a food court? Sorry, sorry.

—He looks off into the distance, because he hadn't considered this motivation. Again another long silence. More close-ups and long shots. Then he says—

—The agent?

—Yeah, the agent says, There's no net set up. But it's going to be very hard for me not to seize the surveillance video being shot over my shoulder from the ceiling, not to mention the camera that got us when we entered. I know you have multiple identities, but it's my responsibility to capture you. Are you confident those images won't lead us to your weapons and your research? The assassin responds, It will take time, though I'm sure you'll track me down. But why won't you tell me what you think? Was I wrong to sacrifice Justin? Only right then the agent's cell phone rings again. He answers. Who else but his father? Only this time the agent allows himself the slightest smile. Yes, Dad, across from the Chinese place. The assassin's eyes widen. He pushes his chair back. The agent clutches his forearm. A fan, he says, sit, don't worry. Just then his father enters the frame. The agent stands, shakes his father's hand, clutches his shoulder, they don't hug, and then the agent drags a chair over. Dad, this is Drew Kelly.

—Drew Kelly works as the assassin's fake name. Bloom, you rule!

—Dad, this is Drew Kelly, we were on a case years back, but he switched agencies. Now he's cleaning up in private security. Nice to meet you. Handshakes, etc. We were just talking about that assassin. My father, do you mind, Dad? My father actually thinks this guy's on to something. How do you figure, the assassin asks the agent's father. The agent's father doesn't speak at first. Honestly, even after the fall he's taken, he doesn't much appreciate being outed like this by his son, he's a proud man, especially not to a perfect stranger who once worked as a criminal investigator. The agent gets a little more serious. My father, he tells Kelly, worked for Donovan Pharmaceuticals for twenty-seven years. Is that so? Kelly asks. Sales? he asks again. Sales and marketing, then just sales, the agent's father answers. Until the mideighties, before the mergers, they were a single division. May I ask, Kelly asks, may I ask what you lost? The agent's father pauses, does something with his mouth and tongue. I was eighteen thousand shy of half a million, the agent's father says. Then the camera sits on Kelly, who responds to the agent's father, in character, Son of a bitch, he says, shaking his head, I'm real sorry to hear that, he's almost affecting some sort of drawl all of a sudden, but then he looks quickly over at the agent with this expression, something between alarm and confusion, only he recovers quickly and turns back to the agent's father and asks, And you support what this man, this assassin is doing? The father turns to his son, possibly to check if it's alright to speak his mind, then says, Well, that Wenders son of a bitch sure had it coming. But he was about to go up on trial, Kelly interrupts him, the case against him was supposedly airtight. They were talking about smoking-gun documents and everything. He would have gone to prison for the rest of his life. Tell me something, the father responds, what are your thoughts on the death penalty?

—I love you, Daniel.

—Kelly thinks for a moment. I've had my doubts, but I support it overall. Good, the father says, you take a man's life, you forfeit yours as punishment. Now I ask you, and I don't mean to belittle murder in the first degree here, but I ask you, the suffering Wenders caused, thousands of employees jobless, three point six *billion* dollars in pension funds gone, evaporated into thin air. I ask you, the suffering of all those people, of their families, that doesn't add up to something worse than one single murder? The worst thing that was going to happen to Wenders was he was going to spend the rest of his days in some white-collar prison, where he'd take up painting or gardening, with me and you footing the bill. The least they could have done was throw him in with the other murderers and rapists, let them exact a little justice. But as it was all going to play out, the punishment would not have fit the crime. Should the man who killed him be killed himself if he's caught? Kelly asks. I suppose, the father answers, I suppose, though I'd have to imagine he knows where all of this is headed. Guy like that, I don't care how crafty you are, you're going to get caught. I'm surprised they haven't caught him already. And what about Justin Grace? Kelly asks. What was his crime, being related to the secretary of state? The father pauses again. Yeah, I can't say I understand quite what the killer was thinking. Which isn't to say I minded seeing the secretary of state taken down a couple notches.

—Well, look who's here. Donny Banderberg. Fancy meeting you here. Daniel, you remember Donny, I'm sure.

—Good to see you, Donny.

—Good to see you, Daniel. This idea, Max, right, it's Max now?

—Max it is.

—Fucking loon. Anyhow, Daniel, this idea Max told me about, I got to tell you, this idea really blew my mind.

—Thank you.

—You did *Helsinki Honeymoon*, right?

—Yeah, that was me.

—Good stuff. Silly name, but good stuff. Pretty intense.

—Thanks. It was originally called *Captives*.

—Fucking directors. Max, you going to finish that?

—Go ahead. Can I interest you in a cinnamon roll?

—Nah, doctor told me to cut down on sugar.

—But not curly fries?

—Yeah, you're right, fuck him. Go get some of those rolls, I want to talk to Bloom.

—So why are you guys hanging out at this food court? Place depresses me.

—Did Max tell you to meet us here?

—That he did.

—Right. I was telling Max some more ideas for the screenplay.

—Like what? You got to tell me. Bloom, I'll level with you, I haven't been this excited about a new project in a while. I can't tell you how fed up I am with what we've been putting out. Here's what my studio does. Sappy, wacky, and gory. That's it. Every one of our fucking movies is sappy, wacky, or gory. It's tiring.

—What about *Destiny's Mountain*?

—And artsy. Sappy, wacky, gory, and artsy. But that was bad artsy. This story you've got, this, I don't know what it is, it sure as hell isn't any of that. How long until the script is done? Because I will buy it and I will green-light the living shit out of it. I spoke to a half-dozen

big names last night, every one of them wants a piece of it. These
Hollywood types who hate the government, they're falling over themselves to be a part of it. You'd have Oscar winners playing bit parts.
We could be in production by September. Shoot in the spring. Out
before the elections.

—Diabetes is served.

—Jesus. If my wife finds out about this, she'll kill all three of us.

—Donny, can I ask you something?

—Absolutely.

—This story, you don't find it a little troubling?

—Fucking right it's troubling.

—No, I mean, you don't think there's anything, I don't know,
morally questionable about the premise? This is a movie about a man
who kills a number of people, some of whom are very bad people,
some of whom might be considered very bad people depending on
your politics, and some of whom really can't be considered bad at all.
And this movie doesn't really condemn this guy who's killing them.
I mean it doesn't really celebrate him, but the movie's definitely about
thinking long and hard about why someone might do this and why
this might not be not just, well, not all bad but maybe even a little
good. Right? And these people he's killing, we aren't talking about
one of those big brother look-alikes, one of those broad brush
strokes, totalitarian, fascist dictators in a tight-fitting uniform leading a reincarnation of the Nazis, one of those unambiguously evil
governments with some bold, menacing, reminiscent of the swastika
symbol they fly on red banners everywhere. That would be safe, no
one would care about that. This story is about our government right
now. I mean we can change the names, play around with the details
a little bit, make the secretary of state the real villain instead of the
secretary of defense or the vice president, but as it stands now, this is
a movie about a guy killing people related to our country's leaders
and a federal agent who can't decide if he should stop him.

—That's why it's so fucking great.

—This could be treasonous. Incitement. I don't know. This could be really dangerous. Plus, maybe it's just wrong.

—Bloom, let me tell you something. My wife doesn't let me watch the news anymore. I'm not allowed to listen to it, either. She cancelled the newspaper, too. I can watch ESPN for scores, but she put one of those V-chip locks on all the news channels. You know why? Because I lose my fucking mind every time I hear what's going on in this country, every time I see what an obscene mess this government has made of everything it touches. Bloom, I'm not a political guy. I'm a movie producer. Lewinsky blew Clinton. Big. Fucking. Deal. I didn't care for Reagan, but whatever, maybe I wasn't paying attention. But I started reading the papers after 9/11. And these guys are a goddamn disaster. Should we shoot their relatives? Probably not. Should we make a movie about someone shooting their relatives? Fucking-A right we should. Fuck them. Let them deal with it getting out in the open.

—You don't think they'll try to stop it?

—They might.

—You don't think we might go to jail?

—I spoke to my lawyer for two hours last night. The movie could get blocked, but nothing more. And you know what? Maybe I'm just talking out of my ass here, but I'd go to jail for this. Not to mention the publicity we'd get from the controversy, it would make the stink over *Passion of the Christ* look like a tiff between a studio and a distributor that gets buried on the tenth page of *Variety*. This movie will be so fucking big, you can't imagine. You'll be rich and famous and make Michael Moore look like a soft-spoken pussy in the process. Bloom, you get me this script. The people will decide what they think of it. Get 'em talking. A little national dialogue. Let the fucking government try to squelch that. Max, what the fuck? You ate the whole damn roll.

13

A few minutes before ten A.M. the next morning, Daniel watches Caroline pull her massive high-end pickup out of the driveway, off to drop Zack at Caleb's, off to work herself. Daniel walks to the kitchen and prepares himself a single egg, scrambled, which he eats with a single piece of toast and a single slice of tomato. He makes an effort to eat slowly, calmly even, using fork and knife, though his tongue and throat have long since learned to hurry everything along. Afterward, despite himself, he looks over the newspaper. The various branches of government appear to be locked in some sort of spat, everyone trying to claim the army for themselves. Not that the army is postponing action until all sides come to an agreement. Turning to the editorial pages, Daniel remembers that his favorite columnist doesn't publish today, which is just as well, enough already. He closes the paper, laying his head on the table.

He didn't sleep much last night. Spent a great deal of time watching Caroline unconscious, she appeared to him to be very good at sleeping. The screenplay seemed stuck, both the story and the project itself. How will he end it? How will he conclude the plot without too neatly resolving all the moral dilemmas? And Donny seemed a bit too enthusiastic about the whole thing, until he finally slipped, mentioning money and publicity, maybe his outraged conviction was just an act, maybe he just sees an opportunity to translate the national rage into box-office dollars. Not to mention, if and when Daniel does finish the screenplay, he'll lose control over it in the moment the contracts are signed unless he and Max are willing to fight and fight and fight some more for creative control. Plus, it has no name.

Still in sweatpants and a T-shirt, he opens the sliding door at the back of the house and walks, barefoot, to the guesthouse office. Once inside, Daniel picks up a small framed photo of Caroline and Zack, taken only hours after the birth, and places it on the footlocker that works as a coffee table for the couch Caroline insisted on putting in the office. There's something calmly heroic in her expression, she'd never been so open, so present, so easy. She hasn't been that way since. This is his ideal Caroline. He looks at the picture daily, it both helps him to continue loving her and prevents him from being satisfied with who she is now. He turns back to his desk, pulls open a few drawers, reaching around in the back of each one until he finds it. He takes out a baseball, looks at the dark scuff mark, almost thirty years old. Buddy Bell hit it 380 feet, and Daniel's own father, in the single superhuman moment of his entire uneventful lifetime, reached up and caught it with his bare hand. The fans nearby went wild, slapping his father's shoulders and back, some guy down their aisle offering to buy him a beer. His father just turned to Daniel and put it in his hand. Said nothing.

Daniel takes the ball and puts it next to the picture on the footlocker. He turns back to his desk and disconnects the phone. Then, lastly, he opens the top right drawer of his desk, reaches in the back, and pulls out a single piece of Kleenex that has been folded into a small mound, unfolds it, revealing the bright yellow octahedron. Dumps it into his hand, holds it up to the light. No markings, extremely sharp corners and edges. Daniel walks to the bathroom, places the pill on his tongue, bends over, and drinks straight from the faucet. A point on the pill carves a line down the back of his throat. He returns to the couch and sits, looking at the picture, then the ball, then the picture, and waits.

A few minutes later Daniel wonders if he shouldn't make one last trip to the bathroom. He rarely sits so still, and the act has made him aware of what may be pressure in his bladder. Just like before watching a movie, one should make sure there will be no interruptions. So he stands back up, returns to the bathroom, takes out his penis, and attempts to urinate. It takes some focused flexing of his lower abdomen to get anything out. In the end it reminds him of filling small paper cups, at the behest of a nurse, less than halfway to the top during a check-up. Still, now as then, better than nothing. He turns to head back to the couch.

When Daniel's left hand clutches the edge of the bathroom door he suddenly stops. Something is different. His hand feels somewhat numb. He looks at it, grasping the door, but he is unable, without looking closely, to determine where his hand stops and the door begins. He attempts to squeeze the door, but seems unable. He tries to release his grip, to let go of the door, but he cannot. Somehow, this does not disturb him. The full weight of the door, though it rests on its hinges, is apparent to Daniel. Four coats of paint cover the door, Daniel knows this without knowing how, without doubt, without having to believe it. Blue, black, white, and yellow. The yellow was painted on thirty years prior to his own birth. The door is eighty-three years old, made of oak. Daniel feels his shoulders grow wide and thin and square and flat and hard. He feels, in what are both his shins and not, the bruises left in the door from the many times he has kicked this door, or himself, in frustration. Daniel, still holding the door in his left hand, is not disturbed by any of this, not even by the bruises he can feel forming in his lower legs.

Other than Daniel, the door has, in the last five years, only been touched twice by Zack and once by Caroline. It has not been cleaned since Daniel has known it, and a thin layer of dust, along with a few cobwebs near a top corner, cover them both. The door doesn't move, even an inch, for months at a time, as Daniel rarely bothers to close it when going to the bathroom. But the door, which has migrated through his hand and down his arm, and has merged with Daniel's body, filling and flattening his torso, straightening his legs, and filling the space between them, removing his neck, molding his head, a head without thoughts, into a wide rectangular extension of his shoulders, the door accepts being the door, aspires to be nothing beyond itself. The door, seldom used as such, has the ability to close off the bathroom in Daniel's guesthouse office from the rest of the guesthouse. It has no opinions about its role in the universe, though it continues to feel the original pain of the trees from which it was cut. For two-and-a-half hours Daniel stands motionless in the shape of this door, unaware of time, unable to move, his mind emptied of all thoughts, his consciousness reduced to this small set of physical sensations and material memories. For two-and-a-half hours Daniel is the door to the bathroom of his guesthouse office.

—**Hello.**

—Rabbi Brenner?

—Who's this?

—Daniel. Daniel Bloom.

—Yes?

—Is this Rabbi Brenner?

—Stop calling me Rabbi Brenner. My name is Ethan.

—Ethan, I took it.

—It?

—The yellow thing. P19.

—Uh-huh.

—What the hell was that?

—I'm sorry, could you repeat that?

—We need to talk. Can I come over?

—Fine. No. Okay, yes, but not here.

—Where?

—There's a small park on Olympic, between Mullen and Muir-field. You know where that is?

—I can find it.

—I'll meet you there in twenty minutes, I need to take care of a few things first.

———

—Hello.

—Hey.

—So. What in the world was that?

—What, P19? You tell me.

—I don't remember. I can't. I took it at about ten thirty, got up to piss at around ten thirty-five, then I remember leaving the bathroom, but that's it. Next thing I knew, I woke up on the floor at about one forty-five.

—What objects did you have with you?

—I took out a picture and a baseball, but I never got to them. All I can remember is holding the bathroom door.

—I told you it acts quickly.

—But what's the point? I don't even recall anything.

—Nothing?

—Just that there was this door.

—What was it like?

—What? The door?

—Yeah, the door.

—I don't know, it was just a regular bathroom door.

—Oh, I highly doubt that there was anything remotely regular about it at the time. Do you have any feelings about the door, normally?

—The door? No. I don't even know if I ever really looked at it before. I never even use it. I'm the only one in the guesthouse. I keep it open.

—That's no good.

—What do you mean, that's no good?

—You're not supposed to choose an item you have no feelings toward.

—I didn't plan on choosing the door. I went to piss. What's supposed to happen?

—I can't believe you really recall nothing.

—I fell asleep right after. I barely slept last night. Maybe if I hadn't fallen asleep I'd remember. But what's supposed to happen?

—You're the first person I've ever heard of who had such an empty experience. If you did it again, right this time, you'd get it. Or at least we'd know that you're the problem.

—What the hell does that mean? What should have happened?

—Perfect intersubjectivity, you idiot. Complete merging with another. The borders of the self dissolve, the ego disappears. You experience absolute oneness with another, and this experience exhausts the limits of your consciousness. There exists nothing outside of this sensation of total fusion.

—Well, maybe it happened, but I just don't remember.

—How in the world can you experience absolute oneness with another and not remember what that feels like?

—Because it was absolute? Because a fucking bathroom door has no feelings? Because I became one with a lifeless piece of wood.

—Figures.

—Figures?

—Tell me something, Mr. I-couldn't-possibly-be-what's-wrong-here, where did that door come from?

—It came with the house.

—It came from the house? Are you retarded? Seriously, have you ever been diagnosed with any severe learning disabilities, are you mildly autistic or something?

—Fuck you.

—It came with the house, great. But, as I expect you know, houses do not occur naturally in the wild. So where did the door come from?

—From a supplier who sold it to the builder.

—And the supplier. How did he get the door?

—From the manufacturer, the distributor, I don't know. It's probably an old door. What's your point?

—Daniel, was this door given birth to by a bigger door? Did mommy door push baby door out her mail-slot vagina?

—You're so fucking strange and obnoxious it's almost entertaining.

—Bloom! Where do doors come from? Here's a hint, where do *wooden* doors come from?

—Trees. Fine, it came from a tree.

—And you experienced complete oneness with a forming, living thing and you remember nothing.

—I never thought about it.

—Clearly.

—And this is my fault?

—You'd have me blame the door? How many hours a day do you spend in that office of yours?

—A lot, but so what? I don't even use the door.

—And use, for you, would be the only measure of the door's worth. This door is an integral part of the office—

—Actually we considered removing it once, I have this filing cabinet we were trying to make room for.

—Figures.

—Oh, lay off.

—I'd offer you another dose, but I'm truly frightened we'd find out it really *is* you, that you're immune to the full meaning, hell, even the partial meaning of the experience.

—I appreciate your confidence. So what now? Hey, why are we meeting here, anyway?

—You didn't hear about last night? No, that's right, Zack wasn't there.

—What?

—The short answer is my short tenure at Beth Israel is going to be even shorter than I imagined.

—What'd you do?

—I had a Who's-the-Stupidest contest.

—And how does that work?

—I gave them a quiz. Extremely, mind-blowingly easy questions about Judaism. Name two of the ten commandments, name one matriarch and one patriarch, was Noah Jewish, who's older, Moses or Jesus? We corrected them together, I was even more disappointed than I expected, so I laid into them a little.

—Meaning?

—I demanded they convince me, in light of their nearly unqualified ignorance, that any of them really deserved to be bar or bat mitzvahed.

—Did they?

—Some tried. They said this was why they came, that this is their opportunity, that they really want to learn.

—And you didn't accept this.

—No, I did. But I forced them to take an oath first.

—An oath?

—I, state your name, admit that I am an ignorant Jew who probably doesn't deserve to be bar/bat mitzvahed, but by admitting this I am taking the first step toward correcting it. I promise to work hard for Rabbi Brenner, who can't believe he's even bothering.

—That last part you're just making up.

—Nope. I admit it, I got a little carried away. Maybe I could see the end already.

—Did they take the oath?

—Did they have a choice? Most of the boys were giggling, but two girls in the back, they did the best on the quiz, too, a real shame, they broke down. It was a mess. There were some meetings this morning. I apologized, the parents left, Rabbi Kaufman and I met afterward. We agreed, or he told me, this wasn't going to work out.

—That's it?

—That's all, folks.

—Makes me feel not so bad that I got so little out of your suggestions.

—It shouldn't. You should feel bad. I'm not perfect, but just because it's bigger and older, you shouldn't conclude that I'm the problem. Temple Beth Israel is the problem. Anyway, I have one more idea for you. Last-resort kind of stuff.

—And what would that be?

—Go to Israel.

—Why would I go to Israel?

—You're a Jew, go to Israel. A lost Jew. That's what it's there for, right? That and the next Holocaust. Go, wander around. You need to get away from here, this place isn't good for you. There's no history in this town. You have no connection to anything, that's why P19 did nothing for you.

—I touched a door.

—You need to remember that you have a past. Take your son. Take Zack, for his bar mitzvah. Father and son. He can read some Torah at the Wall, or at Masada. Float in the Dead Sea. Hear some Hebrew. Listen to Jews argue in a Jewish language in a Jewish street. Feel a part of a community that doesn't spend all day carefully orchestrating simulations of sex and violence.

—Is it safe there?

—Usually. I have a friend, an Israeli guy I met in India, he does private tours. You'll love him.

15

Later that day Daniel and Caroline drop Zack off at Caleb's for a sleepover and then head out to dinner. Sushi. Overordering. Sake. Spirits are high, or highish, for the simple reason that two hungry and affluent people are eating expensive and delicious food. So why not now?

—Hey, what would you think if we took Zack to Israel in a couple of weeks?

—Did you say, Israel in a couple of weeks?

—I did.

—Why in the world would we go to Israel?

—Jews, Jewish state, you know. Plus, Zack's bar mitzvah. I thought he could do some of his portion at the Wall.

—His bar mitzvah isn't until next April.

—But summer's still a good time. I mean, what's he doing all day? He had a bad time at camp last summer, so now all he's doing is hanging out with Caleb, watching TV, playing video games, and asking us to chauffeur him all over town.

—I can't go for another month. This job is going slower than I thought and they're a total pain in the ass. They want me to redo the patina in the kitchen. It'll be September before I'm done. He'll be back in school by then.

—So what if I take him myself?

—Yourself? Daniel, what's up?

—What do you mean?

—Who put you up to this? Since when do you care about Israel, and since when do you want to spend two weeks alone with your son in a foreign country? Does this have something to do with that book you're reading?

—Sort of.

—Was this Rabbi Brenner's idea?

—We spoke about it.

—Who brought it up?

—He did.

—You know he's going to be fired.

—It was a bad fit.

—He's a crazy asshole. Where wouldn't he be a bad fit?

—He's different, that's all. He's got some creative ideas, people just weren't ready for them.

—Insulting a room full of thirteen-year-olds is a creative idea?

—He got carried away.

—I tell you what, you tell me what's going on, and then if you can convince Zack to go to Israel with you, by all means.

—Alright.

Chewing, sipping, chewing.

—Okay, when Zack wanted a Christmas tree or a Hanukah bush a few years ago, why did you say no?

—Have you planned out this conversation?

—No. Answer the question.

—Because we're Jewish.

—So what about a Hanukah bush? That's Jewish.

—No it's not, it's silliness. It's Jewish Christmas, it's an oxymoron.

—So what?

—So what, what?

—I mean, why do you care in the first place? Why should Zack want to celebrate Hanukah and not Christmas?

—Because he's Jewish.

—What if he doesn't want to be Jewish?

—Who says he doesn't want to be Jewish?

—Well, why should he want to be Jewish? Other than the fact that he is right now.

—Because that's who he is, who we are, who our ancestors were.

—So?

—So? Are we about to have a fight?

—What?

—Because we haven't had a good one in a long time. Not since Thanksgiving.

—You want to have a fight?

—Why not? Zack's not here. We could start now, take it home, the whole night's before us. We could really have it out.

—Can we have make-up sex afterward?

—If we both cry first.

—Why do you want to fight?

—Because you're keeping something from me. Because you want to take our son to the most dangerous place on earth for Jews.

—There are still Jews in Syria and Iran, you know.

—Fine, one of the most dangerous places on earth for Jews, and you won't tell me why.

—Well, here's why, sort of. You know in April, when we're all going to be up on the *bima* thing, in front of the whole temple, I'm going to hold the Torah and then give it to Zack and I'm supposed to say something to him first.

—Sometimes the mother does it.

—You can do it, too, but I definitely want to do it. Anyhow, I have no idea what I'll say.

—Tell him you love him. Tell him you're proud of him. What's so hard?

—I will. But I can tell him that any day.

—But you don't.

—That was mean.

—You don't.

—Caroline, dear, am I allowed to ask what in the world is the look you're going for with your eyebrows?

—Oh, you're an asshole.

—I understand some trimming and plucking might be in order, but you're about to run out of eyebrows.

—Fuck off.

—I mean, look at this.

—Don't touch me.

—I loved your old eyebrows, the ones you could see.

—Please stop.

—If I'm going to give Zack a Hebrew Torah scroll in a Jewish temple, don't you think I ought to have something, oh, I don't know, Jewish to say to him?

—So you want to go to Israel to gather material for your speech?

—In a sense, but not only. Don't you think it will get Zack thinking more about it?

—About what?

—About why he's Jewish or what it means.

—What are you working on right now? Is this about a script? Is Holden involved in this?

—He's Max now.

—Whatever, the guy's a nut job.

—He's one of the finest agents in Hollywood.

—Is he involved in this?

—No. He doesn't even know about it.

—And a script? Is there a script behind this? Are you writing something set in Israel?

—No, I'm not.

—I can't believe you brought my eyebrows into this. And speaking of bad hair decisions, are you growing a beard?

—Maybe.

—But you can't grow a beard.

—I can try.

—Your moustache will just float above your lip, you've got no connecting hairs over here.

—Notice how I let you touch my face, even when you insulted the hair growing out of it.

—You shouldn't.

—Can I ask Zack?

—Do whatever you want. If you take him and get him killed, I will kill you. Anyway, how are you going to persuade him?

—I don't know.

—C'mon. Alright, I'm Zack. Mr. Sudden Super Zionist, Israel's stupid, why should I go to Israel?

—It's beautiful.

—I'm twelve.

—Alright, it's cool.

—What's cool about it?

—We can see things that are over three thousand years old. We can see Jerusalem. We can float in the Dead Sea.

—Big whoop.

—Caroline, he'll have a great time if he goes. Rabbi Brenner hooked me up with an Israeli friend of his who's agreed to be our personal tour guide.

—So this is his idea.

—Yes. I told you, he suggested it. So what?

—How many times have you met with him?

—Just a few.

—What, and he gives you advice, tells you to take your son to Israel?

—We just talk, it came up in the conversation.

—Honestly, I think it's a waste of money.

—I'd rather spend money on this trip than a big, stupid party.

—What if Zack wants a big, stupid party?

—Who are the parents, and who's the kid?

—You know there was a bus bombing there last week.

—I promise he won't die.

—No buses.

—Fine.

—Nothing stupid. No rappelling down mountainsides or playing with machine guns.

—Fine.

—C'mon, get the bill. Let's go.

—Did we fight enough to have make-up sex?

—Hardly.

—Can we just have regular sex?

16

The Blooms' backyard, after the guesthouse and a row of plum trees that grow inedible plums got through with it, is but a single long strip of grass. A couple of times a month a man named Carlos or Juan or Juan Carlos, Caroline tends to deal with him, comes riding in on a weathered orange sit-down mower. Five minutes and one pass in each direction later, he rides off, thirty dollars richer. When a much younger Zack consumed just about all his parents' time and energy, Caroline and Daniel allowed Alfred to crap there with impunity, turning the grass into an unnavigable fecal minefield. But no longer. Reclaimed by the humans at this address, the strip now serves one purpose: Pickle.

For those unfamiliar, here's what you need: First, two bases, or base substitutes. The Blooms place, some fifteen feet before the north wall, a cheap, rubber home plate with a black nub in the middle, the home plate once upon a time the bottom section of a combo home plate–tee-ball stand, and, at a safe distance from the south wall, an old squarish seat cushion taken from a long-since-sold set of dining room chairs. Second, a couple of mitts. Third, a ball, or, considering the low wall at the south end of the yard and the strained relationship between the Blooms and the Manfredis, who live on the other side of this wall, a number of balls. Baseballs for purists, tennis balls for those who, like the Blooms, go through a few a game and tend to bean other players in the back during the more chaotic Pickle melees. Fourth, four or more players, two to wear the mitts, throw the ball, and guard the bases, the rest to run back and forth between the bases. Five, a long stretch of grass that can be turned into a dead-end, self-contained, two-way base path. See above.

Today's roster. Presently manning the chair cushion, Zack Bloom, son of Daniel Bloom. Average arm, quick feet, tendency to giggle when all hell breaks loose. At the other end of Zack's throws, for now, Caleb Vaisman, Zack's very, very best friend. Great arm, no acceleration, reckless and argumentative, slides even when entirely unnecessary. And running the bases, for now: Phoenix Senders, this summer's third wheel, never tires, no eye-hand coordination whatsoever, son of notoriously strange parents whose income source is shrouded in mystery; Jack Jay, silent kid from down the street who has managed to live eleven years on the planet without developing a discernible personality in the process, can throw but can't catch, was recruited solely for Pickle and will, in fact, unceremoniously return or be returned home prior to post-Pickle refreshments; Daniel Bloom, great with a mitt, bum left knee, legendary Pickle mentor.

The rules. Guys with mitts play catch near the bases; base runners, standing with at least one foot touching a base, wait for a bad throw, or not, and then take off in the direction of the other base. The decision to run is left to the discretion of each individual runner, there being no teams in Pickle. If a runner is tagged, he takes the mitt of the player who tagged him and the two exchange roles. If the runner arrives safely, play continues. Games last anywhere from five minutes to two hours.

In addition to the pride he takes in having found such a popular use for his otherwise useless, outside of horseshoes and bocce ball, oblong patch of lawn, Daniel consistently finds himself, overall, happily stunned by his son's unwavering affection for Pickle. As a man who writes narratives for a living, Daniel has, somewhat unintentionally, trained his brain to experience the world, the real one, as a boundless collection of linear plots, of conflicts and resolutions with beginnings, middles, and ends. The supremely blatant circularity of Pickle, a game that is nothing more and nothing less than the contrived isolation and endless reenactment of the clumsiest possible moment from the otherwise graceful game of baseball, a base runner foolishly stuck between bases, strikes Daniel as so patently nonsensical that its long-standing popularity in his own backyard is no less remarkable to him than one day finding a cinder block floating in midair. Daniel joins in, then, as an essentially removed ethnographer, trying to comprehend up close the appeal of this exercise, it can hardly be considered a game, in which no one keeps score and no winner can ever emerge. As Jack and Phoenix run with moronic glee back and forth between the bases, while Caleb struggles to extract the ball from a thick tangle of bushes growing along the north wall, Daniel feels a pang of melancholy as he recognizes, once more, his inability to enter the game completely, his failure to truly understand or relate to those who can, and the simple fact that he is, it seems, an adult. Zack, meanwhile, uses his mitt to, apparently, catch Phoenix's head and drag him to the ground. The game seems to be ending, as any game so inherently close to meaningless-ness invariably must, with a willful collective deterioration into mad-cap anarchy. Caleb, ball finally in hand, runs headlong toward the writhing pile of prepubescent boys, hurls the ball into this heap of playmates, causing Phoenix to squeal in pained delight, and, finally, some five feet from the mound, leaps into the air and lands at the top. Daniel offers to round up refreshments.

The clock on the microwave informs Daniel that he's just entered his hundred and twentieth minute of playing with Zack and his friends today. His work, which has no set hours, which rarely ever truly needs to be done, which he himself can almost never ignore entirely, allows Daniel, even on a weekday like today, the luxury, at least in theory, of pretending he doesn't work at all. Prior to Pickle, Daniel, quickly renamed Mr. Suck, joined the other three in a video game basketball tournament, where he, Mr. Suck, was mercilessly trounced by Caleb, aka Trauma's Stepchild, in the opening game, much to no one's surprise. Daniel forces himself to join in and play along like this every couple of months. While Zack seems to like his father enough, or at least endure him without protest, Daniel can't help but feel that his son's childhood is presently passing before his eyes, and that, moreover, he no longer understands who his son is, which isn't to say that Zack is troubled or troubling, just that he's another human being, one growing progressively more complex every day, and in this way coming into possession of an elaborate interior world his father cannot penetrate. So he tries to play with him. Also, and maybe this is the real reason, he wants to take him to Israel, but can't find a way to introduce the idea.

Daniel and the remaining three boys gather in the living room, where Daniel distributes the sugary chilled carbonation. Phoenix locates an oversized coffee-table book on Alfred Hitchcock, and, intrigued by it, will ignore the other three entirely for the next fifteen minutes, his eccentric parents having failed to train him in the fundamentals of conversation.

—Hey, Zack, how would you feel about the two of us taking a trip to Israel in a week or so?

Zack says nothing, drinks his drink. Caleb answers for him.

—Man, why would anybody want to go to Israel?

—What do you mean? It's supposed to be an amazing place.

—My dad says the place is doomed.

—Doomed?

—He said the Israelis are going to have to kill all the Arabs, but that it won't matter because they have so many kids that you can't kill them all.

—Why do the Israelis have to kill them all?

—I don't know, because they're terrorists.

—All of them?

—I guess, I don't know. My dad says 9/11 was just the beginning.

—Zack, any opinion on the matter?

—He says that World War III has already started and that there'll probably be a draft by the time I'm eighteen.

—Zack?

—Why do you want to go to Israel?

—Well, your bar mitzvah's coming up, and I thought you could read part of your Torah portion at the Wall.

—But I barely know my portion at all. I just got it.

—You don't have to. It's just an idea. I was there about twenty-five years ago. It's beautiful, it's fun, it's really cool, there's a million things to see. There's the mountains and the sea and Jerusalem.

—My dad would never let me go. He thinks Israel will be gone in twenty years.

—Are you going to work there?

—Not if you don't want me to.

—He said that all the Israelis should just get out while they can.

—Does Mom know?

—Yes. She said it's up to you.

—They should go back to Poland or wherever they all came from.

—How long would we go for?

—Not that long. Ten days, a couple of weeks. Rabbi Brenner has an Israeli friend there who can be our personal tour guide.

—Rabbi Brenner got fired.

—Who told you that?

—Is that the crazy rabbi guy you told me about?

—Eric Haas told me that he made everybody say they were stupid and that Maya Rubin cried and told her parents and that her parents got Rabbi Kaufman to fire him.

—He made everybody say they were stupid? That's totally awesome. Did they?

—I don't know, I guess. He made them.

—Well, it doesn't matter. I exchanged some e-mails with the rabbi's friend, his name's Nadav, and he seemed like a good guy. Said he could take us camping in the desert.

—You should make sure he's got an Uzi.

—What do you say?

—They shoot like thirty rounds a second.

—I don't know.

—Or maybe it's forty.

—Caleb, shut up, man.

—What?

—Can Caleb come?

—Zack, this isn't a trip to Disneyland. You need a passport—

—I have a passport, we went to Mexico last year for my mom's fortieth birthday.

—And tickets aren't exactly cheap.

—What if his parents pay?

—Mexico's gross.

—Zack, I think this is just for you and me.

—All the food gave me diarrhea.

—Alright.

—Alright, you'll go?

—Alright, I'll think about it.

—My dad and brother got it, too.

Forty-five minutes later Caleb, whose overbite is the stuff of national symposiums, gets picked up for his weekly session with the orthodontist. Daniel heads to the kitchen to begin dinner preparations. Hamburgers, he informs Alfred, who is resting nearby, I've given up. Zack heads to his room to play video games or masturbate, the distinction meaningless. But then he begins visiting the snack cupboards every six to seven minutes, first grabbing handfuls of nuts and cereal and after that selecting individually wrapped granola bars and colorful fruitish treats. He enters the kitchen, he leaves the kitchen, in, out, back again. Daniel's *Hey* and *What's up* and *What ya doing* elicit *Hey* and *Nothing* and *Not much,* until the dad here remembers that sometimes raising a child isn't such a mystery after all, for this is Zack's longstanding mode of unwittingly communicating discomfort, anxiety, and fear. Daniel recognizes the behavior after his son's fourth trip to the kitchen, a silent interface with a bag of salt-and-vinegar potato chips, but lets the routine continue a few visits, a few mouthfuls longer, the predictability too satisfying to preempt. Until finally, a cylinder of processed crap in hand, he decides to interrupt.

—Zack, what's the story? Something bothering you?

Just a look, nearly pouty, nearly guilty, mostly weary.

—You okay?

Chewing. Dad approaches, helps himself to some of the cheese-infused concoction in order to break the ice, and tries again, knowing how much easier it would be for Caroline to persuade their son to speak.

—What's going on?

He reintroduces the carbonation as an additional gesture of goodwill. They drink and, finally, the impatient, if not exactly desperate father belches, because belches are funny. Success.

—Dad, Caleb said that suicide bombers only get on buses with all the windows closed because that contains the air pressure or something and so more people get killed then because the blast is stronger than if the windows were open.

—What did Caleb say?

—So if we go will you make sure that we don't get on buses that have all their windows closed?

Daniel can picture himself laughing softly, putting his arm around Zack, and saying, Of course, son, I'll be sure, no buses with closed windows. Of course, son. Maybe he'd even ruffle his son's hair a bit. Some tender sitcom moment, the family communicates, the parent comforts, the child sighs with relief, everyone's a winner. Do they make sitcoms about a world in which twelve-year-olds sit around discussing the finer points of blowing yourself up in public spaces? Cheese puffs and terror.

—We don't have to go.

—There's an Israeli kid in my class at school, Amir. He goes back every summer. He says it's no big deal.

—But it's scary?

—He says that no one really talks about it, that he's scared when they drive, though, because everyone drives crazy there.

—Look, Zack, I mean in terms of numbers and statistics, you know, and all that, it's like getting hit by lightning.

—But you don't know.

—No. That's the idea. It's random.

—I mean, I want to go, this summer's so boring. And Amir says Israel's way cooler than Los Angeles. He said that the beaches are awesome.

—They are. Why don't we see what Mom thinks at dinner?

—And the girls are hot.

—I don't doubt it.

—Caleb says they give the suicide bombers special drugs that make them not care about what they're doing. It's like they don't even know.

—What drug is that?

—He said it doesn't have a name yet.

17

—**Bloom, you** got a couple of hours?

—Why?

—I've got another audition. Can you come sit with me? I think it'll help me relax.

—What's the part?

—I'll tell you when I pick you up. I'm perfect for it.

—Sure, what the hell. I'm here. Come on by.

—So what's the part? Comedy, drama, what?

—It's a commercial.

—A commercial? You're selling out already. That was quick.

—Because prior to this moment my career was a model of integrity.

—Why do you want to do commercials?

—What the hell do I care? It's all product placement, anyway. You want to guess what it's for?

—What can Murray Stein sell? Are you the main character?

—There's a series of satisfied, some might say lucky, satisfied customers.

—Not cars. Not shoes. Medicinal?

—Close, but no.

—Food, no. Insurance?

—No. I'll give you a hint. I'm a total stud.

—This is a national campaign?

—Yep. But limited to cable.

—Cable? I have no idea.

—One last hint, but this will probably give it away. You put it on your dick.

—Get the fuck out of here.

—I'm getting laid! According to the commercial, anyhow.

—You're hawking condoms?

—I'm hoping to.

—With all due respect to your smashing good looks, might I ask, huh?

—The idea is, even you, yes you, might get some, so be ready. It opens with the handsome guy, but then there's the fat guy and the ugly guy and the weird guy. And we're all getting booty.

—Booty?

—I think that's one of the things it's called.

—So where's the script at? Donny's been leaving me messages.

—Shouldn't you be getting into character?

—Not to worry. You see that assistant?

—With the nose ring?

—Yeah, her.

—What about her?

—She wants to fuck me, badly.

—What'd you take this time?

—Nothing. My breath is fresh, and I've got my finest underwear on. But not for long. Because that little number, that little sweet thang, is going to be riding the Murray Stein train this afternoon. Yeah.

—I see.

—I am sexiness personified. I give the world a boner.

—Please stop.

—Can't stop. Gonna be going all night long.

—I'm going to talk about the script now.

—Don't let my sexy ass stop you.

—The agent. I've been trying to figure out the agent. He's really going to have to be in a bad way. He's still functioning, because that's what comes natural to him, it's the only thing he still knows how to do, but his personal life is a mess. I guess we'll have one of those late-night bar scenes, maybe with his dad, maybe a shot of his fridge, which is 60 percent booze, but we'll need more than that, too.

—How about some other drugs? Make him a pothead. No, coke. Heroin's supposedly making a major comeback.

—We'll see. But here's what I'm thinking. He's divorced, right? Couldn't hold his marriage together. Only his ex-wife still pines for the guy. So there's a scene where they're at a motel. She's remarried, you see her running her fingernails down his back with a wedding ring on one finger. It's the end of the act. He's huffing, she's under him, the light's not flattering, the motel's a dump. He finishes and rolls off, barely seeming to have enjoyed it. She starts talking, mentions some guy who's clearly her husband, clearly another loser, they might give him his job back, she says something like that. The agent doesn't even respond, gets out of the bed, walks to the bathroom, maybe the audience gets a shot of him nude from the back, he's aging and not exactly thin. The audience hears the water go on in the sink, he's probably washing his crotch. She says his name a couple times, he doesn't respond. Gets dressed. She keeps talking. His phone rings and he answers, doesn't even say to her, Hey, I've got to take this, he just answers. She's insulted, but barely shows it, cuts herself off and looks at her nails. He asks some questions, Where? When? that kind of thing, it's another assassination.

—He doesn't even kiss her on the way out, does he?

—Definitely not. Scribbles a note, hands it to her, and leaves, still on the phone.

—Guy's a real charmer.

—It's raining outside the motel. He doesn't even give a shit. Walks indifferent through the rain to his car, makes no effort to keep himself dry.

—An important scene, because it wasn't dark enough already.

—Tell me about it.

—It'll make a great holiday release.

—Fuck the holidays.

—You're not doing too well, are you, Bloom?

—I'm thinking about taking Zack to Israel.

—The next leg of Daniel's tour de spirituality?

—I got to get out of here.

—Yeah, but that place makes the U.S. look like paradise.

—Maybe that's the idea.

—When are you going?

—I don't know. Soon. I still have to convince Zack.

—Can I come?

—What? No. Why would you want to go, anyway?

—I'm not any less Jewish than you.

—So, everyone's Jewish in this town. Hardly qualifies as a reason. Why don't you invite Donny while you're at it?

—He's not Jewish.

—Banderberg's not Jewish?

—It was his wife's name.

—He took his wife's name?

—Career move.

—I see.

—He's Greek Orthodox.

—Obviously.

—C'mon, take me to Israel.

—No.

—The women there are supposed to be incredibly hot.

—Forget it.

—And cruising the bar mitzvah circuit is probably not a bad way to pick up chicks over there.

—Of course. It's all an elaborate ploy to get laid.

—Speaking of which, check her out. Ouch.

—Murray Stein? Is there a Murray Stein here?

—That would be me. Murray Stein, in the flesh.

18

And then, perhaps, a moment of grace. Caroline returns home Friday afternoon all smiles and good cheer. After weeks of unbearable tension and unreasonable demands and unfounded accusations, the long-dreaded Gail Bahmani, underemployed psychotherapist and bitch-client extraordinaire, suddenly changed her tune, confiding in Caroline, confessing to the embattled interior designer her belief that Michael, her husband, is cheating on her and/or addicted to online pornography. In addition to hearing all sorts of genuinely unbelievable and really appalling dirt and details, the personal in personal computer had never seemed so literal, Caroline the confidante found herself repositioned as an ally, a comrade even. Gail, apparently in search of a friendly, supportive ear, apologized to her, offering the theory that her previously, and retrospectively inexcusable, unkind treatment of Caroline was merely displacement or projection or some such explainable thing. Client then offered coffee, designer offered Kleenex and a hug, and just like that Caroline realized she could do no wrong.

Daniel listens to her story with an approving, or at least cooperative, smile on his face, sensing how nothing so rejuvenates an ailing marriage as witnessing, up close, another marriage's dramatic collapse. Son and dog are assembled, a neighborhood walk commences, and soon ice cream is eaten in the agreeable shade of a not-too-warm summer afternoon, the conscious decision to likely ruin their appetite for dinner only adding to the shared pleasure. The Blooms harness this carefree gumption and head to a nearby movie house, not even bothering to see what's playing before setting out. They settle on an overhyped summer blockbuster they've all avoided until now, procure some popcorn to add to the ice cream in their tummies, and assemble in the darkness.

Going to the movies, obviously, is never a simple matter for Daniel. The mere act of exchanging money for a ticket and then walking willfully into the theater itself unleashes inside him a frightening and unruly cluster of bad feelings. A thick clump of frustration and contempt, with a dense core of anger and fear, rises to the surface, easily recognizable for never being far from the surface to begin with. In addition to whatever else he may have accomplished so far in his screenwriting career, there can be little doubt that he's managed to ruin, just about entirely, the experience of seeing a movie, at least those of the contemporary American variety. Before the previews even begin he already knows too well who was involved, what was sacrificed, whose ego prevailed, and once the projector actually rolls it only gets worse. He suffers through the clichés and the shortcuts and the insidious, lowest-common-denominator lack of imagination like he's watching some poor thing already soiled being shamelessly abused some more, until, typically, he rushes out before the credits have a chance to remind him who's responsible. A couple of times a year Max drags him to a small movie house to remind him of what, theoretically at least, is possible. No one speaks, they just read the subtitles or decode the black against white, and once it's over they wait a full week to share their impressions. It's the only way to reclaim some of their otherwise long-dead reverence for the medium.

But today, with a relieved wife and a still adorable son at his side, Daniel decides not to give a shit. He does this from time to time, he decides it might just be a matter of deciding to be happy or content or at peace or resigned to one's own fate, and so he decides. The lights dim and the audience is subjected to an ad for the military. Daniel boos audibly. Caroline reprimands him but doesn't mean it, while his son gives him a confused look that Daniel interprets as being colored with admiration. As for the movie, it stars computer-generated imagery and a superstar's multimillion-dollar cheekbones and jawline. It contains not a single surprise, but the seats are comfortable, Caroline holds his hand, and Zack eats a mountain of popcorn. Daniel allows his negativity to fill up the rest of their vacant row, but otherwise ignores it, along with the unwritten screenplay that, even in the mostly dark, fills his peripheral vision.

At dinner, carry-out ordered from the lobby of the theater, Caroline, at Daniel's behest while Zack was in the bathroom, says,

—So Zack, Dad tells me you guys talked about a trip to Israel.

—Yeah, we talked about it.

—And?

—You can't go?

—No, I've got to finish this job. And that'll take another month at least.

—I can't decide. I want to, but, is it safe?

Dad interjects, There's actually been a ceasefire for a few months, it's been very quiet.

—Except for last week.

—Right, except for last week.

—It's a special opportunity, honey. It's not going to Canada, but you'll be fine.

The conversation continues for a time, but Caroline's confident optimism and calm, loving warmth, a little reassurance here, a nudge of encouragement there, make Zack's eventual assent a foregone conclusion. In truth, Daniel can barely believe his wife's devotion to the cause, he assumes she must have some ulterior motive, or perhaps she's still on his side after all. Whatever the case, once convinced, their son's enthusiasm flowers. If his side of that evening's phone call to Caleb is to be believed, according to Zack it's going to be totally awesome.

The Blooms turn in early, for them, anyhow, and the final event of the day seems all but certain until Caroline announces, apologetically, her complete exhaustion. She hates making excuses and Daniel has no interest in them, but it's been a long week and the conversation with Gail really wiped her out. Daniel tells her again not to worry about it and offers her a sincere kiss on the forehead goodnight. In truth, he's tired himself, not to mention you can only ask for so much pleasure from one day. Still, it would have been nice. And more important, maybe the act could have distracted him fully, if only for a handful of minutes, from the nagging matter of whether or not the agent will ever bring the assassin to justice, that is, of course, if justice has any place in the story to begin with.

19

For reasons good and bad, the Blooms don't watch much in the way of televised news these days. But channel surfing abounds, and occasionally an arresting news image is sufficiently arresting to give a restless thumb pause. The charred carcass of a bus qualifying as such an image. It's a Thursday afternoon at the Blooms', and the late summer date, in combination with the irregular hours Caroline and Daniel, especially Daniel, keep, make this as good a time as any to watch TV for no good reason. Caroline, actually, isn't really watching. Though sitting on the same TV-facing couch as Daniel, her eyes are focused on her lap, where her hands are manipulating a few different fabric samples and some adhesive, all as part of a little experiment, which, if it goes well, will be reproduced on a greater and more expensive scale in the Bahmanis' living room early next week. There isn't a goddamn thing on, just lowbrow program after lowbrow program appealing to the millions of American jerk-offs who watch TV at this hour. Despite his genuine affluence and considerable success, Daniel's gradual recognition of the market audience he's aligning himself with at this very moment is nearly enough to shame him into moving thumb to power button in order to liberate himself altogether from the idiot box's hypnotic inertia.

Until he gets to the bus. Over the course of the last few years, Daniel's once fairly thoughtful approach to the news has boiled down to a cynical, and self-contradictory, modification of an old saying, such that for him, at least when he's going to be totally honest with himself, bad news is good news. The government has outrageous plans, foolhardy programs they've undertaken, and the only way this dangerously headstrong bunch might be stopped, so Daniel reasons, is if they continue to ram the already damaged ship of state into yet rockier shores. So while another part of Daniel regularly tries to remind himself that the steady increase in the number of dead and wounded, or even just the suffering suggested by the more abstract statistics on inequity, means lots of real sorrow for lots of real people, well, perhaps it all does have to get worse before it gets better. The blackened bus, for just an instant then, stops him as just another bit of regrettably necessary carnage. But when he hears the reporter's words, this normally peaceful coastal town just a short ride from Tel Aviv, Daniel is more than roused from his viewing stupor. After all, he's already started packing for this destination, and in less than forty-eight hours is scheduled to take his son, his only son, the one he loves, on an entirely voluntary trip to this land of unrest. The real reasons for this remain cloudy. Indeed, the push, the possibility of simple escape from the all-too-familiar bottom left-hand corner of these unwell United States, has, as it transformed quickly from idea to reality, been more than enough to make it all seem like a pretty good idea. He just wants to get away, this long-ignored but recently welcome urge so surprisingly pronounced that the destination and even the identity of his traveling companion have become afterthoughts. He's purposefully held out against thinking too much about the particulars of the country he's soon to visit, so that his necessarily impossible dreams of perfect relaxation and simple pleasure and complete release and even spiritual self-transformation, the details of which remain entirely vague, might last a few more days. These dreams of his have recently been draped over and tucked into the lines and spaces of the forever strange name of the place itself, which he keeps saying to himself over and over, the optimism of the initial *I*, the headiness of the two powerful English words that almost make up this name, and most of all the mysterious space between the pleasantly atypical *A* before *E*, a welcoming exception that has become for Daniel, over the course of this silently desperate week of preparations, the dense core of his innumerable longings for everything from a perfect cup of coffee to a stable, harmonious, meaningful world in which he no longer has anything to prove.

Caroline's attentive ears have yanked up the rest of her face, and now she knows and, worst of all, sees. In addition to hearing the sobering numbers and the predictably graphic description provided by the bevested reporter, Caroline and Daniel notice the bearded Jewish men, in bright orange vests of their own, slowly combing the site. As the reporter explains in the poetically morbid closing sentence of his solemn monologue, they have gathered at the site of a bombing, as they have done before and will almost certainly do again, in accordance with Jewish law, to collect body parts, scraps of flesh and bits of bone, all taken from the once-innocent passengers of this now smoldering bus.

Then they look at each other. Neither speaks. Daniel, truly caught off guard, senses he ought to backpedal somehow, either apologize or explain or acknowledge something. He feels responsible, if not exactly culpable. Or perhaps he should press on and rationalize, that phrase *otherwise the terrorists have won* coming to mind. Caroline continues not to speak, but she's really looking at him. She hasn't looked at him like this, she hasn't looked at him this much, this intently, in a long, long time. Sure they're married and live together, for nearly twenty years now, but that doesn't mean they haven't managed to find ways to occupy distinct and only infrequently intersecting orbits. Sitting on a couch together but not really interacting being just one example. Only now, with a commercial for a storied investment firm wisely muted, Daniel feels her soft brown eyes, her nearby lack of eyebrows now utterly irrelevant, fix him to the couch and then scan him carefully, searching for some crucial bit of information all their recent conversations have failed to reveal. Her gaze isn't exactly accusatory, her complete focus has calmed her, but there's no mistaking her determination. Daniel would like to speak, but this event has exposed him, so now he can only wait, knowing that when his wife finally opens her mouth the words coming out will declare a verdict. A full minute later:

—He's not going.

—I know.

—You can go. I won't argue. You shouldn't.

—I know.

—Stupid.

And then she's up and out of the room. He hears her climbing the stairs and opening Zack's door. Daniel continues watching TV, sort of, amazed he's going anyway.

20

On his last afternoon before leaving, Daniel takes Zack back to the ice cream spot. They walk, talking some but not a lot. Some sports, some recapping of the summer so far, some inquiries into prospects for the seventh grade. Over the course of the last eighteen months or so it seems to Daniel that Zack has become one of those kids who doesn't talk that much. He wouldn't say antisocial, just very quiet for long stretches. Caleb has gone in the other direction, annoyingly so, and Daniel suspects this has something to do with it. And try as he might, Daniel can't help but wonder if his son's reticence isn't directed toward him, isn't some protest, some initial stage of a long-term strategy designed to strand the father somewhere outside the son's inner circle. Other than his constant preoccupation with his scripts and all the attendant deal making, Daniel can't think up any real good reasons why his son might resent him, though perhaps this is enough. Or maybe it's just Daniel's expectation that he and Zack will replicate the relationship he had with his father. Dead seven years, and Daniel's still pissed at him. But then suddenly:

—Dad, why are you going to Israel?

—What do you mean?

—I mean, I don't know, why are you going to Israel?

—You mean why am I still going to Israel?

—I guess.

—Do you think I have a good answer?

—Probably. I mean people don't just fly to other countries for no reason. Do they?

—No, usually not. Can I ask you a question first?

—You already did.

—Ha, ha, ha.

—Ms. Payton used to say that all the time.

—Good one.

—So yeah, what's the question?

—What do you think of the president?

—The president?

—Yeah, of the United States. What do you think of him?

—I don't know. Sort of seems like a jerk.

—Why do you say that?

—'Cause, um, I mean the war and then the hurricane. He just seems like he doesn't really know what he's doing. He seems kind of stupid, but mean, too.

—Uh-huh. Just a sec, sorry. Hello.

—Bloom?

—Speaking.

—You're going to Israel. What the fuck?

—Who is this?

—Who is this? This is Donny, who the hell do you think it is?

—Hey, Donny. What's up?

—Why in the world are you going to that shithole?

—It's not a shithole. Sorry, Zack, just a sec.

—Pisshole.

—Who told you I'm going to Israel?

—Your mother.

—My moth—

—Max, you moron. Who do you think told me?

—Donny, can we talk later? I'm sort of busy right now.

—With what?

—I'm taking my son to get some ice cream.

—Sounds urgent.

—I'm leaving tomorrow, you schmuck.

—Brushing up on your Hebrew for the big trip, I see.

—I think that's Yiddish actually.

—Which ice cream place?

—Mitchell's.

—You on your way now?

—Yes. But, Donny, don't—

—Save me a seat.

—Donny—

—Who's Donny?

—Some producer. Crap.

—Is he coming to ice cream with us?

—Sounded that way.

—Why?

—I'm not sure. He's interested in something I've been working on.

—What's it about?

—You don't want to know.

—C'mon.

—What would you think if someone killed the president?

—Like what happened to Lincoln? You mean assassinated?

—That's the word.

—Are you working on something where someone kills the president?

—Not exactly. Sort of. What would you think?

—I don't know. I mean, he's a jerk and all, but still. Do you?

—Do I what?

—Do you want him to be killed?

—You really want to know?

—Yeah.

—Let's get some ice cream first.

—Do you, Dad?

—I do.

—Why?

—He's a very, very bad president. The worst ever, I think. I think he's a very dangerous person, and I think he's responsible for a lot of people dying. Americans and people in other places. Plus he's a liar.

—Isn't that illegal?

—What, wanting someone to kill the president?

—No, that he's killing so many people and lying and everything. Isn't there impeachment for when a president is really bad? Why isn't anyone trying to stop him?

—There are, but it's pretty complicated. A lot of people like him, and a lot of people in the government really like him, or at least they support him.

—Does Mom?

—Does Mom what? Support the president?

—No. Does she want someone to kill the president?

—You'll have to ask her. Probably.

—Bloom!

—Hey, Donny.

—And this must be Bloom junior.

—This is Zack. Zack, this is Donny Banderberg.

—Hi.

—A pleasure. Zack, you know your dad's a hell of a screenwriter.

—Yeah, thanks.

—Does he let you see his movies?

—Last year my mom started letting me.

—You like 'em?

—Yeah, they're pretty good. *Helsinki Honeymoon* was pretty cool.

—And what do we call it at home, Zack?

—I mean *Captives*, that was pretty cool. Kind of violent.

—Kind of? Your dad's like the Mozart of violence.

—I prefer the Picasso of pain. Donny, you want some ice cream?

—Nah, can't eat that crap. Hey, how come you're not fat, eating ice cream in the middle of the day?

—It's a special occasion. There's also this thing called exercise.

—So they tell me. Zack, what flavor's that?

—Chocolate peanut butter.

—It's good?

—It's great.

—Ah, crap. I'll be back. Bloom, c'mon here, would ya?

—What's with the script?

—It's coming along.

—Coming along? Give me some of that chocolate peanut butter in a cup.

—How many scoops?

—Just one.

—Two is only fifty cents more. We're having a special this week.

—What the hell, two. Bloom, when will you have a draft for me?

—I'm working on it. I'll finish it when I get back.

—That's no good. Thanks. Keep the change.

—No good? Since when do you put deadlines on scripts you haven't bought yet? I'm going to Israel tomorrow, I'll be back a week from Wednesday. What's the problem?

—Outside of the fact that the place is a fucking disaster and you're going to get yourself killed?

—It's not that bad.

—Whatever. The problem is I've got a hundred-and-fifteen-million-dollar production budget but no script. That's the problem.

—That's an awful lot of money.

—Oh really?

—Who's directing?

—You wouldn't believe me if I told you.

—Try me.

—No. Get me a script. Half the town's in a goddamn circling pattern waiting for you to deliver that script.

—You know, Donny, I never agreed to write this for you. We never even settled on any terms.

—Please. You don't think me and Max haven't ironed something out already?

—He's my agent, he works for me. I still have to agree.

—Whatever, Bloom. I still don't get it. Why the hell are you going to Israel?

—Leave me alone.

—Zack. Why's your dad going to Israel?

—I don't know. I asked him and he started talking about the president.

—What about him?

—Donny.

—What did he say about the president?

—Just that it would be right if someone killed him.

—Zack.

—Do you think it would be, Zack?

—I don't know. Maybe.

—Do you think there's anything wrong with just hoping someone else kills him or kills other bad people that help him?

—Maybe.

—Do you think there's anything wrong with a movie about someone killing the other bad people that help him, even a movie that doesn't think it's wrong?

—Probably not?

—Zack, let me tell you about a conversation I had the other night. Man, this is good ice cream. Zack, you and your friends talk about sex much?

—Donny.

—Some. Not really.

—But you know about it. You know what it is, right?

—Well, yeah.

—And oral sex, you know what oral sex is?

—Donny.

—Oral?

—Yeah, like blow jobs. You know what a blow job is, yes?

—Donny, c'mon.

—Yeah, I know what that is.

—Donny, he's twelve, for god's sake.

—Bloom, please. Zack, you got a computer in your room?

—Yeah.

—With Internet and all that?

—Yeah.

—A fast connection? DSL, cable modem, something like that?

—I think.

—Bloom, trust me, this ain't news to him. He's got the keys to the Fort Knox of whacking off in his very own bedroom.

—Lovely.

—I love it, father and son blushing. So here's the conversation I had. I'm at a dinner party. You know what that is? Adults get together and have dinner and call it a party. Bullshit. Anyhow. So we're sitting around having The Conversation. You know what The Conversation is?

—No.

—Bloom?

—I give up.

—It's like the conversation you and your dad were having. About the president and how much he sucks and how badly he's ruined everything. I don't know what you kids talk about, but that's what we adults talk about. All the time. So you know what Allie Drexel says? You know her, Bloom? Wife of Kip over at—

—I know Kip.

—Allie's really sweet. Grew up in Iowa or Kansas or some place like that. Real sweet, she baked an apple cobbler. Fucking apple cobbler. Real salt-of-the-earth kind of woman. You know what she says, Zack? You're gonna love this. She says, If I thought it would make everything better, I'd blow him if I thought it would make it all go away.

—Him?

—The president. You're laughing. Bloom, your son thinks blow jobs are funny.

—Am I allowed to tell you to stop?

—Zack, am I grossing you out?

—No.

—Lighten up, Bloom. That's what she says. Then this other guy, David Griffin, he says, You would not blow the president. Oh yes I would, she says. You wouldn't? No, I wouldn't, he says. Back and forth. The next thing I know we're going around the table, having a serious conversation about whether or not we'd put the president's cock—

—Donny, enough.

—Sorry, put his penis, that's better, put his penis in our mouths as part of some fellatio-powered time machine. Fellatio's a fancy way of saying giving someone a blow job.

—Dad, isn't that the name of that Italian director you're always talking about?

—No. Close, but no.

—So tell me, Zack, what do you think of that?

—It's pretty weird.

—I'd say. And how many people, out of ten, do you think said they'd do it?

—I don't know. Two or three.

—Not even close. Seven patriots drop to their knees to turn the planet around, three maintain their dignity and let things continue to go to hell in a handbasket. The conversation got complicated for a while. Brian Kosman was there. He's gay, right? Which is cool. Right?

—Sure.

—So he wants to know whether or not some of us, I'm unclear who that was exactly, could have the option of, or would have to, you know what they call it when you do it to a woman?

—Do what?

—You know, lick her—

—Donny.

—Cun-something?

—Cun-something. I like that. Cun-something. So we talk about whether you could cun-something the first lady instead, but then finally we all agreed that it didn't matter who you like to screw normally, that it's got to be the commander in chief this time. He's laughing again. Bloom, your kid thinks this is hilarious.

—It's called nervous laughter, Donny.

—Did you?

—Did I what, Zack?

—Did you say you would?

—Easiest decision I made all day.

—Gross.

—I even said I'd swallow—

—Donny, that's really enough. He's only twelve, c'mon already.

—If we'd get impeachment proceedings, too. I would. Now, Zack, your dad isn't writing a movie about giving the prez a BJ, but he's working on something that the 70 percent of us who would will line up to see. Probably the other 30 percent, too. Only now he's going to Israel. Bloom, why are you going to Israel?

—To get away from people like you.

—Seriously.

—Yeah, Dad, why are you going to Israel?

—What, you're on Donny's side now? I just need a little break.

—From what?

—So go to Santa Barbara for the weekend. You're going to Israel for a break? You got a retard for a travel agent?

—You're not supposed to say retard anymore.

—Says who, Zack?

—You're just not. It's like saying homo.

—Donny, it was really great seeing you again, but is it too much to ask for some time alone with my son?

—Fine. Walk me out to my car.

—Bloom, I need that script. It's in the public interest.

—Donny, I'm truly flattered by all this attention, but—

—Look Bloom, you go on your stupid fucking trip. But you come back without an ending and you'll give me no choice but to buy the idea from you. I got a stable of writers who can take care of the rest.

—What makes you think I'll agree to that?

—Don't be stupid, Bloom. You know how things work.

—Blow me, Donny.

—Get in line. Look, I don't know if you'll have one anyway, but I reserved a cell phone in your name. Pick it up at the airport—

—The airport?

—When you get there. The one named after that dead midget prime minister of theirs. Keep in touch. You want to go pray at that fucking wall of theirs, be my guest, but I need my script.

—Sorry about that, Zack.

—He's funny.

—I suppose. Crap. Hold on a second, I gotta take this. Max. What a surprise.

—What's with the tone of voice, Bloom? I just wanted to say good-bye.

—Thanks.

—When's the flight?

—Seven.

—Ouch.

—What have you and Donny been talking about without me?

—Don't worry about it.

—Don't worry about it?

—Hey, great news.

—Huh?

—I got a part in that commercial.

—Mazel tov.

—Yeah, listen to this. I was auditioning for the ugly guy, but in the end they offered me the part of the weird guy.

—And you were worried about being typecast.

—Versatility will be my calling card.

—When's the shoot?

—Next week.

—Right on. Hey, look, Max, I got to go.

—Last question.

—What?

—Does he catch him or not?

—No idea.

—Figure it out.

—Bye, Max. Sorry, Zack.

—What did he want?

—I have no idea. If you figure it out, let me know.

—Dad?

—Yeah?

—What do you need a break from?

—I don't know. Not you. C'mon, let's go.

21

He can't believe it's come to this, but as the last day turns into the last evening and finally the last night, all Daniel can think about is whether or not he and his wife will have sex. July came and went. Nothing. He can't remember with certainty the last time. Probably in June, but there's no way to date it reliably against the end of Zack's school year, which was on the fourteenth. Meaning May cannot be ruled out. No one need tell him that whatever ails his marriage can't be cured through intercourse, but still, why not start there? If they fail to or choose not to or simply refuse to, well, then something becomes official, because tomorrow early he's off to another country halfway around the world, and married couples, especially married couples who haven't really touched each other in two months or more, would seem to need to, or simply really ought to touch each other prior to one of them putting a whole country and an ocean and another sea between them.

Daniel watches her at dinner, thankful for her diligence in the areas of diet and exercise. She's old enough now that things could really start to deteriorate in this area, which, he must admit to himself, wouldn't be a good thing. As his eyes follow her while she heads to the kitchen for more salad, he actually stares at her ass with unfocused sexual longing. He feels shame. Not so much because his train of thought throughout the day has set off various sensors wired to what some might call feminist concerns. It's more that he's cordoned himself off from contemplating just about every nonphysical feature of their relationship, knowing instinctively that each and every one of them mirrors the possibly fatal stagnation of their joint libido. As Caroline returns from the kitchen, glass of wine in hand, their eyes meet for a moment. Daniel quickly averts his, feeling a painful spark of understanding.

After dinner he finishes packing, orders a cab, checks his e-mail, walks Alfred, who barely makes it around the block, checks the scores, does the dishes, and makes sure his various travel documents are in order. Caroline is elsewhere. Upstairs perhaps. He runs out of things to do and heads to their bedroom. Stopping in the doorway, he surveys the scene, she's on the bed, in sweats and a T-shirt, staring at the small TV on their dresser.

—What you watching?

She doesn't answer at first, clearly captivated. A few seconds later she responds without turning her head or moving her eyes toward him.

—One of those PBS documentaries. My god.

He enters and sits down on his side of the bed. The clock says 11:09, meaning another twenty-one minutes at least. The narrator's voice is serious and thoughtful. He looks at the screen. Still shots of various members of the administration, and then some documents set against unimpressive graphics.

—What's it about?

—The war. Prisoners. Torture. What isn't it about?

She's come late to all this. Absorbed in her new career, in Zack, and not much for the newspaper, Caroline steered clear of it all for a couple years. Maybe overcompensation for Daniel's obsession, for his ranting over coffee in the morning and his bitching over dinner in the evening. But now she's hooked, like everyone else. Talks back to the screen, asks rhetorical questions expressing disbelief, curses.

Daniel tries taking her hand, she lets him. A few minutes later it's back to the studio for a pledge drive interlude, the documentary still has another forty minutes to go. She tries watching the predictable plea for funds similarly enthralled, but can't. Her body relaxes next to his, her hand remembers his.

—Caroline.

—Huh?

—Can I interest you in the pleasures of the flesh this evening?

She laughs.

—It's been a while.

—I know.

—A long while.

She's still looking at the TV. If you give a hundred dollars or more you get an umbrella.

—Well?

—You're very romantic.

—What can I say?

—I want to watch the rest of this.

—You don't know how it ends?

—Not all of it. You don't either, you know.

—When's it over?

—I don't know. Midnight.

—Midnight?

—Shh. It's back on.

The narrator continues with his time line. From bad to worse. Daniel draws his body up to Caroline's. Puts his head on her shoulder. No protest. Soldiers in the desert. International law. She smells great. His head's getting perfect olfactory stereo of hair product and perfume, a little fruity and a little herbal something. The same scents since before he came along. Reminds him, semiconsciously, of when he absolutely, crazily loved her. He closes his eyes. Hears some ex-CIA someone, who's probably sitting in front of a bookshelf, giving his side of the story. Excerpts from a press conference. Daniel turns into her more, swelling up below, seeing what her thigh can offer.

—C'mon, Daniel.

—What?

—What.

—Rhymes with insurrection.

—Shh.

But she doesn't make him stop. So he nestles some more, trying hard to not to press his luck. Just tries to relax in order to enjoy inhaling her. The narration keeps getting in the way. Joint chiefs of staff. Attorney general. Meaningless syllables in Arabic, all those fucking names.

—Caroline, hey, would you put on the headphones?

—No.

—Please. I promise to leave you alone.

—Alright. Give 'em to me.

He dislodges himself and grabs the wireless headphones from below his nightstand. After *Captives,* in an effort to repair things, Caroline bought this TV and these headphones, to encourage her husband to do his compulsive late-night viewing in their bed and not downstairs. He agreed, but the flickering of the screen kept her awake, and soon the experiment was over. She puts them on and mutes the television. Daniel attempts to resnuggle, but the size of the earpiece forces him away from her shoulder and down to her chest. He lifts up her arm, she says nothing, and he rests his head at the edge of her right breast, draping his left arm across her torso. She holds him, sort of. Now he can't help himself. Her smell, her breast, his left hand reporting for duty, and of course, the down below. For a time he caresses her right arm, trying to remember how to do this lovingly, but not sexually. His penis, of course, is running interference, and in a moment of poor judgment he lets his free hand settle on her opposite breast.

—Daniel, you've got to stop. Her voice is loud. The headphones.

—Sorry.

—I'm looking at a corpse packed in ice.

—Sorry.

—It'll be over in ten minutes. Jeez, just leave me alone. Start yourself if you have to.

And like an animal he does. Removes his pants. Tries his left hand, which doesn't really know what to do, but maybe that's for the best. Closes his eyes, tries to listen to her breathing, his nose making a small depression in her boob. Even left-handed things progress quickly. He can't finish like this. Looks up at the screen. A patrol. Hearings on Capitol Hill. The president behind his seal and podium. He hopes these images and all they suggest will dampen his suddenly frenzied passion, like recalling Indians' statistics used to do years back when he first started fucking and wanted it to last forever. But it's no use. There's so much more than an overabundance of seed pent-up down below. There's his son, who if he doesn't hate his father perhaps should. There's the fact that having failed to maintain ties with people from his past, buddies from his hometown and roommates from college, his best friend at present appears to be a business relation who changes his name regularly and aspires to appear in ads for prophylactics. There's the distinct sense that he's witnessing the beginning of the end of something enormous and dangerous, that things are soon going to spiral out of control, that the world is on the cusp of some very dark epoch, that his possibly resentful son may well, if he's lucky enough to survive, tell stories to his own grandchildren of fleeing to the border or hiding out or something unimaginably worse. There's the screenplay, which he both wishes never came to him and wants, obsessively, to finish, if for no other reason than he still measures his self-worth against his ability to resolve an intriguing premise. And finally, according to this haphazard inventory anyhow, there's his nearly foreign wife, with whom, once upon a time, he delighted in all things mutual, a woman he simply loved,

and who, he believes, loved him right back, a woman whose unsus-
pecting knees and shins he now unloads himself upon, moaning despite himself, burrowing, despite himself, into her side, wishing for a
number of unnamable things from her that he now most certainly
won't get, as she rips the headphones off with disgust and attempts
to distance herself from her still-writhing husband.

—Fuck, Daniel. These are new.

—Sorry.

—Fuck.

—Sorry.

—If they stain, every time I see them I'll have to think of the
fucking Geneva Conventions.

She takes them off, turning them inside-out in the process, and
then actually covers her crotch or pubis or whatever it is down there,
behind a pillow. He's no longer allowed to see.

—Get whatever you need and go sleep with the dog downstairs.
Bye.

TEL AVIV

If something is wrong, there will be a reason for it. If it is deeply wrong, then our understanding of it will have to dig deep, force us on journeys we may not wish to take.

—JACQUELINE ROSE,
The Question of Zion

1

—Daniel?

—Nadav?

—Welcome.

—Thanks. Thanks for coming to meet me.

—No problem. You have a cell phone. Nice.

—Yeah, someone back home wanted me to have one.

—You will belong here with that thing.

—Good to know.

—How was the flight?

—Fine. Long.

—You flew with Lufthansa, yes?

—Yeah. Stopover in Frankfurt.

—They are good, no?

—Yeah. Not bad.

—But it is strange, right? You bought the tickets with Lufthansa and you think, this is funny, I am going to Israel, but I am flying with the Germans. And then you don't think about this thing again, not until you go on the plane. And then you really begin to think about this, and you are sure that everyone thinks this, so you decide to not think about it, but you can't stop to think about this thing. And you are asking yourself, am I the only man on this very big and so clean airplane who is continuing to think about Germans taking us to the Jewish state? Are the, eh, how do you say it, are the stewards wondering this thing, too? And you look at them, and they are so beautiful, blond people everywhere in their also blond uniforms, even the man ones are beautiful, but maybe they are little bit too beautiful. And then you feel bad, because you conclude, probably they are homo, but then you don't really feel bad about this, because you remember that the Nazi killed the homo, too, so now you think, the homo is taking the Jew to Israel on the German plane, and this is making you quite happy, this thing, so you smile at the pretty steward and he smiles to you, he is very nice, and you think, maybe he isn't only a nice steward, maybe he is wanting to fuck me, but you see that he smiles nice to everyone and then you decide, this is just the excellent German service on Lufthansa. This is not like the American plane where everyone is tired and not pleasant, no, the Germans we know are very good at this job, everything so, so *chik-chak,* you know, *chik-chak,* just like that, very quick. But then this idea reminds you, too, that so were the Nazis, *chik-chak,* very quick. So you give up and drink your American Coca-Cola and watch your bad American movie, yes?

—More or less. Sure is hot.

—Tomorrow will be *hamsin.* Eh, a heat wave. Thirty-six degrees in Tel Aviv.

—Thirty-six?

—Celsius.

—How many Fahrenheit is that?

—I don't know. It is a lot. The body is thirty-eight. But the air in *hamsin,* even in Tel Aviv, this does not move. You will be sad from this. I will sleep on the floor in your hotel room, my air condition broke and you must wait many days for a man to come to fix it.

—Alright.

—August is a dumb time to be in Israel.

—What can I say?

—Never mind. This is my car. It is a piece of shit. We have this saying in Hebrew, too. *Chatichat chara.* Piece of shit. But I don't think it will break.

—Lots of legroom.

—Legroom?

—Room for your legs. It was a joke.

—A man who has a large car in Tel Aviv, unless he owns a parking space, will never find a place to put his car. Never. He will search until his car stops from no fuel. Like New York and not like Los Angeles.

—Right.

—Plus having a piece-of-shit car, the Palestinians don't want to steal it.

—Palestinians?

—Yes, this is their revenge on us. They steal our luxury cars and take them to the West Bank and make them into pieces and then sell the pieces back to the Israeli, eh, garage men, and then the, how do you say this?

—Mechanics?

—Yes. The mechanics sell the parts to the Israeli customer for a lot of money.

—The Israeli mechanics work with the Palestinian thieves?

—Something like this. It is complicated. And the Wall makes it harder. But yes. So when I see this piece of shit, I don't feel so bad, because even the Palestinian will think, this is a piece of shit.

—Great.

—I don't know if they say *piece of shit* in Arabic.

—Can't help you there.

—Not important.

—I suppose not.

—Good. So here is our choices. We can kill them all, or kill enough of them that they will finally give up and go away, or push them far away, but I don't know where this is, because we push them to Lebanon and see what happens. But we can try, we can do the ethnics cleaning.

—Ethnic cleansing.

—Yes, we can do this. It will not be pleasant, but we can do it. Transfer. And the world will be very mad with us from this, but we can do it still, and maybe then they will not be bothering us so much. We can bomb their houses and put in the prisons all the men and be very mean and make their economy to be very bad and that no one will have a good job and that they are stuck inside their small borders until they say, okay, Israeli bastards, you win, we lose, and we give up and are leaving for Canada.

—What are you talking about?

—Wait, a moment. Or we can believe that they don't really want us in the sea anymore, and we can say to them, yes, you are right, we were very mean to you, we tried to push you out in 1948 and we hit you harder than was nice and we broke your bones and we built the settlements and we took the water and we put in prison many men that were not belonging in prison and we are sorry. And so if you will agree to not explode yourselves on our buses and to not teach your children that in the future you will have not just Ramallah but Haifa also and if you accept that the refugees will not return, we will pay you for this, but they cannot return, not to Yafo, it is just not possible. And so if you agree to all this, we are saying sorry, you are saying sorry, we stop trying to win by bombing and occupation and you stop trying to not lose by terror and the Hamas, then you get your small state next to our small state. We can try this, too, we can say that they are still our peace partner.

—They.

—They. The Palestinians. It used to be the Arabs. When I was a boy it was the Arabs because we didn't want there to be the Palestinians. But maybe now it is really the Muslims. I don't know. And this is a very big problem. If it is the Muslims then we are having to fight for a long time. We will kill many, many Muslims, but there are too many to kill them all.

—Right.

—I am not always talking like this. The Israeli actually does not talk about this all the time. When we got cables, we—

—Cables?

—For the television.

—Cable television. Not cables.

—In Hebrew it is cables. Hmm. Good. When we got the cable, we started to want the American life. The nice car, the nice kitchen, the nice food, the computer. But when you must be killing people all the time, you have to say that you love your country, too, because if you don't then why are you killing all those people, you know?

—I lost you.

—Never mind. I was listening to the radio when I drove to the airport and a very stupid man from the army spoke and then I start to think about this again. I will try not to.

—Don't worry about it.

—You did not know who they is.

—It doesn't sound like you know, either.

—Yes.

—How about something to eat and a nap?

—Food, yes. Sleep, no.

—I'm tired. Why can't I nap?

—Jet lag. If you want to overcome the jet lag, you must not sleep until the night.

—But it's only eleven forty-five in the morning. I've barely slept in two days.

—Never mind. We will get you excellent coffee near the sea. But you must kill the jet lag or it will kill you.

—Kill?

—I know. I need to stop this thing.

2

And then Nadav grows silent. He looks straight ahead at the highway, three pale gray lanes in both directions separated by a flat median. Daniel allows himself to survey his tour guide for a moment. His gray eyes protrude a bit too much, and he missed some spots when shaving this morning. Also, a couple small patches of dried blood near the top of his neck. Otherwise, a little pale. Anywhere from late twenties to early forties. A faded brown T-shirt assumes the shape of a small oval near his waist as it comes to rest on his belly. Old blue jeans. Overall, he looks very Israeli to Daniel, which makes no sense to him, since he has no idea what it means to look Israeli in the first place, so he looks him over again trying to locate the crucial, determining feature. Perhaps the way he holds his jaw, casually clenched. Or perhaps it's nothing more than his affiliation with this car, a white compact manufactured in a country that has yet to break into the American market, a car whose engine buzzes at such a high frequency it recalls Max's Vespa. Or perhaps it's the road they're riding down, which in most ways looks like any other highway, only the lines are just a bit narrower, while the signs are clearly designed by a department of transportation with a radically different, and, Daniel can't help but think, decidedly primitive aesthetic. The numbers and images, the blocky speed limits and clumsily colorful symbols for

exits, suggest the blithe confidence of a formerly bloated socialist bu-
reaucracy not up to the task. Or perhaps Daniel is just very, very tired
and not equipped to accept the fact that he has indeed voluntarily
brought himself to this foreign place.

He thinks to start the conversation up again, but Nadav, staring
straight ahead, seems oblivious to Daniel's presence in his car. The
Israeli has turned the radio on to a station whose format sounds to
Daniel doggedly noncommittal. A casually smooth DJ talks for a
while, then plays two songs, first an Israeli pop ballad and then "Hotel
California," interrupting both in the middle, Daniel can only guess,
in order to continue talking about whatever far-from-urgent matter
he was talking about before. Then out of nowhere a phone interview
with a woman who sounds oddly flirtatious and provocatively throaty
as she draws out her otherwise meaningless syllables. A short tune
that might be some sort of station identification jingle. Then the DJ
starts speaking again, but soon stops all at once. A series of beeps and
then another voice altogether, that of a different woman speaking
quickly and without emotion.

—The news?

—Yes.

—Anything important?

Nadav holds up his right hand with his thumb, index and middle
fingers brought together. A moment, he says. Eventually the woman
stops and the DJ returns, talking over Frank Sinatra.

—Well?

—Everything is okay. Everyone agreed that peace is the best thing
and will not fight anymore. Tomorrow a big, how do you say it, a big
parade in Jerusalem. Candy for the children.

—Seriously.

—Nothing so interesting. No one was killed since eleven o'clock.

They have reached the edge of the city. Their road becomes a
bona-fide urban freeway, snaking just below the paved surface of
dense urban development, massive billboards, buses everywhere,

even a number of, if not exactly skyscrapers, then unambiguously tall, and rather impressive contemporary buildings that have clearly been constructed in the decades since Daniel's earlier visit. Despite an additional lane or two in each direction the traffic has stopped. Nadav remains silent.

What Daniel realized on the plane, it started on the way to New York, continuing en route to Frankfurt and later Tel Aviv, is that the agent's father will have to commit suicide. This might involve darkening his earlier scenes slightly to set the stage. Maybe he throws down the shoes he is polishing in disgust. Maybe that scene opens with a shot of the father sitting motionless, almost catatonic, on his sofa before his son arrives to visit. Maybe his medicine cabinet is overflowing menacingly with three dozen vials of prescription medication. Clearly during the scene at the food court he'll sound a good deal more haunted and furious and, above all, injured. It could just be a matter of casting, finding someone who plays tragedy well, who effortlessly suggests defeat. In any case, he will kill himself not long after he meets, without ever knowing it, the assassin.

Daniel purposely left his laptop at home, he didn't even pack a pad of paper. He knew he'd regret this, but felt it was necessary and really the only way to protest Donny's intimidation. But somewhere over the Atlantic he found a pen in his carry-on and started scribbling notes on the inside cover of a Sam Peckinpah biography. Two main questions. What's the method and how does the audience find out? A gun isn't out of the question. The son's obvious familiarity with them makes it reasonable enough to believe that the father has one himself. And while the cinema loves nothing more than guns, the father's almost paralyzing depression, his dejection, his sense of losing everything he's worked for, his status, his purpose, his very identity, makes the deliberately immediate violence of a gun inappropriate. Plus, he was white collar all those years. Hanging himself, while also deliciously theatrical, is out of the question. Asphyxiation is closer to giving proper expression to the father's gradually expiring will to live, but he has no garage, and while the oven could work, it lacks any meaning beyond itself. Which, in the absence of something totally over the top like jumping off a bridge, leaves pills. Outside of being a perfect fit for the father's weary constitution, is the fact, Daniel celebrated this realization with an extra long sip of his ginger ale somewhere between Greenland and Iceland, that the father, of course, actually worked all those years for a pharmaceutical corporation, bestowing upon the act a second layer of meaning for those really paying attention.

Nadav has exited the highway and is driving recklessly on surface streets. The traffic, both dense and frenetic, suggests an abrupt mass convergence of New York taxi drivers with long-standing amphetamine habits. Obedience to traffic signals, lane designations, and even pedestrians' basic human rights is, at best, inconsistent and reluctant. Every intersection seems to offer up another provocative demonstration of improvisational daring. In particular, the size of these cars, Nadav's is far from the smallest, allows for all sorts of experiments with squeezing and passing that would be unimaginable even in the hurried, dangerous streets of LA. Amid this squeezing and passing are scooters and motorbikes constantly slaloming aggressively between the larger vehicles, among them a high frequency of surprisingly immaculate white taxis operated by seasoned drivers who clearly don't give a shit about anything or anyone, and enormous, intimidating red and blue buses that Daniel sees as little more than bombs on wheels. The soundtrack of this overwhelming set piece is an oppressively thick and absolutely constant honking of horns, so insistent and seemingly groundless that it can only be explained as an act of collective unconscious hysteria. All this frenzied motion and clamorous blare finds its perfect expression in the outrageous proliferation of bumper stickers. One to two on most cars, with a sizable minority plastered with a half dozen or more. While their actual messages are beyond Daniel's comprehension, subtlety doesn't appear to be part of the vehicular discourse. If he was a braver or perhaps wiser man, he'd demand to be returned to the airport at once. Forty minutes in the country and he's seen enough.

—You have money?

—What do you mean? Israeli money?

—No. Money. I mean, can you spend a lot of money here? Are you willing?

—Depends. What are you talking about?

—If you will pay to park, then things will be better for us. It is not far to the sea on foot.

So they park and walk. And sweat. Daniel would like very much to shower, to change his clothes, to, in particular, say farewell, at least for now, to this pair of underwear, which he has been wearing since Los Angeles. Why are they not at his hotel?

—How much farther?

—You complain already. A good American.

—I'm not complaining, I'm asking how much farther. If it's still far, then I'll complain.

3

Despite the debilitating heat, the sun here has a predatory quality, and his nearly complete exhaustion, he can feel himself desperately transferring his full weight from foot to unwilling foot with each step, this is what it must mean to trudge, Daniel can't help but be intrigued by this unmistakably Israeli street. It's too narrow to really matter, he can't imagine any Israeli thinking twice about it when the time comes to nominate streets to represent Tel Aviv in some imaginary national Israeli street-off, but its wholesale difference from his typical idea of a street combined with its simple and undeniable materiality truly captivates him. The storefronts are small and mostly modest, tiny hardware stores with discounted hot plates in their display windows, overstaffed and underdecorated hair salons, corner minimarts crammed with vegetables and newspapers and nut-filled bins and colorful knickknacks hung from retractable awnings, and, finally, actual, genuine falafel stands, some also displaying rather enticing columns of layered meat revolving slowly past an electric coil illuminated in orange. Though the pedestrian traffic doesn't quite qualify as bustling, the narrow sidewalk does amplify its intensity, while the people themselves, in their impossible variety, make Daniel feel something akin to what Zack must have felt the first time they took him to Disneyland. The crowd is mostly young and casually dressed, but includes as well small pockets of miniaturized elderly women, the occasional soldier, and even a couple of religious men, who, on this apparently secular street, seem awkwardly out of place. If there are Arabs, they must look no different from the Jews. On the whole, the crowd is a little darker than LA, and if not clearly better looking, then unambiguously sexier. With the exception of those in their premodern European black, even the men, perhaps especially the men, along with the older women, and perhaps even the older men, seem to possess a certain sexiness-enhancing unmediated physicality that forces Daniel to remind himself to stop gawking. Something in their hips perhaps. Nadav, obviously less mesmerized by it all, keeps almost losing Daniel, turning every couple minutes to say, without much force, *ya'alla.* Daniel tries to catch up, if only because he wants to ask Nadav for some insight or explanation, but each time he gets within earshot he fails to find a way to formulate his question. All he can think to ask is, is all this real, was it all here yesterday, what does any of it mean? Meanwhile, he sweats so much that he looks down to see it soaking through his own jeans, causing a large drop to slide down his forehead and splash onto the right lens of his glasses.

Finally a view of the sea presents itself as they cross a street lined with large hotels. The sight of the water causes Daniel, quite unexpectedly, to visualize his new location on the globe, a little dot at the far right edge of the Mediterranean. So far from home, and for no good reason. But the water, dark blue and nearly smooth and continuing past the perfectly flat horizon, helps him decide not to be bothered by this. Nadav points to a small building near the water, but set off from the actual beach, which continues north for perhaps a mile, its pale sand crowded with a few thousand people who, somehow, have wound up here as well.

—**Ethan told me** you are a scriptwriter.

—Yeah.

—You wrote many movies?

—Fifteen or so.

—This is a lot. You sell them?

—About half of them.

—Really? And they make them?

—Three of them have actually come out.

—Three. This is something. I have seen them?

—I don't know. You guys get a lot of American movies here?

—Of course.

—And you see these?

—Sometimes. Not so much in the theater, but I rent them and then there is the cable. Cable, right? Not cables.

—Cable, right.

—So what is the most famous one?

—There was one called *Helsinki Honeymoon*. Came out a couple of years ago. Pretty big hit.

—*Helsinki Honeymoon*. I don't know this. But sometimes they make new titles in Hebrew. What is it about?

—A man kidnaps a woman, but then changes his mind, but then she takes revenge on him.

—Ah, yes, I think I saw this. He has a moustache, the man who kidnapped her.

—Yeah.

—And she, she is a British.

—Right.

—Yes. This was not bad. Violent. But interesting.

—You liked it?

—Yes, I did. I mean I didn't so much liked the violence, but this was interesting. It was different. It makes me think after.

—Thanks. Hey, by the way, what did they call it in Hebrew? Do you remember?

—What did they call it? Yes. Just one word. *Shevuyim.* How do you say this? Prisoners, maybe.

—Prisoners?

—Yes, this is one translation.

—What about *Captives?*

—Yes. Yes, *Captives* is right, too. What is the difference?

—What *is* the difference? I don't know. Huh, that's interesting.

—It is funny. This word, but not in the plural, is the name of a famous Hebrew story about some soldiers taking an Arab man for no reason during the Independence War.

—Really?

—Yes. They beat him, too.

—Huh. That's strange.

—It is not so strange.

—What?

—That he writes this story.

—Oh, I thought you meant that it's not so strange that they used that title.

—This may be strange. But the story is not so strange, though many people don't like it.

—Is it a true story?

—I don't know. Sometimes I think so. It could be.

—What else did Ethan tell you?

—About you? Not so much.

—No?

—Not really.

—He's an interesting man.

—He is funny.

—Funny? I'm not sure that's the word I'd use. Seems awfully angry to me.

—You are right, but this is because he tries to love the things he hates.

—Why do you say that?

—This is his mantra.

—He told you this?

—Many times.

—So what's funny about that?

—Because he hates so many things. And I think when he tries to love them he cannot. And this is making him to hate them more. Maybe it is not funny. Maybe it is sad. I don't know.

—You're good friends?

—You know, we became close in India, when, three years ago, and he writes me e-mails, and I try to write, too. He is different.

—That he is.

—Tell me, you are writing a movie now?

—Sort of.

—What does this mean?

—I started something recently, but I'm not sure I want to finish it.

—Why not?

—You don't want to know.

—I don't? How do you know this?

—I mean it's not worth getting into.

—No? Is it a bad idea, the movie?

—Depends how you look at it. There's a big-time producer who wants to buy it, so I suppose it can't be too bad of an idea.

—What is it? You must tell me.

—Later, I promise. I'm tired.

—The coffee does not help?

—No, it does.

—It is good coffee, yes?

—Not bad.

—So tell me.

—Later.

—Oh, stop to be a fucker and tell me.

—Later, I promise.

—Tell me or I get up and run away and you are a homeless in Tel Aviv.

—Right.

—You are not believing me? Look, here is fifty shekel. Mr. Agnon, in purple. Not a bad writer, either, even is winning the Nobel, but he didn't write about what we did to the Arab. It is nice that we put him on our money. Good-bye.

—Stop, stop. Alright. The movie. Here's the idea. A guy starts assassinating a series of bad people. Corporate scum, dirty politicians. And then the agent who is supposed to catch him isn't sure he wants to.

—And what will happen?

—I don't know. I just started about a month ago.

—That is all?

—Pretty much.

—This is funny.

—Funny?

—Not laughing funny. Silly or, eh, ridiculous.

—How is it ridiculous?

—It is not a story. Even I know it is not a story.

—Not yet, it's just a premise. There's a little more, though.

—What else?

—The assassin and the agent meet a few times.

—This is interesting. But you must be careful.

—About what?

—It is many years since an assassination in America, yes?

—That guy tried to kill Reagan in the eighties and Lennon got shot in eighty-two.

—It was eighty.

—So?

—We have Rabin's assassination in 1995. It destroyed everything. Maybe everything falls apart anyway. But it did. This is not a game, even to pretend.

—I agree. That's why I'm not sure I want to finish it.

—But maybe I help you finish it anyway. What do you say?

—You think it's a stupid, dangerous idea. Now you want to help me?

—I did not say dangerous. I said you must be careful.

—I write alone. I've tried a few scripts with partners, it never works.

—I won't be a partner. Just, you know, ideas and things like this.

—We'll see. So what's the plan?

—You want my ideas for the script?

—No. For my visit. What are we going to do? What have you planned?

—Oh. Not so much.

—When are we going to Jerusalem?

—Jerusalem.

—Yeah, Jerusalem.

—We are not.

—What are you talking about?

—I cannot go to Jerusalem.

—What, are you on probation?

—I do not understand.

—Why can't you go to Jerusalem?

—I am not like Ethan. I don't try to love the things I hate.

—You hate Jerusalem?

—Not always did I hate it. But now, yes. It is a city for people who demand they win. Not everyone there, but too many, yes.

—But it's such an important city. It's the capital. I mean, you just don't go there?

—And I hate the religious, and I hate the Arab. I try not to sometimes. But I do. Well, I don't try not to hate the religious, I just hate them. Some days I try not to hate the Arab, but it is difficult, because they hate us, even if I am not blaming them for this. And I hate the settlers, and I hate the settlers who live in the new Jerusalem suburbs that are pretending that they are not settlers. If I go to Jerusalem, I just feel very bad. If they ask me, give it to the stupid UN or Switzerland to be in charge. We ruin it. When we had half, maybe it wasn't so bad. But now, even when we cut it in half, we ruin it worse.

—You're a tour guide who won't take your visitor to the most important city in Israel.

—Tel Aviv is more important.

—Whatever. The most important city in Judaism.

—Daniel. I will tell you something. If you are coming here thinking I am your Jewish tour guide, you will be quite disappointed. This country is not a Jewish park of amusements for the bored diaspora Jew or the confused diaspora Jew or the curious diaspora Jew. This country is where Israelis live. I am Israeli. I can show you this.

—But what about all the history? The Bible and everything.

—Perhaps if I am needing money, I show you this and then you think it is important and then you give me money and then I buy a tank and destroy Jenin. But I am not needing that much money.

—What are you talking about? And I am paying you.

—Not so much. If you want, I take you to the minister of touring and we find you a touring bus. You ride with the other Americans.

Your guide, that tells you the funny stories, shows you the handsome
soldier and you will buy them guns.

—You're not making sense.

—No?

—Anyway, I don't want to see soldiers.

—You who write *Prisoners*—

—*Captives*—

—It's the same—

—No it's not—

—In Hebrew it is the same. You love violence, and you don't want
to see soldiers?

—I'll see them on the street, won't I? We already saw some.

—This is true.

—Really, no Jerusalem? What about the big Holocaust—

—No. Stop it.

—What?

—Do not say that.

—Say what?

—What you said.

—What? Holocaust?

—Yes. Do not say it.

—Why not?

—I am trying for a year not to say it and not to talk about it.

—Am I allowed to ask why?

—Just to see if it is possible.

—That's it?

—No, I mean, I want to see if one can live without it, you know.
If my thinking and my talking can not have it.

—Just the word Holocaust?

—Please stop. But no. Also, you know, the other words.

—Nazi, Auschwitz.

—Yes, yes, stop, stop.

—But you said them earlier, at the airport.

—Yes, I know. It is difficult.

—You're doing this alone?

—I have some friends who agree to this when they are with me. Most days I fail and must start over.

—Okay, so we won't go to that place, that I won't mention by name. But what about all the other stuff? The Wall and the Old City and all the ruins. I mean, that's it, nothing from the past? Nothing? You know, it's not exactly coincidence the country's here.

—I know this. I am sorry. But we should have chosen Uganda. Even though they would hate us there, too.

—Great. So what are we going to do?

—I show you my life. Not a tourist trip. I show you Tel Aviv, where the real Israeli lives. We go to the cafés, to the beach, to the bars. There are very good restaurants. There are dramas, but they are in Hebrew, and an art museum.

—What else?

—Are you smoking grass?

—Marijuana?

—Yes.

—It's been awhile. You want to get me high?

—Many young people in Tel Aviv are smoking grass now. It helps us I think to remain here and not become crazy.

—Great.

—The grass here is very good, you will see.

—Ten thousand miles to smoke weed.

—You are married, yes?

—Sixteen years.

—Are you fucking other women?

—Last I checked, no.

—This is too bad.

—I suppose.

—I thought perhaps I could help you fuck an Israeli woman.

—The way you put it, it's so appealing.

—Make love. Would you want to make love to an Israeli woman?

—Nadav, your generosity is humbling. How exactly would you arrange that? I suppose you'll introduce me to a genuine Israeli prostitute.

—No, but I could. No, I take you to a true Israeli bar. You are suddenly very interesting there. I have many friends. Or some, a few. We make jokes together. I tell them, he writes the Hollywood movies. You buy everyone drinks. I introduce you to Ronit and Yael and Carmel. Who knows. Every person loves to fuck in the hotel. This I know.

—Speaking of which, when can we go there?

—I am not fucking you, Daniel. But I can introduce you to Tomer, he will for certain fuck you there.

—I want to shower, Nadav.

—This was funny, no? I am making jokes in English.

—Hilarious.

—Do you write comedies?

—No. Not my genre.

—Too bad. I will help you put some good jokes in this one.

—Because assassinations are so amusing. So what else? Do we ever leave the city?

—We can go north if you like. It is pretty there.

—Alright.

—And perhaps my mother invites us for dinner one night.

—Your mother.

—But she is mad at me now. I am there since my air condition is not working, but we are fighting.

—About what?

—She is my mother, we are fighting. But she will like meeting you. You look a little like Gal, my brother.

—And do I get to meet him?

—No.

—Why not? You hate him, too?

—Actually, he is dead.

—Sorry.

—Never mind. But I am not telling you about this now. And you can't run away, because then where would you go?

5

Daniel speaks to Nadav from the bed of his hotel room overlooking the sea. Nadav turned on the television while Daniel show-
ered and continues watching a channel showing Israeli music videos.

—Nadav, I really need to sleep.

—I cannot allow this.

—I can barely keep my eyes open.

—I know it is difficult, but if you want to enjoy your visit you
must overcome the jet lag. If you sleep now, you will not.

—That's all well and good, but I'm dying here.

—Stop to be a baby. You are hungry, no? I will take you to the
best hummus in the whole world. I will show you my neighborhood,
then I take you back here, we will smoke some grass, and you sleep
the best in your whole life.

—Sounds great in theory, Nadav, but I'm fading.

—No. Do not do this. Daniel, open your eyes! Daniel!

—Nadav, cut it out. What the fuck?!

—If you sleep, I am leaving and not coming back.

—How much?

—How much? What?

—To let me sleep.

—You cannot.

—Just a little.

—No.

—Just a half hour. I promise I'll get up then.

—One hundred shekel.

—How much is that in dollars?

—Twenty, twenty-five.

—Deal. Now turn off the TV and leave me alone.

—No TV is two hundred shekel.

—But the music is loud.

—You said that you are so tired.

—Still, it's annoying.

—So okay, I watch soccer with no sound.

—Fine. Good night, Nadav.

—Good night. Dream fast. It will be good morning in thirty minutes.

6

The best hummus in the world, according to Nadav and soon Daniel, is in Nadav's neighborhood. Here, Daniel can tell at once, the hippest of the hippest Israelis live. They are even better looking, on the whole, than those he passed earlier on the way to the sea, reminding him of the crowd that frequents certain profoundly funky streets in Los Angeles. Only here they're all Jews. But the clothes and the hair and the shoes and the music pouring out the open door of a nearby record store are proof of how globalization and the Internet and who knows what else have obliterated the fashion lag that once kept this place a reluctant backwater. Now he's got nothing on these people.

The hummus arrives, spread unevenly on a simple white plate and topped with olive oil and paprika. Some thick pita in a basket arrives simultaneously. Fading again, Daniel eats eagerly, viewing the food as fuel he'll be able to convert instantly into energy the moment it's swallowed.

—It is good, no?

—Delicious. Jesus.

—They are Arab.

—Cool.

—Sometimes I think this is why it is so good. Then I feel bad. But why? This is their food. But there are some people from Poland who learn to make great falafel. But not like this. Not important. There is something bothering you?

—No.

—Yes there is.

—What are you talking about?

—You are looking around so much.

—So, I've never been here before. I'm just checking it all out.

—No, this is not how you are looking. You are worrying about the terrorists. Will they come here? Is that man or that one or that one with the bag, is that the one that will kill me? I saw it, too, when we are drinking coffee.

—Have there been any incidents around here?

—Not exactly here, no. About ten minutes that way, there was a coffeehouse that was exploded. Three people die. And a bus that goes not so far from here.

—Recently?

—The bus was two months ago. The café, already two years I think.

—Do you worry?

—I think about it, yes. This is another reason not to go to Jerusalem, there they are having many more attacks.

—Why are you smiling?

—It is funny, you have a wife and a son, yes?

—Yeah.

—So you must tell them that the danger here is not so big. Even after the bus in Ashdod this week.

—Yeah.

—And now you are being scared.

—I suppose.

—You are safe here. We are outside and the owner here is Arab.

—They know that? They care?

—I don't know. Maybe.

—Do you ride buses?

—Not often, but sometimes you must.

—Why? You have a car.

—Yes, but sometimes you must.

—I don't understand.

—Never mind. So tell me, what else will be in this movie?

—Oh, you don't want to hear about that. Not now.

—I do.

—You're not going to threaten to abandon me if I refuse?

—No, I cannot do that here. Too many people know me here and then you will find where I live and this will not be pleasant. But, please, this is making me very excited.

—I thought you said it was silly.

—Maybe it will not be so silly when I help you.

—What makes you think you can help me?

—I am smart. Please.

—Alright. So the agent, the one who's supposed to catch the assassin but isn't sure he wants to, has a father that the audience sees early on. He's not doing well. Turns out he lost everything when the company he worked for tanked—

—What is this, tanked?

—They went bankrupt, they lost everything. But it was one of those deals where all the employees, even the ones like the agent's dad who had been there for thirty years, lose all their pension money, you know what pension is?

—Yes, we have the same word.

—Right, so he loses everything, and he's a wreck.

—This is sad.

—So I think he's going to have to commit suicide.

—Why, why, why.

—I'll explain in a moment.

—No, I say that, why, why, why, it means, I don't know, oy, or that is so sad, or what a pity this is.

—Oh. Huh.

—Suicide. Really?

—Yeah. It's going to be important for the agent's motivation later on.

—What will he do?

—I'm not sure exactly, but it's important to push him toward sympathizing with the assassin.

—And this will help?

—Yes, I think so. It came to me on the plane ride over. So the question is, how does he do it, and how does the audience, and the agent, find out? I decided he takes pills, I'll explain why later, but I don't have an answer to the other questions yet.

—Pills is better. You don't need all this blood.

—Right.

—Can I offer something?

—Huh?

—I do not know how the agent finds out, but do not make the cut, that is what it is called, yes?

—Yeah.

—Do not make the cut then, and not to the funeral, either.

—What do you mean?

—In the movies, when a person finds another dead person, after he is making sure that this person is dead, there is always a cut to the funeral, where it is cold and sunny or it is raining. This is bullshit.

—So what do you suggest?

—After the agent finds his father dead, the scene is continuing for a while. The son calls to the police, but then there is not so much to do. The father is dead from some time already, his skin is white already, so the son knows that he cannot do anything for him. So what does he do, he must wait many minutes for the police and the ambulance.

—Why do you show that?

—It is the saddest part. Not the finding out. This is very sad, too, of course, but he cannot do anything, this is sadder. And the camera is seeing this.

—So what, you just have a long shot of the agent standing there?

—Something like this, I do not know. The actor playing the agent will decide what he does.

—What would you do?

—Me? I will be very sad. I am crying. I am trying to fix the body. Maybe there is something from the father's mouth that comes out because of the poison. I am wiping this. I am trying to help the body, but I cannot, so I am then crying more.

—He's an investigator, he'll go to the bathroom to check the pills.

—No, the father knows this about his son, and so all the pill jars are on the table, and therefore the son does not need to look.

—Is there a note?

—No. You say the father is very sad. So we know.

—So what else does he do, the agent? How long does the shot last?

—I do not know, but longer than you want. You understand? You let the audience see him alone with his dead father. He tries to fix the body, but he is a police, and he is remembering then that you cannot do this. So he must stand, or sit, and wait. This is very sad. And so later, when he is not so mad with the assassin, the people watching will not blame him for this.

—Not bad.

—Right? It is not bad. I told you.

—I do not know how you are liking to smoke the grass, so I bring a joint and also my pipe.

—Your call.

—I did not understand.

—You can decide.

—Oh. It is nice to smoke the joint on the, how do you call this thing, the *mirpeset*?

—What, the balcony?

—Yes, right, the balcony.

—We can't smoke outside, there are other balconies right there.

—Daniel, you did not see that the hotel is so empty? In the lobby? Why do you think they are giving us this nice room with the two beds when we are not asking for it? Come outside. Do you see other visitors? Down there I see some people. When they are blowing up buses, not so many tourists are coming. We will smoke the joint here. Sit. And then I let you sleep.

Moments later Daniel can't help but believe, in a manner nearly humbling, that he's a profoundly fortunate man. From his luxurious ninth-floor balcony he accepts the joint from Nadav for the fourth time, slowly reaching toward the other man's hand, still riding out the involuntary coughing fit caused by the first bundle of smoke. The sun is minutes from falling out of sight, and the sea below, which seems to him a good bit friendlier and more serene than his Pacific Ocean back home, appears to relax a bit more with each passing moment. Either his blood now circulates differently, or its purpose has changed. His head certainly feels transformed, a little larger, a little less crowded. The beach has emptied almost completely, creating a soothing pocket of well-earned urban silence. Daniel, inhaling more carefully this time and holding the warm sweetness in his mouth for a few seconds, concludes with some conviction that he is just now realizing, truly realizing, that he is indeed in Israel, which at this moment seems to him a wonderful thing to realize.

—It is really strong material, yes?

—Yup, yes, yes sir. Exhale. Yes siree, affirmative. Oh yeah. Extremely strong material.

And then a grin.

How has he managed this? He makes up stories, turns them into screenplays, revises them, revises them again, and for this he is rewarded, repeatedly, with wealth he never, or almost never, imagined. No set hours, no dress code, no boss. No boss. He has no boss, that whole thing, of someone coming into his office and demanding things from him, ordering him to do things, it never happens to him. He attends doubleheaders on Wednesday afternoons. He goes to matinees and buys more popcorn than he needs, or even wants. Sometimes he imagines things, and then later millions of people pay to see them, not knowing that he imagined them in sweatpants, or even on the toilet. He takes his time, or at least tries, or at least can try, to take his time. He decides one day, okay, it's more complicated than that, but still, he chooses one day to, just like that, okay, not exactly just like that, but regardless, one day he sits down at his computer and buys a plane ticket, putting it on a credit card that he pays off completely each month, and uses that ticket to get on one plane and then another and then another, New York, Frankfurt, Tel Aviv, the three planes together having dropped him off halfway around the world. He could, in fact, were his lucrative imagination so inclined to write or even to begin to develop a screenplay set in this place, write off this trip, which, again, he can afford, anyway. And so now here he sits on the spacious balcony of his beautiful hotel room, digesting a delicious Israeli dinner, getting high with his very own personal Israeli tour guide, watching the Mediterranean sky grow both pink and dark, listening to the newly sedate traffic flow pleasantly below, admiring the fairly impressive architecture of the sturdy buildings crowding, along with his hotel, up to the edge of the nearly slumbering sea.

—Nice, yes?

—Extremely nice. Beyond extremely nice.

—I told you.

—Great time of day.

—This writer I told you about today, many stories he writes happen at this time. He is very good when he is describing the day becoming the night.

—What does he say?

—I don't so much remember. Sometimes I think maybe he is just trying to understand what this time is that is not day or night, you know?

—I don't think I've ever written a scene at sunset or at dusk.

—How do you say what this is, yes?

—Is that possible?

—It is between and always changing.

—I'm a fool.

—Look at those lights there.

—It's so rich.

—Do you see? How the street it becomes a different street every second. When we start the lights are doing nothing. Now they make the street evening.

—But it's hard for a filmmaker. To get the light right. It keeps changing and you have to shoot from so many angles. It would take days to get one scene. Still, I should.

—We do it now. A scene at this time.

—No. No work right now.

—Please. I request from you.

—No. Really, no work.

—This is your work. This is funny. You pretend.

—What can I say?

—You stand your face.

—Huh?

—Nothing. This is how we say this in Hebrew.

—Stand your face?

—Something like this. I don't know why. Maybe it comes from the Torah. I should know.

—Definitely can't help you there.

—Not important.

—Okay, I think I go to sleep now.

—Now?

—Yes. If I am a little tired, it makes me very tired. I did not sleep enough yesterday. I fight with my mom, and then I feel bad and do not sleep good.

—It's only eight fifteen. You don't want to go downstairs, walk around a little?

—Aren't you also wanting to sleep? All day you are asking to sleep. Please, Nadav, give me the permission to be sleeping. Now I let you. Go to sleep.

—Well, I'm awake now. Feel like I ought to take advantage of this, it's been awhile. That strip down there's looking awfully inviting. What do you say?

—You can. You should. It will be interesting for you. Soon the beach is crowded again. There is the bars and the dancing and the music. When I'm young I'm coming here with my friends and we are trying to fuck someone.

—C'mon, Nadav, man. I don't want to go by myself. You're my guide. I'm paying you. Come down. Show me around. Maybe you'll fuck someone.

—Not this night. And I am not making you pay for the grass, and it is expensive. Do not worry. Go down and walk along that street there. You will not get lost because of the sea and this big hotel.

—I don't know.

—And do not go into a bar without a guard there when you go in.

—Why not?

—You should know this. Because of terrorists. Never mind. To-morrow we get up early and go to the *shuk,* the market. It is interest-ing. I will buy you nuts and dates. And the terrorists don't blow themselves up in the morning, because they want to be on TV in America when they do it, but you are all sleeping then. Good night.

A few minutes later it is much more dark outside than not. The edge of the sky, out where it falls to meet the sea, remains blue, but the rest is black. Daniel stands up. His ass feels like it is asleep. Walks toward the balcony railing. He's up high, so he steps back. Looks in through the sliding glass door. Nadav is out cold. He hasn't called home yet. Shit, he hasn't called home. Before it was too early, but it hasn't been too early for a while now. He needs to call this instant. Im-mediately. But Nadav is asleep and the phone is right next to him. The cell phone. His cell phone, he'll use it. Goes back inside, where the air feels different on his skin, removes the phone from his bag and returns to the balcony. Standing or sitting, how should he call? Really isn't looking forward to speaking with Caroline stoned, but he needs to get this out of the way if he's going to enjoy himself. Hope-fully Zack will answer. No, hopefully no one will answer. Leaving a message would be a breeze. Magnificent view. No wonder they fight over this place. Alright, enough. On with it. How do you dial to the States? Ignorant, the phone becomes an utterly useless blinking plastic rectangle. He does recall being handed some documents along with the phone back at the airport, perhaps instructions were included. So it's back inside, rummaging through his bag. Three pages. Back to the balcony where there isn't really enough light to read. But he can't turn on a light in the room, either. So it's into the bathroom, whose much-too-bright light seems indifferent to the needs and underlying values of his high. It's a matter of values, of course bathrooms should have dimmer switches. He catches himself in the mirror and is both amused and ashamed. Is he in fact growing a beard? A little over a week's growth, it's still possible to pretend he was just being lazy. Runs his hand over the hair, which may already be too long to call stubble. An odd sensation, especially when you're watching it at the same time, sense of touch and sense of sight coordinated like that. The instructions. Right. First page, formalities, liability, it's a fucking contract. He quickly looks at the other two. He sees some numbers, but the text is too dense and the bathroom light is just killing him, so he drops the pages on the counter, turns off the light, and exits. The darkness is awfully dark, until his eyes adjust. Heads back to the phone by Nadav. He hasn't slept in a room with another man since college. Over twenty years. Did Nadav even bother to undress? He makes out one sock, white, on the night stand, which is slightly illuminated by the light of the clock radio. Only one. Definitely only one. Crouching to the floor, Daniel can't find the other sock. Not important, but awfully curious. Checks the far side of the bed. Nope. The phone. Pick up the phone and call the lobby. But what about the sock? After a few long seconds of standing perfectly still and looking at, or mostly listening to, Nadav sleep, Daniel lifts up the bottom of Nadav's comforter and lowers himself toward Nadav's feet, hoping the dull, dull glow originating from the street below will be enough. Not really. Either he's still wearing it or he isn't. Either way it doesn't matter. Either he took off one sock and then either fell asleep or decided to go to sleep before taking off the other, or he took off both of them and then the second sock either wound up somewhere out of sight or he deliberately put it somewhere else. A masturbation prop? Sperm receptacle? Unlikely. Daniel can just make out the shape of Nadav's Israeli feet, but nothing more. Touch would answer the question, at least the main question. Risky to be sure. But a best-case scenario would find him touching, very lightly, just one foot and immediately feeling the sock and then that's that. He returns to the sock on the nightstand. Closes his eyes, as if it isn't dark enough already, and trains himself to recognize the material with just the tip of his index finger. Puts his off hand inside Nadav's sock to simulate the quality of the sock when stretched over a foot. Back to Nadav. Right or left? Which does Daniel remove first? No idea. He's done it, what, twenty thousand times, and he can't remember. How can that be? Only one way to find out. Sits on his bed, takes off his shoes and then his socks. Of course it's the right one. No shoes and socks, feels nice, should have done that a while ago. But perhaps Nadav's a lefty, not to mention he reads from right to left. Fuck it, he'll try the left foot. Closes in, slowly lowering the tip of his finger until he feels a foot, a foot still in a sock. Odd. But alright. Now what? The phone.

—Good evening. How may I help you?

Beautiful accent. Wow. Almost sounds French.

—Hi. Yes. How does, what do I need to do to dial, to make a call to the States?

And she tells him, without hesitating. It's quite simple, could have guessed himself.

Back to the balcony. It's going to cost a fortune to call overseas on a cell phone. The strip is really lit up now, the traffic much heavier. He can hear the dull, rhythmic thud of synthetic bass coming from somewhere down below. Only go into a bar with a guard. Do most have guards? Time to dial. He has to start over four times, too many numbers. Finally gets it right. Some clicks and pauses. His breath is making the phone sweat.

—Hello.

Perfect connection.

—Hey, Care, it's me.

—I was wondering when you'd call.

—Yeah. Sorry. Hey, what time is it there?

—Ten something.

—In the morning, huh. It's already night here.

—Your flight was okay?

—Yeah. Pretty long. Frankfurt airport's kind of funky. Something distinctly European about the place. I think it's the clocks or the signs. Hard to put your finger on—

—I'd love to hear about it, but I'm about to run out. So are you happy to be there?

—I don't know. I guess. It seems pretty strange all of sudden. You know?

—Hmm.

—I mean I'm here, you know? I'm, I'm east of Istanbul. I'm like, I don't know, a day's drive from Baghdad.

—And that's a good thing?

—Right. Yeah, so, I don't know. We'll see. Nadav's an interesting guy.

—I'm sure. Look, I gotta run. Zack's out. Be in touch.

—You want the number? Where I'm at and everything?

—Next time. I'm gonna be late. Call when you want. Be safe. Nothing too stupid. Bye.

Be safe. He's alone on the balcony. Where does she have to be in such a hurry? Be safe. They're coming after him. Or they could be. Crazier things have happened. He's heard about it. A handful of them skirt the Israeli coast guard, pull a little dinghy up on the shore, and then just start killing people. Just for kicks they make their way into this very hotel through a balcony. They climb over the edge of this balcony, all raging eyes and bared teeth, and kill him, on their way to a night of religiously motivated political murder. Nonsense, of course. Not a balcony on the ninth floor. But from the hallway, why not? Sure it would be a challenge, the hotel has its own security, but nothing's impossible. They get past security and take an elevator, or the stairs, probably the stairs, up to a high floor. They leave one guy outside. They have walkie-talkies and the guy outside tells them which rooms have lights on. One of them used to work here before the Israelis stopped letting Palestinians come from the West Bank for work, so they all know the place inside and out. They'll break into the rooms with lights on and kill whoever's inside. Actually they'll have some kind of master key. They'll use silencers or something that will allow them to kill people without making any noise. Entire floors of guests before the night is over. After a while, once it gets later, they'll try every room, light or no light. When the news gets out, that fifty-one tourists, from the U.S., Germany, France, England, Canada, and elsewhere, were murdered, many in their sleep, in a four-star hotel, a luxury hotel that's part of an internationally known and highly respected chain, the Israeli tourism industry will truly grind to a halt. Which is why they might try it. Despite the difficulty of getting past security and overcoming, somehow, whatever video surveillance system they must have here, it might be worth the effort. Pretty un-likely. Pretty fucking unlikely. But he goes to the door and makes sure all the locks and latches are in place, anyway. He's a target. That's for certain. He and everyone else here. Sure it's unlikely, but what he knows for certain, unlike back home where he wonders if there really is anyone, anyone inside the country, really trying to kill him at this point, despite all the hype and the color-coded threat levels and the fear and the round-the-clock speculation and the ridiculously con-trived entertainment, what he knows is that here there are most cer-tainly people trying to kill him. Right now, probably. Because every once in a while, every couple of weeks, or at least every few months, it happens. On a bus, or in a bar, or even somewhere random, like a pool hall or a supermarket, it happens. Because the threat in the U.S. has to be overblown, because if it were really so bad, why wouldn't they just send a few guys into a few crowded movie theaters on a Saturday night, kill a hundred people or so with submachine guns, and paralyze the movie industry? Or blow up some buses? How hard could it be? Sure, planes are more dramatic, but how hard would it be to hit the subways? Right there in New York, on the Brooklyn Bridge or in a tunnel. Maybe they're out there, maybe they're not. Maybe they've got bigger plans. Whatever the case, here he knows. Here he knows that he's got an outside chance of dying, even if he avoids the buses. It's stupid to worry about it, it's so fucking random, now that he's here it's stupid to worry about it. What an idiot, coming here. He really doesn't want to die. Of course he doesn't. But the desire seems particularly pronounced at the moment. Not because he has such an amazing life, though it's not bad, and not because of Zack, though that has something to do with it, and not because of Caroline, though he'd sure like to patch things up with her before it's all over. He just doesn't want anyone who wants to kill him to get to him. He doesn't want that moment when he realizes that they've gotten to him, when he learns the identity of his killer, that hideous instant of eye contact before the moment of his death, when he's identified as the doomed object of their refined, limitless fury. Maybe he'd actually never know. Either way, he's not going down there tonight. Much too dangerous.

He's exhausted, but too wired to sleep. So he remains on the balcony for hours, scared, and watches the strip below, waiting for the explosion. Eventually he gives up and gets into bed, where he listens to Nadav snore softly for another hour or two. By the time he forgets that he's trying to sleep and instead just falls asleep, the next day is announcing itself as the sky begins to pale.

8

Daniel stands at a lunch counter, trying to order an egg salad sandwich. The man on the other side of the counter stands about six five and appears to be a Latin American guerilla. Thick, dark beard, fatigues, even two belts of bullets looped around his torso in the shape of an X. Daniel can't remember whether or not he should fear him. When Daniel speaks, his words leave his mouth as words, as actual letters that then dissolve into fog just before reaching the guerilla, who responds to Daniel in regular Spanish, which Daniel recognizes but doesn't understand. Despite this, he begins preparing Daniel's sandwich, removing a two-foot-long machete from a sheath on his waist to chop the eggs. Someone calls Daniel's name. He ignores it, watching instead how the guerilla, who is now asking Daniel in English if he's ever seen the Woody Allen movie *Bananas*, obliterates the eggs with his too-large knife. Whoever is calling his name won't stop, and soon the set, the counter, the overhead fluorescent lights, the guerilla, the fog that was Daniel's response, Yes, of course, many times, great movie, all of it dissolves.

—Daniel.

—Daniel. Please to wake up.

—You must to wake up, Daniel.

—Daniel. *Ya'alla.* Wake up.

And he does. His displeasure at being conscious is complete, there is no part of him glad to be awake. It is bad for him to no longer be sleeping, he realizes with perfect conviction, as he has much unfinished business, sleepwise. He had been, just moments ago, properly buried beneath the full weight of his long overdue sleep, only to be disinterred prematurely, the violence of this act registering all over his body, every bit of which needs more rest. He is a man who, having not eaten for a week, has been allowed exactly four bites before the grand buffet is abruptly cleared. As a last, feeble act of protest, he refuses to open his eyes, groaning instead.

—Daniel, it is almost ten thirty.

—So?

—So let us do things.

—What's the hurry?

—Get up.

—It can't wait till tomorrow?

—We will travel to the north today, so we must do things before we will leave.

—The north will be there tomorrow. Let me sleep.

—I cannot allow this. I cannot allow your jet lag to do this.

—What has my jet lag ever done to you?

And then Daniel's blanket disappears. He opens his eyes to see his guide holding the blanket and looking at the tourist, who himself remains curled up naked near the south edge of the mattress, his unremarkable circumcised penis resting motionless on his left thigh.

—I believe you have something that belongs to me.

—I am apologizing. But you must get up. I will be waiting on the balcony.

Daniel rolls onto his back and takes in the empty room. He can't rule out the possibility that he remains stoned. Everything, as was the case last night, appears to protrude slightly from its place in the world, the dresser, the television, the balcony railing, all unusually vivid, only now each object seems less vibrant than brittle. He will have to be careful.

—What did you do last night?

—Not much. Hung out on the balcony.

—You did not go down to the *tiyelet*?

—The what?

—What we just passed. This path along the sea that we are looking at yesterday together.

—Nope. Remind me why we're walking and why it's so fucking hot.

—We will have an early lunch. Yemeni food. There is a place. And then to the north. You will like it. Why did you not go down?

—I don't know. This humidity, Jesus. Like a bad summer day in Cleveland.

—You were very excited when I went to sleep.

—I got less excited.

—But you must be going to sleep very late to be still so tired this morning so late.

—I had trouble falling asleep.

—So if already, why don't you go down?

—The pot. I don't know, it was a bit much.

—You were scared from something?

—Just a little freaked out.

—From what?

—Let's not get into it.

—You were scared from the terrorists.

—No I wasn't.

—This is not good.

—I wasn't.

—Here.

And Nadav puts his hand on the small of Daniel's back and

pushes him toward a long blue bus, whose design seems inspired by the bendable straw.

—What are you doing?

—We will go up on the bus.

—No.

—Yes.

They are just outside the doorway at the front of the bus. More or less standing in a short line that is waiting for a few passengers to get off.

—Nadav. Cut it out.

—We will go on the bus a little. There is a better Yemeni place near Allenby in any case.

—No.

But then the line is moving onto the bus, and Nadav has suddenly taken hold of Daniel's hand and wrist in such a way that he must join the Israeli in walking up the black, rubber steps and into the bus.

—What the fuck?!

—Please to be quiet.

Nadav offers some money and then says something to the balding driver, who sits indifferent behind a giant steering wheel almost parallel to the floor.

—Come, let us go to the back. It is fun to be there on the long bus.

The bus is perhaps 40 percent full. More women than men. Some small children. A couple Asian women. No male soldiers, no Hasids, though there is one tiny old man, clean shaven, wearing a worn black suit and a fedora. Some reading, a fair amount of cell phone activity, but most of the passengers just sit quietly, their bodies now bouncing slightly with the motion of the ride. Daniel and Nadav, having walked the length of the bus, sit down along a row of seats at the back. The windows are closed. Air conditioning. Almost a consolation.

—You're a fucking asshole, you know that.

—I am sorry you think this.

—You think this is funny.

—No, I do not.

—You know I have a family. A wife and a son.

—You really think you will die here.

—I'm not a fucking idiot, Nadav. I know I probably won't. But, still, it's not a fucking game.

—No, you are right. It is not.

—Dick.

—And I will not make you to do this again. But you cannot be worrying about the terrorists all the visit. This is even more bad than the jet lag.

Daniel looks straight ahead. Scans the passengers again, half curious, half vigilant.

—This is a very famous Tel Aviv street we are on. Dizengoff. Named from the first mayor of the city. Once this is the fanciest street in Israel. There is a word we make up to say that you are going to walk on this street, *l'hizdangef*. But people are not so much using it anymore. It is a nice street still, but not so nice.

—Now you're a fucking tour guide all of a sudden?

—Do the New York people say let us go Fifth Avenueing?

Not many single men on the bus. Maybe five. A couple are way too old. One is thankfully pale, blond even. Of the other two, one is reading a Hebrew newspaper and listening to headphones. The other, perhaps, fits the part, but wears shorts and a tight white tank top and carries nothing. Daniel's cell phone rings, startling him. Every time the bus stops he must check to see who is getting on. Mostly middle-aged women.

—Hello.

—Hey, traveler, it's Max.

—Hey.

—How's it going over there?

—Alright.

—Just alright?

—I don't know.

—Where are you?

—On a bus.

—A bus?

—Yep.

—Why in the world are you on a bus? Are you crazy?

—Don't ask.

—Caroline would kill you.

—I know.

—What else?

—Well. Got really high last night. Good food. Not allowed to go to Jerusalem. Or sleep.

—Wow.

—Don't trust the brochure.

—But then again, no one's blown you up yet.

—This is true. Not yet.

—And the screenplay?

—That's why you're calling?

—Not really. Just wanted to see how it's going.

—The screenplay?

—No, the trip. I called Caroline, but she didn't have much to report.

—How'd she sound?

—The same. In a hurry.

—Right. What's up with you? Donny been bugging you?

—I've been ignoring his calls.

—Wise move.

—Other than that, not much. I think I'm divorcing my iPod.

—What was that? Your iPod what?

—I think I'm going to get rid of it.

—Okay. Why, exactly?

—Or at least figure out a way to get rid of the shuffle feature.

—Because?

—I got, like, six thousand songs on it. Maybe more, I don't know. And you know, at first it was fun, every song I've ever had all on that one little device, and who knows what might come up next. It's amazing, simply mind-boggling. But then it's like, I got to decide again if I want to hear this song right now? I mean, of course I could just let it play, just let whatever song comes on play, but sometimes it's not something I want to hear. And isn't the point to hear exactly what you want whenever you want? So now I've got to make a decision every three to five minutes. Another thing to deal with. Plus, a lot of times, I don't know, I feel bad when I skip to another song, like I'm insulting the artist, and even when I don't go to the other song I worry, maybe I'm not really listening to the song I want—

—Daniel.

—Max, just a sec. What?

—We will get down soon.

—Who's that?

—Nadav, the guy who's showing me around.

—You like him?

—Later.

—Where's the bus?

—Tel Aviv.

—Nice place?

—It's alright.

—Do you feel cool?

—Why would I feel cool?

—You're riding a bus, tough guy. Staring down danger.

—Yeah, me and some moms.

—The terrorists shall not prevail!

—Your iPod.

—Right, so and then sometimes I don't really seem to like anything I've got on the thing, and I think to myself, Max, you pathetic urban single male with all sorts of disposable income, you loser, you have this vast music library and still you're not satisfied.

—Maybe you shouldn't listen to it all the time.

—But I love music. I really do. At least I thought I did.

—So go out and buy some new stuff.

—Well, that's the problem.

—How is that a problem?

—Well, because if I'm going to be totally honest with myself, then I'm going to have to buy stuff I really don't want to buy, or that I didn't think I wanted to buy. I mean, I realized, I don't like Johnny Cash. I have, like, seven of his CDs, but you know what? I just don't like him. I've been telling people for years that he's brilliant and underappreciated. You gotta check out Cash. But you know what? He's annoying. Honestly, sounds like a southern retard. Same with Ray Charles. Annoying. He's blind. Big fucking deal. And you know what terrifies me?

—What?

—I don't think I like the blues, Daniel. I thought I did, but I'm pretty sure I don't. That's a lot to admit.

—No shame in that.

—No shame? Bullshit. What is cooler than the blues?

—Jazz.

—Jazz is basically the blues. A subcategory. If I don't like the blues, what chance do I have? And it gets worse. There's this Greatest Hits of the 80s disc I have on there. A client gave it to me as a joke once. As a joke. Early Madonna, Duran Duran, Prince—

—Nothing wrong with Prince.

—And Huey Lewis. I like Huey Lewis. This is who I am, Daniel. I like to sing along to Men at Work.

—Daniel, this is our exit. Please to get off the phone.

—Max, look, can we talk later?

—Sure. But you won't tell anyone?

—What, that you like REO Speedwagon and Journey?

—I do not like REO Speedwagon. Journey's body of work, however, is, in its way, impressive.

9

Daniel doesn't care much for the montage. Actually, he'll admit, the original French auteurs, okay, you can't really argue with their approach to the technique, fair enough. But the contemporary American montage, the ubiquitous, inevitable, overused, give-the-editor-a-weekend, a soundtrack, a-couple-bottles-of-wine-and-let-the-good-times-roll montage, this Daniel dislikes. Filmmaking as music video. Cinema as visual mixed tape. If his duty, ultimately, as a storyteller is to give some shape to time, to, above all, chart change over time, then the montage suddenly seems awfully obvious and more than a bit lazy. Which is why most of his stories are, in terms of the time represented, pretty short. A couple of days, a week at the most. You need to show the transformation, the audience needs to witness it, as it happens, more or less, in real time. And it isn't easy, to locate and enact that precise moment when something, or someone, is no longer as it, or she, or he, was. He has no illusions that anything he does is, in the final account, particularly realistic, let alone original, but still, he's trying. Resorting to montage is to give up or at best plug in a worn-out if nonetheless reliable formula.

Which is why Daniel's distinct sense that he's going to need montage to get through this merits mentioning, a feeling that comes to him as he listens, sort of, to Nadav narrate the emergence and evolution of Tel Aviv's homeless problem not far from a homeless man sitting cross-legged on a mat of Israeli cardboard in front of a Yemini restaurant that has recently gone out of business. It's not that he's not enjoying himself, though, of course, at this exact instant the urge to complain and bemoan his reality requires little explanation. Rather, it's all just a little too much. Each and every moment so far, each and every thing, in its very existence as a distinct, and a distinctly different thing, or moment, well, if he's going to endure the next week or so, there will simply have to be some significant filtering, some aggressive editing, some wholesale ignoring of people and places and experiences, because he's been here less than twenty hours and it feels like a month. As it stands it's all just a little too intriguing, from the high frequency of Asian women paired up with aging Jews in walkers and wheelchairs slowly navigating the cluttered city sidewalks, dog crap everywhere, to the strange patterns, combinations of white and blue and red and yellow, adorning street curbs, some sort of mysterious parking code, to the endless variety of Hebrew fonts, curved and block, colored and black, crowding menus and posters and signs and billboards, fonts meaning something to everyone, including, somehow, him, to the sizable role played by coins in the Israeli currency system, as demonstrated by a taxi driver's decision to give Daniel almost forty shekels' worth of change in the form of a towering stack of coins both big and small, silver and gold, rounded and not, to the way the topography noticeably changes not forty-five minutes north of Tel Aviv into a beautiful rolling green plain made so by the simple reality of Israeli agricultural prowess, to the fact that for their unduly late lunch they eat delicious kosher lamb on skewers and thick, oven-warmed pita and pickled radishes and something alarmingly yellow and seven types of salads but not a bite of lettuce at a restaurant attached to a gas station, where full serve is the only option and the young attendants all wear green overalls and a tank of gas in Nadav's undersized automobile, if Daniel's confused and hesitant math is to be believed, costs about sixty dollars, to the fact that most

Israeli toilets give you the option of the half flush, a shortened, often gray handle running below the longer black one, which, if pulled, dispenses only half the basin's water, to the strange shape of street-lights and doorknobs, of public telephones and electrical outlets and bottles of soda, to the abundance of small and not-so-small memo-rials at city corners and along roadsides, which Nadav at first points out reluctantly and in the days following not at all, most of them sad and brutal and ugly and reminiscent of Soviet-era sculpture, clumsy welding and jagged edges, to the cramped, isolated Arab villages with their massive, half-finished cement villas, to the tanned, graying ruins, the slender aqueducts and the Ionic columns and the massive amphitheaters and the neglected, slowly crumbling walls that are in-deed thousands of years old, to the hills and mountains and valleys and a single, perfect lake, all part of a landscape so ridiculously var-ied it seems to be some kind of oversized topographic mosaic, to, fi-nally, his overwhelming impression that many of these people either are not Jews or are Jews of another sort entirely, and not merely be-cause many of them, and not just the Ethiopians, are undeniably and really swarthy, or wearing uniforms and carrying machine guns, or clearly impoverished, or intensely religious, or seemingly stupid, or originally from a continent he's never visited, or operating a tow truck or handing out a speeding ticket or taking a piss against a wall, or re-turning his perplexed and dumbstruck glances with weary gazes of their own. In short, he feels nothing and everything between himself and this place and these people. He reminds himself that this is all, in some sense, his, or even worse, him, or at least an inexorable part of him. An option, an obligation, a birthright, a duty, a last resort. After three long days, he is fully captivated by a coarseness and a despera-tion and a fading beauty that altogether repulse and implicate him that much more for his uneasy association with the first or sober identification with the second, or wistful longing for the last. Fol-lowing the first night's high, and others like it in the days following, and dragged along past night after night of shallow, insufficient sleep, he has since stopped dreaming here, Daniel feels things inside him, things both recognizable and utterly unexpected, gradually drift to the surface, until nothing about himself here surprises him anymore, least of all his ineluctable, if possibly meaningless, tie to this amazing and disastrous place.

10

And then there's Nadav, who at the moment is quietly driving his marginally adequate automobile, the air conditioning of which, even on max, can only get the inside of the car within about four degrees of what Daniel would describe as comfortable. Sweating has been a main activity of the visit so far, you step out of the shower and instantly feel like it was a waste of time. Nadav takes yet another hit from a small, mobile pipe that appears on first glance to be nothing more than a filtered cigarette and pulls up to a dull cement bus station at the side of this mostly deserted two-lane highway to pick up a couple of hitchhiking soldiers. Overall, Daniel would say he likes Nadav. He's clearly bright and typically kind and occasionally funny and quite capable of finding great places to eat, but his qualifications as a tour guide don't seem to extend much beyond this. It's not that he's uninformed, it's more that he prefers not to talk about, let alone elaborate on, most of the many things he apparently knows. Daniel asks questions, lots of questions even, while Nadav typically ignores them or says things like Forget from this. When Daniel persists, as he does on occasion, such as right now, Nadav occasionally relents and offers dark and brief explanations like the following:

—In the past many people are picking up the hitchhiker, because we are supposed to be helping one to the other, but then there are some girls being raped, not many really, but enough, and the news makes from this a big story, and then worse there is the soldier who gets a tramp, eh, this is what we call getting the hitchhiking ride, but it is from an Arab or Palestinian, and they kill him and take his gun. So now not so many people, especially not the soldier is hitchhiking, not alone at least. So, good, I will pick them up and tell them first where I am going, because if I am a bad Arab, I can just ask them first and then say that I, too, am going to where they are wanting to go even though I am not only in order that they will get in the car, and then I can kill them and take their gun, even though I probably am not doing this if there are two of them.

—You're not worried about picking up two guys you don't know who are carrying machine guns?

—They are not loaded, even I can see this.

—Still.

—Are you wondering if perhaps the bad Arab could dress up like the soldier and get in my car so he can kill me?

—Maybe, I don't know.

—For my piece-of-shit car? And you are here, too. I will talk to them now and will hear their accent, do not worry.

The two soldiers agree to get in the car. They're extremely young, but fairly sizable in their way, and it's unclear how they and their leather boots and machine guns and duffle bags will fit. Daniel brings his seat up so far that his knees are pressing against the glove compartment. Nadav moves a few things into the already crowded hatchback. The soldiers, smiling gamely, pile in, making a series of cramming and pushing noises and possibly taunting one another. Eventually they set off again, though it takes a good minute for the car to reach its previous speed. Daniel wants to study the soldiers, to just look at these two new human beings who are sharing this space, two human beings who happen to be, on the one hand, soldiers presently training to kill people or at the least doing something, some administrative or technical or intelligence work, that helps or sets the stage or enables other soldiers to kill people. And Jews, on the other hand. And also not all that much older than Zack. But after the initial greeting he gave to each of them, to the tall, rail-thin one with the small round glasses, and to the slightly shorter, much larger one with no more than twenty longish whiskers growing out of random places on his face, he actually said *shalom* to them, Daniel realizes he can't just turn around again and stare at them, especially considering he just exhausted his Hebrew lexicon and so would be staring at them only. Partially out of exhaustion and a discomfort stemming from his newly contorted position, Daniel closes his eyes and rests his head on his knees. He can still see one of their guns, which is resting on the small armrest between him and Nadav. The sun seems unusually bright today, the sky abrasively blue. Perhaps, somehow, he will fall asleep. The three Israelis have begun speaking quickly to one another, making their foreign sounds, especially, it seems to Daniel, the guttural *ch* that all three produce with astounding regularity and apparent ease. For a minute or so Daniel focuses on this only, this mild storm of seemingly meaningful throat clearing, which is slightly more irritating than it is interesting, until Nadav addresses him in English.

—Daniel, I tell them that you are writing the movies and that you write *Prisoners*—

—*Captives.*

—Yes, I tell them you write *Captives.* Tzachi, who sits behind you, he says he likes this movie very much, he says, what a movie. Uri, he is sitting in the other place, he did not see it, but now he says he wants to see it.

—Thanks for the publicity.

—Can I tell them about the new movie I am helping you with?

—No.

—Please.

—Not now.

This is the other main feature of their time together. Nadav, who seems, beyond food, marijuana, and misfortune, difficult to excite, difficult even to get to talk, especially about his own life, has demonstrated a steady, and fairly annoying, interest in Daniel's latest project. He brings it up two to three times a day, typically at meals, but during their more lengthy car trips as well. Daniel often refuses, but at times relents, in part, of course, because he himself has continued working on the screenplay in his head, whether he wants to or not, regardless of whatever else he happens to be doing.

Since the father's suicide, Daniel has, or Daniel and Nadav have, decided that the agent is officially taken off the case. His own various destructive and worrisome behaviors, drinking and not even bothering to pretend that he's taking care of himself, which were already increasing prior to the father's suicide, obviously spike after it, until the agent's superior, some director of a division, played by a large graying man whose arms are invariably crossed over his chest, who clearly takes no shit and doesn't beat around the bush and who was already concerned, both in general and in regard to the admittedly obvious conflict of interests suggested by the agent's father's predicament and the assassin's targets, now decides that the agent needs to be reassigned, if not ordered to take leave and possibly undergo some serious and intensive psychological evaluation. The agent, naturally, protests, but his superior, during a scene set in his office that contains very little dialogue, just the two staring at the floor a lot, refuses to reconsider. And then, in the middle of a real bender, the agent gets a call from the assassin, who's apparently unaware that the agent's been taken off the case. The assassin tells him to meet him in some random city. Daniel suggests Cincinnati. Nadav, not familiar with Cincinnati, suggests Chicago, which isn't random enough for Daniel. This is as far as things have progressed over the last few days.

Nadav is doing most of the talking now, speaking with considerable animation, slapping the steering wheel from time to time, while the soldiers in back, at least one of whom smells not good, ask the occasional question or interject with a short comment. Then after Nadav's long monologue the soldier behind Daniel begins his own monologue. When he finishes the other says, Yo. Nadav speaks to Daniel, who responds to him without lifting his heavy head from his knees.

—Daniel, Tzachi has a wonderful idea for the movie.

—Great.

—No, really it is a great idea.

—He's in a screenwriting unit, I assume.

—No, tanks, actually.

—Tanks.

—Yes. Listen to this. The assassin tells the agent to come to meet him, they don't know what this Cincinnati is either, Uri says he has a cousin that is living in Miami so it should be there—

—Miami's all wrong.

—Never mind. The assassin tells him to come to meet him because he actually did know about the father, and so now he is going to kill someone in charge from the company that his dad worked for in the past.

—What, and he wants him to watch?

Tzachi speaks from the back.

—It will be great!

—But what's the point?

—Well, we have said before, yes, that perhaps this assassin is wanting to be caught. Maybe he wants this to stop also. So he will have the agent there and then maybe he is getting caught. But maybe, too, he just likes the agent or feels very bad about the father and so thinks that this is the right thing to do.

—So what, the agent gets into the assassin's car and they go and wait for the target? Who exactly is he, anyway?

The Israelis, mostly Nadav and Tzachi, talk for a moment, until Uri, quite excited, interrupts them in English.

—From the, eh, the jail. And now, how do you say this, *teepul*?

—Therapy.

—He is going to the therapy, because he is feeling bad still from what that he did.

—They shoot him as he's coming out of his therapy appointment?

—He is going at the same time each week, so the killer knows.

—Okay. Does he actually shoot him? How could the agent, even after everything that's happened, just let him do that? He's a federal agent.

The Israelis consult one another some more. Uri and Tzachi, suddenly locked in a crescendoing, staccato back-and-forth, scream excitedly at one another until Tzachi, triumphant, begins chanting something over and over. The two soldiers break into song, perhaps a marching tune. Nadav offers his hand to the backseat. High fives can be heard.

—Daniel. What will happen. *Walla* Tzachi is genius. Simply genius. It is something. The assassin speaks to the agent while they are waiting. He says, this man, he tells on the other men that run the company, so they go to jail, but not him, not for so long. Even though he is really the bad one. Or they are all bad. And he says, I don't know, maybe this is not the right thing what I am doing. You will decide. But letting this to happen this time, it doesn't mean that you think that the other times are okay. This is for your father, that is all. One time, maybe, it is right one time. And the agent is not saying anything. He can't say anything. He can't say that this is okay, these are not words that he can say. But maybe as, eh, passive he can let it.

—Tzachi said this?

—I am adding some things.

From the backseat:

—It is good, no?

—And?

—So they sit there for some time. No one is saying anything. And then a man steps out of the building into the parking that is in back and is empty almost. He is dressed very nice. Nice clothing. He walks to his nice car. Stops and is talking on his cell phone. The assassin takes the gun, but just as he is shooting the agent grabs him.

—He shoots?

—Yes. He does shoot.

—And?

—He shoots the man in the shoulder.

—But doesn't kill him?

—No. And then the man sees them. He is trying to yell, but it is hard for him to do this. The agent says, kill him, but the assassin will not. Give me the gun, he screams at him. But no. The assassin starts to, eh—

Then Uri starts speaking in Hebrew. Tzachi says something, and soon all the Israelis are arguing. Nadav pulls the car over.

—What are you doing?

—Tzachi wants to show us.

—What?

—How this scene should be.

—Here?

—We are getting to the road to Netanya soon and then they get off. Who do you want to play?

—What are you talking about?

—Do you want to be the assassin, the agent, or the man that they are shooting?

—I don't want to be any of them. I want to get back to the hotel.

—Oh, you are so much the American pussy, you know this.

—Fuck off.

—Why not? If you do not like this, then you do not use it. And if you do, then great.

—I am going to play the rich man you are killing.

—Okay, Uri is the man we shoot. So who are you?

—I don't care.

—I do not believe you. But okay. I am the assassin. You are playing the agent.

Tzachi and Uri get out of the car, which grows unbearably hot the instant the engine stops. Uri walks across the two-lane highway into a field. Daniel doesn't recognize the crop. Whatever it is, it's green and almost knee high. Tzachi tells them to sit in the car and be quiet. He gives Uri's machine gun to Nadav.

—Please don't shoot Uri.

—We are just pretending. There are no bullets.

—*Ya'alla.*

Uri walks in the field. Takes out a cell phone. Starts talking in it. Tzachi turns to Nadav and points at him. Nadav lifts the gun to his shoulder.

—*Ya'alla!*

—Why are you not grabbing me?

—This is silly.

—Why?

—It just is.

—Do you know how this scene should end?

—I don't know that this scene should be in the movie.

—It is a good scene. It is forcing the agent to decide. He must decide, no?

—But what's the point?

—This is your movie, I do not know. Tell us, what is the point of the movie?

—I don't know.

—Yes, you know the point.

—I don't.

—So, okay. Never mind. Play this and we will see. Then after we drop them off, to your hotel. I let you sleep in the afternoon. Okay?

Daniel doesn't say anything. Nadav lifts the gun again.

—*Ya'alla!*

Daniel sits still. Uri looks up from his phone and yells, *Nu.* Tzachi walks around to Daniel's side of the car.

—If you are not playing, please to get out. I will play.

—Nadav, let's go.

—Please, mister, I will play.

—Nadav.

Tzachi opens the door and puts his hand on Daniel's shoulder.

—Get your hand off me.

—Daniel, let him play if you will not.

—No.

—This is not nice. He is wanting to help. That is all.

Daniel slams the door shut and sits still for a moment, sweating so much there's no point in being bothered by it.

—Alright, let's go.

—No, let us play the scene.

—That's what I meant. C'mon already.

Tzachi walks back across the street and screams something to Uri. Uri walks across the field talking on his cell phone.

—*Ya'alla!*

Nadav lifts the gun. Daniel grabs him and pushes the gun, somewhat on purpose, into Nadav's head.

—Ow! *Koos umek!*

Tzachi screams to Uri, who falls and then can be heard moaning.

—He's not dead. Shoot him.

A small line of blood is running from above Nadav's right eye.

—No.

—Shoot him.

—No.

—He saw us. Shoot him.

—No.

—Give me the gun.

Nadav drops it out the window. Tzachi raises his hands and begins to say something, then stops himself and puts his hand to his mouth. Daniel opens his door, gets out, walks around the car, and picks up the gun.

—No, no.

Tzachi is walking to him.

—What?

—He makes the gun apart. You cannot.

—What?

—The gun is not working now, he makes it apart.

—So what do I do?

Tzachi screams to Uri. Uri screams back.

—You will use his, his, eh . . .

—Revolver!

—Yes, his revolver.

—Like the Beatles!

—The guy coming out of therapy has a gun?

—No. Maybe. No, you are using Uri's revolver. It is yours. The agent gun. I bring it to you.

Tzachi runs across the street. Uri's arm rises up out of the field, holding a handgun. Tzachi runs back.

—Here, take.

—It's not loaded?

—No, look.

Tzachi points it at the road and pulls the trigger a few times. Nothing.

—Here.

Daniel takes the gun. Starts walking across the street toward the field. Tzachi grabs his arm.

—No. Eh, sorry. From the beginning, yes?

—Why?

—It will be better.

—He is right.

Daniel turns around to give Nadav a blank stare, tucks the gun into the back of his pants, and goes back to the car. Tzachi screams to Uri, who stands up smiling. Daniel hands the machine gun to Nadav and then gets back inside. Tzachi screams.

—What?

—There is a car coming, Daniel, we must wait a moment.

—Sorry about your head.

—Never mind. It is not so bad. Soon you will shoot the man who because him your father killed himself.

A small van passes by.

—*Ya'alla.*

Uri walks across the field. Stops. Removes his cell phone and begins talking. Nadav lifts the gun. Daniel grabs the gun, pulling it toward himself. Nadav struggles and the gun slips from his grip, hitting Daniel's nose.

—Fuck! Fuck.

Uri is moaning from across the road.

—Fuck. Shoot him.

—No.

Daniel can feel his nose bleeding.

—Shoot him. He saw us.

—No.

Daniel wipes his nose with the palm of his hand.

—Give me the gun.

—No.

Nadav drops the gun outside the car. Daniel gets out. Slams the door. Pulls out his gun. Tzachi walks toward him, an actual handkerchief in his outstretched arm.

—Here, mister. Are you—

Daniel pushes Tzachi's arm down and walks to Uri, who, seeing Daniel's face, stops moaning and asks:

—What is happening?

—Moan.

—Your nose. What is happening?

—Uri, moan. You're bleeding to death.

Daniel stands right over him, extends his arm with the gun and points it at Uri, who says, No, no, in heavily accented English. Daniel tries to decide if the agent should say anything. He tries to decide this for some time. Uri moans and says no many times, occasionally opening his eyes to look at Daniel, whose arm remains perfectly straight despite the weight of the gun. The palm and fingers of the hand holding the gun are unevenly red. Every few seconds he can feel a drop of blood leave his left nostril. He can feel the sun burning his neck.

—Sorry.

And he squeezes the trigger. The click frightens him. Uri becomes silent.

—*Yofi!*

A moment later Uri extends his arm to Daniel. Daniel stares at it for a few seconds, then takes it and helps pull him up. Uri is heavier than he looks, and Daniel bends down slightly to lift him. As he raises his head, too quickly, white lines begin snaking across the field, quickly taking it over from left to right and from bottom to top. Then the bright sky darkens.

—Mister!

11

In a whisper:
—Nadav?
—Yes.
—Just seeing if you're awake. I can't sleep.
—Me either.
—Fuck.
—How is your nose?
—Fine. Your eye?
—Fine also.
—Fuck.

—Here. I have an idea.
—What?
—Let us smoke the grass and then we will swim in the sea.
—Nadav. Man. I can't keep up with you. I'll swim, but enough with the weed.
—You will do what you are wanting, but you should.
—Why?
—Because it is most good to be high in the day. We learn to smoke the grass at night, correct, there are reasons why for this, but

it is, eh, preferred with the sun. It is more easy to be deriving the benefit from it.

—We'll see.

—Maximum, you are high for a little while.

—Maximum?

—Maximum.

—Maximum, what?

—Maximum, you are high.

—That doesn't mean anything.

—But this is English, no?

—Yeah, but we don't use the word like that.

—Oh. This is how we are using it.

—You say the word *maximum* in Hebrew?

—Yes.

—Maximum?

—Maximum.

—But it doesn't mean maximum.

—No?

—What the hell are you trying to say?

—So you are high for a while. That is all. It is not so bad.

—Maximum?

—Yes.

—Use it in another sentence.

—No.

—C'mon.

—I am tired.

—You're tired.

—I am.

—I'll smoke if you use it in another sentence.

—You were to smoke in any case.

—A sentence.

—Maximum, I am smoking the grass every day.

—Still doesn't make any sense.

—Never mind.

—I tell you, yes?

—Dude.

—The sea and the sun and this smell of the salt, it is nice, yes?

—Whose idea was it to walk in sand?

—When we get to the water you will not be able to complain.

—Nadav. My good man. A question.

—What?

—Are you happy living here?

—What?

—Are you happy living here? In Israel.

—Yes, I hear this. Later I will answer, okay?

—What? It's such a hard question? Yes or no?

—No. And then yes, almost.

—What does that mean?

—I will answer in the water.

—C'mon.

—Go into the water, and I answer you.

—I'm liking this sand. Just standing here, my feet are extremely satisfied. Is sand a liquid or a solid?

—The water is better, you will see.

—I'm sure I will.

—Jew. Into the sea.

—What?

—Into the sea.

—What are you doing?

—I am pushing you into the sea. I am the Arab, you are the Jew. Into the sea!

—Nadav, what the fuck? Alright, alright.

—No, you must fight, and then I must push you into the sea.

—I'm going.

—I am winning! I am winning! I am pushing the Jew into the sea. Viva la Palestine!

—Great, now what?

—Be in the sea.

—Good, so here is what you will do. Go on your back so you are looking up to the sky. Breathe strong and deep.

—What about my question?

—After. But only if we are also talking about the assassin.

—Is your middle name quid pro quo?

—I don't have a middle name.

About eight seconds later Daniel, who now feels importantly alone, giggles slightly. He tries not to be concerned by this, by the way it snuck up on him, by the fact that clearly it came by way of nerves and exhaustion and not from anything particularly funny. Instead, he continues looking through his eyes at the pale, pale, almost white blue sky with the eleven small clouds that constitute his entire field of vision. His ears register the muffled hum and suggestive drone of their submersion. Nose and mouth, salt and, perhaps, some birds. But mostly his body draws to the front of his attention, so weary he wonders if there's any chance his limbs could start falling off soon, one by one. Buoyed like this, Daniel senses just how much work is typically involved in holding oneself, one's body, together, in maintaining posture and managing weight and simply not falling over. He doubts very much he can fulfill his obligations in this area much longer if sleep continues to refuse him entry. Nevertheless, the sensations, right now, are intensely pleasant. Following Nadav's instructions, he inhales deeply. He can feel the mysterious, hidden, probably pink flesh of his lungs expand in the hollow of his chest, while his mouth curls up into a foolish grin. His breath gives the activity an extra boost, so he inhales deeper yet, enabling him to perceive the slight movement of the clearly three-dimensional clouds that were perfectly still not a moment earlier in the far-off sky. Children's voices are coming to him through the water. Though their Hebrew is flattened and warped, he identifies their laughter. It's a shame he's not naked. Why, he's not exactly certain, but it's a shame. But never mind. Arms and hands are falling open at the wrist, pointing straight up to the sun. The still water now rises, and with it, himself, only not enough, so he's forced to give up and return to standing.

—It is good, yes?

—Pretty awesome.

—You are like the happy floating Jesus.

—He walked on water.

—Not important.

—So answer the question.

—If we can talk about the assassin.

—Later.

—But we must. We are ignoring from him.

—But he's not important. It's about the agent.

—Yes, but perhaps it should be about him as well.

—Perhaps, but you're cheating. Answer. Are you happy living in Israel?

—I tell you. No, and then yes, almost.

—And this makes no sense.

—If I am to tell you I must be the happy floating Jesus first.

—So.

—Daniel, you know what this means.

—I don't.

—I am not happy. I don't like to be saying this, because I am a little happy now. In the water and after the grass. But I am not a happy man. Most of the time. For many years I am fighting this. I am saying no, I am pretending, I am trying very hard that it will not be true. When I am finally happy I am saying, finally, and saying, this is it, yes, finally. I am sitting and trying the yoga and the tai chi and the sex to be more happy, to be more often happy, but in the end I am not so happy. Mostly. So then I am thinking, maybe it is Israel, it is guilty of my unhappiness. The shouting and the hate and the Arabs and the wars. And my mother. Therefore, of course I am not happy. Good, I am going to London, and then to India. Am I happy there? A little more, for a short time. London, it is nicer, not so much screaming. And the parks. More space to be alone. And India, the people are gentle. And the food. But I am still there. Nadav in London. Nadav in India. And soon I am seeing the things I don't like. That people are dumb, too, in London. Very dumb. And that in India so many poor. It is my guilt, that I see these things. And suddenly I am missing Israel. Because if I am to hate things, then I should know them and they should be my things. Yes? The Israeli newspaper, it is so stupid. It screams. You hold it and it is screaming at you. But some of the writers are good, and I like to read about our bad soccer. And there are rules here, but no one is listening to them. Everyone is pretending that the rules are not for them. Because we are all Jews, perhaps. But then, here I am, it is mine. I belong, almost. Not away. I hear the way people break Hebrew, and it is my, how do you say this, alienation. I see the stupid police car that always has its siren turning, why? But it is my police car, and I am not so scared of the man in it. In London, it is different when I see the big police car. I walk in Tel Aviv, and I am a little sad, but I am not a stranger also. And sometimes I can be happy. With friends a little. In the bar that I know a little. Floating in the water like the Messiah. Drinking chocolate milk from the plastic bag like when I was a boy. In Tel Aviv on Friday in the afternoon, for a couple hours all the people are quiet and slow, I love this time. You will see it today. Before we go to my mother's for dinner.

—We're going to her place for dinner?

—Yes.

—I'm going to be high with your mom?

—You are wanting to smoke again before this?

—No, I'm still going to be high then. From this.

—No, we are not going so soon. You will not be high then, it is just the water. But she will bother you in any case.

—What's with you and your mom?

—Oh, no. I already am telling you about being unhappy. Not also my mom. You can ask her. She will be happy telling you.

—Fair enough.

—The assassin.

—What about him?

—Why?

—Because.

—No. Why?

—Because there is someone out there who is actually doing what everyone else wants to do.

—That is all?

—Pretty much.

—But how?

—Does it matter? He's independently wealthy. He was in the army for a while and was a sniper. He has some land in rural Montana. He practices there. He only drives. No flight manifests. No passenger lists. He doesn't have a job. He slowly accumulates enormous amounts of cash so that he doesn't need to charge anything. Can't be traced. He's a computer wizard and uses this knowledge to cover his tracks and to accumulate false identities. He has no siblings, no wife, no children, no relatives, so no one notices when he disappears. This is all he does. He's patient and meticulous. Very intelligent, but very alone. This lets him decide to actually do it. No one to talk him out of it. And no original trauma. None of that bullshit. His father didn't molest him. His brother wasn't killed in the war. Just another angry person with a lot of spare time and money. That's who he is.

—He is interesting.

—He's necessary to the story. But it's about the agent. Who's now a fugitive from the law to boot.

—Do you like ice coffee?

—Ice coffee?

—When they put it in the blender with the sugar?

—You guys got that here?

—Of course.

—Sure. I could drink one.

—And we sit on the beach and look at the women and pretend we are sexy.

—You're very sexy.

—Yes, you are funny. If I was homo, my life would be easier.

—How so?

—It would. I don't know how to talk to the women, really. Only men.

—Have you tried it?

—What? Fucking the man?

—Yeah.

—I don't want to. I am just wanting to want to.

—Right.

—Good. Let us drink the ice coffee and wish we were homo.

12

Enjoying their drinks through a straw, when they notice a crowd over in the sand. Large and standing in a dense, slowly widening circle. Nadav and Daniel head over. Lots of pointing and mumbling. Then policemen arrive. Loud sirens and louder orders and the sudden erection of low metal fencing.

—What's going on?

—A suspicious object.

—Here in the middle of the beach?

—Yes, do you see this carton box?

—That one?

—Yes.

—Let's get out of here.

—No, it is okay.

—How is it okay? Are the police telling us to leave?

—Of course.

—They're shouting. C'mon.

—It is not so dangerous. We will watch. Enjoy the coffee.

—Unbelievable.

Daniel's phone rings.

—Hello.

—Bloom.

—It is.

—Donny.

—Donny, what's up?

—What's up there?

—You know, just watching some kind of bomb-squad robot being lowered from a truck.

—You're fucking with me.

—Nope. An actual robot with treads. It's heading over to the sand. It can maneuver on sand.

—You're at the beach with the bomb squad?

—I am now.

—Get the hell out of there.

—No, they set up a perimeter with some metal fencing. I've been told we're alright.

—By whom?

—My guide. A very trustworthy man.

—Sounds like you're having a great time.

—Possibly. Having trouble sleeping.

—What now?

—What?

—What's the robot doing?

—Some guy with a remote control is sending it over to this cardboard box.

—Shit.

—Now it's just standing there.

—What's it look like?

—You know. Treads, a couple of arms. Probably has a camera on top. More *Blade Runner* than *Star Wars*.

—What a fucking place.

—Has its charms.

—So what's up with the movie? You working on it still?

—You know. On and off.

—What do you got?

—Father kills himself. Agent sort of teams up with the assassin and winds up shooting his dad's old boss.

—Great, great. And the ending?

—Nothing yet.

—Nothing. Bloom, I need this ready soon.

—Yeah, you told me before.

—No, I mean it. I'm starting to get a bad feeling.

—What?

—I don't know. People don't seem as pissed as they were about everything a few weeks back.

—What do you mean?

—I run into people, we talk, it doesn't even come up anymore.

—Are you're worried that the world is improving? That it will hurt box office?

—Shit, Bloom, nothing's getting better. It's getting worse. But I'm sensing fatigue. People can't maintain this level of indignation forever. And this budget won't last forever, either.

—I see. Can't really help you there.

—Yes you can, finish the fucking script.

—Oh, wait, the robot is leaving the perimeter.

—What happened?

—Nothing so far.

—I can't believe you're just standing there.

—Now they're moving the fences back.

—Great.

—Every single person here is on their phone. I feel so Israeli.

—Wonderful.

An explosion. Some screaming. A brown plume fills the air and all at once disappears, falling back to earth.

—Bloom, what the hell was that?

—Holy shit.

—What?

—They just blew it up.

—Jesus.

—Speaking.

—Huh?

—Some men in uniform are entering the perimeter.

—Army or police?

—Both. A couple of them are laughing. Most aren't. The robot is being returned to its truck. Here goes the fencing and the perimeter. Shutting down the set. Truck with robot driving off.

—You need to get out of there.

—Here we are, moving closer to the scene of the crime. Very brown. Nadav, what is this?

—Tea biscuits.

—Tea biscuits.

—Tea biscuits?

—A forgotten box of tea biscuits. Obliterated. Sort of looks like graham crackers. Some half circles around the edges. Like oversized, edible postage stamps. Quite a mess. What's that, Nadav? Oh. Nadav is informing us that the birds will clean it up. So everyone's a winner. Except the tea biscuits and whoever originally planned to enjoy them with their tea. Otherwise, a little suspenseful entertainment, a little training exercise, and the birds get a treat.

—Bloom, you don't sound so good.

—I'm fine. Just admiring the view from the corner of tea biscuit and counterterrorism.

—Get some sleep, alright?

—I'm trying.

—Finish the script and come home.

—Will do. Hey, one last thing.

—What?

—Now that you're on the phone. I was thinking the other day. Actually night. Couldn't sleep. Is he a fucking idiot or a fucking asshole?

—Who?

—Who? The president.

—Is he what?

—A fucking idiot or a fucking asshole. Because at first, back when he first got elected or whatever that was, I figured like everyone else, the guy's just a fucking idiot. A total moron. An intellectual lightweight. *Being There* meets *The Manchurian Candidate.* Only now I'm not so sure. Seems like more of an asshole, or at least not only an idiot. Suddenly very cruel and heartless and not compassionate and pretty damn conniving. An awful lot of collusion for one idiot, you know? Any opinion on the matter?

—Right. I see what you're saying. How's all of the above sound?

—Probably about right. Look, Donny, it's been a pleasure, but I gotta go shower. I'm off to my tour guide's mother's house for Shabbat dinner.

13

For some reason it's going to be a bath and not a shower. Maybe he's hoping to reclaim some of the aquatic bliss he briefly enjoyed back in the sea. Or perhaps he's just looking for another opportunity not to stand. Slow down the process. Escape from that stoned Israeli for a while. He can't tell how he feels. Outer layer, caffeine buzz, fairly pronounced, thanks to his decision to accept Nadav's offer to finish the guide's still half-full frozen coffee confection. He couldn't sleep now even if he wanted to, even if he could. Fingers and toes, in particular, quite animated. Could have something to do with whatever happened to him back there on the phone with Donny, suddenly emboldened, suddenly sarcastic about that, of all things. Below this, his high. Dissipating, but a factor all the same. Keeps reminding him, along with the fact that he's not wearing any clothes, of his body. Finally, fatigue. It's starting to make his eyes hurt and joints ache, starting to make him want to hide more than sleep. The number of acts he feels confident he can perform has been dwindling steadily. No longer fit for public consumption.

The water runs. The waiting and the noise of the tumbling water irritate him. Daniel's perched on the edge of the tub, naked, his both hard and soft ass unable to decide if this is a comfortable place to sit. The cold porcelain, just bearable, barely. More interesting than comfortable. He's facing the mirror and getting a long look at himself. His hair, a good bit bigger than normal, is doing all sorts of strange things thanks to the work of dried salt water and sea breeze. In general, he looks better and worse, depending on your perspective. Tanner than normal, and therefore more vitally physical in some culturally informed, rugged, masculine, and/or natural sense. But a closer look, especially at the eyes, suggests that all is not as it should be. He stands and approaches the mirror. Though a bit bloodshot, the white part and the iris and the pupil overall seem fine. But the outlying skin is starting to give up. Not exactly wrinkles, not bags, not sagging, just some vague deterioration. Perhaps it has something to do with some complicated layers, all with *derma* somewhere in their names, just below the surface, that are beginning to decay. Where skin and veins and glands have lost interest in one another after all these years. Decides to attribute this, like everything else that's bothering him, to his lack of sleep. He steps back to finally consider his beard in progress, the main attraction. It's official now, he's way past mere stubble and the laziness of long weekends. On his way to caveman. Does it look good? Hard to say. Mostly just different. Makes his jaw more imposing, obviously. The moustache is a bit thinner than the rest, but not so thin as to doom the project. What surprises him is the gray. Entire patches on both sides of his chin that highlight the otherwise easy-to-miss gray on top of his head. He's old, or may be. Possibly well into the second, and thus last, half of his life. It seems so impossible, if only because he still believes, more than knows, that he circumvented adulthood, meaning he's gone straight from adolescence to old age. He walked into a James Bond movie at age thirteen, *The Spy Who Loved Me,* okay, not necessarily one of the franchise's highlights, he can't help being born too late to have caught Connery in the theater, and decided, then and there, this is what he would do. His tastes evolved, no, matured, in the coming years. *Dog Day Afternoon,* the second *Godfather, Taxi Driver,* and, of course, *The Deer Hunter,* he always had a thing for the darker side of suspense and action, for a person pointing all that violence back at himself, but regardless, he knew this is what he'd do. Not so much because he refused to consider a more conventional career path, architect was always the back-up plan, choice number two, but it didn't matter, he was crazy for the movies. So elaborate, so real, so impossible. His parents, or his mom, anyway, tried to be supportive, he's not sure he'd do the same for Zack. Thankfully, his success saved him from having to confront his own father's stubborn disapproval, which he knew stemmed from a principled refusal to take seriously a profession, in quotes of course, that involved sitting at a typewriter in your bathrobe and figuring out new ways to have people pretend to shoot one another. His father's tastes in movies were actually not far from his own, but Daniel's vocation had him denying this until the end. Once he died, Daniel let himself admit it, even said it to Caroline a few times, that despite all the hard work, the insane persistence required, there was an awful lot of screwing around involved, a whole lot of unchecked mischief, a potentially unhealthy dose of never knowing and never having to learn what it was, exactly, real grown-ups do all day. And now he's growing old, on the hopefully long downhill toward death. He was lucky to inherit a favorable metabolism, so in clothes he looks young and fit. But standing here naked, the sagging is impossible to miss. Again, his skin appears to be the first to give up. He's deteriorating, diet and exercise and all that are only going to retard what's already under way and irreversible. Had he lived a few centuries ago, at his age he'd already be dead. If he trimmed the beard, gave it some definition, he'd look distinguished, or at least less feral. But he feels required to let it run its course, to not interfere. Caroline, whom he really should call, would never allow such disregard for his appearance, even if he argued that it wasn't disregard at all, not to mention however casual his milieu, he'd get a lot of shit and strange looks. So this might be it, his last chance to not bother.

The bath doesn't quite work. First too hot, then too cold. Tries laying on his side for a while, curled up, hoping to sleep but not drown. He should have such problems. Shivers violently when he gets out, his body unable to regulate its own temperature any longer. Could really use a hug, one can only demand so much affection from one's towel. Sits on the toilet and runs a small black comb through his beard, wondering how the prophets groomed themselves, if at all.

Daniel exits Dahlia's unbelievably clean bathroom and pauses for an instant in the hallway, unable to decide which way to go. He should, of course, turn left and head back to the living room and the kitchen, to speak with Nadav's mother, to offer to help, or at the least to look out again over the darkening city.

The two men had waited a couple of minutes inside the lobby's glass and plaster walls for the aging elevator to arrive, for the long translucent rectangle on the elevator's outer door, which Nadav would soon pull open himself, to fill up, from the top down, with the white light of the descending cab. Inside the slowly ascending, cramped lift, with no more than ten square feet of floor space, Daniel had felt his fading high continue to bleed into his long-standing exhaustion, until the mobile surface he was standing on stopped an inch and a half below the building's eleventh floor. Almost right across the elevator, Nadav's small mother had stood in her own doorway, already greeting them. She was smiling, wearing black, accepting the bouquet Daniel had insisted on bringing, with densely packed layers of enthusiasm, surprise, and gratitude. And then, even before he'd stepped inside her apartment, he saw the far wall of her living room, an enormous window offering a mostly unobstructed view of the city. Nadav and his mother had quickly gone bickering off to the kitchen, she hobbling noticeably, the kind of limp that starts in the hip, her right side dipping down briefly with every other step, an apparent misunderstanding regarding the time they were supposed to arrive serving as a springboard into the muddy pool of their first Hebrew argument of the evening. Daniel crossed the large room to look out the window at the silent, calm city below, the largely white buildings pleasantly interrupted by the green of an occasional small park, the newly unimposing, distant streets gradually emptying of buses in the run-up to Shabbat, the scattered clusters of motionless yellow and orange construction cranes rising off in the north, the sudden end to all this dense development at the sea's edge, the placid water appearing to have cut the city down the middle. He gladly ignored the escalating fight in the kitchen, deciding he could manage with a view like this, could be happy with a view like this, could simply relax and be himself with a view like this.

Assuming Dahlia's still busy in the kitchen, Daniel figures he can take his time returning to her. Nadav has already gone back down to the car, his pathetically contrived excuse transparent even to Daniel. So he turns right to investigate, briefly, of course, the rest of her apartment. He passes a small study filled with books, a computer on a desk overflowing with papers, next a guest bedroom, a man's clothing, T-shirts and jeans, neatly folded on the bed, and then arrives at Dahlia's bedroom. He catches himself before crossing the threshold, he'll just peek inside and turn back. But then he sees the pictures and is soon standing near the base of her bed.

The walls of her room are filled with photographs, hundreds of eight-and-a-half by eleven-inch pictures in unremarkable, identical cheap black frames, arranged in precise, dense, uninterrupted rows that, starting from knee height and rising to the ceiling, cover every available inch of the four walls not already claimed by window, doorway, or furniture. Faces. People and their faces. Mostly the same people, the same faces. Nadav's quite frequently. Dahlia's prominent as well. And a couple of others. Daniel turns around once and then twice, scanning the thousand-plus human faces that crowd the still-inanimate walls. He would be unable to sleep here, but then again he's unable to sleep anywhere. Near the end of his second spin he notices that the right wall is almost entirely in black and white. Not just black and white, but old as well. Rounding her bed to examine a cloudy, expressionless family portrait of exclusively pale people with dark, dark hair in black dresses and black suits, their faces uniformly strange in the early days of photography, the severe patriarch still clutching his old-world beard and head covering, everyone gathered around him on a sofa handcrafted in the midnineteenth century. Two individual portraits, the only oval-shaped photographs in the room, the lighting different, the edges smudged and discolored, the people possibly from the family portrait, only grown up, one of whom, the man, with Nadav's bulging eyes. A wedding shot, a farming shot, and a picture of three men in an ancient Jeep, two clutching rifles manufactured for World War I. The one in the backseat later marries a woman who, in a faded photo up by the ceiling near the entrance to Dahlia's bathroom, is standing by a tree with a younger, smiling woman in a long pleated skirt, who for some reason holds a cane. He wears a white short-sleeved shirt at the wedding, she a white blouse. A couple of years later, still living in black and white and barely a third of the way to the room's second corner, they have a daughter, who stands with a one-armed doll in front of a small cottage surrounded by dense vegetation. The girl, who smiles to expose her teeth, grows in increments of two to four years per picture, joined by a sister around the time her perfectly straight hair reaches her waist. Above a dresser a new man appears, quite young, dark curly hair and a barrel chest, maybe not yet a man, standing at a beach in leather sandals, and then on a hill holding a metal canteen, and then, almost smiling, next to the girl with the black hair, no longer so long, no longer a girl. He poses in uniform, first alone, and then again, saluting a paper-thin officer. At their wedding, in sharper, possibly professional black and white, he wears a tie and a jacket that was either brown or gray and a hat over his unambiguously black curls. She wears a white dress, her hair now shoulder length. They laugh for the first time in family history. They move to a modest apartment with a small balcony, and on the same late afternoon or early morning, the shadows dramatic, she takes four pictures of him with a new moustache reading a Hebrew paper and drinking from a mug, the pictures taken within minutes of one another, he ignoring the photographer in each but the first, his face partially obscured by the headlines in the fourth. Then he's back in uniform, no moustache, three small bars on each epaulet, being saluted. She is pregnant and smiling, her hair is long again. Nadav, the black-and-white infant Nadav, the eyes are unmistakable, appears one vertical row away from the room's second corner, held by his father, who remains in uniform. His first couple of years are nearly a dozen photos long, his grandparents and then an uncle reappear to hold him, he crawls with one foot flat on the kitchen floor, the attached knee pointing toward the ceiling, his tiny white shirt stained gray down the middle. He stands, he holds a ball, he plays with two girls, he pretends to cook, he draws on his face, he naps with his ass in the air atop his father, out of uniform, who naps as well. He touches his mother's pregnant dress. A brother arrives two pictures before the first color photograph. The father, his curls still black, his bars replaced with a single circular something, holds the newborn, nearly smiling. Nadav, his gray eyes touched with green around the edges, considers his brother asleep in a crib, his pink hand reaching through the bars toward a bare, yellowish foot. Mom and firstborn stand on a sunny city sidewalk before a storefront sign in red Hebrew, Nadav holding his mother's thigh, the two of them next to a stroller and an old blue sedan. Nadav stands in a brown swimsuit on the beach looking beyond the frame to the left, his brother sits at his feet, naked, his hands buried in the sand, this day at the sea arching over the doorway leading to the rest of the apartment. The father, hidden behind plain black sunglasses, wears tight trunks, his torso and thighs thick and firm, no muscles, no fat, and plays with his small sons, in the water, at the shore, on a large sheet next to a plate of pale green melon. Some time passes. The younger brother, nearly as old as Nadav was at the beach, reading a book on the floor, Nadav, his back to the camera, stands near a desk at the edge of the frame. An older woman appears with some frequency for a brief stretch as the pictures near the third wall, her hair rigid and nearly orange, always touching one of the boys, typically failing to smile. Nadav begins school. He wears white and stands with other children in white, an Israeli flag raised behind them. Daniel grows curious and then anxious, scans ahead to verify. He rushes past one corner to the next, past Nadav's first bicycle, past his younger brother's broken arm at what might be age ten, past Nadav's graduation from high school, past the brother, now a half head taller than his older brother, in uniform, past the two with long, wild hair in frayed cut-offs and worn-out T-shirts. No father since the day at the beach. A group photo, just above one edge of Dahlia's headboard, with the younger brother back in uniform, bars on his shoulders, contains three graying grandparents. Daniel considers his feet for a moment, listens for something from the rest of the apartment, he should leave, but there is only half a wall left. Mostly Nadav and his brother. Once in Europe, possibly France, maybe Spain. From time to time Dahlia stands between them, the top of her head reaching just past their shoulders, her hair now permanently cropped short, smiling the exact same large smile that pulls the corners of her mouth up and out. Nadav's brother, confident, handsome, and mysteriously blond, begins wearing a tie without a jacket, standing near an older man who, Daniel can't be quite sure, may have been a politician of some significance. Nadav remains in jeans. He sits and reads and smokes cigarettes, often refusing to face the camera. And then just Nadav. Nadav and sometimes Dahlia. Not three vertical rows from the corner where the family first began. He looks the same, so does she. He gains some weight, he loses some weight, his hair gets bigger and then smaller. Nothing changes, especially not her smile, though they return to Europe, definitely London, standing in public spaces, occasionally touching. Just the two of them.

Daniel turns and leaves the room. In the hallway his field of vision grows suddenly white, his head filling up with blindness, but he continues walking by recalling how to move his feet, by focusing on the reliable flatness of the floor. When he can see again a few moments later, he stops, finding himself no more than an inch from the left wall.

—What is your opinion of our country?

Her voice, though not quite nasal, originates more in her mouth than her throat, her vowels more European than her son's. Either she smiles or appears poised to smile, always, or at least this evening. Her right shoulder bouncing rhythmically in response to her atypical gait, she shuttles back and forth between the kitchen and a table in the next room, the table steadily filling up with dinner, each time passing the stationary guest, whose fairly sincere offer to help was dismissed by a quick flick of her wrist. Accepting a glass of wine from his hostess with a smile of his own, Daniel tries to gather his mouth and mind together so that they might formulate an answer to her question. He wants to respond, and not solely, or even primarily, to meet the minimum standards of good manners, only he finds himself incapable of settling on the basic form, let alone assembling the main ingredients, of an answer. Perhaps a single word, wonderful, lovely, or two, truly impressive, absolutely amazing, would do it, would satisfy her, would get him, and her, would get them to whatever lies waiting for them beyond this opening exchange. But maybe she wants more, maybe she would press him, No, what do you think of this place, what do you really think? Or maybe after all it's not the country she wishes him to judge. Maybe the link connecting them, the absent link who disappeared to smoke yet more pot, or kick his innocent car in obstinate rage, or simply stand alone somewhere breathing in the Sabbath air of this enormous Jewish city, maybe she wants an answer for him. Either way, Daniel fails, trying to catch her lively eyes with his own in an effort to communicate that he really is trying, despite the disappointing results.

The front door opens and two people enter, Nadav and a younger man, recognizable to Daniel from Dahlia's wall. This is Kobi. A cousin. He shakes Daniel's hand with great excitement, It is great, man, to meet you, man. His pale head is shaved clean, though the contours of his natural balding remain visible. A small gold loop hangs from each ear, his mostly white shirt is unmistakably tight, he wears strange boots, not quite cowboy boots, not quite anything else. Aftershave applied in a manner well beyond generous. Kobi studies film at the university, Dahlia continues. Great, man, he says again, still shaking the American's hand, smiling and meaning it. Daniel turns to Nadav, whose expression betrays no affiliations, no respon-sibilities whatsoever, their joint entrance merely a coincidence.

Dinner consists of approximately seventeen dishes, most just above room temperature, most nearly tasty. Something with cabbage and tomatoes, something with peppers and olives, something with eggs and noodles. A cow's worth of dairy products, cream cheese, cottage cheese, sour cream, and a few bowls filled with things white that have no names in English. No candles, no prayers, though Dahlia says Shabbat Shalom. Daniel echoes her. Kobi says, Yes. Nadav eats a slice of bread, tearing it into three pieces first.

—I love your movie.

—Thanks. Thanks a lot. Which one?

—You know, what are they calling it?

He turns to Nadav, they confer in Hebrew.

—*Prisoners*? Dahlia offers.

—*Captives*?

—The man with the moustache, you know?

—Yes, *Captives*.

—This is fucking great, I tell you.

—Thanks.

—At the ending, when she shoots in his leg. Man! Where does this come from? Dahlia, did you see this *Captives*?

—No, I am sorry. I will.

—Oh, you must, really.

Daniel smiles at her. You didn't miss much.

—That is bullshit! Hey, you like Tarantino?

—Hmm?

—Tarantino, you like him?

—I thought *Reservoir Dogs* was interesting.

—Yes. And what of *Pulp Fiction*?

—It was okay.

—Okay?! It was fucking great! The fucking greatest, I tell you. Daniel blushes under his beard, grateful for it.

—I am writing a movie like this. Well, not so much like it. Six soldiers that are, how do you say this?

He and Nadav confer again in Hebrew.

—Smuggle, Dahlia offers.

—Yes, they are smuggling the guns and the drugs, near Lebanon, but the movie is not in order.

—Drug-smuggling, gun-running soldiers.

—And a whore, I forget, there is a whore.

—You'll probably be able to get some funding from the government.

—And two are homos.

—Alright.

—But the four not homos don't know this.

—Of course.

—I can show you a scene we shoot already.

—You brought something with you?

—We shoot it when I am doing the *miluim,* how do you say this?

—The reserves.

—Yes, the reserves. My officer is permitting me.

—Um, okay.

—Kobi, Daniel is writing a movie now that I am helping to him.

Kobi responds instantly in Hebrew with a question. Nadav answers him. Another question. Another answer. Back in forth in accelerating Hebrew. Dahlia asks them, in English, to speak English. Daniel drinks more wine, scans the table, tries to recall which of the dishes he liked most.

—Daniel, what do you say, I am helping to you, too, okay?

—Is resting on Shabbat an option?

—Man, you are fucking working on us, I know you are fucking working on us!

Eventually dinner ends. Daniel goes to the bathroom and takes his time. He'd like to finish soon in order to clean up, he'd insist on helping this time, but that would involve interacting with Kobi, who throughout the rest of dinner used the word *fucking* like it had recently been surgically attached to the definite article, like someone was paying him to say it. So he hides for a time, browsing through a Hebrew women's magazine. Near the end, partial nudity.

—Where are Nadav and Kobi?

—I do not know. They no longer request permission.

—Oh.

—Would you like some mint tea?

—Sure, that would be great. What can I do?

—No, please. Just go to relax in the den. You are the guest. Just a moment.

He chooses a slim, black leather recliner. The accompanying end-table and reading lamp, the former piled with magazines, newspapers, and even a small scissors, tell him this is Dahlia's place, but she'd insist all the same. An extremely comfortable chair. A perfect chair. Soft at the surface, but firm below, it holds him flawlessly. Blaming it on the wine, he removes his shoes and puts his feet up on the matching ottoman. Notes to himself that there are no photographs in this part of the apartment. Humming in the kitchen. Need to call home. Quite a chair.

She is spreading a blanket over him. He jerks, startled, embarrassed. Begins to sit forward.

—Shh. Sleep. It is okay.

She has turned off the light. The very top of the city, partially illuminated, stands silent outside the window. The palm of her hand is on his left shoulder, gently pressing it back into the chair, where the rest of him waits heavy and warm, possibly still sleeping. She is close, closer than she's been all evening, but all he can make out is a slight glint across a lip, perhaps another smile. He wishes she'd keep her palm on his shoulder. Then something almost melodic in Hebrew, he can hear the aging flesh of her mouth making the sounds. He thinks to nod, to agree, but is already unconscious again.

—Yo! Daniel, man, you are, you are gonna, yo!

The lights are on, Dahlia's voice, loud, comes racing in from somewhere else. Nadav responds. Then Kobi. They argue. Daniel tries to open his mouth, though not to speak. In his dream, the first he's had in days, Zack had a beard, had Daniel's beard, though he was no more than eight years old.

The three Israelis come toward him. No one has stopped talking since they started. Nadav addresses him:

—Daniel, we make some of the movie. The next part. Okay? We show you. Okay?

His mother reprimands her son.

—Not now, Nadav. What are you doing? And then some Hebrew.

Kobi is in the far corner, cords in his hand, a large digital video camera resting on top of the nearby television. He appears to know what he's doing. Nadav continues addressing Daniel, while Dahlia stands between them, blocking the American from her son's view.

More Hebrew, all of it contentious. Finally, Daniel gets his mouth open.

—Dahlia, it's alright. It's alright.

—I am sorry, Daniel, no, it is not alright. It is rude. It is very rude. I am sorry for this.

—Never mind.

—See, Ima?

—No, this is not okay, what you are doing. He was sleeping. With jet lag, you wake him up. Not okay!

—Please, Dahlia, don't worry about it. I'm awake. It's alright.

—I bring some tea. I am sorry.

—Nadav.

—My mother is a pain in the ass.

—But you're a saint.

—You will like this.

—What?

—We make the next part of the movie. Now we show it to you.

Kobi, clapping his hands with excitement, says something from the corner.

A close-up of Nadav, his face unevenly lit. The digital image filled with patches of shadows, some like dark puddles. He is upset. Looks down. Closes his large eyes. Opens them, looks back up, turns to the right.

—Get out. Get out from the car!

The beginning of some Hebrew.

A line across the screen. Then it's blue. Then Nadav, in close-up, his face partially lit. Upset. Looks down. Exhales. Bites his lip. Turns his whole body to the right.

—Get out, get out from the fucking car!

A line. A blue screen. Kobi, shot through the window, sitting behind the steering wheel, smoking a cigarette, mildy concerned at most. Off screen, Nadav:

—Get out from the fucking car!

And then again. And then Kobi, removing the cigarette:

—Get in the car. What if the police are coming?

—Get out from the fucking car!

The frame drops for a moment. Nadav says, Shit. A line, a blue screen.

—Get into the car. The police are coming!

—Get out from the fucking car!

A small black gun enters the frame.

—Fucking get out!

Dahlia makes a sound. Starts screaming at her son. Kobi rushes to the TV and freezes the image. Nadav screams at his mom. Says, quite loudly, what sounds like the word *die*. She stands up but doesn't leave. Kobi rewinds a bit.

—Fucking get out!

—No.

The gun moves closer, the frame dips, then rises.

—Get the fuck out! We can't leave this thing. They will use the bullet and find that it is my weapon.

—This is not my problem.

A couple of lines and blue screens. The ground, for a second. Then the frame pointing toward the car again, but it's a wider shot, coming from below, the car at least twenty feet away. The lighting is different, even poorer. Kobi behind the wheel, Nadav enters the picture, his enormous foot stepping into the frame from above. He recedes toward the car, pauses for a minute, then takes out the gun and points it at Kobi, who says, faintly

—This is not my problem.

Nadav quickly stuffs the gun into the back of his pants, opens the car door, yanks Kobi out, pushes him onto the hood of the car, and punches him.

—I am making it your fucking problem.

Dahlia makes another sound, then speaks. Kobi rushes back to the TV.

—No more, not here. I do not want to see this anymore.

—Ima, we are almost finishing.

—No.

And then more Hebrew, though no one screams. Finally, Dahlia addresses Daniel.

—Daniel, it was a pleasure meeting you.

—Thanks for having me.

—Perhaps we will see each other again before you travel home?

—Sure, I'd like that.

She stands up, limps away. Daniel gets up and follows her.

—Hold on, guys, let me use the bathroom.

He stops her in the hallway.

—Dahlia, I'm sorry about this.

—What? She doesn't smile.

—I don't know. For falling asleep like that. For the movie.

—You don't apologize.

He extends his hand to her, and she takes it. He thanks her again. They kiss one another on the cheek, her face, which smells like a flower or a berry, pressing into his beard. She asks, before pulling back all the way, How is Nadav?

Daniel pauses, still holding her hand, the skin loose.

—You know, I like him. Trying to sound sanguine all of a sudden.

—But how is he? How are you finding him?

He pauses, she hasn't let go of his hand.

—I'm sure he's going to be fine.

—But he is not now? Yes?

—I don't know. Hard to say.

—Can you say something to him?

—What?

Pause.

—What would you like me to say? Not sarcastic, not even rhe-torical.

—I do not know. Remind to him that he was close to, to, eh, his plan—

—His plan?

Pause.

—Not important. Just say to him, will you tell him, that he, you know. She smiles. Releases his hand and looks down.

—No problem, I'll give him a little pep talk.

—He is so smart, the smartest boy in school.

—I don't doubt it.

Nadav appears in the doorway.

—*Ya'alla*, Daniel.

She kisses his cheek again and disappears. It was lavender.

The two men walking away from the camera, which again shoots from the ground, heading toward a slight, dark mound on a small dune spotted with the long blades of a grassy weed. They stop in front of the mound and stand motionless for a few seconds. Kobi turns around and jogs toward the camera, kneels, and extends his arm. A line, a blue screen. A dog. A dead dog. A German shepherd, but a mutt, its ears oversized, its snout strangely rounded, lies still, eyes closed, dried blood on its ears and neck.

—What the fuck?

—Wait, Daniel, you will see.

A line, a blue screen. Nadav bending over, grabbing the dog's corpse below the shoulders, struggling under its possibly imagined weight. A line, a blue screen. Kobi, cigarette in mouth, bending over, grabbing the dog around the thighs. Speaks in Hebrew, releases the dog, waves his hand. A line, a blue screen. Kobi, cigarette in mouth, bending over, grabbing the dog around the ankles. A line, a blue screen. From the ground up, the two men carry the dog's fairly stiff body toward the car, which waits with trunk open. They drop it into the trunk, a minor thud. Kobi turns around and jogs toward the camera, kneels, and extends his arm. A line, a blue screen. A close-up of the dog in the trunk. Almost the entire frame is black, just a couple spots of light reflecting here and there off its black, black lips. Nadav speaks in Hebrew. Kobi responds. A line, a blue screen. A close-up of the dog in the trunk, the lighting improved. A dead dog, blood around its neck and the back of its head, in the trunk of the car, for ten long seconds. A line, a blue screen. Nadav inside the car, staring straight ahead, wiping what might be blood off his hand.

—Now what, you asshole?

Kobi off screen:

—I am leaving the bodies. I do not know, asshole.

—Well, this body you are taking.

—To where?

—I do not know. You are planning this, so tell me.

—I did not plan this.

—Fuck. Fuck!

A line, a blue screen. Kobi inside the car, hand on the steering wheel, smoking a cigarette. Nadav off screen:

—Now what, fucking asshole?

—I don't know. I am leaving bodies, asshole.

—This one you are taking.

—Where?

—I do not know. This is your plan, you tell me.

—I did not plan this.

—Fuck. Fuck! Fuck!!

A line, a blue screen that stays blue. Kobi walks toward the television and turns it off. The apartment turns dark, but then gradually begins to glow with a soft light, coating everything in a faint, yellowish ochre. Kobi, grinning, hands in pockets, walks up to Daniel's chair.

—How are you liking it?

—Interesting.

—No. Tell us.

—It's interesting. It is.

—Not so bad, no?

Daniel looks at Nadav. A couple of minutes later, after giving Kobi his e-mail address, Daniel announces, You know, guys, I'm sorry, but it's way past my bedtime.

15

Though they've expanded it modestly over the last decade or so, nationalizing Friday afternoon and even Friday morning in most cases, officially the Israeli weekend is a brief affair. Mercilessly, biblically brief. Sunday may as well be a Tuesday as far as Tel Aviv is concerned. Which leaves the tail end of Friday as the only night of the week not brushing up against a routinely sobering morning of alarm clocks, coffee, and unappealing trips to the office. So they've learned to make the most of it, this Friday night, the Israelis have. Without the luxury of a weekend night run-through, without the option of turning in early on Friday to refuel for some serious bingeing on Saturday, the secular Israeli has no choice but to dive headlong into Sabbath eve's shallow pool of freedom. And so he does. As Nadav's car tunnels back into the city during what would seem to be a rather late hour, the still-dense traffic suggests that from some other, more immediate points of view, things are just getting under way. The air, nearly cool, encourages the lowering of windows, releasing music, laughter, raised voices, and cigarette smoke into the night. The faces in these cars are mostly young, with a high concentration of young men sporting close-cropped dark hair. Recently, and temporarily, liberated from their uniforms, they are unapologetically focused on the task at hand, that of living it up, of letting loose, of eating and drinking and smoking and dancing and scheming and hugging and cursing and kissing and screaming and brawling and screwing and forgetting themselves altogether, of letting all of whatever's left of them hang out in its entirety, if only for the sake of verifying that something, some endangered part of them, remains available for this most vital of purposes. In short, the mass migration to the city's center, which began hours ago and will continue for hours to come, is that of a populace that in the area of fucking around does not have time to fuck around. Self-restraint, inhibitions, second-guessing, anticipated regret, repression of any sort will just have to wait until Sunday, all this, depending on whom you ask, being either Zionism's greatest achievement or an entirely unintended side effect.

Not so the travelers in Nadav's car. They've been on the road for over twenty minutes now, inching along, watching each traffic light change a half-dozen times or more before passing through, surrounded on every side by legions of revelers, but not a word between them. Nadav stares straight ahead, the various parts of his mouth occasionally moving for reasons unclear. Daniel is slouched against the door, arms crossed at his chest. He wants to sleep, both for the sake of sleep and in order to escape from the present, external reality of the car's interior, but his discomfort and concern and general annoyance keep him awake. So the two simmer while the minutes pass them by, the abbreviated weekend evaporating before their very eyes. Not that either has anything pressing to do come Sunday morning. Finally:

—You know, you are not treating nice to Kobi.

—How's that?

—You are not being nice to Kobi.

—You're giving me pointers on manners?

—He is so excited to know you.

—The way you treat your mother, and you're coming to me with complaints about my effort to survive Kobi Ben Tarantino?

—He is worshiping you. This is his dream, you know this.

—Tell me something, is your mom that unbearable?

—You can help him with the connections in Hollywood, but you just ignore from him.

—Because she seemed awfully kind and patient and even loving from what I could see. But you treat her like some royal bitch.

—The scenes we are making are great.

—You argue with her, you disappear, you don't help out, and then you burst in screaming so you can force her to watch you picking up a dog's corpse.

—This is a great scene.

—Whatever.

—What does this say, *whatever*?

—Whatever.

—Whatever what?

—It means, it means it's alright, but that's it.

—Alright? Just alright?

—Honestly, I wasn't that impressed.

—Oh, you are being so full of the shit, you know this.

—Are you suggesting I missed something?

—There was nothing to be missing. This is why it is a good scene. There are the two men and the body. And the blood. And we are showing it, for many seconds we are showing the body. This is what the movie now is about, and so then we show it.

—It's not what the movie is about.

—No?

—No.

—Yes. But yes. It is.

—It's not about a body. It's not one more fucking movie about where to hide the body.

—You have a body in the movie, you must put it somewhere.

—Who says that's what's going to happen? Zacky?

—Tzachi he is called. And it was something of an idea.

—Whatever.

—Again this *whatever.*

—Look, this movie is about whether or not it might be justifiable for someone to kill people, even people who may have it coming. That's the idea, anyway. It's bigger than where to put a body.

—When he starts killing them, then it no longer is just an idea. Then there are bodies that are now dead.

—Why do you treat your mom like shit?

—And you must find a place for them.

—Why do you treat your mom like shit? You can't stand being in the same room as her.

—Why are you not calling your family?

—I've called them.

—Yes. How much times?

—I don't know, three or four times.

—I remember only there is one time.

—I've called when you were asleep.

—So four, we will say four. You are lying, but we will say four. Even this number is not so much. You are rich, it is not because of the money. You go to a place your family is thinking is very dangerous, but you are not every day calling them. If I am you, I am calling more.

—How did they die?

—Who?

—Who? You know.

—Tell me.

—What is this place?

—I have to throw something.

—Why are we stopping?

—You can help or you cannot. It is not mattering to me.

—What are you doing? Where are you going?

Daniel gets out of the car. Follows Nadav to the trunk. Nadav opens it.

—Nadav. What the fuck? We've been driving with this fucking

thing in the back the whole time? Why the hell did you keep it in the trunk? Jesus.

—Kobi think he saw a police coming, so we shut the trunk and go. Will you help to me?

—Jesus, it really stinks.

—Take the legs. No, here.

—Fuck, Nadav, this is really fucking nasty.

—Do not talk like this about one of your players. The dog, she is giving a great performance, yes?

—We're just putting the thing in a dumpster?

—But instead what?

—I don't know. But just throwing it out.

—If you like, perhaps we are driving away from the city to a field. We get one of those, what are you calling it?

—A shovel?

—Yes, a shovel. And we make a hole and are putting her in it. And when we are finally finishing the sun is back in the morning sky. This is like a movie, no? It is very dramastic.

—Dramatic.

—There is no word *dramastic*?

—Or drastic.

—Not dramastic?

—No.

—There should be.

—I'll be sure to put it in the suggestion box when I get back to the States.

—Do you want to do this?

—Do you have a shovel?

—No.

—No shovel, no hole.

—We can make the effort to get one.

—It's almost midnight.

—We are in a nation of farmers and pioneers. We can find a shovel.

—What do you think?

—I drive us to the dumpster, this is my opinion.

—You think it was someone's pet?

—Is this making a difference?

—Man, what is that smell?

—I do not know the word in English. Her body is beginning to no longer be a body, yes?

—It's disgusting.

—You are not being around dead bodies often times.

—And you are?

—Come. Let us throw this. If a police is coming, we will become, eh, very tied up.

—You didn't answer.

—Come. I answer to you in the car.

—Damn, it's heavy.

—Yes.

—How are we going to—

—Put your hand there. I will count. When I am saying three, up and inside. One, two, and three.

—Shit. Sounds like the dumpster is empty.

—Come.

—Should we say something?

—Something?

—Yeah, I don't know. Like a prayer or something.

—For the dog?

—Yeah, like the mourner's *Kaddish*.

—Are you mourning for her?

—That's just what it's called.

—Do you know it?

—Some of it. A little. You don't?

—I do, mostly. But I don't want.

—Me neither. But we should say something.

—So say it.

—Alright.

—Sorry.

—This is all?

—I guess.

—*Ya'alla.*

—So how did they die?

—Who?

—Your father and your brother.

—Okay. My dad dies in 1973, in the Yom Kippur War. In Sinai. Second-highest ranked soldier who is being killed. My brother.

—What?

—He killed himself.

—Ah, shit, Nadav.

—Never mind.

—No, I'm really sorry. Shit.

—It is funny, almost. When he dies, my brother, it is such a bad time in the country. Always there are being very severe terror attacks then. And my brother, he is first commando, and then officer, and then, what do you call it, head, no, bodyguard, and then he is going to the reserves in dangerous places, and when he is back he is saying, no, I will keep traveling on the bus, and then he dies, not from the terrorist, but from himself. He decides, I think, to kill himself.

—Sorry.

—Though maybe it is not so funny.

———————

—What was he like?

—It is late.

—C'mon.

—He is funny. I am more funny, but he is funny also. Excellent in football, I mean soccer. He is the good one, you know. I am the disappointed one. I complain. He is silent.

—And then he kills himself. Damn, Nadav.

—Sometime I think I knew this could be, sometimes I don't. I am so smart, but this I don't see. When we talk, it is about my problems.

—When was this?

—Four years ago. Almost four years.

16

—**Hello.**

—Caroline?

—Yes.

—Huh, it didn't sound like you. You sounded different.

—It's me.

—Hi.

—Hi.

—So what's up?

—Nothing new.

—Where are you?

—Where am I? Home. You called the house.

—No, I mean where in the house.

—In the laundry room.

—Right. I'm on the balcony of my room.

—So how's Zack?

—Fine, I suppose. At Caleb's.

—He's been there a lot recently.

—What can I tell you, I'm very busy.

—No, I just mean it's great he's got such a good friend.

———————

—Everything okay?

—What?

—Everything okay? You sound, I don't know, like something's up.

—Nothing major. Running late, again. Got a second job heating up, this one's going to be a real pain.

—Who's the client?

—You don't know them. Not industry people.

—You'll be fine.

—Let's hope.

—Caroline?

—Huh.

—I'm so tired.

—Leaving your family behind to travel to a war zone can be exhausting.

—C'mon, Caroline, I mean it. I don't think I've slept more than ten hours since I got here. It's three in the morning, and I'm out on the balcony because I can't sleep, again.

—Have you tried napping during the day?

—Nadav won't let me.

—Look, Daniel, I gotta run.

—Care, if I don't get some sleep soon, I don't know what I'm going to do. I'm lightheaded. My teeth ache, I swear to god, my teeth ache I'm so tired. My vision has been clouding over with something white every time I stand up or move suddenly. What am I going to do?

—What do you mean, what are you going to do? Do what everyone else does, Daniel. Say good-bye to me, hang up, walk to your bed, and lie down.

—Can you give me Zack's cell number?

—I don't remember it offhand, it's stored in my phone.

—Can you go get it?

—I'll have him call you.

—You will?

—Yes, he'll call.

—Alright.

—I gotta go.

—Please have him call me.

—Bye, Daniel.

—Hey, wait. How's Alfred?

—What?

—The dog, how is he?

—Fine. Old. He pissed on the kitchen floor yesterday morning.

—Alfred. I miss him.

—Bye, Daniel.

—I miss him, I do.

—Bye.

—Alright, bye.

17

A couple of mornings later a faint metallic click wakes Daniel, who only three hours earlier was down on the strip, an insomniac drinking a not-so-horrible Israeli beer after being swiped by an impassive security guard's flat metal wand at the bar's entrance. Now he lifts his furry, rumpled head, already amused by how little it takes to rouse him. He turns to Nadav's bed, expecting to find him asleep, if only to augment his self-pity, but the bed is empty.

—Nadav?

Another click, coming from the door leading out to the hallway. Daniel gets out of bed, wraps a sheet around his waist, hurries to the door, opens it, and sees Nadav heading toward the elevators.

—Nadav.

The Israeli stops, but hesitates before turning around.

—Nadav.

He takes a couple of steps toward Daniel and stops.

—In a few hours I'm coming back.

—Where are you going?

—I leave you a note.

—Where?

—Next to your head, not far from the light.

—What did it say? Where are you going?

—Go to sleep. I am sorry that I wake you.

Daniel steps out into the hall, turning the lock to keep the door open.

—Nadav, what's up?

Finally the guide walks the rest of the distance back to the tourist. His hair is still wet in places, he's recently shaved, two roundish red spots below his jaw on the right side. Shirt tucked in.

—To the cemetery.

—To the cemetery? How come?

—Please, Daniel, go to sleep.

—Who's at the cemetery?

—Today, it is the fourth year of Gal's death.

—Your brother.

—Yes.

—Sorry.

—Never mind.

Daniel, still holding the sheet to his waist, looks up and down the hall. It's empty, but nevertheless. He takes Nadav's elbow and leads him back into their room.

—Do you mind if I come?

—It is not necessary.

—I know, but, your mom will be there, right?

—Of course.

—I'd like to, it'd mean a lot to me.

He has no idea what this sentence means.

—You can do what you like, but if I am you I am staying and resting.

In the bathroom, Daniel quickly wets his face, hair, and armpits, runs a damp towel over and around his scrotum, brushes his teeth. While emptying his bladder, partially onto the floor despite his four decades of practice, he feels the refreshing qualities of this recent effort to clean himself instantly evaporate. Turning to leave, he bangs a knuckle on the underside of the marble countertop. He examines his hand, a small oval of bright blood where skin used to be. He is rotting from fatigue, parts of him, possibly the entire system coordinating sensory input and motor response is beginning to malfunction.

In the elevator, Daniel leans in toward Nadav and inhales.
—You didn't smoke.
Nadav continues to stare straight ahead.
—No.

—Does it feel different?
—What?
—Not smoking.
—No. Not so much today.

—It is for my mother.

In the lobby Nadav suddenly stops.
—You will need a hat. Do you have one?
—No, just my sunglasses.
—Come.
They head to the gift shop. A couple of minutes later they exit, Daniel now the owner of a khaki fisherman's hat with the word *Israel* in different-colored English letters across the front. It was all they had in his size.

Driving south, first on the big highway, then on a major surface street. The sun, already hot, pours in from Nadav's side of the car, their sunglasses barely making a difference. The street is lined with white apartment block after white apartment block, four or five stories each, recessed balconies, their plastic shutters closed. Some are off-white, or tan. The development remains dense here, but not quite so crowded. No more streets lined with cars parked half-up on the curb, the intersections have become more generous. Laundromats, a post office, bakeries, a large drugstore. Compared to Tel Aviv, the pedestrians are varied, more elderly and children, a little darker as an aggregate. They strike Daniel, somehow, as utterly normal, profoundly typical. Nadav is silent, the radio is off. Daniel closes his eyes, feels a line of sweat run diagonally down his chest. Can't sleep. Opens his eyes, looks at Nadav.

—Hey, Nadav, you want to try and figure out an ending for the movie later?

Nadav turns to him, no change in his expression, then turns back to the road.

—Perhaps. We will see.

Daniel closes his eyes again.

After Nadav parks, he removes a large piece of cardboard from his trunk, unfolds it, and inserts the plain rectangle inside the windshield. The asphalt of the parking lot smolders. The entrance stands some hundred feet away. Through it Daniel sees some white gravestones, but it's difficult to make much out with the people everywhere. Most are going in, a couple are heading out, while a few groups stand and wait. Nearby there's some sort of small, flimsy booth with a religious man in front. A number of stray cats, most undernourished, claim the dwindling shade against the outer wall. A kiosk selling flowers and bottles of water.

Their group is to the right of the kiosk, most everyone has arrived. Daniel sees Dahlia, then Kobi and a dozen others, a few he recognizes from the photographs. Two men must be well into their eighties, canes, handkerchiefs, matching straw hats. Nadav greets his mother, Hi, Ima, they kiss each other, she wraps her left arm around his back. Daniel shakes Kobi's hand, Kobi smiles, touches Daniel's hat, says, Nice. Dahlia calls out the American's name. She grasps his hand and smiles, slightly. He is introduced to most of them, two cousins, an aunt, an uncle, a couple of friends, their names immediately forgotten. Three more people arrive, including a very old woman. Daniel stands at the edge, then drifts over to the kiosk and buys two large bottles of water covered in condensation. Suddenly his phone rings, peeling him away from the group. He thinks to answer, almost midnight in LA, but feels it's inappropriate, so he turns the thing off instead. Looks back at their party, disturbed by the thought, What's my motivation here? Obviously, it isn't about him. So he'll simply be here, solemn, respectful, a utility man, offering to buy bottles of water and fulfilling other sundry tasks that may surface. Nothing more. Nadav will notice, as will Dahlia, and maybe, somehow, that will make them feel better, or at least a little less worse. The sun is ruthless. Nadav stands near Kobi, five relatives and a family friend from his mother.

Through the entrance and inside. The group heads down a central path, still wide enough for two or three across, Dahlia hobbling steadily in front, Nadav not far from Daniel. The outsider brings up the rear, sipping absentmindedly from the water, both here and not, nearly excited to be nearing the final destination, until he gets his first look at the graveyard itself, one giving rise to a bristly chill that runs down his neck and spreads out along his shoulders. He shudders, wanting to turn back. All he can see is white stone, flat and boxy, for a half mile or more in every direction. He hasn't seen an open space like this since the trip up north. How many? One hundred thousand? Two hundred thousand? A quarter million? The great Israeli necropolis. Row after row in nearly straight lines, like a farmer's field, an occasional irregular or oversized shrine disrupting the dense, uniform grid, the land rising modestly in a few places. The graves nearly touch one another, in this overcrowded land death is no different, because they're above ground, the tombs. Instead of a simple headstone, a marker for the dead body but thankfully separate from and merely suggestive of it, each tomb here includes both a headstone and a large raised rectangle, containing, Daniel can only assume, the body itself, or whatever is left of it. Or maybe, hopefully, not. Were his guide, now wading into the vast white burial ground, not presently spoken for, Daniel would ask for, would demand, an explanation. How come? Why? What for? The explanation can't be solely Jewish, since among the Jews back in the U.S. it's just an upright slab, isn't it? Vertical slabs and grass. The group turns off the main path, heading, according to the still-rising sun, his neck is blazing, due west, walking now in single file. Vertical slabs and soothing, calming, pastorally reassuring grass back in the States. The ground here, what little of it remains unclaimed by heavy white stone, is plain brown earth that's already beginning to cover his shoes. Not a single tree in sight, nothing more than the occasional neglected, overgrown shrub. They stop. The elderly, and some of the not so elderly, remove their hats, wipe their brows, rest against their canes, drink from the bottles. Daniel looks intently at the nearest grave, wonders if it might belong to Gal, looks like a pinball machine with the legs chopped off. An awful lot of trash everywhere. His effort to make eye contact with Nadav fails, since the guide stares out in the opposite direction, standing a couple of tombs away from the group. More walking, past a startling plot of children's tombs, miniaturized pinball machines for premature deaths, all clustered together for reasons unclear. Past five more rows, ten rows, twenty rows, past the occasional group, small or large, assembled here today because their son or father or husband or uncle or daughter or mother or wife or aunt or cousin or friend died on or around the same day, probably according to the Jewish calendar, that Gal died. They aren't stopping, how are the old men and that woman able to continue, especially in this, the ugliest, hottest, most cramped place he's ever been? His head seems to fall forward every few steps, not as if he's falling asleep, but as if he's falling. Thinks briefly about the agent and the assassin. Tries not to. Says to himself, It's for Nadav, for later, the rest of him unconvinced. But still, all he can think, a thought-question that refuses to budge or evolve in any way, One of them has to die, does one of them have to die?

Finally they stop again, one of these graves must belong to Gal. The tombs are so close together it's not until everyone has found a place to stand that Daniel can be sure which is his. The group spills out along all sides, with a few of them, including Daniel, forced to stand a death or two away, looking out at Gal's tomb from beyond the monument to someone else altogether, an ex-body or two between him and this massive substitute for Nadav's brother. And indeed, among the largest of the black letters carved into the upright slab, at the far right where the name most likely begins, is the Hebrew letter *gimel*. Daniel recognizes it from the face of a dreidel, it's a letter that has something to do with Hanukah as well. Must make the *G* sound. Dahlia stands at the base of the tomb, her black hair pulled back under a tan hat, her mouth held together tight, her eyes, like everyone else's, hidden behind sunglasses. Nadav is up near the lettering.

For a moment, for more than a moment, everyone is silent, a few remove hats and wipe off sweat. Daniel looks back toward the entrance, they've walked at least a quarter mile and are perhaps only halfway to the far wall. Not a sea of death, just a very large and very dense lake of it. One of the old men begins to speak. Or sing. He chants something. Daniel wonders if he is hearing some of the *Kaddish*, but the recitation is only partially audible and even Daniel can detect a marked accent. A woman, a youngish woman, late twenties perhaps, effortlessly beautiful like just about every other woman in this country, removes a piece of paper, unfolds it, and begins reading, her Hebrew soft and steady. Most likely a poem. She cries near the end, two or three tears her left thumb quickly erases not long after they reach her cheek. More silence. A middle-aged woman sings, two others join in, all three taper off. Dahlia removes her sunglasses, her eyes nearly impassive, and calls to Nadav. He turns to her, doesn't move, remains silent. She says, Bo, extends her hand, which seems to quiver against the hot air. The people between them look at one another, until an uncle and then two cousins step back, forcing another four people behind them to relocate, the creation of a seven-foot path for Nadav requiring the coordinated effort of a half-dozen others. He finally walks toward her, she takes his hand, pulls him close, rests her head on his upper arm and begins weeping softly, a slight tremble in her left shoulder. Nadav's face is still. He removes his sunglasses, slowly places them above the brim of his hat, scratches briefly at a spot behind his neck. A moment later, standing at the base of the oblong stone box containing and/or marking his only sibling, he takes his arm, places it around his mother, half of whose tears are now absorbed into his shirt, and very slowly closes his eyelids around his enormous eyes. At which point Daniel begins crying, uncontrollably.

He doesn't see it coming, it just comes. He turns and begins walking away swiftly, soon turning in the opposite direction of the tomb and thus away from the group's probable gaze, calling upon his quickly dwindling reserves of self-control in order not to run, in order to make it seem that nothing out of the ordinary is afoot. But not ten seconds after he senses something rushing to the surface, he's deep, deep within it, well past deciding whether or not he should cry, well past maybe crying, well past knowing why he's crying, well past just taking a deep breath and collecting himself, well past being able to respond appropriately to his knowledge that while now is not the time, it is, undeniably, the place, to begin unraveling in this way, well past having any say in the matter at all. He's been seized by something, a sudden, pronounced reaction to the introduction, in large quantities, of a potent and possibly dangerous foreign body into his system, and only through enormous effort does he succeed in withdrawing quickly, almost violently, from the group, turning, then walking swiftly, and soon simply running through the heat toward a patch of tombs without visitors, until deciding, if that's the word, that he's far enough away to unclench his jaw, at which point a noise comes out that is technically a moan, but could well be confused with the sound a person makes when emptying his stomach through his mouth.

Now he's on the ground, parts of him touching the back of one tomb and the front of another. His legs just won't support him any longer, so most of his weight falls into his knees, the rest into his right hand. A small part of him resurfaces for an instant, a part that expects the rest of him to follow, a part that could be the beginning of him recognizing that this was just an episode, this recognition synonymous with his awareness of the episode ending, this part then supposedly the leading tip of the inevitable and surely imminent process of Daniel reassembling himself. Only just as fast this small part disappears, sinking back into the blur of the still-swelling episode, which obliterates Daniel's instinctive effort to draw himself out of its expanding reach. Soon nothing that is Daniel is beyond it, which from an outsider's perspective translates into a grown man convulsing on the ground in a graveyard, half on his side, half on his front, his damp, nearly muddy face buried in his right arm. His insides are in the process of becoming undifferentiated, as whatever it was exactly that first set him off now conquers and colonizes every last bit of him, an uprising flattening the typically well-policed boundaries separating the various regions of his self into fairly ordered and thus relatively manageable territories, such that soon Daniel is crying about, the following presentation being regrettably, but necessarily, linear and thus essentially arbitrary: his work, his wife, his fear, his father, the script, his marriage, his son, the specter of divorce, his future estrangement from his son, his exhaustion, his loneliness, his helplessness, the state of the world, his place in the world, his guilt, his shame, his relative good fortune, his failure to believe in God, his stubborn mortality, his obvious limits as a storyteller, and his inability to be someone else, ever. This lasts between two and three very long minutes.

Throughout most of this time Daniel is convinced, to the extent that he can form any opinion about the matter, that he is in fact getting further and further from the very possibility of gaining control of himself, as his sense of himself, his version or understanding of his very own identity, melts into a formless, inchoate sludge of feeling quite bad. It ends only once Daniel is drained of the energy required to sustain such hysteria, in fact, the next stage, brief to be sure, has him falling into unconsciousness for a few seconds. Then he resurfaces again and by way of reflex begins the process of putting himself back together again, starting with his body. He sits up, he wipes his face with his shirt, he takes a number of deep breaths, he looks around. Then he cries again, but only briefly, so he wipes his face again. Eventually he stands up and begins walking toward the entrance. The group is gone, thankfully no one came looking for him, at least no one found him. He begins to take inventory of his inner self, his breath still all over the place, a decidedly unpleasant task when conducted in a cemetery and of a self in such disarray. It's all there for him to see, or understand, the good and the bad, the likely, the regrettable. His marriage is in deep trouble, his relationship with his son totters on weakening legs, he's an overpaid hack, the world is a growing disaster, and the most he can do is get rich riffing on people's possibly ironic desire to have their collective sense of doom translated into ninety minutes of overproduced, nonsensical violence.

He makes out the group as it nears the entrance, a good hundred and fifty yards from him. He's really trying to hold it together, to come up with an explanation, but neither project is going well. Were there a little red button to push, one that would instantly relocate him to a random site anywhere else on the planet, he'd take his chances, such is his interest in facing Nadav, Dahlia, and everyone else. Now he's crying again. He doesn't want to hold anyone up, but neither does he want to face any more people than absolutely necessary, so he buys some time, turns his back to the entrance and works on his breathing.

A few minutes later he decides he's reached a semistable plateau on the long trek to composure and heads toward the entrance. Thankfully, only Nadav and Dahlia remain. He takes another deep breath and once he's within twenty feet of them tries to put on a playful, self-deprecating smile, but just like that his shoulders begin bouncing and shaking and soon he's falling apart all over again. Despite his pure humiliation, Daniel accepts Dahlia's invitation and collapses into the offer of her embrace. She holds him, rubbing his back, which heaves. Eventually he pulls away and begins talking or sputtering, his nose dripping.

—I'm so sorry. I don't know what happened. I haven't been sleeping much—

—It is okay, this is what happens sometimes.

—Nadav, man, I'm sorry. I guess you're right, I should have stayed back—

—Forget from it. It is nothing.

And back and forth like this for a minute more, Nadav patting his shoulder throughout. They get him some water. He drinks, he splashes his face, he takes some deep breaths, he says, Whooo, loudly, he decides it's over. They walk Dahlia to her car, where he hugs her again and apologizes once more. She just looks at him, smiles, and reaches out to his face.

—What is this that you are growing here?

—I don't know.

—You will decide. Good-bye, Daniel.

They walk to Nadav's car and then stand next to it while Nadav tries to cool it down.

—I feel like a total idiot, Nadav.

—No, this is the idea, to be sad. You are doing an excellent job. I think you make my mother happy.

—Sorry.

—Not important.

Nadav removes his phone.

—Who you calling?

—The man who sells me the grass. He lives on the path home.

Daniel remembers his phone, removes it from his pants, and turns it back on. Three messages. The first voice is Deb, Caleb's mother, Caroline's best friend:

—Daniel, hi, this is Deb. Everything's okay, but, but Caroline's been in an accident. She'll be okay, but please call here as soon as you can. Bye, Daniel.

LOS ANGELES

This time no more lofty words about humanity, this time it's in your hands. This time it's not someone else's wickedness, this time it's on your conscience. Let him go and you've saved him. Today the choice, that terrible and great choice, the one we always spoke about with such awe, all of it sits in your two hands. This time there's no escape in "soldier" or "order" or "what if they catch you?" or even "what will my comrades say?" Naked you stand facing your duty. All of it is yours.

—S. YIZHAR,
"The Captive"

—**I want** a divorce.

—Oh.
—I do.

—Alright.

What he sees. His wife of sixteen years, in a hospital bed. His wife, pale and puffy, almost virginally pale, except for the long bruise that connects jaw, cheek, and forehead on her left. The lighting is poor on that side, the window is to her right, so it's hard to know what's shadow and what's bruise. Based on what he can recall from the proximity of his initial stunned cautious embrace, most of it is bruise. Swollen either way, though not quite freakishly so. Not quite. She'd call it freakish. Bluish green hospital gown. Tube running out of her right hand and up toward the IV sack, which drips steady. Her nails are professionally colored a very light red. Left leg in full cast, from thigh to ankle, the tips of her toes unpainted. She looks extremely clean.

—Your beard is hideous.
—I know.

———

—I'm not mad at you.

—Okay.

He has a stomachache. Not nausea or gas. Not some vague discomfort. It hurts. Might not be his stomach. One of his organs, just below his ribs, hurts, as if there is something sticking into his middle. Plus his hands, if he tries raising them off his lap, shake.

—I could be. I suppose I am. But that's not the point.

—Care, I'm so sorry.

—But once I recover, I don't think we should stay together. We know what's possible for us, and I don't want that.

—Well.

He knows he's done traveling for now. For over thirty hours he was struggling westward, struggling in foreign airports, struggling at thirty-six thousand feet, struggling at passport control, asking and double-checking and trying another desk and calling international offices and wondering, during a seven-hour German layover, what else he could be doing to obtain a single seat anywhere on one of the many planes flying its human cargo to New York. All that pushing, almost none of it physical, aimed at nothing more and nothing less than transporting his body from a cemetery in Israel to this very hospital room. He should stop now, should forget about the cruelty of his meaningless impatience while waiting in a purposeless line, and those affectless European clocks that display ridiculous times like 21:47, and the fifteen times he locked himself in an aseptic German bathroom stall to cry once more, and the scandal of his weary determination to find a phone willing to talk to his credit card, and the near comedy of his glaring inability to influence the thousands of other things that proved to be beyond his control, he should stop concentrating on wanting to be somewhere else, and just be here, caring, finally, for his badly injured wife, even though she no longer wants to be.

—Now that I'm not dead, I want to live. You know?

He nods. He's concentrating with everything he's got on not cry-ing. Not because it would be inappropriate, because at the least it would be understandable, and not because at least some of him doesn't want to, because it does, just because he has this pretty clear sense that it would be even worse this time. Daniel retreats quickly from the already tangled sources of his exhaustion, pain, misery, fear, and shame, only to find that they're tangled and scattered, tangled and scattering, then suddenly snowballing and heading right back toward the him that sits opposite his lucky-to-be-alive, soon-to-be ex-wife, who either is taking advantage of the license one gets to un-ceremoniously broach the unpleasant after having nine titanium screws drilled into one's ankle and knee or is simply articulating what must be said, her near brush with death having thoroughly educated her in how one must live one's only life. He looks at the floor, takes a deep breath, and wipes away a couple tears that broke through his defenses. A small victory.

—We had a good thing for a while, but it's over. Zack is going to be gone soon. I have my career. You have yours. We're not the kind of people who put those aside for the marriage. And that's what it would take. You're not. I know you're not. You can't, Daniel. Fine. I don't hold it against you. I won't anymore. And even then, even if we could, it wouldn't be worth the effort. I wouldn't choose you now, and you wouldn't choose me.

He looks at her now, at her white cast that he can't believe has been formed exclusively to help the five breaks along her left leg heal. Had he ever thought about her bones before?

—How do you feel?
—Numb and achy.
—Shit. Care, I'm sorry. You want to talk about it?
—What? The accident?

—Yes.

—No.

—Can I hold your hand?

—Not right now.

—Alright.

—How's Zack?

—Moved in with Caleb.

—Right.

—How'd he take it?

—Hard to say. He's closed up. I told him I'd be fine.

—Daniel, I'm serious about this. I'm not talking about therapy or counseling or separating. Clean break. That's it. As little negotiating as possible. I'll take less if that's what it means. I'll rent a small place. You can have the house. I don't mind living modestly. I want less. We'll figure out Zack.

—You're sure this is the time and place to make it official? Between us?

—It's official.

—It is?

—Yes.

—This is something you decided here?

—I made it official here. But no, I've been thinking about it for a while. I was thinking about it when the accident happened. I just needed the courage. Now I have it.

—Can I ask why?

—I don't love you. The last year, whenever I said, I love you, every time I said it I realized I was trying to convince myself or encourage myself to believe it.

—I see.

—I want you to be happy. I don't think you're a bad person. But I don't love you. I'm sorry.

—Don't apologize.

—I am.

—Hi, Ma.

—Hey, Margaret.

—Is this a bad time?

—No.

—Daniel, I didn't know if you wanted anything, so I brought you something anyway. I figured you're probably exhausted from the trip.

—Thanks, Marge.

—Look, I'm going to go see Zack. He's at Caleb's, right? I'll bring him back.

He stands up, the pain in his side somehow gone, though his knees buckle briefly. After walking the four cautious steps separating him and Caroline, he leans in to kiss her. For some reason she kisses him back, her lips dry. In the elevator, he puts on sunglasses and cries until the third floor, when they come on with an empty stretcher.

2

He gets lost on the way to Caleb's. Quite lost. Extremely lost. He does not know where he is. Must be west of point A, south of point B, actually, he's less sure about his location in relation to B. Whatever the case, he has no idea how to get to point C, or, more pressing at the moment and certainly related to the earlier information, which exact point, let's call it D, he presently occupies. For seventeen years he's lived in Los Angeles, he's been all over, driven thousands and thousands of miles within this city that so loves, that so demands driving, and now he's absolutely unclear about where he is, doesn't even know the name of this street. First a canyon, then a valley, then an unmarked right, then oblivion. Seems like a fine place to cry.

Strange thing is, Daniel's not entirely sure how he feels, having pulled over onto an unpaved shoulder, about having misplaced himself like this. Certainly not proud, nor would he say it was his plan all along, but as an excuse, an opportunity even, not to be in either of the two uninviting places he ought to be, origin and destination, perhaps this has its advantages. There's shame here, too, in recognizing his reluctance to face Zack, to then support him in a manner sufficiently reassuring, such that his son might be able to confront his mother's suffering in order to then feel whatever it is he might then feel, to, in short, be a father in one of the more expansive senses of the word.

Now's the time, apparently, to be loving, to be patient, to be steady, solid, and strong, to be the sort of man he most certainly is not here on this otherwise placid, tree-lined strip of neglected gravel. Daniel regards himself in the rearview mirror of his anonymous, indifferent rental car. He sees a lost man, an isolated man, a weak man, a weeping man who needs a nap long enough to be measured in days.

Four minutes later, and after first blowing his nose into a napkin he acquired in the Newark airport, he turns the sterile American sedan around and retraces his path, driving, he's almost certain, in the exact opposite direction of Caleb's house, this nevertheless his only reasonable chance of ever reaching his supposed destination. Despite the distinctly first-world character of these northern Los Angeles streets, the wide, smooth lanes, the spacious, ordered intersections, the traffic lights expertly timed by well-trained engineers, he resents having to drive himself and suddenly misses Nadav. Did they hit it off? Perhaps. Did Nadav actually like him? Hard to say, probably. But by the end, at least most of the time, there was something comfortable, comforting even, about getting into that puny white piece of shit and waiting to see where the Israeli might take him next. Turns out passivity suited him.

Once Daniel had finally managed to explain to his guide what had happened, after Nadav silently helped him pack his own bags and aggressively worked the phones to get him on the next flight to Frankfurt, the Israeli, sitting on the hotel bed that he would not sleep in again, spoke, for the first and only time, about how to cope with bad news. There is nothing you can do, he told him, what will make you sad is keeping to look for something to do. He rose, walked to Daniel, who had been standing aimlessly in the middle of the room since they entered almost an hour earlier, put his hand on the visitor's shoulder, squeezed it firmly, and looked right at him, the Israeli's expression momentarily transformed, brow softened, jaw slackened, Nadav's previously incessant effort to produce or maintain his own face suspended for perhaps a second, until Daniel saw, for just an instant, traces of Dahlia in the eyes of her only remaining son. Then he took Daniel to the airport, allowing him to get to within a half hour of Jerusalem. At passport control things got complicated, the outrageous beard, the lone traveler, the obvious signs of distress, the incomprehensible story about why he had come and what he had done and why he was returning right now, and soon he was escorted to a small, windowless office where he sat for fifty slow minutes staring at a giant, expressionless woman in an undersized tan uniform who sat behind an undersized desk and who betrayed only the slightest interest in his papers and even less in him, occasionally talking into her plastic phone, twice summoning a miniature Ethiopian woman into the office for reasons unclear, until finally, without an explanation or an apology or even wishes for a safe trip home, he was given permission to return to his life in the diaspora.

Deb, Caleb's mother, opens the door. She's greeting him warmly before she finishes registering the version of Daniel Bloom about to enter her home. After enduring the fluctuations of their erratic hug, first perfunctory and meaningless, a loose embrace, just the kind of thing friends and parents of friends do around these parts, then focused and sincere, Deb clutching and holding him, her small arms squeezing his bent back, an effort to communicate and act on her recognition of all that has happened, then finally removed and reluctant, a hug endured, her forearms politely resting on his shoulders, this woman having belatedly put man and beard and red eyes and, above all, smell together, recalling as well, perhaps, who knows, her necessary, impending alliance with Caroline, they return awkwardly to their initial positions, attempt to smile, before she finally leads Daniel to his son. Up a flight of stairs, Daniel mindlessly scanning Deb's slight frame and nearly shapeless bottom, her weathered gardening gloves hanging out of a rear pant pocket, her sexuality, such as it is, suddenly a little less off-limits than it used to be, this involuntary, unlikely observation, the first manifestation of his recently altered marital status.

Two aging boys on the floor in beanbag chairs, showering themselves in the sights and sounds of an unmistakably violent and relatively interactive digital world. The obscene volume of their game has prevented them from hearing the stairs or the door, and Daniel gets a split second to examine his son before being noticed. Same dark hair, same round eyes, same full cheeks, his chin, perhaps, beginning to extend out into the world in search of adulthood, his limbs, especially compared to those of his lanky friend, short, almost stubby. Daniel, looking at this person he'd like to consume affectionately, that he'd like to merge with, that he'd like to freeze in order to remove from time, feels his love for Zack rise up. The recently deflated Daniel Bloom begins to inflate, behind his beard something resembling a smile forms. He hopes that this will be enough, though he already knows it will not. As the two look up, he speaks:

—Hey, fellas.

—Dad.

—Hi.

It doesn't quite earn an exclamation point, what Zack said. Enthusiastic, but guarded, and then abruptly muffled near the end, just as he was reaching the final punctuation-determining portion of his utterance, by the sight of his father. Even so, the game is paused and son rises awkwardly from his beanbag, approaches father, and participates in the physical counterpart to their verbal greeting. Another hug, simpler, though incomplete, the younger of the two Blooms pulling back just as Daniel notes the mature nature of Zack's body odor. His son smells like a Greek salad beginning to spoil. Daniel imagines he's likely rancid altogether.

—How you doing, big guy?

—Alright.

—I just saw Mom.

—Yeah?

—Yes, how is she, Daniel?

—You know, okay. She's going to be alright.

—Yeah, I know.

—Good, good. Right.

—Daniel?

—Yeah, Caleb?

—Your beard's nuts.

—I know.

—It's really nuts.

—Caleb.

—It's alright, Deb. I'll probably shave it when I get back to the house.

—No, good nuts.

—Well, thanks. Zack.

—Yeah?

—I mean you sort of look like a homeless guy.

—Caleb, that's enough.

—I told Mom that I'd bring you back to the hospital. You—

—No, it's cool. The way homeless guys can look cool. You look tough.

—Caleb, why don't you go downstairs and set the table.

—Zack, you want to go?

—'Cause my dad would never do something like that.

—Zack?

—Though I guess no one would let a guy like that clean their teeth.

—Caleb, c'mon, honey, come downstairs, I'll help you set the table.

—Uh.

—Doctor Mad Dog, Dentist of the Streets!

—Zack, you want to come?

—Um, Daniel, we spoke to Margaret just about twenty minutes

ago, you must have been on the way over. We were all just going to head over there tomorrow morning.

—Oh.

—They changed some of her medication and Margaret made it sound like Caroline's going to sleep early.

—I see.

—I was going to take the boys over.

—The boys?

—Yeah, Dad, I was going to stay over again.

—We thought that after all that flying you might like a night to yourself, what with jet lag and everything.

—Oh.

—Of course, if you want Zack, you know, to go back with you, of course.

—No, it's not—

—Though I think he'll want to stay for dinner, I'm making chicken fingers.

—Chicken fingers.

—Yes, from scratch.

—From scratch.

—Zack put in the request this morning, we didn't know when you were getting in exactly.

—My mom's chicken fingers rule.

—Of course, you're welcome to join us.

—I, uh.

—Kevin should be home any minute. Really, Daniel, we'd love to have you.

—Chicken fingers with a little barbecue sauce, *D* to the double-licious.

—Zack, so you want to stay here for another night?

—Can I?

—Sure. I guess. If you want.

—Cool, Zack, we'll get to level eight for sure!

—Would you like to stay for dinner?

—I. Well.

—What am I saying? You're probably exhausted and want to rest. Let me run downstairs and make you a plate. We can all meet up at the hospital in the morning. Boys! Does it have to be so loud?

—Zack. Zack.

—What?

—So I'll see you tomorrow at the hospital?

—Yeah, Dad.

And he walks over to the beanbags, bends over, and kisses the top of his son's head. Soon he's reversing out of the Vaismans' driveway, the car quickly filling up with the smell of chicken breasts breaded and fried. Unfortunately, he knows exactly how to get home.

3

His house is dark, silent, empty, and odorless. Alfred enters through a flap in the back door and slowly drags his rusty haunches toward his owner. Though slowed down considerably since his early days, when he would bark and leap and nearly bend his vertical, airborne self in half when any human, much less a human he loved, entered, Alfred makes it clear to Daniel that his side of their greeting will be anything but perfunctory. Maybe it's the time away, maybe the beard, maybe the smell, maybe his loneliness, whatever the case, the dog demands a full debriefing, pressing his wet snout deep into his owner's hands and soon his hairy face. A few seconds later, once it's clear Alfred is only getting started, Daniel gives up, chuckles, and says, Jesus, as he sits down against a wall. While the only member of his household who seems to give a shit about his return tries to understand his new scent, Daniel looks at his house and thinks of boxes and movers and the foolish, pitiful optimism of thirty-year fixed mortgages.

After filling the empty bowl of his last remaining housemate, who has already disappeared through the flap, Daniel elects not to search for mail or check for messages, he doesn't even bring in his bag. Throughout his shower he worries he won't be able to fall asleep.

Shaving is postponed. He climbs into bed, and for most of the eighty seconds before he slips into unconsciousness remembers the imaginary corpse still hidden in an imaginary car, which waits, along with the two men who put bullets into this body, for a proper ending.

Daniel sleeps for seventeen hours. In the only dream he'll recall he sits all alone in a dentist's waiting room, poring through photo albums filled with people crying. For the first time in twenty-eight years, he wets his bed. Despite this, it's Alfred, politely barking downstairs, that wakes him.

He feels both much better and very bad. The densely packed layers of exhaustion that first accumulated around his eyes and feet, and later grew past his hands and lower back, until finally overwhelming his shoulders, neck, and even the muscles in his cheeks, seem to have melted away, though it will take some time for their thick residue to dissipate entirely. Unfortunately, with his body back above the surface, Daniel has no trouble discerning the ravaged state of his life, in the figurative, that is, nonphysical, sense. Moreover, he's hardly optimistic about the likelihood of assembling the mental and spiritual tools necessary for rebuilding something meaningful and sustaining out of the fragments and scraps of what used to be, let alone returning things to their original form.

Theirs was never, not even during those stretches of perhaps coincidental mutual satisfaction and even joy, a model marriage. In addition to a whole lot of other things, it really came down to the fact that despite all they did share, meals, beds, cars, trips, finances, fluids, and perhaps even parenting, each ultimately remained in his or her own camp, failing and/or refusing to genuinely cast his or her lot with the other. Daniel wanted success, Caroline wanted happiness. For many years, without a doubt, Daniel wanted Caroline to be happy, Caroline wanted Daniel to succeed. But at a certain point, perhaps when Caroline went, in order to be happy, back to work, or when Daniel began cutting off nearly all communication with wife and son during his ever-lengthening risky voyages into the dark, dangerous inner circles of the film industry, with an eye on even greater success, some serious doubt crept into the conjugal equation. It wasn't so much that Daniel stopped wanting Caroline to be happy or that Caroline no longer hoped for Daniel's success. Rather, Caroline started having great difficulty convincing herself that Daniel cared enough about her happiness to have his concern for her happiness make any meaningful claims on the enormous investments he made toward his own success. Similarly, Daniel began to wonder if Caroline would allow herself to truly experience, with him, those unmistakably unhappy periods of uncertainty and anxiety that one invariably encounters on the road to success. And so it was less, at least at first, that the one stopped supporting the other. Rather the one stopped believing that the other's support was either reliable or authentic. After a while both Daniel and Caroline simply stopped looking for signs of mutual support, having trained themselves to decide in advance that sincere or hollow, frequent or rare, such gestures were ultimately of no use to them. After a, say, four-year period of each thus ignoring unambiguous overtures of concern, of underappreciating explicit acts of encouragement, but, remarkably, still enjoying a satisfying amount of happiness (Caroline) or success (Daniel), the two pretty much no longer bothered to give or take in a way that ever went beyond polite or civil. Throughout all of this they may have still loved each other in some necessarily abstract sense, but neither one did much about this, thus hollowing out their twenty-year-old bond to the point that eventually all it took was for one of them to say, I want a divorce, just those four words spoken aloud, for the whole thing to collapse so quickly and completely that years from now their once fondest shared memories of the ever-receding past will likely be recollected only under the dim, distorting light of wounded skepticism.

———

Daniel thinks, or at least senses, some of this as he peels away the piss-soaked sheets, which he does with an admirable lack of shame. Alfred greets and sniffs him at the bottom of the stairs because he can no longer climb them. Daniel hears a slight whimper, perhaps the dog is trying to alert his owner to, or apologize for, the fact that he has urinated on the kitchen floor. It's already midafternoon and Daniel still hasn't eaten a real meal on this side of the ocean, the plate Deb fixed for him remains on the passenger seat of the rental car, so Daniel enters the kitchen and eats over a half pound of various food-stuffs that require no preparation, or even a plate: two bananas, seven slices of low-fat turkey breast, sixteen bite-sized pretzels, a couple of handfuls of dried cereal, three granola bars, and an ice-cream sand-wich. He craps. Then, in lieu of other more aggressively marketed therapies, counseling, medication, prostitution, meditation, Daniel showers. Still dripping and with towel around his waist, he searches the house for a scissors so that he might remove, in what will have to be a multistage process, the long hairs that continue growing out of his face. Standing opposite the bathroom mirror with implement in hand, Daniel takes a long look at himself for posterity's sake. A loud knock comes from the front door. Then the doorbell. Then another knock. Finally, a holler:

—Caroline, Bloom, anybody here? Hello? Hey, c'mon. Open up!

5

—Holy crap.

—Hey, Max.

—Holy shit.

—What?

—What the hell is that?

—What?

—That thing you're growing. It's astonishing.

—I was about to shave.

—Oh no you're not. You're on to something. That, my friend, is authentic. It's authenticity. Do not touch it.

—Alright.

—Looks especially nice with the towel. Mr. Natural. Nice.

—So you're back. When did you get back? Hey, aren't you back early?

—Yeah.

—I thought so. I called your cell phone over there. Some guy named Udi answered. Kind of a prick, to be honest. What's up, why did you cut the trip short?

—Caroline was in an accident.

—Oh shit. She alright? Where is she?

—In the hospital.

—The hospital, fuck. Bloom. Shit. What, what happened?

—I don't know exactly. She was turning and someone didn't yield, or someone else was turning and she didn't yield. She didn't want to talk about it.

—Shit. Well, well at least you're back and she's going to be okay. She's going to be okay, right?

—Yup.

—You heading over there?

—Probably. Soon.

—Mind if I come along?

—Be my guest.

—Shit, Bloom, that's awful.

—Hey, do you mind if I change the subject?

—To?

—Well, okay, admittedly not the easiest thing to segue into considering the circumstances, but it's why I came over. It's why I called Udi.

—Huh.

—I got a girlfriend.

—Really?

—I do.

—Congratulations.

—Guess what she does.

—No.

—C'mon.

—Give me a hint.

—She's totally hot.

—An actress.

—Nope. Hotter.

—A model.

—Sort of.

—Sort of?

—Not really for clothes and not on catwalks, and she's not a six-foot-tall anorexic.

—But she's a model.

—That she is. On magazine covers and everything.

—But not a regular model.

—No.

—I give up.

—C'mon, be a sport. Ask some yes or no questions.

—Max, I don't feel like it.

—C'mon.

—Please, Max.

—Please, Max? Bloom, what's up?

—Beyond my wife being in the hospital?

—Yeah, beyond that.

—You're kidding.

—Not only.

—Fine. She wants a divorce.

—Caroline?

—Caroline.

—What? A divorce? Why? That, that bitch.

—Nice, Max. Lovely.

—Shit, and she just had a car accident, so you're not even allowed to be mad at her. That crafty bitch.

—Please stop.

—That's so unfair. That's cheating, isn't it?

—I'm going to get dressed.

—You still haven't guessed.

—Max, my wife, who doesn't want to be my wife, is in the hospital. Zack is holding himself hostage at Caleb's.

—Huh?

—Never mind. If you're going to tell me, just tell me already.

—Fine. She's a yoga model.

—A yoga model?

—Yeah, you know, she models yoga poses in books and magazines and videos. And she does magazine covers. She was on the June cover of *Yoga World*.

—*Yoga World*.

—Hey, don't pooh-pooh *Yoga World*. Circulation has quadrupled in the last two years.

—Up to twenty?

—Bloom, she's amazing. She's nice, and she's smart, and she is so hot she ought to be arrested.

—And she's with you?

—I know! It makes absolutely no sense.

—Where did you meet her?

—Ah, you're showing interest, like a good friend. You'll see, I'm going to help you through this divorce. I'll even help you negotiate Zack's release.

—Where'd you meet?

—Gas station. I was filling up the Vespa, she pulled up in her hybrid, we started talking about gas mileage, I had a spare helmet, I offered her a ride, the rest is history.

—I'm happy for you, truly.

—Damn, I was going to suggest some sort of double-dating event, but now you're third-wheel material.

—Thanks.

—That's alright, just don't be too much of a downer. Hey, you know what? She's probably got totally hot yoga-model friends! This'll be great. You won't believe how hot she is. I have no idea why she's with me, but she really likes me. She says she's never met anyone who knew where their kidneys are like I do.

—What the hell are you talking about?

—I don't know. It's a thing in yoga. There's a lot of poses where you're supposed to do something in relation to your kidneys.

—And you know exactly where yours are.

—Right here. And here.

—They're not lower?

—Nope. That's what everybody thinks.

—So you're doing yoga now?

—Check it out.

—What?

—What? This.

—You're sitting cross-legged on the floor. Big deal.

—Do you have any idea how difficult that used to be for me? Do you know that I considered suing my father because of the tightness in my hips? Do you have any idea what summer camp is like when you can't sit Indian style? My mom can touch her elbows to the floor without bending her knees, and this is what I get. That and my nose. This represents enormous progress on my part.

—And all in, what, less than two weeks. Well, I'm happy for you.

—There's more. Check it out. She's half Indian, half African American. She's like a super babe from another planet. And, needless to say in light of her profession, or her professional qualifications, she's extremely good at having sex.

—Wonderful.

—Her combination of flexibility and core strength. I tell you, she should win a Nobel Prize in humping.

—What's her name?

—Ananda.

—Ananda?

—It means bliss or ecstasy.

—Is that her real name?

—I'm not sure. We're not there yet.

—So where are we at with the screenplay?

—Please, Max, give me a day or two.

—Are you done?

—No.

—Are you almost done?

—Maybe.

—Maybe probably, or maybe I have no idea?

—You coming with me or not?

—To the hospital?

—Yeah.

—Sure.

—C'mon, get off the floor already. We'll take the rental.

—You didn't answer.

—I don't know. Probably. I don't know.

—What's the last scene you got?

—The agent and the assassin just put a body in the trunk of a car. They each shot it. Arguing about what to do next.

—You're kidding.

—What?

—From the brilliance of the opening and then all the stuff in the food court to two guys arguing about a body in a trunk?

—Look, it wasn't actually my idea.

—You're outsourcing your screenwriting to the Israelis?

—Leave me alone.

—What's this?

—Dinner, from Caleb's mom. Forgot to eat it.

—Chicken fingers?

—From scratch.

—No shit. Do you mind?

—They've been sitting there since yesterday evening.

—I'm willing to take the risk. One thing about Ananda, she's not much for meat.

—Can't have everything.

—Damn, these are amazing.

—What the? Why the hell is someone pulling into my driveway?
Ah fuck, it's Donny.

—Get out of the car! Bloom, get out of the fucking car!
—Stop banging on the window, Donny. For christ's sake.
—Get out!
—Oh boy, he seems quite displeased about something.
—Shit.
—Don't worry, I'll tell him about Caroline, he'll feel bad.

—Why didn't you tell me you're back?
—I just got back yesterday afternoon.
—I call your cell phone, get some son of a bitch named Udi.
What the hell is it with those people, they don't got a word for man-
ners in Hebrew? No wonder that place is so fucked up. Why didn't
you call?
—I wasn't planning on coming back early.
—That wasn't my question.
—I was going to call, trust me.
—When?
—Later today.
—Don't give me that bullshit.
—Donny, his wife's in the hospital.
—What the hell are you talking about? What's your wife doing in
the hospital?
—She was in a car accident.
—Bad?
—She's in the hospital, Donny.
—Right. Sorry.

—Bloom, that sucks.
—Thanks, I know.
—She's going to be alright?

—I think so.

—She's not unconscious or anything fucked up like that?

—No, no. Just a couple of broken bones in her leg.

—But no brain damage, right?

—Jeez, Donny. No.

—So full recovery, right?

—Yeah, hopefully. She might have a slight limp. They had to put some screws in her leg.

—We were actually on our way over. You wanna tag along?

—That's very kind of you, Max, but I'll pass.

—Alright. Here's what I'm thinking. I feel bad for you and your wife. That's really a shit deal, what happened to her. I'm sorry she's got to suffer like this, I'm sorry you had to cut your stupid trip short. But it looks like the worst is over, am I correct?

—Let's hope.

—Actually, Donny, his wife wants a divorce, too.

—Max, please stop.

—A divorce? This a new development?

—What? Yeah, she told me yesterday, in the hospital.

—Damn, Bloom, that's hardly fair, springing it on you like that.

—That's what I said.

—Well, alright, I'm sorry about that, too. Unless, of course, you were looking for a way out all along. I can't say, having never met the woman. But Bloom, damn it, none of that helps me out, and I need some helping out. As it happens, my little talk with Udi wasn't my first unpleasant trans-Atlantic phone call of the day. You know when I woke up today?

—No.

—3:46 A.M. You know why?

—You got an unpleasant trans-Atlantic phone call?

—Very perceptive, Max. You know who it was? Forget it, why would you know. It was a couple of my Dutch investors with some questions. Where's the script? You said it was going to be ready last week. Where is it?

—Why'd you tell him it was going to be ready last week?

—Because it was.

—But I never told you that.

—You're right, I told you that.

—Well, Donny, c'mon. Then that's your problem, not mine.

—Not your problem? I'm not so sure about that, but yes, it's definitely my problem. These two Dutch bastards have liquidated thirty-eight million dollars thinking they're getting in on the ground floor of this guaranteed blockbuster of yours, and now, two weeks later, I got nothing for them. Nothing. Dick all. You know what independent Dutch producers do when you hang them out to dry like that? Unless your idea of Dutch culture is slashing a guy's tires and ruining a guy's reputation and possibly even making some additional middle-of-the-night phone calls to Los Angeles to enlist the services of the kind of guys, Dutch or otherwise, who beat the crap out of even big, intimidating, former Division III college linebackers like me for a living, then let's say that they're about to do some things very much not in the Dutch spirit of things.

—You played linebacker in college?

—Max, shut up. Bloom, where's my fucking script?!

—Donny, I really need to go visit Caroline. I should have been there hours ago.

—She can wait. Sounds like she doesn't want to see you, anyway. Where is it?

—I'm almost done.

—Almost? Where are you at with it?

—Donny, let me take him over to the hospital. We'll be there for a half hour, forty-five minutes, then straight back here. I promise, I won't let him leave the house again until he finishes.

—Where are you at with it?

—Donny, please, just let him go.

—Bloom.

—Fine. There's a body in the trunk. The assassin and the agent are arguing about what to do with it.

—You're kidding. This is a joke.

—Well, I'm not sure the scene won't get cut—

—A body in a trunk. Unbelievable. Gimme your keys.

—What?

—Gimme your keys.

—No. Hey. Donny! Give those back.

—You want a body in the trunk, I'll show you a body in the trunk. Let's go.

—You're crazy, I'm not going in there. Give me my keys back.

—I'm going to count to three. When I'm done, either you're in that trunk or I put you in it.

—You're insane. Bye, Donny, good luck with the Dutch. C'mon, Max, we'll take the Audi.

—You think I'm kidding.

—Hey, get your hands off me. What the? Hey! Max, get him to stop!

—Sorry, he's too big. Don't worry, Daniel, I won't let him doing anything real bad.

—You got your cell phone with you?

—Fuck you.

—Do you?

—Yes.

—Good. C'mon, Max, let's take a ride.

—Fuck you, Donny.

—Can you hear me, Bloom?

—Go fuck yourself.

—I'll take that as a yes. Good. We've got Max on the line as well, a little conference call.

—Hi, Daniel. You okay back there?

—You drove across my lawn, didn't you?

—It'll grow back.

—You're a son of a bitch.

—Guilty as charged. Alright, let's get down to business. You've taken this story to a very dangerous place. This started as a big idea movie, a movie about the fucked-up state of the world, and now it's about a corpse in a trunk. That won't do.

—Donny, if you think I'm going to work on this from the trunk of my rental car, if you think I could work on this from the trunk, you're out of your mind.

—Bloom, trust me, this wasn't my plan. But honestly, I got all day. In fact, it's all I got. I told Vesha and Koenrad that I'd have something for them by the end of the day. So let's get working.

—C'mon, Daniel, I'll help.

—I'm hanging up. I'm calling 911. Bye.

—911.

—Yes, hello. I'm locked in the trunk of a car.

—Are you injured or in any immediate physical danger?

—No, no, I don't think so.

—Is the car moving?

—Yes.

—Do you know where it's heading or where you are?

—Somewhere in North Hollywood probably.

—In which direction are you traveling?

—I don't know, we turned a few times.

—What's the make and model of the car?

—I don't know, it's a rental. A Ford, maybe. Or a Chevrolet. Could be a Chrysler. Definitely American.

—What color is it?

—Green. Or gray. Maybe light blue. Depends on the lighting.

—Do you know the men who put you in the trunk?

—Yes.

—Are they criminals?

—Not really. No.

—Do you believe they're dangerous? Do you feel you're in immediate danger?

—No, probably not. But they won't let me out.

—Sir, if you don't know what the car looks like or where you're located, I'm sorry, but there's very little we can do.

—Can't you trace the location of my cell phone?

—Sir, that requires additional resources. In light of the fact that you yourself do not believe you are in immediate danger, I cannot request those resources at this time.

—You're kidding.

—Sorry, sir, I am not.

—Can't you set up a perimeter or something?

—A perimeter?

—You know, when you establish a perimeter around a certain area in order to prevent a suspect or a suspect's vehicle from getting away.

—Oh, that's actually called an encasement.

—Encasement?

—Yes sir. You must have heard perimeter on television or something.

—Unbelievable. Can, can you hold a moment? I got another call.

—What?

—Max and I are still waiting.

—Fuck you, I'm on the phone with 911.

—Really? Are they coming?

—Max, where are we?

—Max, open your mouth and we're going to have problems.

—Max! Where are we?

—I want to say, but Donny's doing this thing to my pinky that really hurts.

—Ah, fuck, we're getting pulled over.

—I told you to stop running stop signs.

—Shut up, Max. Bloom, do not make a sound, I'm warning you.

—Driver's license and registration.

—Here you are, officer. Max, check the glove compartment for the registration.

—Is this your vehicle?

—No, officer, it's a rental.

—Here's the registration.

—I need to see the rental agreement.

—Here, officer.

—This vehicle has not been rented in your name. Are you Daniel Bloom?

—No, sir.

—Where is Daniel Bloom?

—We're on the way to pick him up.

—Where is he?

—Help! Help!

—Bloom. Damn it. Son of a bitch.

—Open the trunk! Get out of the car slowly and keep your hands in plain view.

—Thanks, officer.

—Are you alright, sir?

—Yeah, fine.

—You two, keep your hands on the car. Are you Daniel Bloom?

—Yes.

—You two, you're under arrest for kidnapping and theft. You have the right—

—Officer, really, that's not necessary. Please. It was just a joke, a prank. I lost a bet.

—A bet?

—Yeah, we're friends. Just screwing around.

—Actually, officer, we were trying to figure out an ending to a movie he's writing.

—Industry guys, figures. You guys think everything's a movie.

—I apologize.

—Officer, you go to the movies?

—Sometimes.

—Did you happen to see *Helsinki Honeymoon*?

—Of course. One of my favorites. Fine film.

—Well, you're looking at the man who wrote it.

—No kidding. You wrote *Helsinki Honeymoon*?

—It was supposed to be called *Captives*.

—Wow. Great stuff. When she kisses him on the forehead at the end before shooting him. Damn. I'll tell you what, that scene haunted me for weeks. My wife gave me the DVD for Christmas last year. One of my favorites.

—Thanks.

—Hey.

—Yes, officer?

—The new one, what's it about?

—A sniper.

—You don't say. Huh. Listen, I got a buddy over in the SWAT unit downtown who's a sniper. You need any technical questions answered, here's my card, give me a call. I actually got some great movie ideas I've been tossing around for a while.

—Thanks, I may well give you a call, Officer Pelfrey.

—Kip. Call me Kip.

—No problem, Kip. Look, do you mind if we go? Production on the new one is supposed to start in September, and we still don't have an ending.

—As you wish, gentlemen, but how about everybody rides in the cabin this time?

—Sure thing.

—By the way, what's the new one going to be called?

—How does *Captives* sound to you?

—Sounds good to me. Alright, you fellas take care.

—Give me my keys.

—Make him sit in the back, Daniel, and don't let him near your fingers.

—Quiet, Max, or I'll be looking for new representation soon.

—You wouldn't do that.

—Try me. Donny, you owe me more than you can imagine.

—Fine, but you still owe me an ending.

—Go screw yourself, I got your ending.

6

Ninety minutes later Daniel enters the hospital alone. He doesn't want to be here, surrounded by this sad, reluctant, helpless convergence of the unfortunate, the infirm, the expiring, especially since the various indirectly empowering means, sympathy, empathy, pity, blind faith, stoicism, lament, belief in a higher power, that a person might call on, once forced inside these 500,000 square feet of bad news, turn their backs on Daniel, refuse him access. Max revoked his earlier offer in order to join Ananda on a photo shoot, a sun salutation series for *Yoga Age.* Said he promised her. Still, Daniel has every intention of trying, with words or without, to communicate to Caroline his regret at what happened and his hope that she'll make a full recovery. Just inside the main corridor, flanked by somber gift shop and solemn cafeteria, a sharp scent of disease-induced decay lingers, despite the steady application of industrial-strength disinfectants and cleaners. He'll try this even though she may not want it, even though he's unsure he can. Three parts bleach, one part death. Daniel shares the elevator with a wheelchair that's been forced to hold and transport a woman with thigh-wide ankles, the skin discolored and taut. A single article of clothing, a poncho, a tarp, or a sheet with a hole cut in its middle, has been pulled down over her thirty-pound head. The feeling he gets in this place is so bad he experiences some confusion regarding the underlying causal relationship between sickness and hospital. In other words, which comes first. A very slow elevator. To be here is to be vulnerable, and not merely to contagions long ago isolated by the medical community. The indifferent lighting on Caroline's floor complements the pale Formica surrounding the nurses' station, aptly highlights the sickening stainless steel waiting patiently in each and every corner. Bad luck and misfortune filling up the air.

Her room is empty. The bed unmade.

Caroline Bloom, room 5129, let's see. Says here she was released just before lunch. Yes, quite certain. 11:50 A.M. this morning. Yes, sir. No, sir, I'm not sure, that information is not recorded in our paperwork, we just have the doctor's signature authorizing her discharge. What's that, Renée? Oh, a woman with a couple of teenage boys. That's right, yes. You're welcome, take care.

This time Deb doesn't hug him, which isn't to say she's unfriendly. Obviously, she knew this was coming, she knew he would come, she knew she volunteered for this as well. He's welcomed into the Vaismans' uncluttered, well-lit kitchen, where he's offered coffee and a slice of homemade banana bread. He accepts. Deb, ever efficient, her face just big enough to contain the necessary features, all pleasantly symmetrical, all of it rounding quickly into chin, jaw, hair, and skull, answers his questions, offers additional, relevant information. Caroline's resting, probably asleep, in the in-law unit, they had suggested an extra dose of Vicodin after the move, the boys are upstairs, just got back from a walk down to the corner to get a movie, a taxi came for Margaret a couple of hours ago, four-thirty flight, Continental. She has, more or less, taken sides by facilitating his wife's desire to begin severing her life from his. When you leave the hospital, you go home. So she knows, Deb does. Probably knew before he did. May have known long ago. Certainly knew yesterday, knew they'd be having this conversation. But she's not hostile, even though after years of receiving Caroline's confidence, her honest opinion of the man sitting opposite her couldn't be all that favorable.

—I'm sorry about all of this, Daniel.

She looks right at him, right at his eyes, and she means it. There's nothing dramatic in her delivery, this isn't a performance for him or for her. She simply regrets that it has come to this, and she's telling him so. He wonders if she thinks Caroline has made the right choice, if she tried to talk her out of it, if she thinks this is irreversible, final. He'd ask, but she might refuse to answer, and somehow that would make everything even worse.

—Thanks. It's alright. I'm going to grab Zack, see how he's doing.

—Good idea. Tonight's turkey burgers. He didn't seem to care for them last time.

Zack and Caleb are at Caleb's computer. Caleb sits, Zack stands next to him. Their cell phones are out, Zack points at the computer monitor. Daniel approaches and places his hand on his son's head, something his own father used to do on rare occasions. Zack, possibly startled, turns to him, nearly smiles.

—What you guys up to?

—Downloading new ring tones.

—Cool.

—Check this out.

And they run through more than forty different options in about three minutes. Songs, sound effects, famous lines from well-known movies, even one from *Helsinki Honeymoon,* when the female lead says, near the end, Something to remember me and your old self by. The boys giggle and say, Cool, and voice their disbelief and rush to claim their favorite before the other can beat him to it. Daniel waits for them to finish.

—Zack, what do you say you and I go grab some dinner?

In hopes of guidance, Zack looks at Caleb, who does something unclear with his shoulder.

—Can I still stay here tonight?

Daniel nearly opens his mouth to offer something sarcastic, something including the words *moving in,* but wisely catches himself, not wanting to embarrass his son, not wanting to expose himself.

—'Cause Mom's here.

—Right. Sure. No problem.

Caleb extends his cell phone to Zack, Hey, take this, see if you can figure out how the ring tone override works.

Zack debriefs with Deb in the kitchen before leaving. Daniel stands in the foyer, keeping his distance, more or less watching the accelerating attenuation of his already paltry paternal authority. He thinks to assert himself, to seize his son, to march in there and remind Deb that he hasn't been reduced to weekend visits, not yet anyway. But he waits, however impatiently, since there's no advantage in getting on Deb's bad side. Too bad Kevin Vaisman, DDS, is such a one-dimensional, self-assured bore. If they were closer Daniel could mount a counterattack through the rear flank, not that he could ever actually prevail.

—So where do you want to go?

—I don't care.

—C'mon. Anywhere you want. Burgers, Chinese, pizza. It's up to you.

—I don't know.

—Are you hungry?

—Sort of.

—Because if you're not we could go do something first for a while. Check out a movie, hit the batting cages, go to the ocean. Whatever you want.

—Nah, I don't feel like it.

—Well, what do you want to do?

—You can decide.

—You're awfully indecisive today. What's the story?

—Nothing.

—Hey, will you put down Caleb's phone already?

—Dad?

—What?

—Why did you go to Israel?

—There were a few reasons.

—Like what?

—Well, they're kind of hard to explain. I kind of needed to get away. I wanted you to come with me.

—But you still went when I couldn't.

—I know.

—And then Mom got in the accident.

—Zack, I'm really sorry about what happened, but you know that Mom's accident didn't happen because I went to Israel.

—But maybe she wouldn't have been driving there that day if you didn't go.

—Maybe.

—What's with you and that phone?

—I don't like your beard.

—I'm going to shave tomorrow. I meant to shave today, but something came up.

—It looks dumb.

—Zack, enough. Where do you want to go?

—You know, a couple nights ago we went to Chili's for dinner and we were waiting for our food and Caleb found these little cards for comments and we filled them out and then Caleb said, Why do they only have these at restaurants and hotels and stuff and why don't they have them for the important stuff, like why don't they have them for schools and teachers and parents and stuff like that? And Kevin said, Pretend that's for me, and so we were about to rate him but then our food came. And we forgot about it, but then last night before I went to sleep I remembered it and I started thinking about it.

—Yeah?
—Nothing.
—C'mon. What?

—Dad, you'd get a lot of fairs and even some poors.

—I know.
—You would.
—I'm going to get better. I'm going to finish this screenplay soon, and then that's it, for a while.
—That's what you said last time.
—It's true this time, I mean it. I think I'm done after this.
—Kevin's kind of dumb sometimes, but I don't think he'd get any poors.

—How about pizza? And then some ice cream? What do you say?
—I don't want to go.
—Zack.
—I don't.

—Aw, Zack. Come here.
—No.
—You know I love you. I do.

Daniel loves to watch his son run, always has, it's the moment when the biological impossibility of it all, of an actual, self-contained, properly functioning flesh-and-blood son grown from his own seed seems most wonderfully real to him. He tries to appreciate this once more as Zack, likely still crying, runs right back up the Vaismans' long driveway, his very own two legs carrying him swiftly down the gray pavement until he disappears, just like that, inside this other house that two-thirds of the family once called the Blooms now calls home.

Two days of nothing. He doesn't leave the house. He doesn't talk to anyone. He doesn't shower or change his clothes. He sleeps, to the extent that he sleeps, on a couch downstairs. He lives on granola bars and sunflower seeds and small packages of peanut butter crackers intended for his son's school lunches. Every time a car drives down his street, which isn't often, he assumes it's Donny, or someone sent by Donny, coming to punish him. His opinion on this possibility is one of alarming indifference.

He tries a few times to convince Alfred to take a walk, but apparently the dog's joints will no longer allow it, so it's back to letting him relieve himself in the backyard. Midway through the second day, Daniel notices, finally notices, that the dog is doing this, letting himself out through the yellowed, once-translucent plastic flap near the bottom of the kitchen door, with atypical frequency. In and out, or rather, out and in, and then out again. From where he sits Daniel can see Alfred leave, but after that nothing, making it impossible for him to draw any definite conclusions.

It takes approximately four hours for Daniel to stand up to investigate. He passes Alfred's double-bowl dog dish on the way out, the food side remains half-full, while the water has long since been emptied. The owner steps outside and into a small puddle of what he will later decide was urine that has for some reason been left right outside the door. Daniel scans the backyard for a few moments until he spots Alfred, good old Alfred, who has lowered himself down to the top step of the pool, where he is now busy lapping up its water. In Daniel's absence the pool has been completely neglected, and the nearly greenish water level has dropped to just an inch or so above this first step. As Daniel nears the dog standing in his oversized water bowl, Alfred stops drinking, urinates briefly, and then lies down on this same step, apparently unconcerned by the water-urine cocktail that now covers the bottom 20 percent of his brown-on-white fur.

—What are you doing?

Alfred turns his head just enough to make eye contact with Daniel. His expression recalls the kind of look he would offer after being caught, in his younger, wilder days, after letting his teeth and jaw have their way with some defenseless piece of furniture. The dog's face is still, his big dark eyes expectant, almost pleading.

—Well, I apologize for the poor service. No shame in being thirsty. What do you say I put some water in your bowl and bring it out here?

Which he does, to no avail. Moments later Alfred slowly stands up and drinks some more from the pool. Urinates again. Lies back down. Daniel watches this routine two more times in less than twenty minutes, noting along the way that today's clear midafternoon sky has the makings of what many would consider a lovely day, until, after first walking listlessly to the far end of the stair, Alfred, while barely arching his back, releases what appears to be a frayed brown ribbon, spotted in red and over one foot in length, from the small opening located directly beneath his tail.

Daniel grabs Alfred's thirty pounds and change from the pool and carries him across the yard, holding him up against his right hip like a small log, feet and head sagging clumsily. The dog couldn't like this, he hasn't picked him up in ten years, not since Alfred outweighed his in-house contemporary, Zack, but the human detects no protest.

By the time they return inside, to collect keys, wallet, phone, and a few towels from a downstairs closet before heading out again, a wet circle two feet in diameter covers much of the human's side.

He puts Alfred down on the pavement next to the car in order to spread the towels over the passenger seat, having elected to otherwise disregard the leather. The dog pees on the driveway. Daniel considers getting a bowl for drinking, but after measuring the distance to the vet against the uninviting logistics, Alfred and his towels would have to be moved to the floor, and even then it's likely the bowl would spill, he concludes there's no point. A minute later they're off, Daniel patting the smooth, waistless, curled-up canine lump on the beach towels next to him. His hand likes this, there's some tight evolution-informed symbiotic fit to this owner's-hand–dog's-body connection, so he keeps it up, nearly enjoying its meditative flavor. But only for so long, because soon enough he wishes he had blinders on, he wishes he were nothing but a driver, a driver with some sturdy, inanimate cargo, a driver with no meaningful past and no discernible future, whose consciousness reaches out only far enough to monitor the road right in front of him. Instead, he gives the dog one last pat, removes his hand and strikes the steering wheel twice, cursing first with regret and then again with dread.

Daniel allows Alfred to relieve himself in the parking lot of the freestanding clinic before entering. This time the dog walks, albeit very slowly, the thirty feet between the car and the building, though his owner needs to lift him up the stairs leading to the entrance. The reception area is a simple square with a few upholstered benches. An abundance of kitschy nonsense, macramé, needlepoint, and shell art, much of it, of course, animal themed, covers the walls, along with photos of pets, notices for missing cats, and advertisements for dog walkers. Alfred finds some unclaimed floor, while Daniel approaches the rectangular opening in the wall that frames the torso of a young woman dressed in blue scrubs. He waits as a middle-aged woman, who attempts to verbally soothe a mysterious, silent animal hidden in

a plastic crate at her feet, settles her bill and instructs the young
woman to give Peggy her best.

—Can I help you?

—I, I think there's something wrong with my dog.

—Do you have an appointment?

—No.

—Okay.

—He's urinating constantly.

—Just a moment.

—And some diarrhea.

Nothing.

—He needs to see someone.

Her eyes don't approve of his face, and the rest of her doesn't
know what to make of the rest of him and his manner. She turns her
head and consults a computer monitor, thus presenting to Daniel the
two cropped ponytails sticking out from the two bumps at the base
of her skull.

—Why don't you have a seat while I speak with the head tech-
nician?

—Can you see him?

—We'll fit him in, it may be a while.

And so after giving her his name and that of the dog, he sits down
near Alfred, and they begin to wait. A couple of minutes later Alfred
cautiously rises, walks to the entrance, lifts his right paw perhaps
three inches, and softly scratches at the door. Daniel alerts the recep-
tionist that he's taking the dog out but that they're not leaving. She
says nothing. He lifts the dog down the steps, placing him off to the
side, where Alfred immediately pisses. Just as he leans over to pick
him up again, the dog lies down, right there on the warm pavement
near the base of the stairs, no more than an inch from the urine, his
not-so-moist, leathery brown nose glistening faintly in the sunlight.
Daniel looks at him for a moment.

—Alfred, I'll be right back, okay?

No response.

He goes inside and approaches the rectangle, which now frames a different, slightly older assistant, whose scrubs present a flowered pattern. He tells her his name and the situation.

—We'll be outside, we're not leaving, do you think you might be able to give us a bowl with some water? I'm pretty sure he needs to drink.

She obliges, not graciously.

Back on the steps Daniel alternates between wishing Caroline were there and wishing he were Caroline. She would demand to be seen, she would say, her voice a few decibels louder than necessary, I don't think you understand, and then she would make them understand. She wouldn't mind the confrontation. Maybe he should call them, maybe they'd want to know. But he has no news yet, and maybe it's nothing, maybe this is the kind of thing that happens to old, rickety dogs, maybe they'll give him some shot or supplement and that'll be all, maybe the vet will say, as they shake hands good-bye, Don't worry, he'll be back to his old self by the end of the week. Instead of being Caroline he watches the cars passing back and forth, warming himself in the late, late afternoon sun, wondering how many of the drivers are as wealthy and miserable as him. Then he thinks of the screenplay, which he has been thinking of throughout. All that's left is the final showdown between the agent and the assassin. How did it get so small? He shouldn't be thinking about this now, he should be figuring out how to reclaim his family, or at least should be gathering up the nerve to go inside, it's been at least forty-five minutes by now, and make a scene, he should, in short, be someone he is not. Perhaps one of them will shoot himself in the head. If one of them shoots himself in the head, it will have to be the agent, that's the only reasonable resolution in regard to suicide. Unless they shoot each other as part of some tacit understanding. Years ago, Caroline would listen to these deliberations, would offer suggestions, would help. He should really call her. How to resolve something like this? Someone does something to make the world better, or someone does something to make the world worse. And what would be the measure of either? Caroline wouldn't know, but if she were willing to listen, that would count for something. Etc., for almost another hour.

—Alfred?

Daniel turns.

—Come on in.

Back, dog in arms, through the waiting area and into a small room. A third woman, tall, thin, no breasts or hips, asking him all sorts of questions. He answers, he watches her for clues, he gets nothing. She pets Alfred. She leaves. A few minutes later a man enters, stocky, broad shoulders, black curls, very tanned, dressed in dark denim overalls and a green T-shirt. Vaguely familiar. Looks like an aging high-school wrestler.

—Daniel.

His voice is deep. The man extends his hand and smiles. Strong, warm grip. Handsome, though his nose, chin, and forehead are nearly too big for the rest of his face. He has a soul patch, a perfect, meticulously groomed equilateral triangle right there under his bottom lip.

—Hi. Thanks for seeing us. I'm sorry, I—

—Not to worry. Dr. Kamden.

—Right. Hi.

—The beard's new?

—Yeah.

—Impressive. A courageous decision.

—Thanks.

—You're in the industry, right?

—Yes.

—Screenwriter?

—Yes.

—Thrillers, right? Action? Suspense?

—Uh-huh.

—*Helsinki Honeymoon*, if I recall correctly.

—You do.

—Great stuff. Truly enjoyed it. Okay, I'm not sure *enjoyed* is the right word. It was powerful. Really stuck with me.

—Thanks.

—Though I never did figure out what that title meant.

Daniel looks at the man's perfect smile.

—The reason I mention this is that my younger brother, Marty, who you might call the troubled child, get this, he's training to be a stuntman. Can you believe that?

—Huh.

—Guy's a lunatic. But you know what, I bet he'll be good at it, I bet he will, so long as he doesn't kill himself, right?

—I suppose.

—He's searching, maybe he finally found what he was looking for. Who knows, maybe he'll be in your next one. Are you working on something?

—Sort of.

—What's it about?

—Uh, it's hard to explain. Could we, do you think?

—Of course, of course. Dramatic inhale. Alright, let's see why you and, he looks down at the file, why you and Alfred are here today.

He reads the files, asks a couple questions, takes a few notes, performs a quick physical on the dog.

—I am going to take Alfred in the back, and we'll run a couple tests. Blood and urine. Ten minutes and I'll have an idea.

—Fine. Should I wait here?

—If you'd like. We're at the end of the day, so it's up to you. Alfred, what do you say you and I head back and see what's what?

The man and the dog disappear. From the other side of the wall Daniel hears the doctor.

—Kelly, I need a blood and urine screening on this one. Possible CRF. And then something unclear.

He waits, trying desperately not to think of a single thing. He fails.

Ten minutes later, the doctor returns, holding a towel and Alfred. The doctor places the towel and then the dog on a high, wide counter in the middle of the room. The two men stand on opposite sides of the counter, petting Alfred. The doctor's forearms are enormous.

—Daniel, he purses his lips, I do not believe in beating around the bush. Alfred has chronic renal failure, also known as chronic nephritis. Alfred's kidneys are gradually shutting down. That's why he's thirsty and that's why he's urinating with such frequency. Could be cancer, which I doubt, a heart condition, possible, or just age and genetic predisposition. That's my guess. His numbers aren't too bad yet. Yet. He looks down at the file. But the process is most certainly under way.

Daniel doesn't say anything.

—How old is Alfred? Twelve?

—Almost thirteen.

—Almost thirteen.

—What can we do?

—CRF, assuming that's what we're looking at, I'd have to do some exploratory surgery, which I can do, or run an MRI to confirm, but I'm 90 to 95 percent certain based on his symptoms and these tests and my experience. CRF is irreversible. With medications, which are not cheap, you can alleviate Alfred's suffering somewhat. I can provide medication that will decrease his thirst and with it his frequent urination, I can give him pain medication. None of which does anything to retard the progression of the condition itself. But it should give you and Albert and your family, a son, right?

—Yeah.

—It should give all of you another, we're looking at a range of three weeks to two months before complications are no longer treatable without a transplant, which at this age I cannot recommend.

—So what happens after the three weeks to two months?

—He'll need to be euthanized.

—Oh.

—I am sorry. But you need to understand that even with medication there will be symptoms, visible complications, all of which will steadily worsen.

—Such as?

—Weakness, weight loss, depression, diarrhea, vomiting. Quality of life will be moderate at best.

They're petting Alfred. Then the doctor removes his hand, opens a cabinet under the counter, takes out a towel, lifts the dog a bit, removes the towel from under him, which is wet, and replaces it with the new one. They resume stroking the dog, the doctor looking at Daniel, Daniel looking at Alfred, whose eyes are closed.

—So, so what do you—

—It is not unreasonable to consider euthanizing sooner.

—How much sooner?

—Next week, a couple days, tomorrow. Today.

—Now?

—I regret that I must tell you this. I am truly sorry.

—What do you recommend? What would you do?

The doctor stops petting Alfred. Takes a step or two away from the counter, crosses his arms, leans against a different counter running along the wall behind him. He smiles, perhaps wistfully.

—Have you ever wondered what it would be like if dogs lived seven times longer than us instead of the other way around? Can you imagine that? Dogs would become family heirlooms. They'd be in our wills. We'd inscribe our family trees on their sides. For generations. Or put a little microchip in their collars with all sorts of information for posterity. Four-legged time capsules. When a dog got run over, it would be like a giant redwood felled by some lightning. Imagine having a pet that was born at the time of Washington, or even Shakespeare. Look at the giant tortoise, it's not impossible.

Daniel doesn't respond.

—I was in my third year of vet school before it hit me: Kamden, you're going to have to tell a lot of people that their pets are dying, you're going to see a lot of pets die, you're going to kill a lot of pets. They just don't live long enough. Fucking dogs. Fucking Alfred, look at him, not even thirteen and that's older, when you do the math, than anyone in my entire extended family. Thirteen. Can you imagine if you had to wait until you were ninety-one to have a bar mitzvah? Son of a bitch.

—You think I should do it now. That's your opinion.

—I don't have an opinion. I don't know Alfred. I don't know how you feel about him. If you take him home, I won't go with you. I won't be living with him for two weeks or two months. I don't know what kind of place you and your family are at right now, what kind of people you are, how quickly you like your Band-Aids removed. I can give you some medicine, some sodium-based pills, it will keep him from urinating so often, you can take him home, tell your family, make a decision, decide if you want to come in tomorrow, next week, next month. You'd have to wait at least twenty-four hours, though, we only perform this procedure at the end of the day.

The two men look at one another.

—Let me give you some time alone. I'll be right back, excuse me.

Daniel, left alone, stares into space for a few minutes. Then he leans over and kisses the front tip of Alfred's head, on the spot just above and between his eyes, something he's never done before. The dog looks at him, appears to know. The dog lifts his head and rests it back down on a different paw, blows a bit of air through his snout. Daniel recalls the weight of his cell phone in his pocket, removes it and calls Zack's cell phone. He gets voice mail. After the beep Daniel waits a second and then hangs up without speaking. Could call the Vaismans or even Caroline's cell, but decides not to. Probably a bad decision, but Alfred's been his dog for years now, and he never was Caroline's anyway. He was the only one, almost thirteen years ago, who thought it might be fun to have twins. The doctor returns.

—Have you made a decision?

—Can we do it now?

—I see. He nods. Are you sure?

—Yes.

—You're certain?

—More or less.

The doctor actually chuckles.

—That sounds about right. Damn. Did you speak with your family?

—No, I didn't.

—You're certain about that? About this?

Daniel doesn't speak.

—Your decision. What would you like to do with his body afterward? I can keep him and then arrange burial or cremation. Or you can take him yourself, if you want to bury him at your home.

—I'll take him home.

—Alright. I am going to round up what we'll need. You can think about it more. You can still decide to postpone up until the moment before we give the injection. I will be right back.

And he is, with a mat folded under one arm and a syringe in the opposite hand. The contents of the latter are pinkish purple. He opens the mat and spreads it on the floor.

—Are you ready?

—Yes.

The doctor lifts Alfred and carries him down to the mat.

—Take a seat by his head. I will insert the needle into this foreleg. In less than ten seconds he'll start breathing deeper, then it'll slow and soon after it will be over.

The two men are on the floor around the dog.

—Are you ready?

—Yes.

—After I find the vein, if you prefer, I'll let you depress the syringe. If you want to be the one to do it.

—Me?

—Yes, you. If you want.

—Is that legal?

—I am willing to decide that that is irrelevant at the present moment. Would you like to?

—Have other people done it?

—Not important. Do you want to? Do you want to be the one to euthanize Alfred? If not, I will do it.

—No, no. I'll do it.

—Ready?

—Yes.

The doctor, on his knees, leans over Alfred and raises one of his front legs. With his thumb and forefinger he searches for a vein. He reaches his off-hand back up to the counter and grabs the syringe. He slowly inserts it at an angle into Alfred's leg, the thick skin rising up and gathering around the thin needle. The dog lurches slightly. Daniel continues petting him. The doctor removes the needle.

—I didn't get the vein.

He tries again, an inch or so higher up the leg. Inserts it, then removes it.

—I apologize.

A third time. For the first time all day, Alfred whimpers.

—I am sorry. This happens on rare occasions. There, it's in. If you want, take the syringe from my hand, try not to move it. Depress it steadily until you reach the end.

Daniel reaches out for it and takes the plastic tube. It's extremely light, virtually weightless. He lifts his thumb and places it on the plunger, removing and returning it a few times in order to center his thumb exactly. Finally, it's in place. He's motionless, hoping to think of something.

—Go ahead.

He searches for something to think. His jumbled mind sits remote and silent, somehow far away from this room. Finally, a small, powerful wave of anger surfaces. He lowers his teeth into his bottom lip and pushes down quickly, with more force than necessary in order to kill his dog. His thumb slips off the plunger at the end. He struggles to slow his breath.

—Pull the whole thing out without changing the angle. Good. You did good, real good.

Alfred sighs. Then nothing. Daniel rests his hand, the one that held the syringe, on the dog's upper ribs, feeling the dog's individual hairs against the tips of his fingers. He thinks he senses something, probably a heartbeat, and then Alfred is completely still. The doctor slowly stands up.

—I'll give you a few minutes alone with him, then I'll return to help you out.

Daniel waits for the crying, has been waiting for a few minutes now, but nothing comes. He takes a few deep breaths, wondering when he'll falter, but he does not. Eventually he removes his hand from the dead animal. He considers saying something aloud to it, but decides against it. Instead, he stands up, takes a few steps, and sits down in a chair near the corner. Leans over and rests his forearms right above his bent knees. Waits for the doctor, who returns a minute later with a large black plastic bag.

—If I had any wisdom about any of this, about death or grieving, I'd offer it now. But I don't, sorry.

—Don't worry about it.

—You'll figure out how to deal with this, we all do. You might be at the pound tomorrow picking out Alfred Jr. You might find some other stuff coming to the surface, you might realize in a few days that you've been going through a trying time but hadn't recognized it or admitted it until now. Just be honest with yourself. Don't rush the process.

—Thanks.

—I will hold this open and you can put Alfred inside. Or we can do it the other way if you'd like. Or I can do it by myself.

Without speaking, Daniel walks over, picks up the warm corpse, and puts it in the bag. The doctor gathers the top of the bag and ties it into a knot. Then he hands it to Daniel. At first he senses the urge to sling the bag over his shoulder, but feels it would be inappropriate, so he just holds it in front of him.

—You need any help out?

—No thanks, I think I got it.

—You haven't moved recently?

—No. Why?

—The invoice.

—No. Same place.

—Be well, Daniel. Let yourself feel what you are feeling.

Daniel turns, opens the door, walks back through the empty waiting room and then through the front door. Once outside he stops before going down the first step. The absolutely clear afternoon is now dusk. Thick blue to soft orange in the darkening sky, a peaceful moment has snuck into Los Angeles while the city wasn't looking. He lowers the bag onto the stoop and gathers it all in. Just before descending the stairs he looks down and sees the bowl Alfred was drinking from not an hour before. Daniel considers this for a while, then crimps and crunches up his suddenly hot face. He lifts a hand to his beard, clutches it, gathers it, attempts, briefly, to rip it right out of his skin. A few moments later he reaches into his pocket, removes his phone, scrolls through a few menus, and dials a number. Almost four rings later,

—Hello?

—Rabbi Brenner?

—Ethan?

—Who is this?

—Daniel. Bloom. I was wondering, do you have a minute?

—**You're back** from Israel.

—I am.

—You want something.

—Can you meet me at my house?

—I had to sell my car.

—Why?

—Can I pick you up?

—Tell me what you want from me.

—Can I?

Eventually, Daniel gets an address and cryptic instructions for finding the guesthouse. He hangs up and carries the bag to his car. Moments later he places it in his trunk, instantly aware of and unmoved by the inescapable irony.

Daniel works his way around the unlit stucco wall of another enormous Hollywood home and makes out a small bungalow in the far corner of the yard. Other than a couple of vertical strips of dull light coming from the edges of a single window, this hut is completely dark. He makes slow progress toward the structure, approaching carefully, his steps uncertain. Finally he reaches it and knocks, two soft, slow beats. Fifteen seconds later the door opens. Rabbi Ethan Brenner, unevenly lit, faces him. He presents the kind of expression that follows a very long sigh, the look someone gives after being found at the end of a simple game of hide-and-seek that has gone on for two weeks, his face saying, Okay, I give up, yes, I know that was uncalled for, and alright, let's get on with it. Still, a touch of the playful remains at the edges of his red, swollen eyes and badly chapped lips, which are threatening to curl up into a full-blown smile. Perhaps, despite the assorted varieties of disrepair informing his appearance, the exclusively rumpled hair, the small drop of clear snot resting in the raw rim of his right nostril, the overgrown, tangled beard, perhaps this was just as he planned it, or even more unnerving, perhaps he has convinced himself, no, is in the process of convincing himself, right this very instant, that this, that all of this, is just as he planned it. And then his greeting, such as it is:

—I see your beard.

The rabbi steps back and allows Daniel to enter the single-room dwelling. Looking past a bare futon bent in half and pushed up against a wall, he spots the room's only source of illumination. On a card table in the far left corner, what might be a large flashlight, covered by what might be a pale green pillowcase, points straight up to the ceiling, its luminescence highly compromised. Under and around the table, and then spilling out all the way to the next corner, boxes, some closed, some open. Along the far wall, a folding chair, a yoga mat, an old bookshelf overflowing with oversized dark leather volumes, a very small cassette recorder, a door to the bathroom. A footlocker occupies the center of the room, a footlocker on which sits a thin jar holding a bundle of something slowly burning. Finally, to the right, a tiny kitchenette long since overwhelmed by neglect. Daniel tries to decide where to put himself, the rabbi is presently claiming the chair, so he takes a couple of steps toward the futon. As he sits down he notices, on the card table, propped up against the wall and standing on its thin wooden legs, an actual Torah scroll, naked and bound with a bit of frayed twine. The two men look at each other. The rabbi licks his lips.

—Tell me why you are here.

—I just killed my dog.

—Tell me how you want me to respond.

—Will you help me bury him?

—Tell me why you chose me.
—Why are you talking like that?

The rabbi closes his eyes, opens them. Smoke from the smoldering bundle reaches Daniel. Sage, and marijuana.

—I want to be certain there are no misunderstandings.

———

—You're not well.

—Your family.

—What's happened to you?

—Where are they?

—They're not here.

—Of course.

—Of course what?

—Information. Do you know that three days ago I walked seven blocks to my bank, where I have left in my account exactly eighteen dollars, I recognize this not to be an arbitrary or accidental figure, and I used my credit card to obtain a safety deposit box, and in this box I placed no less than six types of drugs, six a meaningful number, perhaps, as are seven and three, drugs that I brought to the bank in a plastic bag inside another plastic bag, both of which I later disposed of in the lobby, drugs that include thirty seventy-five-milligram tablets of Demerol, fifty microliters of liquid acid, these numbers mean nothing, a small Baggie with a variety of powdered amphetamines, like the sand of the sea, an ounce of psychedelic mushrooms, and two, yes two, exactly two blue tablets of MDMA, which you may know by its street name, Ecstasy. *An* is not a number.

—Why a safety deposit box?

—You should know that animals cannot be given a Jewish burial.

—Fine, it doesn't need to be Jewish.

—Look, maybe I should leave.

—I wonder if you were surprised when Caroline told you she wanted a divorce?

—How do you know she wants a divorce?

—I wasn't ready to throw them out, but I needed to put them at a distance. A safe distance, a safety deposit box. A safe. Safety in numbers.

—I asked you how you knew that she wants a divorce.

—Yes, I know. One question at a time.

—Well?

—She told me.

—She what?

—She found me, I don't know how, after you left. She demanded a great deal of information, everyone wants information.

—What did you tell her?

—As if I am an authority. As if there is such a thing.

—What did you say?

—But not wisdom, no one wants wisdom.

—What did you say?

—She is not like you. She got right to the point. What happened to Daniel? What had I done to her husband?

—What did you tell her?

—I attempted to articulate my impression of your situation.

—What the fuck?

—It took some time.

—You motherfucker.

—I may be willing to help you bury your dog, but not in my capacity as a rabbi.

—What did you tell her?

The rabbi, his right leg draped snugly over his left, appears to be reviewing a not unpleasant, mildly curious memory, his eyes resting absently on the wall over Daniel's head. He starts to say some word slowly, something close to *yes*, but the utterance doesn't really go anywhere. Daniel rises.

—What the hell did you tell her?

Nothing.

He approaches the chair, begins speaking faster.

—What the hell did you say to her? Did you encourage her? Did you advise her to leave me, did you say that I was inadequate, that I, what, that my, my spiritual aura had dulled? C'mon, what did you say?

—She was not in a good place. Neither were you, of course, but her place, it wasn't good.

—What happened?!

The rabbi finally looks up at him, right into his eyes and nearly smiles, almost pleased with himself, but a bit troubled by something as well.

—I think I provided a space in which she could make some very difficult decisions, I think I did. No encouragement, just space.

—You son of a bitch.

And then, for the first time since the one and only time Daniel lost his self-control with Zack, some nine years earlier, Daniel tries to injure another human being. He leans over and grabs the rabbi. He doesn't quite stand back up. The rabbi resists, but not with much conviction, and so his weight, once off the chair, begins to fall toward the floor. Not ready for this, Daniel starts to lose his grip, but without thinking much at all about it, still manages to direct his semi-closed fist to a place near the center of the other man's face. He briefly feels the bones of his hand up against the hard parts of the rabbi's nose and mouth. There's a sound, something between a pat and slap. Then the rabbi is on the floor. Daniel, arms at his side, stares at his host, waiting for this punch to echo against his own body. A spasm in his shoulder, a snort, a scream, a rushed exhalation, a forearm lifting to wipe away a dangling band of saliva, something. But instead, nothing. Rather, he feels a bit calmed, if only a bit.

The rabbi touches his own face and finds some blood. Not a great deal, nothing is flowing, just a spot on his lip and a small, already-stalled trail from his nose.

—I wonder if that was uncalled for.

—You're a son of a bitch.

—I'm not convinced it was.

—I'm sorry, but you're a son of a bitch.

The rabbi begins standing up and eventually returns to standing in what turns out to be a five-part, nonlinear process, at which point

Daniel steps back, feeling his hands close back into fists. Then the rabbi sits back down, crossing his right leg over his left once more.

—Do you see that paper towel under the table, in that box, I would like it.

Daniel throws it to him.

—Thank you.

—Why did you encourage her?

—I said I did not encourage her. I let her reach her conclusions, I allowed her to figure it out herself.

—Figure it out?

—Daniel. Let us review the order of recent events. Your wife tells you she would like a divorce, then you kill your dog, then you come to me.

—So?

—This is why she left you, and you still don't understand. And then you hit me.

—Sorry.

—Forgiveness is a beautiful word.

—Why do you have a Torah here?

—Here's what happened. First, I took some acid. A single drop on a single sugar cube. A few days after leaving Beth Israel once and for all. I hiked up into the hills overlooking a canyon with a couple bottles of water, an orange. To clear my head. A profoundly sunny day. Or fill it up. But a very dry day. Everything is dying. Dying and drying right up. And I have no future. Withering. We have no future. I keep trying to focus on something positive, the plants, the shadows, the birds. But there were no clouds, not a single one. So there were no shadows. The birds were in a panic. Everything out of balance. I can't find a flat surface, it's all slopes and inclines. Up or down. Up and down. Up then down. I can't stop looking at that band of brown, apocalyptic smog. After many years and many attempts, I always find it virtually impossible to recreate these experiences with anything approaching verisimilitude. A word I learned in my Bible-as-literature course. At the time, the connections are not merely evident, they are obvious. In any case. I feel the vessels shattering. Shattered and shattering. Lucid visions of my death, the gradual extinction of this and every other city. I see the city emptying out, contracting, decaying. If I had to summarize the experience, or the experience of the experience, in two words, I would choose these words: of course. I didn't learn anything per se. Rather, I admitted a number of things, things I already knew. I make it home in utter darkness, I still don't know how, and survive four days, barely. Just barely survive. I wonder, which organ will fail first, my heart, my lungs, my liver? I try to sleep. Meditation, enormous amounts of meditation. I travel deep to the center of my ravaged consciousness. Again, I cannot explain what I found there. I wept. None of it surprised me. For hours at a time I wept. Somehow I sleep enough to find the strength to try some X, as I can find no other way to escape the hole I am in. So I take two, just to be sure. And then, wonders of wonders, I feel great. I believe in the future, I believe in my future, I believe in our future, I know that everything will work out. But I know, at the same time, I'm cheating. Ethan, you're cheating, this isn't real, this isn't a mirror, this cannot be your consciousness, this cannot be the world, this is an enormous, merciful, miraculous pharmacological crutch. A magical, fleeting illusion. Ephemeral. I don't recall when I learned that word. But I enjoy it, enjoy it and wait, this being my weakness. That was five days ago. I'm so flat. Flat and empty and barren. I am scorched earth. I am dry bones. I try some speed, just to put something back in the tank. But there's nothing there. There is no tank. I am a shell.

—I don't know what to say.

—In the past, I used to believe I could be the Messiah. The Messiah. But not any longer. It was quite a disappointment. Realizing you are just another person.

—Can I do something?

—Such as?

—Get you some food, get you out of here, take you to rehab.

—The problem with these therapies. I know. Some of them, the therapists, have extensive education and training, but I know what they have to tell me, I know what I should do next. Why is this insufficient? Why am I who I am? I have spent too much time exploring this line of thought.

—Tell me, do you know what a *genizah* is? No, why would you? If a text is in Hebrew and has the name of God and gets worn out, one cannot simply throw it out. One is required to bury it. I will switch to second person. But you don't just bury one thing at a time, rather you wait, and then you have a ceremony when you bury a number of such texts. Before you bury them, while you wait for a number of such texts to accumulate, you put them in a special storage unit, called a *genizah*. Beth Israel shares one with a few other temples. One day Kaufman takes me to the ark in the middle of the day, we open it, without any prayers, and remove this one, this tattered scroll. He asks me if I would like to take it to the *genizah*. I agree, and I'm on my way in my car, when I look at it and think, why, it's good enough for me.

—You stole a Torah.

—Just reusing it. I care for it. I read the weekly *parashah*. Would you like to discuss this week's portion?

—You're kidding.

—Not at all.

—You want to know if I want to read from the Torah.

—It's a fascinating portion.

—Sorry, not interested.

—Were that I was surprised.

—How is it if your life is such a total disaster that you're judging me?

—Why did you come here?

—Because I wanted you to help me bury my dog.

—Why me?

—You're a rabbi.

—But there is no such thing as a Jewish burial for a dog.

—I didn't know that.

—But you're still here.

—And I have no idea why.

—You may leave if you like. If that's what you want. Or you may stay. I leave it up to you.

—Fine.

—What do you want?

—I want you to help me bury my dog.

—Nonsense.

—No.

—Yes, misdirection. Bullshit. What do you want? What do you really want?

—What do I want?

—Yes. Since we first met I don't believe I've heard the truth.

—You want to know what I really want?

—I do.

—What I want right now?

—Yes. Speak. First, wait, come here. Hold on. Okay. Come lie down on this mat. Focus on a spot on the ceiling and tell me what you want.

—I don't want to lie down.

—You're a fool if you don't. Do it.

—Fine. Jesus.

—Good. Just pick a spot. Forget your limbs. Take a few breaths first.

—Alright. Here's what I want. More than burying Alfred. This is what I want. More than convincing Caroline to have me back. More, even, than getting Zack to want me in his life. At least right now. Right now, here's what I want. I want to finish this fucking script. That's it. I want it resolved. I want resolution. I want to know that I can set all this in motion, all this unlikely, contrived, insightful absurdity, all this over-the-top bullshit, and then I want to know that I can tie up the loose ends and make the right decisions about the characters and the plot and do justice to the underlying themes and just end the god-damn thing. That's what I want. Closure. That's what I've wanted. That's all I've wanted. That's what I wanted back in your office and in Israel and not five minutes after I heard my wife almost died and right there in her hospital room after she told me it was over. I even wanted it when my son told me I was a crappy father. I did. Okay, it wasn't the only thing I wanted. I wanted her to be whole, I wanted her to still love me, I wanted him to be glad I'm his father, but I wanted that, too, all along. It's been there for, what, two months, this stubborn urge, this giant fucking thing squatting right in the middle of my head. Right fucking here at the base of my neck. I just want to finish it. And I don't want to be ashamed about that, I don't want to feel that there's something wrong with me because this is the most im-portant thing in the world to me right now. I want to finish it, because maybe when I do I'll be able to want all those other things that I should want. Only those things. And I want to stop worrying about what it means that I know that this script, even if it's perfectly real-ized, isn't going to fix the world, isn't going to so much as leave a tiny scratch on this other fucking thing, this monster or machine or what-ever it is that none of us can seem to do a thing about. But I do want it to matter. I wish it would. I want to incite a riot. I want a violent up-rising. When they clean up the carnage in the streets afterward, I want them to find bloodstained ticket stubs from my movie. I want this script to tremble in the hands of every director and producer in this city. I want this movie to be anything but a diversion, I want it to be the thing itself. But I know it won't, that's my disappointment. So I just want to write it, and I don't want to have to worry about its im-potence or whether or not it's art or whether or not some producer or director or megastar is going to disfigure it beyond recognition the moment they get their hands on it. I just want to write a good story, because that's my last remaining consolation. And I don't want to be haunted by the question, Why does this matter to you so much, Daniel Bloom, why can't you just drop it? I want to say, You know what, this is who I've become, this is what I do, this is, this is all I can do, this is who I am. I write stories. Often ridiculous, always violent, sometimes brilliant stories. And I want to finish this one. Because you know what? When I finish a script, before I sell it, before someone else begins to do things with it and to it, when I know I got it, when I know that I solved it, when I can imagine every scene, every line, every moment just as it should be, the lighting, the frame, the edits, then I have this moment, a couple of hours even, when it's absolutely perfect, and then I'm free of it. I'm absolutely, 100 percent liberated, I don't feel any need whatsoever to prove myself to me or anyone else, it lets go of me, it lets me be, this fucking stupid compulsion to write movies. It lets me go. And what I think every time, and I'm thinking it right now, is that maybe, just maybe, this time that feeling, that moment, won't just be a moment. Maybe I'll finish this one and I'll be done, totally and completely and forever done. Maybe I will have finally repaid some debt or fulfilled some duty. Maybe the insatiable will be satisfied. Maybe that moment will last, maybe this dream that somehow, how I don't know, this dream that became a curse will just disappear, and I'll be able to love my son and my wife or love some new wife, and then maybe I'll be able to decide what to do about everything else, the fucked-up world and my place in it. I doubt it, but maybe. That's what I want. That's all I want.

—Excellent. Keep breathing. You know, I've never met someone who says the word *want* with such conviction. It's amazing. It's like when Moses says *God.*

—Oh, go to hell.

—No, no. Don't get up, please, don't go.

—Go fuck yourself. Asshole.

—No, please. I say this as praise. This is your great strength. If I could say it and feel it like you I wouldn't have my problems.

—No, you'd have mine. Bye.

—No. Wait. Here. Look.

—A gun. Of course.

—Come. Sit back down.

—What? You're going to hold me hostage?

—No, no. I just thought it might help. There's a gun involved, right?

—Why in the world do you have a gun?

—I want to help. Come. Sit down.

—Why do you have a gun?

—My parents are survivors.

—So?

—Next time.

—What? You'll shoot everyone?

—As many as I can, as I must.

—Amazing. Is it loaded?

—What the fuck! Jesus! Brenner! Why the hell did you just shoot your futon? Jesus.

—I never actually shot it before.

—Are you out of your fucking mind?

—That felt wonderful, though my sphincter feels like a fist.

—Please just put it down.

—There's no need to worry. Look, I put the safety on. There's that word again.

—Just don't point it at me.

—I thought perhaps it would help you finish your script.

—Somehow, I'm not in the mood all of a sudden. It's been a pleasure, but I really ought to go.

—You're going to bury your dog in the dark?

—It can wait until the morning.

—Will you come to pick me up?

—Sure.

—In all honesty, I'd prefer it if you didn't leave.

—It's late. I'm tired.

—It's been good to have you here. Don't go. I believe we're making progress.

—Progress in what?

—Of course.

—Do you know what I would like more than anything right now?

—What?

—A little *dvar Torah*.

—A what?

—A brief, I promise it will be brief, talk, not a sermon, just a talk, on this week's portion.

—Look, why don't I pick you up around nine tomorrow morning, okay? Afterward, or before if you like, I'll be happy to hear your sermon.

—I told you it's not a sermon.

—Whatever.

—No, not whatever. You see, this is the problem. It's not even a talk, it's a conversation, a dialogue. This is how I teach. But you need the right student. Someone who isn't passive. Come, sit. We'll read the relevant parts of the *parashah*, I'll translate, and then we'll discuss it. I promise you won't regret it. Interpretation is a great pleasure.

—Rabbi, why can't this wait until tomorrow?

—Will you just sit the fuck down?

—Don't point that at me. Please.

—Sorry. Just sit.

—Fine.

—Excellent. Pull up the chest. Great. We'll put that over there. I'm going to remove the pillowcase, the light may be a little harsh at first. Ouch. Alright, now we can read. And here's our text, the real deal, too.

—Don't you have to say a prayer first?

—We can.

And just like that the rabbi chants something for about ten seconds, his voice cracking only once.

—Amen.

—*Tov.* Okay. This is quite exciting. So, if you notice, almost the entire scroll is wrapped around this pole on the right. Why is that, do you think?

—Because we're near the beginning?

—Well, sort of, but not exactly. Here's a hint. You read Hebrew from right to left—

—We're near the end?

—Great. Yes. Right. The high holidays are coming up, and so we must be nearing the end. Which puts us in which of the five books?

—Of Moses?

—Yes. Good. Which one?

—The last one.

—Which is called?

—Not Genesis?

—No. Good. Genesis would imply beginning.

—And not Numbers.

—Impressive.

—My bar mitzvah was in April.

—Which leaves?

—Exodus. And something with an *L.*

—Leviticus.

—And one more.

—Starts with a *D.*

—Deuteronomy.

—Good. Good. So which is it?

—I don't know.

—Well, okay, process of elimination. These are the Five Books of Moses. What happens in his story?

—I don't know.

—C'mon. Think Passover.

—Plagues. Let my people go—

—Good. Another word for going, or leaving, actually.

—Exodus.

—Right. So that's pretty early in the story, so it's not Exodus. Which leaves only two—

—Will you just tell me already?

—Fine. Deuteronomy. I can't believe you didn't know that.

—Spare me the guilt and disappointment.

—No, no, I don't mean it like that. But two hundred years ago you would have known the entire thing by heart. And now you don't even know the names of the books. This is why you need sermons, because you know nothing.

—Do you know what mise-en-scène is? Or the 180-degree rule? Or what deep focus is?

—Are you asking me to compare Spielberg to Moses?

—Hardly. But I'm not a moron, so spare me the old-world song and dance.

—Fine. Okay. Deuteronomy. What is it? Unlike many of the other books of the Torah, it's not a story for the most part. After wandering in the desert for forty years, the nation is gathered just east of the Jordan River. Moses has brought them together to give them, in his last book, his last words. The once-reluctant stutterer delivers his valedictory address. He reminds them in a series of dramatic speeches where they came from and what awaits them and what they must do. And again, just like at Sinai, there is a covenant, a second covenant. Quite a book. True rhetorical brilliance. And this week, do you see those two words, *Ki Tavo*, when you will come, that's the name of the portion. When you will come, or enter, the land Adonai your God is giving you. That's how we begin this week. But that's not what interests me. Let's skip ahead a couple of chapters. It's not marked in the actual scroll, but the portion starts with chapter 26 and goes through 29. Twenty-eight is the one I want to talk about. Take a look at this. Twenty-six is from here to here. Twenty-seven from here down to here somewhere.

—Why do you keep pointing at the Torah with your gun?

—You're not supposed to touch it with your finger, the oil on your finger will damage the parchment.

—But a gun is okay.

—For now it will have to be. Anyhow, look, 29 is this little pisher from just here to here. And then there's 28.

—A lot longer.

—Sixty-nine verses. I don't know if that's the longest one or not, I wouldn't be surprised if there's some mind-numbingly boring longer chapter in Numbers or Leviticus. But this has got to be one of the longest. Okay, so big deal? It's long, so what? Well, what's this chapter about, why is it so long? What couldn't be said in, say, thirty verses, or even fifty? As I said, this is all about the covenant. You know what that is, right?

—Like an agreement.

—Right, it's a contract. A *brit*. Same word we use for a circumcision. Because it was Abraham's original covenant with God, to cut off his foreskin. So when your parents cut off the tip of your prick and when you did that to your son, you barbaric motherfucker, well, it's all part of the covenant. But what are the terms? What are both sides getting? If it's a contract or an agreement. Any thoughts?

—I don't know.

—Think, where are they?

—The land.

—Right, with a capital *L*. The Land of Israel. The people are going to get the Land. For doing what?

—Being good?

—Sort of. For following God's commandments. And that's where this logorrheic chapter comes in. It opens with, here, If you obey, literally, if you hear, really hear, the voice of the *Adonai* your God and keep his commandments, then guess what?

—You get the Land?

—You don't just get the Land. You enter the bonus round. You get all these blessings. From here to here. The blessings. Great stuff. You prosper, your family prospers, your enemies don't. It's a nice package, honestly. But that still leaves from here, all the way down and over to here. What do you think that is?

—What happens if you don't?

—What happens if you don't. Exactly. The curses. Fifty-odd verses of all the horrific shit that will happen to you if you don't. Starts off obvious enough. In standard biblical fashion we get the negation of all the blessings, you won't prosper, your family won't prosper, etc. Up to this point, fairly straightforward. If you keep the commandments everything will be great, and if you don't everything will be very bad. But for some reason that's not enough. So where does God or Moses or whoever wrote this go from there? Any guesses?

—You got me.

—C'mon, you're a storyteller, if you really want to make something horrible, what do you do?

—What do I do or what do most people do?

—Either.

—Graphic violence is a favorite. Excruciating detail. I'm partial to focusing on emotional trauma myself.

—Well, my friend, we've entered all-of-the-above territory. And then some. Over here the people are threatened, I kid you not, with hemorrhoids and boils and sores. Down here, where is it, you will be crazy from what your eyes see. Oh, and right after that, because apparently the hemorrhoids and boils weren't bad enough, burning rashes. What else? How's this, here, you will eat the fruit, not of the vine, you will eat the fruit of your womb, the flesh of your sons and daughters that *Adonai* your God gave you.

—Cannibalism?

—Cannibalism, infanticide subclass.

—No way.

—I mean, how fucked up is that? And where do you go from there? Well, it's got to be something each and every person can relate to, but keep in mind of course that this is the national story, so we get all sorts of details about what happens to the nation. Back here, just a bit before the cannibalism bit, the Lord will bring a nation from the end of the earth, like, hmm, I don't know that word, like an eagle, a strong nation, blah, blah, blah, he'll eat the fruit of your beasts and the fruit of your soil, never mind that we've already been told that your beasts will perish along with your crops. And on and on. And here's my favorite, about ten verses from the end, way after it's all gotten totally pornographic and redundant and self-contradictory, we get this little gem, and every sickness and plague, the what-I-did-to-the-Egyptians-I'll-do-to-you motif is everywhere here, every one of these *not* written in this Torah, *Adonai* will bring upon you until you are wiped out. As in, and if I forgot to mention anything, if somehow I left something horrible out of this horrible list, if there's anything you can imagine that I haven't said, well, then that, too.

—Great.

—And that's chapter 28. Any thoughts?

—Some nasty stuff. Pretty intense. Would give the special-effects department plenty to work with.

—But why? Look, here's why this fascinates me. Most of the time, when we speak to people like you about Torah, we try to make it about you. About what you should do, about how you should interpret some story and apply it to your life. But when I read this, all I can think is, what kind of pathology is behind this chapter? I don't care if we attribute it to God or Moses or some anonymous writer or redactor centuries later, I want to ask them, what is wrong with you? You can't be serious. I can understand this as an initial rant, a first draft, but how about some self-restraint, how about some editing, for god's sake? What ever happened to the logic of *dayenu*? Hemorrhoids aren't enough, we need boils, boils aren't enough, we need to eat our children? There is some serious overcompensation at work here, and I want to know why. We're way past simple emphasis here. We're even way past intense threat. Whoever is narrating this, they have an itch they can't scratch. So my question to you, what's the source of the itch and why can't it be scratched?

—You got me.

—No, c'mon, don't just give up. You can do this. Think. Why? What is going on here?

—Well, okay, there's certainly an excess of negative reinforcement here. It's like a parent who is either addicted to his authority or is really angry or really hates his child or is convinced that his son isn't going to listen no matter what.

—Right, good. I mean what does it say about this particular authority?

—You mean God?

—I suppose. Or this representation of God. Or God's interlocutor. Or God's interlocutor's interlocutor.

—Lack of faith. Doesn't seem to believe that his people can be trusted to do the right thing.

—Because soon they're going to get the Land. The Promised Land, promised as part of the covenant. Right, God is going to pay up, but they're getting it on credit, on the promise that they'll obey his commandments in the future. I get the sense that God is already regretting this.

—He knows it's not going to pan out.

—Don't say *he*.

—Whatever.

—No, not whatever.

—Fine.

—When I read this, other than being amazed and even surprised, I get very sad. I read this and I think, whoever's responsible for this text, this person or thing knows this isn't going to end well. This book, the Torah, is a lot of things, it's a story, it's a set of instructions, it's a contract, it's an autobiography of the nation. And it oscillates between them, because it wants to tell the story of a people who follow the instructions and get what's promised in the contract. But they never do, at least not for long. So over and over, get the Land, lose the Land, Abraham comes, Joseph goes, Joshua conquers, First Temple falls. Back and forth. Be good, be bad. Get the Land, lose the Land. But this just tells me, it's not just back and forth, it's not just get it and then lose it, it's get it and lose it and lose it some more. People have justified this chapter in all sorts of ways. Rhetorical, philological, historical, ethical, anthropological. But I read it and I think, there's no answer for how to get people to be just, there's no answer for what to do when they're not. Have pity on the prophets. And so I just feel like something is doomed. Either we're doomed, or the religion is doomed. I don't know, or both.

—That's it?

—I don't know, maybe the problem starts when you put the authority outside of yourself. When you need to make a deal with someone else in order to live properly.

—Though we don't live alone.

—We don't?

—I mean, most people don't.

—True.

—There's no such thing as a one-person religion, is there?

—I suppose not.

—Isn't there a prayer for afterward as well?

—I don't feel like it.

The rabbi carefully rolls up the scroll, reties the twine, and moves it back to the table.

—Well, that was uplifting.

—You're supposed to say *yosher ko'ach*.

—What does it mean?

—More power to you. Right on. Reverend. Something like that.

—*Yosher ko'ach.*

—Was it too preachy?

—You're a rabbi.

—I know, but I've never felt comfortable with that part. I'm extremely uncomfortable with my authority.

—I'm sorry to hear that.

—Are you? Are you really sorry to hear that?

—Yes, I suppose. It's not something I've given a lot of thought.

—Authority? You haven't given authority much thought? Your son doesn't want to see you, his own father, and you haven't thought about authority? You write movies about murderers and kidnappers and detectives, but you don't think about authority?

—Are you going to insult me again?

—What do you think about?

—In terms of what?

—Your choice. Your son, your screenplays. Anything.

—I don't know, with the scripts, I just think about the story, the events, the characters. When I have those right, then the other stuff will follow.

—Though not this time.

—No, not this time.

—Fine, so figure it out.

—What?

—Get it right. You said before that all you want is to finish this script. Finish it.

—Here?

—Why not?

—I'm too tired.

—Please.

—I am.

—You said you want this more than anything else. Here I am, inviting you to finish it. I know you don't have anything else to do. Finish it.

—I don't have my computer.

—We can write it down.

—That's not how I work.

—Enough with the excuses. Your life is a total disaster—

—Whereas yours is in perfect working order.

—I do not deny the state I am in, but remember, you came to me and not the other way around.

—I tried to leave, but you made me discuss the Torah portion at gunpoint.

—You're exaggerating. Anyhow, you enjoyed it. I could tell you enjoyed it.

—It was interesting. Still.

—Look. I'm going to turn off the light and do some stretching on the mat. Make yourself comfortable on the futon and tell me about this script. I barely know anything about it. Just talk. When you get to the end of wherever you've gotten to, either you'll keep going, or you won't.

—And what if I fall asleep?

—Then you'll fall asleep.

Which is what Daniel, lying motionless in the now complete darkness, feeling his true exhaustion fill up the almost absolute silence, attempts to do for a while. Every so often he hears the rabbi's breath, hears him change positions. Daniel is certain he'll pass out any second. But after a short time, he senses, with some dismay, a certain restful, alert focus settle over his mind. For the first time since the initial premise dawned on him, he's thinking about the script without straining toward it. Without impatience, without ambition or greed or even simple, understandable desire, he just considers it, as an idea, as a story, as something that might be, that might already be. He feels how it's out there, independent of him, distinct from him, this recognition spreading calm over his entire body. Moments later he wonders if he had or has in fact been sleeping. Unable to decide, he instead begins to speak.

He tells it, all of it, every last bit of it, from the beginning. He narrates the opening scene, his voice soft and precise, recalling every detail, adding new ones, describing the layout of each shot, the timing and logic of each cut. He finishes that scene, feeling once again the utter perfection of his opening, somehow untroubled by the real-world grief, the global and the personal, that preceded and followed this initial imaginative spark. He calls out to the rabbi, asking him if he follows, seeing if he approves. The rabbi, if he responds at all, seems to purr. Daniel hears him moving and fumbling for something on the opposite wall. He hears a click and sees a small red light illuminated.

He continues like this, speaking aloud scene after scene. He's in no hurry, he doesn't even feel like he's trying, trying to speak or trying to remember, he just does. The scenes follow one another in an order and with a seamlessness that feel purely natural, unmistakably organic. Daniel's not reading from a script, he's describing an actual completed movie projecting itself behind his closed eyes, he can see and hear all of it in his head, the sets, the lighting, the wardrobes, the sparse music, the voices and interplay of the actors. Without hesitation he translates all these images and sounds into words, the false security of a cheery food court, the spoiled glow of a single, aging fluorescent tube in a sad, lonely kitchen, the call to 911 made without even a trace of urgency. His own limbs are emptying, he grows weightless. At some point there is a click. The rabbi moves, the red light disappears, only to reappear a couple clicks later. The plot flows forward, the screenwriter's voice steady. The two primary characters come alive to him, the weary stoicism of the once powerful agent, his dark eyes, his thin lips, his massive hands, the private, anguished rage of the assassin, his slight frame, his deliberate motions, his wounded gaze. As Daniel recounts their conversations, his own voice alternates slightly. Without imitating them he captures some core feature of each man's speech. Without knowing how or what it means, he simply performs their dialogues, locating effortlessly each nuance in diction and cadence.

But around the time the assassin asks the agent to meet him in Houston, it will be in Houston, Daniel feels something shudder inside him, just below the center of his ribs, the only part of his mass that hasn't evaporated. Though the movie itself continues vivid and uninterrupted, there has been an intrusion nearby, as if an usher has opened a door near the rear, letting in daylight and bleaching the image up on the screen. But Daniel continues, describing the parking lot, the assassin's portrait of his next, and perhaps final, target, the body language of the bitter, long-since-jaded agent, the crescendo in the soundtrack that is finally interrupted by the assassin's shot, itself interrupted by the hands of the agent. With the light gradually consuming the full space of the theater, Daniel tries to hold on to the lifelike brilliance of the action on the screen. He manages right up to the moment when the two men reluctantly place the new corpse in the trunk of the assassin's car. Daniel, his body returning to him, slowly opens his eyes to see the rabbi's room now outlined in the pale light of a late-summer morning.

—So how does it end?
—I don't know.
—You're near the end. How will you end it?
—I don't know.
—You hoped for more, didn't you?
—I suppose.

—You thought you were writing a movie about something grand, about attacking straight-out something vast and invulnerable, and so now you're disappointed. It is only a screenplay. But don't be. The agent's predicament, at this moment, is meaningful. What are his choices?

—Arrest the assassin, turn himself in, turn them both in.

—Or try to escape.

—Right. Or kill the assassin. Or himself.

—What will be his relationship to the law, to the system it sustains? His decision answers these questions. The ending resolves these matters. Will your movie merely investigate such violence or actually endorse it?

—Right.

—So which is it? What does he do?

—I don't know.

—Take the gun. Take it. He has one. What does he do with this gun, with this, his only tool, the symbol of his authority and the authority of the system he represents? What do you want him to do with it? I think you know. I really do.

Daniel, sitting up on the futon, considers the gun for a few moments, feels its cold weight in his hand, and begins speaking again, eyes open.

—The agent says, The cops are on their way, let's go. No, the assassin says. It's over, I'm done, no more, you go. I can't, the agent answers, one of those bullets is mine, the second one, the one that killed him, they'll find it, they'll find me, drive, let's go. But the assassin doesn't move. Up to this point the camera has been cutting back and forth between the two men, now comes a head-on shot capturing both of them. They are silent, no one moves. Finally the agent pulls out his gun and points it at the other man—

—Show me.

—What?

—Show me what he does with the gun.

—Go, he says.

—No, point it at me.

—No.

—Point it at me.

—No. This is my screenplay, goddammit.

—Of course it's yours. I was just trying to help.

—It's mine.

—The assassin turns, looks at the gun, faces forward again and says, No.

—No.

—Stop.

—Sorry.

—Dammit, go, the agent answers. Back and forth, until the agent gets out of the car, rushes around to the assassin's side, opens the door and furiously drags the other man out of the car, throwing him to the ground of the oil-stained parking lot.

—Do it.

—Shut up. Go, he shouts, go, you can still get away, down that alley, go. The assassin stands motionless and defiant, perhaps he wants to be shot, captured or shot. Sirens can now be heard, the sound engineers will place them at the right edge of the theater toward the front. Extremely faint, but detectable all the same. The agent points the gun toward the assassin, but his arm is bent, the gesture lacks conviction. Go, please go. The day is getting late, there are shadows, long shadows, cutting across the screen and each man's face, shadows from the agent's arm, the assassin's body, the small office building, a nearby fence, a row of telephone poles. Suddenly the agent points the gun at his own head.

—Do it.

—I said shut up.

—Point it at your head.

—No.

—Point it at your head. Please. Thank you.

—Go, he says softly, almost begging. The assassin holds his arms out to him but doesn't say anything. The agent cocks the gun, like this, pressing it to his own temple. Go. The assassin closes his eyes for a long moment, his head framed by the agent's shoulder and head, the camera shooting from behind the man with the gun. The sirens are growing louder, very gradually moving from the side to the front of the theater. Finally, the assassin opens his eyes, inhales, begins to raise his hands out toward the agent, then quickly puts them down, turns, and walks away. After a few moments he breaks into a light jog and soon disappears down an alley to the right. The agent lowers his gun and gets back in the car, sitting down behind the steering wheel. He places the gun on the dashboard and reaches into his pocket to remove a handkerchief, a monogrammed silk handkerchief, his father's. In some earlier scene with the father, perhaps in a few earlier scenes, the father will be shown with it, blowing his nose, cleaning his glasses, removing some spittle from the edges of his mouth. The agent takes it and begins wiping down the sniper's rifle, the steering wheel, the door handle, the gear shift, the buttons on the dashboard, putting his own hands and fingertips on each of these things after first wiping it down. The sirens continue growing louder as they close in, the sound will seem to originate from just behind the screen. The agent reaches out with the handkerchief, its letters visible, toward the review mirror. The previously steady, businesslike motion of his hand stops as he catches his own reflection. He stares at himself, his eyes dark and plaintive.

—Great word.

—Shut up.

—Sorry.

—After returning the handkerchief to his pocket he extends his arm once more toward his own gun. Picks it up and cocks it. Cut to a bus, headlights on, pulling up to a stop. The doors swing open, and the assassin, along with a few others, a couple of chatty teenagers, a middle-aged man in a bad suit, an elderly woman with a bagful of groceries, step onto the bus. The camera follows the assassin inside as he pays the fare and finds a seat by a window. He's the most nonde-script man on the entire bus, the one you'd trust the most. The final shot of the movie shows the bus from overhead, pulling away from the stop. As the bus drives off, the camera begins pulling back verti-cally, steadily taking in a wider and wider view of the city at dusk, the grid of partially illuminated streets, the steady flow of light traffic, the pedestrians gradually blending into the dark gray of the side-walks. The bus, shrinking with each frame, turns right and begins traveling down a street that runs perfectly parallel with the long leg of the movie screen, about a third of the way toward its top. Soon, with the camera now perhaps two hundred feet off the ground, flash-ing sirens come into view near the bottom-right corner of the screen and congregate around a car in a parking lot that lies between a small office building and a narrow alley. The camera stops at three hun-dred feet and the credits begin to roll up the left side of the darken-ing frame in the moment the bus disappears beyond the screen's right edge. A few minutes later, just before the credits end and the screen goes black altogether, a second ambulance joins the cluster of sirens that dominate the nearly dark cityscape.

Daniel puts the gun down on the footlocker and sits back on the futon, looking at his feet, chewing on parts of his beard.

—*Yosher ko'ach.*
—Huh?
—*Yosher ko'ach.* You did well. This is good. It's powerful. It is.
—It's okay.
—No, it's better than okay.
—They'll never keep that ending.
—But you said that doesn't matter. You finished it. You imagined

it perfectly. You're done with it. You must feel better. I feel better having just witnessed it.

—You don't feel better? No relief, no lightness, no liberation?
—No.
—Nothing?
—Nothing.
—You must feel something.
—I'm done. That's what I feel. I'm done with this. My family is done with me. I'm done. I've expired.

The two men sit in silence. Daniel doesn't move. The rabbi, suddenly animated, stands and paces the room.

—Daniel. I have one last recommendation. One last idea, one last bit of advice. It will require great courage. But I believe it may be your only chance.

Daniel looks up at the rabbi.

—Let me ask you something. Why was *Helsinki Honeymoon* such a success?
—It should have been called *Captives*.
—I know, Daniel, I know. But why was it such a success? It made a great deal of money. Why did so many people go to see it?
—Aggressive marketing campaign. Good performances. Good story. It was a good movie. The director was an asshole, but it was a good movie.
—Here is my theory, one that I cannot prove. The violence in that movie was unusual, it was, in its way, instructive. When the man, quite early in the film, puts his gun to her thigh, what does he say to her?
—Would you like me to give you something to remember me by?
—Right, he isn't threatening to kill her. He places the gun away from the center of her leg, he tells her this, he's avoiding the main artery.

—So?

—He does this a number of times. He says this line a few times.

—Four times.

—And then after she tries to free herself, near the beginning of the final act, she cuts herself with the glass. He cleans her. Things have already started to turn. She's emboldened, he's fallen for her, or believes he has, he's searching for some way out of this. And when he cleans her, he does it with remarkable care, with compassion, with affection. He says, what does he say to her about the scar?

—I'm sorry, but this one will last.

—And then he shows her one of his scars. And then another. He tells her the stories behind them. They're very touching stories. You really feel for him at this moment. The one from his father on his back. And then he asks, Where are yours? Where are your scars? But she doesn't answer. Not at first. But he is persistent. Not threatening. He simply wants to know. You must have scars, he tells her. Just one, she says finally. And then she doesn't say anything, but neither does he, he simply finishes dressing her wound. Then finally, she volunteers it, My C-section. And he looks at her after she says that. He has love in his eyes. Your scar, he says, you accepted it so another person, your son, could be born. She begins crying, he has reminded her again of her son who she misses dearly, who she has mentioned throughout the film. You must love this scar, it must be so beautiful. He begins crying, he apologizes. Two people were born from this scar, she says. My son and myself. I was so weak until that moment, until he was born. He transformed me.

—And then he asks her to show him the scar.

—Such audacity! How could you have written that? How could you have possibly imagined that two actual human beings could have that exchange in that situation and for it to be even remotely believable? But it worked, it did. He asks, Please show it to me. And she doesn't answer. She doesn't say no. Please, he asks again. You must. I must see it. He releases her hands, the hands she has been trying to free throughout the movie, so that she can. And she stands up and undoes her jeans and lowers them partway down her hips, revealing her panties, her plain yellow panties with a single small flower, a daisy, I think, sewn onto the hem, and then she looks at him, she has this remarkable look in her eyes, as if she's daring him to pay attention, to truly pay attention, and then she folds her panties down. And there is the scar, this dark purple line, this bulge, and just below it, I thought this was a wonderful decision, we see some of her hair. He is mesmerized, and so are we, we don't know what we're seeing. She's so beautiful, her body is magnificent, but this isn't sexual, is it? Could it be? And the man asks, Do you touch it, when you touch it, what does it feel like? And she runs her index finger along its length and says, without emotion, Smooth, a little stiff. Then, after a pause, the man asks, May I? She doesn't respond. He approaches her, asks again. She nods, it's almost imperceptible, but she nods, she assents. And he takes his hand and gently runs it along the scar. He is inches from her, from her genitals, but his hand, we see this in the close-up, his finger never strays from the line, his finger never wavers. He is interested only in this scar. And after this, everything changes. She has all the power, while he has truly fallen for her.

—How many times have you seen this?

—Oh, many times. I own it. Though I had to sell my television recently. It's an amazing sequence. It nearly redeems its own violence. And then, about five minutes later, after she has his weapon, she points it at the same spot on his thigh and says, just before she actually kisses him on the forehead and shoots him, something to remember me and your old self by.

—And?

—It took me some time to make sense of the end of this line. Perhaps I'm just dense. But then I realized it, it was running through the entire movie. Violence is transformative. Violence can be a creative force.

—That's nonsense. I was just trying to be provocative.

—You're not serious. How can you misread your own work so completely? People went to see this movie, people told their friends to go see this movie, because it gave them some hope in this fucked-up world. Maybe they weren't conscious of it, but when you left that movie you couldn't help but think, or believe, or simply feel, that all the bad things that have happened to me, the things that have scarred me, they were opportunities, they were formative in the most positive sense, they changed me, they are who I am, who I have become.

—Okay, fine. So what?

—Daniel, I think you should shoot yourself in the leg.

—You smile, I amuse you. I know, even coming from me, this sounds like madness. But you said it yourself, not five minutes ago. You're expired. There is no you. The present you has no future. He barely has a present. You finished an impressive script and you take no pleasure from that. Your family, your wife and son, they send you away and you do nothing to assert your place in their lives. You have no will. You kill your dog, you put it in your car, you come here and leave it there, this creature of God that shared your home for years, you leave it rotting in your trunk for hours while I talk my nonsense about Deuteronomy.

—It wasn't nonsense.

—Daniel. The Daniel that you are, and I don't say this as a slight, he's run his course. You have no answers to any of your questions, to any of your problems.

Daniel's nose has begun to run, some liquid flows into his moustache.

—How will shooting myself fix that?

—We can't say. We don't know who you'll be after this, but you'll be someone different.

—Different.

Daniel lifts his shirttail and wipes his nose.

—Why do you think so many people get tattoos and put holes in their bodies? Because it feels good? Self-mutilation is a powerful force. We demonstrate who we are, or were, or no longer are, we demonstrate that we have control over our bodies by wounding them. We make ourselves into someone else, someone different.

—What about you? You haven't done any of that stuff.

The rabbi points to his head and smiles.

—You can't imagine what I've done to this. Trust me, you cannot imagine.

The rabbi hands the box of tissue to Daniel, whose nose continues to run. As Daniel blows his nose, his eyes cloud over.

—There is a hospital four blocks from here, they have an excellent emergency room, I know from experience. You'll give me the keys to your car. We'll have you there in two minutes. We'll say it was an accident, I was showing you my gun and it went off accidentally. It will hurt like hell, but you'll heal, Daniel, you'll heal into someone else, another Daniel Bloom. Hopefully a better one. But at the least, a different one.

Daniel, his body temperature suddenly spiking, stares at the rabbi, wishing his vision would clear. Sweat pours down from his forehead. He tries not to blink, and when he finally does he feels a number of large, full tears quickly spill over the rim of his eyelids. He cries. But his crying in no way resembles the hysteria from the cemetery, or even the aftershocks during the days following. This is the crying of calm release, the crying of sober acceptance. His still-thickening beard grows heavy as it catches everything running out of his face. He tries to speak.

—Is this really it? Am I that bad?

—Daniel, this has nothing to do with my opinion. I'm merely telling you what I've observed. There is no shame in this. The first Daniel lasted, what, forty-two—

—Forty-three.

—Forty-three years. If the second Daniel lasts as long, you'll have lived a full life. And it only took one bullet to get you there. Daniel, we both know this one won't last much longer. He can't. But Daniel, remember, this act, too, this act is an act of love. A creative, loving act. You will do this out of love for your family, out of love for yourself, for the you that you will say good-bye to now and the you who will take his place. You can do this. You must do this.

The rabbi walks to Daniel, helps him up off the floor, and leads him to the folding chair. Then he walks to the footlocker and picks up the gun.

—As you do this, I will chant a simple prayer, what I feel is our people's most wonderful prayer. Not the *Shema*. Not the *Ve'ahavta*. Not even the *Kaddish*, though perhaps it would be appropriate as well. No, the *Shehecheyanu. Baruch ata adonai eloheinu melech haolam, shehecheyanu, v'kiyimanu, v'higiyanu laz'man hazeh.* Blessed are you *Adonai* our God, ruler of the universe, who has given us life, and sustained us, and brought us to this moment. It's a prayer of gratitude and appreciation. We say it with joy and humility upon the arrival of any long-awaited or any precious occasion. Perhaps there is some irony in our recitation of it now, but I don't think irony, in our case, is such a dirty word. Before I switch off the safety, your keys.

Daniel, his face wet and shiny, hands the rabbi his keys and accepts the gun. The rabbi begins chanting, his voice swelling with power, and moves to stand behind his last remaining congregant. Daniel continues crying softly as he points the gun down toward his leg and brings the muzzle to his thigh. His hand shakes, but only slightly. The shaking stops altogether once the rabbi places his warm and surprisingly strong hands down on Daniel's shoulders. The rabbi sings the prayer over and over, bellowing louder each time, emphasizing each word with perfect conviction. Daniel presses the gun deep into his thigh and closes his sopping-wet eyes. He cocks the gun and wraps his finger around the trigger. And just as he was taught, he squeezes until he hears a click.

Nothing.

Daniel drops the gun, or it falls from his hand. He pulls himself away from the rabbi, and turns around to look at this other man. The rabbi is smiling the peaceful smile of satisfaction, of long-awaited and well-earned and much-needed satisfaction. The rabbi is beaming. The rabbi is redeemed. Daniel sobs for a moment, nearly laughs, his teeth bared, the last of his fluids on their way. His expression is one of plain chaos, since his face is now resetting itself.

—Allow me to say this, Daniel. You and I, we're good Jews. We are. Indeed, Daniel, we are not merely good Jews, we are good for the Jews. We are. I truly believe we are.

—You may be right, Rabbi. I sure hope you are.

10

Five **minutes later** the two men walk out the front door of the rabbi's hut.

—Daniel, hold on, I forgot something.

The rabbi disappears. He returns holding two small microcassettes.

—These belong to you. Your work.

Daniel takes them, stares at them for a moment, and places them in his pocket as he begins walking in the direction of his car.

—Daniel, hold on, one more thing.

The rabbi disappears. He returns holding the Torah.

—In a second hole, of course.

They pull into Caleb's driveway twenty minutes later. Daniel turns off the car and looks at himself in the rearview mirror. Tries to do something with his beard, but soon gives up, shaking his head. Before he gets out he turns to the rabbi.

—I think you better stay here.

Daniel walks straight up the driveway and knocks. Not five seconds pass before Deb opens the door.

—Daniel.

—Hi Deb. Look, I know I look like shit. But I won't soon. I'd like to speak with Caroline and Zack.

—They might both be sleeping.

—That's fine. I'm happy to wake them up. Where's Caroline?

—Out back. Wait, Daniel, she doesn't—

But Daniel is already walking through the Vaismans' house toward the door that leads out to the guesthouse.

—Daniel, please.

As Daniel reaches for the doorknob, Deb inserts her body between him and the door.

—Daniel, I'm sorry. She doesn't. I promised.

Daniel, not exactly smiling, takes a step back and rests his hand on the kitchen table.

—You know, Deb, the new me would throw you aside. He would. It wouldn't be out of character. Because I made some promises, too. To Caroline, to myself, old promises and new promises. But I won't. Instead, I'm going to pick up this piece of paper, which you may need for other reasons, I don't care, and I'm going to write a short note to Caroline. And you will deliver it to her, and when you do so, you'll tell her she must see me soon.

Daniel turns around to look for a pen. He can't find one.

—I need a pen. Deb, I need a pen.

Deb walks around a counter and brings him one.

Daniel, standing, writes quickly:

Dear Caroline,

I wish you would agree to see me. I hope you are healing. I had to put Alfred to sleep. He was very sick. I didn't call you or Zack first because I didn't think you wanted to speak with me and because I often make bad decisions. I did call Zack, but he didn't answer. I am taking Zack back to our house to bury Alfred. I will return with him later. I want you to see me then.

I am done writing movies. I don't know what I will do now. But I think I'm done. I hope I am.

Love,
Daniel

Daniel folds the paper in half, hands it to Deb, and before turning toward the stairs, asks,

—Deb, would you do me a favor and round up a couple shovels while I'm getting Zack?

Sure enough, Zack and Caleb are still asleep in the bunk bed, their room warmed by the serious work of adolescent sleep. Daniel sits down on the edge of Zack's bottom mattress and places his hand on the boy's naked back. He says his son's name three times, softly patting and shaking his body each time. Zack turns over, opens his eyes, sees his father, then curls back up, still sleeping.

—Zack, wake up.

Zack opens his eyes and keeps them open.

—Hi. C'mon. Get up. We need to go home to do something.

—Mr. Bloom?

—Hey, Caleb.

—What's going on?

—I'll explain later.

Zack starts to move, slowly.

—Do you still have your beard?

—Yes.

—Good.

—Zack, let's go.

———

They're on the front steps before Zack speaks.

—Dad, what's going on? Where are we going? Why do you have those shovels?

—I took Alfred to the vet yesterday. Something was wrong. They told me he was very sick. Zack, I put him to sleep. I called, but you didn't answer. Sorry for not leaving a message.

—Oh.

—C'mon. Let's go.

They walk.

—Dad?

—Yeah?

—Why is Rabbi Brenner sleeping in your car?

—He's been helping me, he's going to help us.

—Is he using a Torah for a pillow?

—He is. C'mon.

They drive quietly back to the house. The rabbi continues to sleep in the front seat. Daniel shifts the rearview mirror to keep an eye on Zack, who stares out the window, concentrating on something he cannot see.

—Zack.

—Yeah?

—How are you doing?

—Alright.

—How's Mom?

—Better, I think.

—Good.

—She walked around a little yesterday. On crutches.

—You still having fun with Caleb?

—Yeah.

—You like it there?

—Yeah, most of the time.

—Good. But we're going to need to talk later, when this is over today. We're going to talk.

—I know.

11

The dog stays in the trunk, the Torah goes to the kitchen, while the three of them look around the backyard for a place to dig two holes. They settle on a small, neglected patch of dirt and weeds between the long strip of manicured grass and Daniel's office. Daniel comments to Zack that they've salvaged the Pickle field. Zack nods his head.

The sun is hot today, and after a few minutes of loose topsoil the digging proves difficult. The three of them take turns with the two shovels. No one speaks, everyone sweats, everyone smells. They finish. Daniel takes his car keys from his pockets, begins heading back to the car, but suddenly stops.

—I need to go inside for a moment.

He finds a scissors in a kitchen drawer, heads upstairs, runs hot water into his bathroom sink, and places a wastepaper basket on its porcelain edge. The snipping takes some time. He applies shaving cream, picks up the razor. His cheeks and chin and neck reappear, the shape of his face marvelously unfamiliar, the skin soft and pale, this undeniably the closest shave he's ever had. He rinses and runs his hand over the smooth skin a few times, taking true pleasure in rediscovering his own recently hidden face.

He returns outside with the Torah scroll to find that Max has ma-
terialized in his backyard.

—Bloom, your face is two totally different colors.

—Hey, Max.

—It's amazing. Too bad, I liked the beard. This is interesting, too,
but mostly unnerving. What's going on here? What's with the Torah?
What's with the holes? And who's this?

—We've got some burying to do. That's Rabbi Brenner.

—Pleasure.

—Nice-looking holes. Wow, you guys really stink. Zack, you
smell like a man. Like a very smelly man. What's going into the holes?

—Alfred. I had to put him to sleep yesterday.

—That's a shit deal.

—It is.

—And the Torah. The rabbi breaks his silence.

—Right. Of course. Listen, Bloom, before the ceremony begins,
which I'd love to stay for, assuming I'm invited, I thought I should let
you know that Donny kidnapped my Vespa. He left a ransom note
and everything. The script, or the Vespa gets it.

—Donny ought to leave you out of this. He knows where to
find me.

—No he doesn't. The ransom note, it was kind of rambling, it
says he came by here first, but couldn't find you or anything to
kidnap.

Daniel doesn't say anything, just turns to hand the Torah to his
son. He looks at Zack for a moment before passing it to him, trying
to think.

—Zack. My son. Hold this for me, alright? He passes the scroll
and kisses his son on the forehead, holding Zack's face in his hands.

Daniel walks to the car and returns with the bag. He places it on
the ground and turns to Zack.

—You want to put it in?

—The Torah?

—No, Alfred.

—Is the bag heavy?

—A little heavier than the Torah.

—No. You can.

Daniel places the bag in the biggest hole. Zack and the rabbi look at each other.

—Go ahead, Zack.

Zack places the Torah in the other hole. Daniel addresses his son.

—You want to say anything?

Zack thinks for a few moments and then declines, shaking his head.

—Okay. Alfred was a good dog. He was. He'll be missed. A very good dog.

Daniel looks at the rabbi.

—I suggest silent meditation. Focus on your relationship to life's creative force.

The four of them stand there without speaking, facing the two holes. Daniel and Zack are near each other, but not touching. A last bit of nervous energy has Daniel probing in his pants pocket. He feels something, two things. He fishes them out and stares at them in his hand. Then he looks over at the rabbi, who looks back at him and seems to grin.

—I don't know which hole to put them in. Neither seems right.

—You can dig a third.

—What are those, Dad?

—Something I've been working on.

—Bloom, those aren't? You're not? Don't tell me.

—It's over, Max. Sorry, but I'm done. No more.

—No more?

—No more.

—What about Donny?

—You want to tell him where to find them, that's your business.

—And what about us?

—What about us?

—Will you still be my friend if I'm not your agent?

—Do you promise to keep changing your name?

—That I do.

Daniel picks up a shovel and digs a third, smaller hole. He drops the cassettes inside and turns to the group.

—Anything else? Last call.

—I wonder if I should have brought the gun.

—What gun?

—Nothing, Max. You can bring it by later. And maybe that stuff from your safety deposit box.

—Perhaps. Unlikely, but perhaps.

—Zack, anything you want to add?

—No.

—Max?

—I got some stuff, but not with me. I'll dig a hole back at my place this afternoon, assuming I can borrow a shovel. I think you guys might be on to something. You're welcome to come along.

Daniel picks up a shovel and begins filling up the smallest hole with dirt. The rabbi grabs the other shovel and does the same with the hole containing the Torah. When Daniel finishes, he hands his shovel to Zack, who begins covering up Alfred. He does this for a while, but hands the shovel back to his father before he finishes. Daniel completes the task a few moments after the rabbi finishes. They put down the shovels and together all four of them stand opposite the graves. Daniel lifts up his right arm and places it on his son's shoulder. Zack looks up at Daniel. They make eye contact, and just like that, Zack begins to cry. Perhaps embarrassed, he buries his head into his father's side, crying and shaking. Daniel holds him closer and places his left hand on Zack's head.

Just as this hand makes contact, something, an idea, begins to surface. Daniel ignores it as best he can, holding his son close, looking at the graves, making no effort to bring it into focus or attach words to what remains, for now, a nebulous idea. But as his son wraps his arms tightly around him, as Daniel looks from the rabbi to Max and back to the rabbi again, he realizes it's no use. There's nothing Daniel can do, he realizes he has no say in the matter. It will be a period piece, set long, long ago, in an era with no ties to today, in a time before history, if such a thing is possible. No, not exactly. Just the opposite. It will be postapocalyptic, after everything finally falls apart once and for all. On a boat or atop some horses, out at sea or somewhere far-off in the mountains. Pirates or bandits or a small fighting force, searching for something they're reluctant to find but need nonetheless. A father and his estranged son at the story's center.

Acknowledgments

For helpful doses of interest, encouragement, and thoughtful comments: Nina Caputo, Eric Kligerman, Jack Kugelmass, Suzanne Levin, Adam Lowy, Jordan Lowy, Ron Lowy, and Naomi Seidman.

For his veterinary expertise: Todd Grand.

For multiple readings and extended conversations: Jonathan Cohen, Mitch Hart, Adi Hasak, and especially Matthew Rohrer.

Thanks to Coffee Culture for quiet music and free wireless.

Thanks to my editor, Tina Pohlman, for putting her good name on the line after only three weeks, for convincing me to leave out the dialogue tags, and for being the kind of reader who makes me want to write in the first place.

All the gratitude I can muster for my agent, Simon Lipskar, who waited patiently through the Blocks to get to the Blooms, who had more than a few prolonged "second book" conversations with me, who always made it seem like he knew this would get written all along, and who is simply really, really good at his job.

All this and more for Taal, who gracefully convinced me to convince myself that the first novel wasn't working, who cleared out vast tracts of our lives for endless talks about this story and these characters, who offered up, however tentatively, more than a few key ideas herself, and who is responsible for preventing our lives from devolving into something that would then turn my protagonist's story into rather regrettable autobiography.

Inordinately large portions of this novel were written while listening to Part I of Keith Jarrett's *The Köln Concert*.